The Last Visit to Berlin | Ruvik Rosenthal

D1566885

Producer & International Distributor
eBookPro Publishing
www.ebook-pro.com

The Last Visit to Berlin
Ruvik Rosenthal

Translation from the Hebrew by Tal Keren

Contact: ruvikr@netvision.net.il
ISBN 9798637090570

The
LAST VISIT
to
BERLIN

RUVIK ROSENTHAL

CHAPTER ONE: GERTRUDE

1.

One summer day in 1902, a mail courier arrived at the door of Doctor Moritz Freyer, Chief Physician of Pomerania Province and Crown-appointed Officer for Public Health, carrying a telegram. The telegram was received by the housekeeper, who then tiptoed to the office of Moritz Freyer and presented him with it.

Moritz Freyer, a compact man whose face was adorned with a thick handlebar mustache and a beard meticulously trimmed in the Prussian style, opened the envelope containing the telegram and learned that his father, Simon Freyer, the rabbi of the eastern town of Marggrabowa, is very ill. He immediately asked Fräulein Brigitta Saranow, the devoted nanny and housekeeper, to cancel all his appointments, and summoned his eldest daughter Trude to see if she'd like to accompany him. Trude flitted to her room and packed a suitcase with a week's worth of clothes, as well as toiletries and a few books, and Herr Holzfuss, the family's regular coachman, drove them to the train station.

The train from Stettin to the City of Lyck, on the east border of Prussia, ran for many hours. Trude and Moritz exchanged few words and dozed often. Occasionally they glanced out the window at the small Prussian towns or attempted to fathom the enigma of the dense woods. The sun shone on harvested wheat fields, and farmers straightened their tired backs as they watched the train go by. At noon they got off at the Lyck train station and found a small hotel, where they washed up before heading out for a lunch. Later, Moritz led Trude down the streets of the comely city and through the gates of the secondary school. He eagerly skipped down the stairs, peeked into the classes which remained nearly unchanged over the past forty years, and even met an old professor and spoke with him briefly. The professor's face shone when he told Trude, "Your father was an exceptional pupil, a student of the utmost aptitude!" And her face shone as well.

The following day, Moritz and Trude set out toward Marggrabowa, which was perched nearly on top of the Russian border, in a small coach drawn by two horses. The coach carried them through the thick of the woods. Moritz, his face jubilant, was enthralled by the view. Suddenly he spoke: "Here, this is where it happened."

"Where what happened, Father? What are you talking about?" asked Trude, and Moritz replied,

"Why, the Egg Miracle, of course."

Trude looked at him, bewildered. "But that was just a story."

"A story?" Moritz grimaced in mock offense. "How can you say such a thing, Trüdchen. It was nothing of the sort, nothing but the absolute truth. This is where the coach crashed, and they found me here, on that very tree, swinging like a pendulum in a clock." He asked the coachman to stop for a moment and they got off. Moritz happily pranced around the small clearing, bounding about like a child until Trude became concerned that someone else might drive by and think him mentally unwell.

The Egg Miracle was a matter of great importance at the Freyer household. Moritz recounted the tale to each of the children upon their seventh birthday. Trude heard it from her father as she

accompanied him along the Oder River to a visit at the Bergquelle Neurological Hospital. Excitedly and in great detail he told
her how on one Ascension Day, which according to Christian
tradition is a time of miracles, Simon Freyer's family, with its
eleven children, took a coach to their new home in the town of
Marggrabowa; and how all of the passengers fell asleep, and the
coachman did as well, and the coach crashed, children flying
everywhere; and how four-year-old-Moritz, the youngest of the
boys, was found hanging from a tree branch; and how among the
pristine egg basket that Mother Zerlina had brought, not a single
one had so much as cracked. Regarding the eggs, Trude and her
brother Kurt were confident that such a thing defied possibility,
while Erich claimed that such a miraculous happenstance could
occur, though special circumstances might be necessary. Despite
their skepticism, Moritz had made Trude swear to impart the
story upon her own children, and they would tell it to theirs, as
the story was in itself a talisman for good fortune and success.

Come evening, Moritz and Trude had arrived in Marggrabowa.
Zerlina was waiting for them at the front door in a loose mus-
lin-hemmed dress, her face small and concerned. Moritz inquired
as to his father's wellbeing and she replied, "He's sleeping right
now." They sat at the table and Zerlina served them the roast beef
and hot dumplings she had labored over that entire day.

Grunts and gurgles arose from the nearby room. Moritz went
to stand at his father's bedside while Trude leaned against the
doorjamb. Simon's face was ashen. Moritz sat beside him and
took his hand. Simon opened his eyes.

"Theresa didn't come with you," Simon said weakly.

"She needs to look after the house," said Moritz, "and Käthe is
still too young, but here is our Trude."

Trude placed her hand in Simon's translucent and somewhat clammy one. Moritz asked, "Are they taking good care of you?"

Simon replied, "I have no complaints."

Moritz said, "Tomorrow I'll have words with your doctor."

"That is completely unnecessary," said Simon. "I want for nothing – pray with me, Moritz."

Moritz took the large yarmulke from the bedside table, wore it, and together they murmured a prayer.

"You haven't prayed in a long while," said Simon.

Moritz, shifting his weight uncomfortably, said, "That isn't important now, Father."

Some men wearing white tallit came into the room and blessed Simon. They seemed to hold him in high esteem. After they left Simon was plunged into an uneasy sleep. Placing his hand on his father's forehead, Moritz started and called to Zerlina. She brought wet towels and Moritz placed them on the heated brow. Simon opened his eyes, which now seemed agitated, begging in the way the eyes of the deathly ill often are, yearning to say the words which for so long escaped them, words of resentment or forgiveness, of all times now, when seemingly nothing could make any difference.

"We'll get the doctor," said Moritz. "Perhaps the medicine is ill-suited."

Simon shook his head and said, "One must have faith," and again muttered fervently, "one must have faith, Moritz."

And Moritz said, "Yes, Father, of course."

Simon suddenly rose up in his bed and stared at his son with small, red eyes, and said, "Who do you pray to, Moritz, one must have someone to pray to."

Moritz said, "Not now, Father, you need to rest."

Simon fell quiet, and his face lit up as he said, "One must pray every day."

Moritz was growing somewhat desperate. Trude approached the bed, leaned close to Simon and said, "Father believes in good living and in family, he prays that people are healthy and happy."

Softly Simon whispered, "Life, Trude, is but a passing shadow, and men are rotting flesh."

Trude attempted to lift his pained spirit and said, "We follow the holidays and eat kosher, Grandfather, and that is also because we love and honor you so."

Simon waved his hand derisively, saying, "That won't do, Trude. Great destruction cometh."

Moritz became genuinely alarmed at that, saying, "Father, do not overexert yourself."

Simon said, "Mortal danger is upon us, I hear the voices, children, here in Marggrabowa they curse the Lord's name and there is no one to fight back, not even a minyan to beg for mercy, sound a prayer before the cataclysm comes." His lips instantly formed a prayer: "Judge me, O Lord, for I have walked in mine integrity; I have trusted also in the Lord, therefore I shall not slide." And his voice echoed yet again, "I will wash mine hands in innocence, so will I compass thine altar, O Lord, that I may publish with the voice of thanksgiving, and tell of all thy wondrous works."

Moritz responded, "Amen," and a darkness came over his proud face.

Trude looked anxiously at her father and gripped his hand. He responded with a light squeeze. Simon's gaze lingered over Trude and he said, "In a year, you shall be wed." Trude backed away slightly, disturbed by this, and he went on, "It will be a lovely wedding, Trude – I will handle the matchmaking in heaven."

"Don't say things like that, Grandfather," said Trude. "You'll get better and come to my wedding in the flesh."

"You must beget children, Trude," Simon said. "Many of them – a man must have many children," and he heaved a great sigh and wept a bit and said, "It was a fine life, I had a fine life." He then rose from his bed despite Moritz's protests and stumbled toward the small, bent front gate, and looked for a moment at the sky, at the people walking past on the cracked tiles, at a carriage driving away. He listened to the sound of bells and the chatter of children and the horses neighing and clacking on the pavement, raised his hands toward the heavens and fell. Moritz ran to him, cradled him in his arms and wiped the froth from his silent lips.

2.

Simon Freyer was buried in the Jewish cemetery of Marggrabowa. The family congregated in Moritz Freyer's large house in Stettin, including seven of his brothers and sisters who haven't yet left for North America or Palestine, to reminisce over Grandfather Simon, whom they had all loved dearly. After that they each returned to their respective business, and his father's prophecy of doom seemed to Moritz as no more than a dying man's folly.

Trude was occupied with her numerous suitors, who had been relentlessly storming the walls of her home, hoping to win her heart and her hand, nearly all of whom hailed from Pomerania Province. Among them were classmates, who suddenly recalled how very fond of her they'd been during their school days. Several of them were the sons of Stettin Jewish community bigwigs.

One of her suitors was even a Christian boy, the son of a highly decorated officer in the Red Order of Nobility, which included among its ranks the Pomeranian elite and close associates of the Kaiser, and of which Moritz was the only Jewish member. Trude's was a subtle beauty – she was not like those glamorous, gorgeous young women. In her heart she knew that it was not her the boys sought, but a way into the prosperous household of Moritz Freyer. She did not outright reject these men but remained timid in their presence and provided them with little conversation. At times she grew morose, and eventually they stopped coming.

More than once, Trude pondered the possibility of traveling to a faraway town, getting herself an education and a profession, and there – where no one knows her, surely she would meet a bright-eyed young man who had never heard of one Doctor Moritz Freyer of Stettin, nor ever visited the colossal house, or wandered the dozen rooms and the dining hall, and the huge kitchen, and the sausage larder and wine cellar in the basement, or peeked into the experiment laboratory that served as an excuse for several medical students to drop in on Trude and attempt to probe her intentions. Together they would walk the streets of an unfamiliar city and sit and laugh with friends at some enchanted plaza. But at this Trude was gripped by a terrible anxiety, and she hurried to put these thoughts out of her mind.

Her two younger brothers, Erich and Kurt, had very little in common with Trude. Kurt had left for Munich, to study art; Erich was apprenticing in a small shop in the Lastadie quarter, near a large laboratory in which Moritz spent his spare time searching for a chickenpox vaccine. The magical strolls the three of them used to take along the streets of Stettin—with Fräulein Sarnow to the statue of Sedina, the goddess of Stettin, on the riverbank, and the weekend trips to Buchenwald—had gone up in the smoke of time.

The year predicted by Grandfather Simon as her wedding year had passed, leaving Trude to deduce that, seeing as this prophecy fell flat, perhaps his prophecy of doom will disappoint as well. She spent her days working as a clerk in the mayor's office – a job given to her by the mayor as a gesture of goodwill toward province physician Moritz Freyer. Sometimes he would even stop by her desk and make small talk with her. On the weekends, Trude would walk along the river with her younger sister Käthe – a clever, opinionated child. With her mother, Theresa, she conversed mostly on everyday matters. Teresa was a somber, heavy-set woman who ruled the large household with an iron fist. Trude sensed that her mother was eager for her to make her move, to choose the man she would marry; but she chose the standard Jewish-German course of action and told her daughter nothing of this, explicitly.

When Trude was 26, the community was abuzz with talk of Moritz Freyer's daughter rotting away in her house and is well on her way to officially become an old maid. She now rejected the notion of going to university, since she could not stand the idea of studying with men and women so much younger than she – it seemed to her not only insufferable but unconventional. Käthe grew up and they no longer went on their weekly excursions by the river. In the evenings, after returning from her tedious work at the mayor's office, she dined with Moritz and Theresa. She felt herself growing fat and dull, fading away. In Marggrabowa, standing over the freshly laid tomb of her grandmother, Zerlina, who had been buried beside Simon, her husband of 60 years, Trude wished for the release of death.

As the days went by, her prospective suitors grew scarcer, and her fondness for them diminished. Her colleagues at the mayor's office were mostly gaunt old women who either fussed over the details of office etiquette or muttered and grumbled about the visitors and passersby. The department heads were usually men, taciturn and brimming with self-importance. One day, she noticed a young-looking man in the hallway. His name was Gerhard, and though he was not particularly handsome, Trude could not seem to look away from him as he passed by her, carrying mail for distribution and papers for signing. Upon investigation, she found that he had arrived in Stettin less than a month before and replaced the retired mailroom courier.

When Gerhard walked by her desk, he would say pleasant things, such as, "Fräulein Freyer, you've brought a piece of sunlight into the office today," and Trude would giggle self-consciously and lightly admonish him. One day he waited for her in the broad lobby of the town hall and, in a sort of excited stutter, inquired whether he could walk her home, and immediately added, "My deepest apologies for asking to accompany you."

She said, "No, it's fine, it's perfectly fine."

They started walking, and her way home grew uncharacteristically longer. They went down to the riverbank and sat there.

Gerhard told her, without the haughtiness that usually accompanies young people's telling of their own exploits, how he left his parents' house in Frankfurt am Main and settled in Weimar for a year or so, to soak up the spirit of Goethe and Schiller, but to his disappointment found nothing of the sort in the provincial city. "Not so much as a single poetic word still dwells there," he said. He then spent a year in the bustling Berlin, leaving when he grew tired of the glittering city lights and the constant swarm of subjects surrounding Kaiser Wilhelm. Then he said, "Perhaps Stettin on the riverbank will grant me some solace."

After that they continued to the Freyer estate, on Königstorstraße, where Gerhard bid her good night. Trude felt light as a feather. At dinner Theresa asked her if everything was all right. Trude laughed, and Theresa looked at her, her eyes knowing.

The following days, as well, Gerhard was waiting for her. They walked along the river again, and he recited poetry for her. In the mornings she began dreading her reflection in the mirror in the large bathroom with the polished green tiles, thinking to herself that he would soon leave, soon he will no longer want me – this is nothing but a cruel game. At meals she hardly ate. The hunger made her eyes burst out like deep wells of sorrow, leaving her more beautiful than she had been. Theresa would ask what was wrong with her, but Trude divulged nothing, and Theresa said simply, "I know everything, Trude, just talk to me, I can help."

Trude ran off to work, and that evening, when Gerhard waited for her in the lobby of the town hall, she told him, "I must go home now; please, I ask of you, do not speak to me again." He smiled and went away but did not return to work after that.

Trude spent the following few evenings secreted away in her home, until eventually she came to her senses and come evening, went down to the bank of the Oder. Gerhard was sitting there, his feet nearly touching the water. He glanced at her, and she smiled, and with a small gesture invited him to come sit beside her.

"I'm sorry," said Gerhard. "I went too far."

And Trude said, "All these days I'd been thinking of you," and they were again silent for a while.

"I've been thinking of you for a long while, Trude," he said. "You know this."

And she said, "I am neither young nor attractive, not this fairy-tale princess you seem to imagine."

"All that is meaningless," said Gerhard. "I see into your heart. You are a caged bird, Trude."

Trude felt bitter tears threatening to burst from her. Fear gripped her and she fell silent and wished to leave.

They met again near the river over the following days and gradually their bodies met as well. One time he told her, "Next month I'm leaving this place." Alarmed, she asked where to, and Gerhard said, "Germany suffocates me; rot spreads deep within it."

She asked, "And what of us?"

He said, "Come with me, you'll come with me, Trude."

They were silent for a long while after that, until Trude got up and heavily went home, to toss and turn that entire night in her bed. For a week, she spoke to no one. Several times she walked to the sea and watched from afar as Gerhard looked at the boats in the harbor until one day he was gone, and she sat at her desk and wrote a letter to the medical student Martin Hendelson, who had asked several times for her hand in marriage and for whom her heart felt nothing. In the meantime, Martin had become a young physician and opened a small clinic in Stettin. In her letter Trude inquired whether he would accept her acceptance of his marriage proposal, though it had been three years since last they spoke. She sent the letter in the hands of their regular coachman, Herr Holzfuss, who had been happy to carry out this mission.

The following evening, the young physician Martin Hendelson appeared in the home of Doctor Moritz Freyer. He was dressed impeccably, and his goateed face was tense. He stared at length at Trude, who stood unmoving in the lobby, and then walked over to Moritz, whose eyes glistened with the wisdom of age, and asked for the hand of his daughter, Fräulein Gertrude Freyer, in marriage. The two of them withdrew to Moritz' study, and when they emerged from it both shared an air of deep satisfaction. Martin approached Trude and kissed her right cheek, then her left, exchanged some pleasant words with her, and left.

Three months later, the town of Stettin celebrated the wedding of Chief Physician of Pomerania Province Doctor Moritz Freyer's daughter – who had already started down the old-maid path – with Martin Hendelson, also of Stettin, of whom it was said that his strange ways and sharp tongue would put him in the grave wifeless and without sons to say kaddish over him, which did not bother him in the slightest, as the man ate pork as if to spite, and shunned the synagogue even on Yom Kippur. At Moritz' explicit behest the wedding took place at the Great Stettin Synagogue, and was conducted by the community rabbi, Heiman Vogelstein.

Many of Stettin's aristocracy had been in attendance: Community leaders, the members of the Red Order of Nobility in their finest uniforms – the ones they would wear upon meeting the Kaiser and his representatives – as well as guests hailing from hospitals and clinics all over Pomerania. The president of Stettin made a brief appearance and was received with much reverence and veneration. Kurt came from faraway Munich, where he had been studying art history. He now had the appearance of an educated young man, with a small goatee trimmed in the same style as Martin's, and he observed the guests with great attentiveness and fascination. Erich came all the way from Antwerpen, where he had been learning French, so that he could assimilate more easily into the culture and commerce of Europe. The guests dined on delicacies diligently prepared by the resourceful Theresa. Moritz strolled among the guests, greeting and blessing, while

Martin seemed somewhat troubled and surly, avoiding nearly all conversation. Barely noticeable under her glittering white dress and bridal bonnet decorated with white flowers, Trude's sad eyes now blurred, after long years of heartache, with the mist of new hope.

3.

The Great War, which had been declared with great pomp in the spring of 1914, soon became a vile, fruitless ordeal. Kaiser Wilhelm deflated his puffed-up chest and holed up in a series of well-dug headquarters, attempting to solve one bad strategy with another. Doctor Moritz Freyer, a peaceful man by nature, had always treated Wilhelm's war habits as he would the mischief of a child playing with a new toy – but now the game had gotten out of hand, and Moritz grew solemn and dour, stooped in stature, and his gleaming copper cheeks yellowed.

The wounded, those who could no longer contribute to the war effort, were flowing into Stettin from the front. They filled the recovery homes and the Bergquelle Neurological Hospital. Moritz came to call and found men staring at ceilings, terrified, shrieking in their sleep. The postmen carried in their satchels letters from the Ministry of War informing of a son who heroically fell during a crucial battle, a husband who had vanished or was buried in a mass grave in faraway earth, or interred somewhere and marked with an austere cross, nameless, dateless.

Moritz would return agitated from the hospitals. He no longer went out in the evenings, instead opting to remain in his study, reading medical books and making notes. The local theater was no longer operating at any rate; neither was the concert hall. The Red Order of Nobility dispersed. Some of the younger members left proudly for the front and returned with limbs missing or unsound of mind. The elderly remained in the city, gradually graying, their jutting mustaches wilting.

The sickness progressed in a slow crawl through Moritz' body. Theresa still directed the house on Königstorstraße with a firm hand, but it had become nearly vacant, most of its rooms uninhabited, and even Fräulein Sarnow was reluctantly sent away, having been compensated handsomely and provided with glowing recommendations. Nearly every day Theresa sat down to write to some family member or other, many of whom had scattered across Germany or left for America or Palestine.

Every Tuesday afternoon, Theresa would visit her daughter Trude at her house on Lindenstraße. There they would sit and sip afternoon tea and discuss current affairs and family matters. An envelope sent from the northern town of Flensburg contained small photographs of the children of Anna and Kurt Freyer – Lotte who was three already, and one-year-old Minchen dressed like a little angel, and Anna with her warm, pleasant face, holding them next to Kurt and his pointed goatee. Trude's eyes shone slightly when she looked at the photographs, and Theresa looked at her daughter and shook her head.

"It's no good, Mutti," said Trude, sensing her mother's gaze. "We've tried everything, I honestly don't understand."

Theresa asked, "It's Martin, isn't it, Trude?"

"We spoke to Doctor Gershon," said Trude. "He says it's a mystery, that there's a great deal of mystery in matters such as this."

"I don't believe in such mysteries," said Theresa. "Everything has an explanation." Trude was perhaps about to reply, but Martin came in, as he did every day at six o'clock sharp, after the last patient had left. He bowed slightly toward Theresa and sat down silently.

Martin, who was not particularly young and prone to all manner of illness, was not drafted to the army. He opened a small ENT clinic in their apartment. It seemed that, during the war more than ever, the clinic was always brimming with old men and women with difficulty breathing, all waiting patiently and inertly for their appointment. At noon he would nap briefly, then return to the clinic. After supper he would meticulously read the local newspaper, which provided news from the front along with commentary pieces. Then he would flip through large books of sheet music, occasionally playing several notes on the piano, or humming along. More than anything, Martin enjoyed playing parts from Wagner's *Der Ring des Nibelungen* When the mood struck him, he would accompany his playing with poignant, exhilarated singing.

All his life, Martin Hendelson played Wagner. He read his congested, meandering books, and went to every lecture on Wagner given at the local music club. He went to listen to Wagner's concerts in the Stettin opera house, as well, though he barely listened to other composers, apart from Beethoven, whom he considered "The spring from which the fountain erupts." Trude shared but little of Martin's love, and he would make a point to share with her his mockery of others.

"Mozart," he would say, "such sweet, sentimental, vernal beauty, the music of a plump Austrian metropolitan, but we are after all of the forest, and this Mozart, even when he goes into the forest he finds there dainty ministering angels making love in a lush drawing room amid glasses of white wine and foie gras."

The royal symphony from Hamburg came to Stettin once, part of a concert tour in East Pomerania, playing Bach concertos and chorales. Martin sat grimacing in the concert hall and during the break left and walked back home, leaving a mortified Trude in his wake. She returned home to find him pounding the keys.

"This time, Martin, you truly went too far," she said to him, angrily.

"Ach, please," said Martin, "the whole world kneels in front of this spoiled servant of the church."

"But how can you say such a thing, Martin!" said Trude. "Bach is divine!"

"Precisely!" fumed Martin. "Precisely! God, God everywhere! you all run to him, to this so-called god, make petty arguments of who owns him, the Jews or the Christians, of whether he sired a bastard or did not."

"And what does any of this have to do with music?" said Trude. "Your Wagner has a dire beauty and Bach has a divine beauty, and you pit them against each other in some absurd competition."

Martin stopped playing for a while, retreating into his thoughts. Eventually he gazed at her at length and said, "Wagner screams from the bowels of my soul. I scream through him. It is the only way I know to scream, my precious Gertrude." She shuddered, because he so rarely called her that, 'my precious Gertrude,' and stroked his hair. Then they quietly made love, and he rolled over and fell asleep, moaning in his sleep, as was his way.

The funeral of Moritz Freyer, on a summer day in 1916, was attended by a small gathering of mourners. The mayor and some state representatives appeared at the Freyer estate to pay their respects, after which life quickly returned to its usual course.

The Great War lasted another two years, then ended as well. The men returned defeated from the front, and the women received them with warm embraces and open legs. In the larger cities the music halls reopened, and the theaters dazzled audiences with new plays. The cabarets were overflowing. It was a time for new dreams.

The large and mostly empty Freyer estate, parts of which had been rented out as clinics, had once again been permeated by children. The next generation of Freyers had arrived upon Grandmother Theresa and Aunt Trude and Uncle Martin. Anna and Kurt came from Berlin with their daughters, Lotte and Minchen and little Susi, and they would go with Trude to the town square to buy groceries for the family lunch, which had regained something of its former glory, in the finest Freyer years. Trude would take them to walk along the Oder, where she told them, as dictated by family tradition, The Legend of the Egg Miracle – adding and subtracting details as she saw fit, inwardly snickering over the liberties she had taken.

When the girls came to visit the Hendelson home, Trude would bring out the collection of toys, games and dolls she had kept just for them. The living room carpets were filled with miniature painted wooden buildings, processions of soldiers and dolls, small musical instruments – xylophone and triangle and drums, and the shrieks of children. At 6 p.m. Martin would leave his clinic, which was once again attended by men, women and children, and his reputation spread throughout the region as a meticulous physician, who always imparts the accurate medical truth – even when said truth is unpleasant to its receiver. He would linger in the rumpus room, examine the girls with a light, amused frown, and say, "Well – and the earth was Tohuwabohu."

He would chuckle to himself and then traverse the room with extreme caution, entered his study and pound the piano keys. Once he started playing, the three girls would cluster up against the door of the study, listening.

"What are you playing, Uncle Martin?" Minchen was first to dare ask.

"The compositions of the wonderful Richard Wagner. Do you like it?" Martin replied, awkwardly.

"Not very much," Lotte admitted. "It's a bit scary."

"Ah," said Martin. "But 'Hansel and Gretel' is also a bit scary, isn't it, Lotte? But still – you like it, don't you? Do you like 'Hansel and Gretel'?"

"I like it a lot," said Lotte. "But that's only a children's story, only a fairytale."

"Wagner writes fairytales, too," Martin explained. "Only, he writes them in music – usually it's older children who enjoy it, like you'll be some day."

"But you and Aunt Trude don't even have little children," Susi piped up, as the mortified Lotte and Minchen scrambled – and failed – to silence her, "so how will you ever have older children?"

"Well, Suschen, I'm afraid that probably won't be happening," said Martin, "and I suppose you find that unfortunate, as well, because otherwise you'd have someone to play with when you come to visit."

"So why not make some little children, like us?" Susi persisted.

A dark spark of mischief glinted in Martin's eye. He turned away from the piano, ponderously stroked his goatee, and said, "Well, it is a long story, too long for so late an hour." The girls widened curious eyes at him, and he cleared his throat and added, "Indeed, it is also a fairy tale of sorts." The girls were now utterly spellbound, even daring to come closer and sit at his feet. Martin furrowed his brow and said, "Once upon a time, there was a city by the name of Stettin, on the famous Oder River.

"What kind of fairy tale is this, Uncle Martin," Minchen protested. "There really is a city named Stettin, and it's really on the Oder, and we are here right now as we speak, all of us, in Stettin."

"Wait till the end – or I'll pluck off your head!" Martin rhymed playfully. "Well, is this town of Stettin, many children were born – too many. The city was packed full of children – there was no more room in the schools, or in the playgrounds, or on the ships in the river, and even the forest paths were so crowded and full of children that there was literally no room to step in!"

"That *is* a fairytale," Lottchen declared. "The forest is room enough for all the children in the world, even if every child from China comes to take a stroll."

"One day, the head of the kingdom, Kaiser Wilhelm himself, came to Stettin," Martin carried on with the tale, himself wondering where it would lead him. "'It is time,' he said, 'to solve this famous Stettin problem, or else other towns will follow this dangerous path, and that will be very unfortunate indeed. There will be so many children in Germany, that no one would be able to move at all – how, then, will we go to war if necessary? How will we work the factories? Who will grow the apples and wheat to feed all these children? From now on,' decreed the Kaiser, 'there will be no more children in Stettin! It will be a special city – a childless city. Anyone who dares parent children regardless, will be unceremoniously tossed into the Oder, and their children will be sold to slavery!'"

The girls listened, mouths agape. Martin, appearing slightly discomfited by the dark turn the story had taken, cleared his throat once again and said, "Well, then, this is why everyone who lives in Stettin, like your Auntie Trude and your Uncle Martin, is childless – by royal decree. One cannot go against the Kaiser, now could he? And now, girls, I require some peace and quiet."

The girls scattered to their affairs, pensive. Martin raised his head and saw Trude, who had been standing by the door all that while, looking at him intently. Martin returned to pound the piano keys and thunderous notes filled the house.

4.

In the spring of 1924, Erich and Hilde visited Stettin with their daughter, Yvonne, a cheerful, golden-haired toddler. She had just turned three and immediately enchanted everyone who saw her. Even Martin went out of his way to read fairytales to her from the books that were slowly piling in the Hendelson home.

Erich frolicked through the streets of Stettin like a boy in love. He and Trude rediscovered the riverside path they used to walk with Fräulein Sarnow. The Great War had scored deep gashes in the people, but left the streets untouched, and now cars were driving through them, procured by the town's wealthy upper class. The gates of Stettin stood true. New ships were still built and launched from the Oder shipyard, though now the launching ceremonies were modest affairs, with none of the military and orchestral splendor which accompanied them during Wilhelm's heyday.

Erich and his little family lived with Theresa, who was growing ever more tired, though she was not yet seventy years old. Mostly she would sit around the house and reread her favorite books, organize and sort the gold and silver cutlery, the candlesticks, the embroidered pillows and the pearls, necklaces and earrings and rings, and even help the housekeeper scrub the heavy wooden furniture that age seemed only to improve.

Now, lounging with Hilde and Erich, she was saying, "This is what's left; who remembers us? What do we leave in this world? Things."

"Come now, Mother," said Erich. "Look – Father wrote at least one notable book on the use of animals in human vaccination. Surely it will serve many generations to come."

"Tomorrow someone will invent a better vaccination," sighed Teresa. "Who will remember Moritz Freyer? Only these will remain," she added, gesturing at the large library whose shelves carried the ranks of black books, thick of binding, the complete works of Goethe, the complete works of Schiller, Hölderlin, Heinrich Heine. "And what became of the Torah books that your grandfather wrote with his very hands in the Marggrabowa Synagogue, now that there is no one left to pray there, and who knows what sort of goy barbarian is using them as kindling?"

"Your Moritz left many behind who owe him their life," said Hilde, "and the city archive keeps a record of his works, and surely they will name a hospital after him. I am truly heartbroken that I never had the chance to meet him. We are what we give to our fellow men – it is our only remnant."

"Ach, that's nice. That's very nice, what you said," said Theresa, and her eyes were soft and wet. She blew her nose. Erich became uncomfortable, as he often did, and went to sit by Yvonne, who fell asleep in his childhood crib, clutching a frayed old teddy bear.

"Erich, why don't we go for a stroll?" Hilde suggested. "Get some air."

The evening Stettin air smelled of spring. Winds from the ocean and the river and surrounding valleys converged to fill their lungs with the scents of the forest. Hilde suddenly embraced Erich, as she hadn't in quite some time, saying, "Ach, Erich, I'm in love with this Stettin of yours! This is a city made for children – these streets, and the river, not like that silly Spree back in Berlin, and Yvonne is doing so well here." Her elation infected Erich, as well, and he took her into the Kuhberg wine cellar.

Several groups of burly young men were sitting there, singing rowdily and guzzling beer by the mugful like farmers, boastful and desperate, and Erich recoiled momentarily, nearly tripping over the stairs, but quickly composed himself and said, "Well then, here is where we founded the October Thirteenth Association, and in two years we'll be meeting here to mark our twentieth anniversary, and anyone who dares miss it will be held fully accountable!"

Hilde and Erich wandered the streets of Stettin. They found themselves on Lindenstraße and knocked on the Hendelson's door. Trude opened it, and a glint of cheerfulness ignited in her sad eyes and she called out into the apartment, "Martin, dear, look who's come to visit."

Martin came out from one of the rooms, appearing slightly troubled and bewildered, saying, "Well, how nice, how very nice indeed, please won't you come in, well this is most unusual, we've only just finished dinner, but this is a perfect time, a perfectly fitting time for a little glass of schnapps and some of Trude's magnificent butter cakes, and a cup of frankincense tea, yes? Won't you say, Trude?"

And she said, "Settle down, Martin, and I'll take care of everything."

Hilde spoke at length of the beauty and wonder of Stettin in spring, and Martin, who had poured several consecutive glasses of schnapps down his throat, muttered something about spring being nothing but a transient fantasy, and Hilde said, "What's so wrong with a bit of fantasy."

Trude, who was slightly apprehensive about the bluntly argumentative nature of her 'exemplar' – as she would call Martin during occasional moments of grace, asked about Berlin which is the subject of so many newspaper articles.

And Erich said, "Really, Trude, you simply must come and visit Berlin, there is so much to do there." And after that, more silence.

"Why don't you play something for us, Martin," said Hilde, "I hear that you are a superb pianist."

Martin, who by this point had become quite inebriated, replied, "As you wish, madam – and what shall I play for you, ladies and gentlemen?"

Hilde said, "On a spring day such as this – only Vivaldi will do!"

Martin's face grew dark, and Trude could sense the oncoming storm, but was relieved when he did not raise his voice but hoarsely replied, "Vi... Vivaldi, here you have it, a flower blossoms in a rose garden, a butterfly flutters in a beam of sunlight, and poof, it is gone."

Embarrassed, Hilde amended, "Only if you wish to, of course, Martin..."

Martin raised his voice; Trude's dread rose along with it. "If I wish?" he giggled, an eerie sort of sound, "If I wish? Perhaps the lady wishes that I chirp some Meyerbeer for her? An operetta for demure Parisian mademoiselles? Candy music? Or perhaps, if I could be so bold, Ro... Rossini? Fun little quintets?" Martin was coming threateningly close to Hilde, now, saying, "Or, perhaps, he-he, Tchaikovsky? The very one? A fistful of honey?!"

"This is unnecessary, Martin." Erich spoke, annoyed. "You, as far as you're concerned, only what you love exists, just one obsession alone, and nothing else matters."

"Correct!" Martin replied, "I don't flutter about from one flower to the next, a bit of Zionismus pollen, a little Socialismus nectar, not I, my dear Erich!"

"I do nothing of the sort," Erich protested, "but study every subject profoundly – nothing that is human can be foreign to me."

"Clichés, Erich, clichés!" Martin maintained his assault under the combined astonishment of both Hilde and Trude, "The Jew's final refuge, and who better to employ it than the long-distance Zionist Erich Freyer, who set out to travel to Palestine with Doctor Herzl and Doctor Landau, and on the way found a blushing *shiksa* bride!"

Erich grew exceedingly pale, and Hilde feared he might collapse to the floor. Trude desperately tried to herd Martin into the bedroom, her arms flailing about, but he was flushed and livid and sweating profusely. Intently he marched toward the piano and began to slam the opening notes of *Tannhäuser*, crying out, "Here is your Vivaldi, here is your Tchaikovsky!" Erich stared at him with mounting amazement as Martin whispered into the music, as if orating some ancient spoken poetry, "And what are you now, my wandering brother-in-law? Where do you sojourn today, second-rate socialist, book peddler, and tomorrow, who knows? Maybe some petty bourgeois in New York, a Manhattan furrier? The Jew does not touch the soul of things, he floats above them, the Jew is unaffected by the mythical power of music, and the two of you, Erich and Kurt, the brain and the heart, David and Jonathan, you are the Jew, because of you we are vomited, expelled, spat on, and what do you say to that! What do you say!"

Silence fell. Hilde stared at Martin, horrified. Trude dropped her head into her hands.

Erich, whose nearly bald head sported an array of bulging veins which now threatened to burst, faced the slightly taller Martin, shook his head and quietly said, "I look for answers, Martin, I haven't sold my soul to anyone, I go to where I see good people working for the benefit of mankind, and that is where I found Hilde, and if the Zionismus will not permit me to marry a good woman such as her, then the Zionismus can go to hell, yes, Martin?"

"Yes, well," Martin muttered, "Humanismus, Socialismus, good people all around, the new face of Judeo-Christianity, you've made man into a god but still that pale mantle remains, words without spirit, a beautiful house founded on lies, yes, beauty for beauty's sake, morality for morality's sake, and where is the root? The root of the soul, where? It is in the darkness, that is where it dwells, but you search only in the light because it is comfortable, it is pretty in the light, but there is nothing, Erich, nothing there, eh? Only fanciful ideals, fantasies, Hilde, fantasies."

"But this is preposterous," said Erich, and his customarily tentative, hesitant voice grew sure and clear, "this talk of the dark root of the soul is nothing but your fantasy, Martin. That darkness holds nothing but decay and death." Martin stared at him, staggered. "I hear this nonsense of dark roots from people you never want to meet, Martin," Erich said, distraught, "yes, yes, vulgar, boorish people. They fill Berlin, like rats in a colossal burrow, and for some reason wherever they are Wagner is never far behind. Your Wagner makes my stomach turn. Yes, Martin, great music – but poisoned, evil."

"Wagner is Germany," said Martin. "Take Wagner away and Germany is gone, faded away, a soulless abomination."

Erich looked at Martin once again, briefly, then turned toward the door. "We're leaving now, Hilde," he said. "Let's go to Yvonne. I long to see her face. I'm so sorry, Trude. We should not have come like this, unannounced."

Trude stood there, eyes moist. Martin seemed dazed and dumbfounded, and Trude led him to his bed. In the morning he woke up, horrified, and ran breathless and gasping down the streets of Stettin to the Freyer home, wishing to apologize, but Erich and Hilde and their little Yvonne were already at the train station, headed for Berlin.

5.

The years went by, Theresa passed away, and of the proud Freyer family, the heart of Stettin's Jewish community, only the childless Trude and Martin Hendelson remained. Germany had suffered quite the ordeal, and nearly half of its Jews packed their bags and scattered to Europe, America, and Palestine – among these were Trude's sister and two brothers, along with their children. The effects of the new regime were evident in Stettin, but Martin and Trude's life seemed unaffected by the changes, and the possibility of following their kin never seemed to come up during the brief, fragmented conversations they had over their evening meals.

In the summer of 1933, as they did every year, Trude and Martin traveled to the Wagner festival at the Bayreuth Festspielhaus. The

annual voyage to the festival was facilitated by extensive prepa-
rations which had begun back in winter, when they received the
program and mail-ordered their tickets, as well as a room in
their favorite guesthouse. This year, the entire duration of the
festival was dedicated to Martin's favorite piece – *Der Ring des
Nibelungen*.

They spent nearly an entire day on the train, and they had to
switch in Berlin and Leipzig before finally arriving at small, rural
Bayreuth, nestled in woods.

Each summer the sleepy streets of Bayreuth awakened for the
Wagner festival, celebrated by admirers and enthusiasts from all
over Europe. This year, however, the bustle was notably greater.
Every government building displayed flags and placards bearing swastikas, and the image of Kanzler Hitler glared from every
display window. Groups of men in brown uniforms marched
through the streets, carrying flags and slogans denigrating the
Jews and the enemies of Germany. Martin looked at them, disgusted, and said to Trude, "Playing music for these people is like
feeding liverwurst to a pig."

Trude grasped his hand and he patted her arm and she said,
"But Martin, you've read what they've been writing there."

"Poppycock," stated Martin. "Nothing but nonsense and the
folly of adolescence."

It was late at night when Martin and Trude arrived at their
guesthouse. The clerk at the reception looked at them intently
as he wrote down their names. They stopped by their room and
then found a small café, nearly empty, where they nibbled on
a ham sandwich and took some solace in coffee and whipped
cream before heading back and falling silently to sleep.

The next morning Martin and Trude made their annual

pilgrimage to Wagner's grave, which was uncharacteristically deserted – perhaps because the other festival attendees were still sleeping off last night's drink. They ate a hearty breakfast and prepared themselves for the wonderful voyage, which was to start in the afternoon and end only toward midnight. At the foot of the stairs a tightly packed mob clustered, some dressed in eveningwear and others in those brown uniforms, and from the heart of the circle a shriek rose which grew louder, deafening, until there was no longer a doubt in Trude's mind that in there, amid that tight ring, stood that man whose name was never uttered in the Hendelson house. The man whose name was shunned like an ancient sorcerer's curse, whose voice was cause only to turn off the radio; from his mouth the German that Trude loves so much had lost the murmur of waves and the whisper of the forest until all that remained was the clanking of axes against steel and the hard cracks of explosions. Now she could see his arm rising and falling. In between shrieks, the crowd exploded into rhythmic cheers.

Martin edged closer, Trude remained behind. For a moment it seemed as though he was engulfed by the crowd, then Trude looked, horrified, as several people surrounded him and expelled him from their space, shoving and pushing until he lost his footing and fell to the ground. A tight ring of people, shrill with profanities and laughter, encircled his prone form. Trude ran to him, her face ashen, and crouched beside him. He looked at her, agitated. A thin stream of blood flowed from his forehead and she took a small handkerchief from her purse and dabbed at it. Somewhat unsteadily, Martin rose to his feet.

"What did they want from you, Martin?" Trude asked.

"I tripped," said Martin. "Bad luck, nothing more."

"But, Martin," said Trude, "this is inconceivable."

Martin shot her a hard look, then turned to face forward. His graying goatee trembled when they walked into the concert hall, which hummed with the last whispers and murmurs before the curtain rose, final coughs, the racket of instruments. Trude's heart was no longer with the music that soon filled the hall. Again and again she glanced at Martin, who sat there, his face expressionless, even during the intermission, as though he had been paralyzed.

The next morning, they took the first train to Leipzig. As the train hurtled through the woods between Berlin and Stettin, Trude said, "Martin, we cannot stay. We'll sell the apartment before the month is out, go to Amsterdam, to Kurt and Erich, or to America. Or London, perhaps."

Martin glanced sharply at her, then muttered, "Well, yes, certainly," folded his pale hands together and looked at his wristwatch. Evening had fallen by the time the train crossed the Oder River.

Trude began making arrangements for their departure. She wrote letters to her brother Kurt in Amsterdam, and to her brother Erich, whose wife Hilde had in the meanwhile separated from and returned to Germany, and to her little sister Käthe, who had just left Berlin along with her husband Albert and their children Rachel and Gabriel, to Palestine. She wrote her beloved cousin Leo Freyer in Brooklyn, and even purchased a small ad in the local paper, where she had put up for sale 'A cozy flat, with option for private office and nursery, 29 Lindenstraße.' Strangers began turning up at the Hendelson home, making inquiries and taking interest, and never failing to be confounded by the owner, who vanished into one of the rooms instead of conducting the tour.

After a great deal of inconvenience and many potential deals that fell through, one Brukenthal, Esq. informed Trude that he had taken an interest in the house, "Which perfectly suits his needs both as a family man whose sons have set out on their own paths, and as a lawyer who requires an office." Overwhelmed by enthusiasm and hope, Trude told Martin about the buyer, saying that this time, he would unfortunately have no choice but to come at the agreed upon time to sign the sales contract. Once they receive payment, they could travel to Amsterdam, and from there plan their next steps.

Martin stared at her, unseeing, and left. For hours he wandered the streets of Stettin. Patients who arrived at the clinic found the door closed, and the lawyer Brukenthal also noticed the distinct absence of the house owner. After spending an interminable hour nibbling on butter cookies with the deeply embarrassed Frau Gertrude Hendelson, who had assured him several times that any minute now her husband should be back from work "which for some reason is taking so long today," he got up and left, not without adding a perfunctory insult.

Trude felt the blood draining from her body and her throat becoming a crucible of tears and her chest filling with lurching sobs, but she could not cry. She stood by the window instead. From the darkness, shifting in and out of the quivering light of the gas lamps, Martin returned to the house, sat down, looked at her, and then got up and went to the piano, but Trude stood in his way.

"Enough, Martin," she said, "say something, now, you cannot stay quiet all the time, I won't bare this silence any longer."

He sat down in front of the piano, but she was there shutting the piano's lid and saying, "Stop that, stop running away," and he burst into laughter, a loud, shrieking laughter.

"Come now," he said, laughing, "stop running away, really, stop running, well, isn't this just delightful, this hardly bears listening, Trude."

"What the hell is wrong with you, then!" Trude yelled, "What is it you want, just speak plainly."

Martin got up from the piano and began pacing back and forth across the room, frantically shaking his head and striking his beard, "Indeed someone here is running, Trude," he spoke in precise, clipped sentences, "but who is running? Am I running? I am not running anywhere, Trude. And you, it is you who are running, up and off you go, like all the pale Freyers talking themselves to death, fleeing alongside them from a passing shadow, from a mob of loud thugs, they run from the barbarians and thus grant the barbarians their victory! Victorious is the barbarian at last, over the Jew and the German in one fell swoop! And I, Trude, I am not going anywhere, and when the screeching Austrian will be wiped from the face of the earth I will be here to spit on his grave."

Trude was stunned into stillness, while Martin appeared reborn. He roamed the house noisily consuming a sweet roll with cream cheese. When he noticed her sitting, his eyes softened. He sat facing her, placing a long, translucent hand on hers, and said, "My precious Gertrude, everything will be all right. These challenging times are bound to pass, and Kurt and Erich will come back, their very souls are rooted here. There is nowhere else they will find their books, their hidden gems, their museums, their music. They are running from themselves, Trude, and your Käthe, she will flee Palestine screaming bloody murder once the first Arab charges at her on camelback."

Trude raised her head, and Martin saw moisture and misery in her eyes. "But I'm afraid, Martin," she said, "so afraid. They burned Erich and Hilde's books at the Opernplatz in Berlin, and they've been drawing swastikas on the storefronts, and here in Stettin, well – it must get here at some point, and what will we do then? I'm already afraid to go to the market, even to take an evening stroll! And what will we do when they shut down your clinic?"

"There wouldn't be a decent lawyer or doctor left in the entire town," said Martin, sucking his teeth, and Trude thought she heard a measure of contempt. "Even these imbecile Stettinites cannot afford that."

Trude did not reply. They went to bed and made love slowly, as if it was their last act of love, and Trude felt the descent of old age which for so long had been waiting on her doorstep and cried that entire night tearlessly.

6.

It was a winter day in 1935. The skies bombarded the streets with hard salvos of rain, and the cracked pavement was blacker and muddier than ever. Trude went out to the curb, just for a moment, to check the mailbox. In it she found some letters from the bank and the medical insurance company, as well as a thin booklet sent from the Pomerania Ministry of Employment titled "Stettin Businesses by Occupation." And beneath that, in smaller print, the subtitle: "Do not accept any treatment, consultation or craft from these businesses." She leafed through it, skipping to page 45. The category "Free Professions" consisted of five names, and the category "Chemists" of another three, and the architect Siegfried Pavel from No. 8 Friedrich-Karl-Straße, whom she knew from school. Her eyes spotted the title "Physicians", which was a larger category.

Trude traced her finger down the list of names, all of them familiar. Adler, A., an ENT specialist from No. 2 Hohenzollern square. Aaronheim, L., A general practitioner from No. 9 Bismarckstraße. She went through the names quickly, her heart pounding. Ehrlich, P., A nurse. Gershon, A., an obstetrician whose name pierced her heart. She used to frequent his clinic on 29 Parade Square, back when she was still trying to get pregnant, and he knew her deepest secrets. Hammerschmidt, H., a general practitioner, No. 73 Oberstraße. For a brief moment, a mist of hope shielded her eyes – but there the letters were, yelling out from the page, Hendelson, M., general practitioner, 29 Lindenstraße. She read it and reread it, the small booklet burning in her hands.

Trude ran to the clinic where Martin was examining a thick-necked, paunchy man. She stormed in and smacked the booklet down in front of him. Martin glanced at her and said nothing. He returned to his patient and waved her away. When the man left, Martin walked slowly to the empty waiting room. For a moment, he was so old and so green. He sat on a large floral-patterned sofa in the middle of the room, and Trude thought that he would expire right then and there. She tried to say something, but he silenced her with a gesture, went to his bed, and did not leave it for a week.

Dr. Erich Weltmann, 43 Kaiser-Wilhelm-straße, an internal physician who would occasionally come to visit, and whose name was the very last on the list, was summoned urgently to examine

Martin. He determined that Martin was suffering from tension and anxiety "on levels far exceeding the ordinary, which can affect and possibly harm the immune system," and recommended that Martin avoid all activity until further notice, especially seeing as he was 62 and close to retiring age. The doctor supposed that "he wouldn't exactly be drowning in patients, even if he was fit as a fiddle," said Dr. Weltmann, laughing drily.

After a week, Martin rose from his sickbed and even ventured out on morning strolls again. He was visited, furtively, by the occasional Jewish patient, who apologized in advance for not being able to pay his full fee. He even returned to the piano, to his Wagner. Now that he had time to spare, he returned to the colossal sheet music books, their bindings adorned with drawings of angels, musical notes and ornately illuminated letters. He would play and play, book after book he would play, and between books he would mutter to himself with an odd sort of exasperation, "They took him to themselves, the barbarians, but I'll guard him, the geniuses must be guarded, so they don't fall into the hands of the ignorant and the vulgar," thus he would drone.

Trude would comment from the other room, "Martin, if you've something to tell me, please speak up so that I can hear."

But again and again he would be back at it, after a while, muttering, "They took Germany, and they bought it cheap for such a treasured gift." And he would make little speeches at the piano about "the squealing Austrian with the dive-bar-German," talking and playing to himself. Even when he sat with Trude for dinner he would mumble as if no one was listening, until she would snap at him and he would fall silent like a child scolded. On the date of the festival in Bayreuth he paced the apartment like a caged lion for a full day and then fell ill, burning with fever.

Dr. Weltmann came at once and prescribed sedatives.

Trude wrote to her family in Palestine and they sent back concerned, sad replies. Whenever a letter came, she would read it to Martin over dinner, and he would listen attentively, making his comments. He was not fond of Käthe, saying that she was "a bigger Zionist than Herzl." Erich was staying at Käthe and Albert's house, in Kiryat Bialik in northern Palestine – when his name came up, Martin would only say that Erich was "a wretched man." He felt sorry for Anna, wondering "what can she possibly have to do in that desert, this girl who never learned a trade, perhaps her brother can build her a bank there." For it was known that Otto Heymann, Anna's brother, was a highly successful banker who worked all over Germany, and even the Nazi leadership sought his financial counsel.

In one of the letters from Kurt, he'd told them how he hopes to become involved in the profound academic research of Israeli art. Martin chuckled and said, "Well, finally he can become a museum administrator – the only trouble is that he's arrived at a country where no one has heard of such an institution!"

Trude, who usually avoided offering a response to Martin's comments, could not help herself this time and said, "And you, you never wanted this family, but it is your family, the Freyer family, and it is nothing to be ashamed of."

"Oh yes, proud people," said Martin, "but not always justifiably, Trude – not always justifiably."

"If things would have been different, Kurt could have been a great scholar here in Germany, respectable, renowned," Trude protested.

Martin said, "I suppose we'll never know, now, will we?"

Finally Trude erupted at him, "Then why the hell did you

marry into this family that you so despise?!"

He sneered. "Well, nothing to do about that now, is there, a bit late to discuss it at this point."

Trude said, "You wanted to be close to Doctor Moritz Freyer, didn't you, to be well-connected, the young doctor caught the scent of a fat, juicy bone." Martin flushed a deep red and retired to his piano, pounding the keys with a vengeance until she came to him, contrite, and again the coughing and the frailty overtook him.

They usually weren't inclined to talk much, and so the days passed slowly. Trude would occasionally bring up the notion of leaving Germany, always indirectly, telling him incidentally about "Bruno and Rosa Fischer, who had just left thanks to their daughter Carolina, who found a husband in America." And once she spoke at length of a friend her age from Berlin, who "despite having no children received a scholarship at a London research institute, securing him an entry visa."

Martin listened absently and suddenly spoke, "And why tell me all this, Trude, when it is nothing but idle talk, when different men have different fates and there is nothing else to it?"

"Perhaps something can still be done, Martin," said Trude.

"And for what," he said, though no longer livid as he was in the past. "What else could happen to us which has not already happened, Trude? And after all we are here, in Stettin, at the heart of the kingdom, eating three meals a day, are things really that terrible?"

"But all these rules, all these restrictions, we barely have a life," said Trude.

"This is our life thus far," stated Martin. "There wouldn't be much to the lives of old relics like us even if we were heirs to

the House of Habsburg, and if we are to spend the rest of it im-
prisoned I prefer a prison on the bank of the Oder rather than
be exiled to the east, don't you? After all, the eastern sun would
eradicate you within the week."

Trude giggled lightly and smacked his beard playfully, but the
sadness never left her eyes, not since that cursed morning in the
winter of 1935, when someone placed the booklet in their mailbox listing the boycotted Jewish businesses of Stettin, or perhaps
since that damned festival at Bayreuth in the summer of 1933, or
perhaps since Martin's hard words drove away Erich and Hilde,
or perhaps since the death of her beloved father during the Great
War, and perhaps that sadness had always remained there, with
her, all her life.

July 18, 1939, Trude sent a letter to her family in Palestine, in
sharp, scrambling letters, chasing one another as if fleeing the
armored footfalls of soldiers.

16.7.39

My Beloved Dears!

Your last letter, and its heartwarming abundance of good
wishes, brought me immense joy. Thank you for all of it.
When I read your words, I forget about the distance, and
feel unconditionally close to you. But after that, when I
feel it so strongly, the separation is that much more painful. It hurts that now, when I so urgently need one of my
siblings here with me, like I've never needed you before,
I can't reach any of you. I know it is hard for you, as well,
having no option to stand by my side.

But fate halts for no one! Who would have thought I
would ever present such a problem to the family? Now

it is my life you discuss on your strolls, and you will un-avoidably reach the same conclusion as I have: It is hope-less. The route to emigration is fraught with obstacles, especially for us. Even if we could get somewhere, there is still the problem of income, livelihood. We would al-ways need people to vouch for us, and where would we find those?

Moreover, we are old, and can only live someplace where we have some connections. Under no condition can the two of us wander the world alone, especially with Mar-tin's health being how it is. This is different, of course, when you have children who can somehow carry their parents along.

And now, all these new restrictions! I was shocked when I read of them. It was as if the thin twig I had been clutching suddenly blew away in the wind. Everything disappeared into the distance, hidden in mist. No point in thinking or planning until something new turns up. It seems mad anyway, that I have not suffocated these wishes yet, when my mind tells me only that there is no solution. And so I oscillate between dreams and hopelessness.

My greatest concern is Martin's health. For a while he was better, and then deteriorated again, and again with all this uncertainty. He ran a fever, and one can never know what that leads to. During those hours I go through hell. Anxiety eats me alive, and there is no one, literally no one I can call for help. I wonder, where are all the people who used to be here, who used to help us – how alone we are these days. Better no to think of it at all.

I've heard nothing about Hilde. I thought Erich should know. He might be suffering quietly, wondering what happened to her, even more so wondering about Yvonne. He should be spoken to cautiously and reassured. Kurt, please write to me about Erich, since you've met him a few times. Käthe wrote a bit about him, but I'd like to hear from you as well. His letters are a bit odd – some seem confused while others are fine, perfectly pleasant. All very loving. He is the same kind, considerate, loyal and devoted man he has always been. We all carry with us a chapter of a broken life, some longer, some shorter.

Trude

7.

On February 12, 1940, at around 8 p.m., the large brass bell hanging above the front door of Martin and Trude Hendelson rang. Trude was a bit startled, as they had no company planned for that evening, and people tended to keep to their homes in the evenings ever since the war started. Martin was lying in bed. The night before he scarcely slept and in the morning his fever rose, and he would not eat. Trude opened the door to find an officer who introduced himself as Oberleutnant Kurz, accompanied by two soldiers.

Officer Kurz greeted Trude and she replied courteously and asked if they'd like to come in. "That won't be necessary, Frau Hendelson," said the officer. "I've been instructed to inform you that by special decree you and any family residing with you must leave Germany within ten hours."

Trude looked at the officer and did not reply. Snakes of ice slithered in the veins of her legs.

"In order to carry out this decree," Kurz continued, "you will be provided with transportation services from the eastern train station starting early next morning."

"My husband is lying in the next room," said Trude. "We have no children; it is only the two of us."

"In that case your instructions are clear, Madam," stated Kurz. "You and your husband are requested to follow these instructions and bring with you two suitcases, one for each of you, measuring no more than fifty centimeters in breadth."

"But my husband is very ill," said Trude.

"Regarding that," said the officer in the same measured monotone, "I can merely assure you that your husband will receive the best available treatment once you have passed the border and reached your new destination in the Polish territories."

For a moment Trude was assaulted by new hope, though she knew it must be as fruitless as all the other sparks of hope which ignited in her life only to be extinguished again, all those years with despair as an ever-present houseguest, dour and burdensome. Poland seemed suddenly like a mysterious new world, an unknown universe of small, distant cities, whose streets perhaps are not so filled with the constant march of soldiers. Perhaps there would be some forgotten corner, some hidden place where they could find a home and lay down the tired and sick body and go to the marketplace without fear.

Trude looked at Oberleutnant Kurz and his soldiers, seeking some sort of confirmation for her new hope, but the door closed after them, and she heard them muttering the details of the next address across the street. She stumbled to Martin's bed and heard herself groan in a voice not her own, Oh, God, oh my God, and she sat beside him, and he woke, startled, from his troubled sleep.

"Tomorrow we are leaving, Martin," she said.

Martin shook his head and she did not know what he tried to say. "I must pack," and again he could not reply and she said, "they said you would be taken care of, that people who were unwell would receive medical treatment, it said so in their orders."

She got up and went to the walk-in closet, opened two suit-cases and stared at them for a long while and wondered, what does one pack for such a journey, how many pairs of underwear will they need in the east? She tried to recall the trips they used to take to her grandfather Simon and Grandmother Zerlina, but those always took place in summer, when the air was clear and wet with dew. After she had packed a few trousers and shirts and underclothes and still had plenty of room in the suitcase, so she rummaged through the floral chests of drawers in which the treasured jewels and pearls had been collected over the genera-tions. She gathered them in her hands and tossed them into the bags, then took them out again, silently furious, and sat there helplessly. Eventually she changed her mind and placed a thick brown envelope inside the suitcase, filled with photographs and letters she had kept, an empty letter book, some envelopes and a pen, and a half-full inkwell, carefully wrapped.

Martin was fast asleep. He had not slept so deeply in a long time, long enough that Trude was momentarily alarmed, but he was breathing soundly, warmly. A small, peaceful snoring rose from him. On the dresser by the piano there was a tall, dusty stack of books upon books of sheet music, with the names of pieces and melodies in heavily crowned Gothic script. She tried to pick two or three of them to shove into the suitcase, but promptly muttered to herself, "Ach, nonsense." She went to arrange a small medicine bag to last at least a week, until Martin is brought to a hospital where he could receive proper care, like Oberleutnant Kurz had said.

By the time she was done packing both suitcases it was 1 a.m. She lay on the sofa in the living room which barely accommodated her height, tried to sleep but failed, and got up to look out the window. The heavy rain was still bombarding the streets and she thought, *What will be of Martin, how will we walk in this rain, perhaps the rain will show lenience and abate in the morning?* She was startled by a loud, hard cough from Martin's room, and she ran to him. He had woken up. She served him a spoonful of thick medicine. She then hurried to the kitchen, set the pot on the stove, and came back.

Martin lay on the bed, his eyes wide, his face white and heavy. "Well," he said, "it is still raining."

"I wish it would stop. It has to stop sometime," said Trude.

"And you are not sleeping. Perhaps you could try and get some sleep," said Martin.

"I've tried to, Martin, but no matter, in any case it will be morning soon," she said. "I'll probably sleep on the train, maybe we could find a decent seat, well, we have to find a decent seat so you can be comfortable, it will probably by a long ride."

"Yes," said Martin, "we'll leave on time, no other choice. And if the rain persists, my raincoat is highly effective even in pouring rain, and it is vital that we bring the large umbrella with us. Best to have all of this prepared in advance."

"Everything will be ready, Martin," said Trude. "We should have a cup of tea, perhaps eat something around five-thirty, so that by six we'll be ready to depart. That way we can be among the first to board. After that it will be hard to find someone to talk to about providing you with appropriate seating."

"Five-thirty, good," said Martin. They were silent for a long while, and suddenly he coughed, a sharp, deep cough, like a harsh scream, and his body writhed on the moist sheets, and she leaned toward him and placed a cloth on his forehead until he became calm. He held her hand like an adolescent boy touching the hand of his beloved, tried to say something to her.

She said, "I know, everything will be alright, we will stay together, no matter what happens we will always stay together, I will sit by your side, in the hospital hallway if I must, and stay there." But Martin was shaking his head in disagreement, swaying from side to side, and she said, "Martin, what is it?"

His eyes filled with tears. "My precious Gertrude," he said, "I ask for your forgiveness. From the depths of my soul, with everything I hold dear, I beg for your forgiveness, will you forgive me, Gertrude?"

Trude looked at him, astonished, and said, "But Martin, what is all this, there is nothing to forgive."

But he shook his head again and this time impatiently, with an anger that intensified, his white face reddening, and he yelled, "Forgive me, Gertrude, my beloved Gertrude, I have brought you so much sorrow, I am a blind man, Trude, a blind man who deserves neither forgiveness nor love, and still, forgive me, Gertrude!" The words flowed jumbled from his mouth and became a lingering, keening sob, slowly waning. Martin fell to the mattress, defeated, and fell asleep once more, but yelled in his sleep and moaned and groaned.

Trude looked at his sleeping form, concerned at first, then

astounded, and her eyes which had been accustomed to stopping the tears were now overflowing with them. She wept, violently, a ceaseless rhythm of heaving sobs. She hadn't cried like that in years, in all her years. She wept for her barren womb, for her days which had been used up between the restaurants and the market-place, for the books devoured and forgotten and for the sounds of music that faded away in the river air. She wept for her brothers, Kurt and Erich, and her sister Käthe, who had gone to Palestine, whom she will never see again, and for their young girls who used to come every spring and walk to the market with her or stroll through the picturesque forest paths of Pomerania, and for the image of Gerhard which also flickered momentarily through the river mist and dissipated. She wept for her love for Moritz, her beautiful, proud father, an endless lament, a fire consuming the breast, many waters cannot quench it.

When Trude's crying died out so did the rain. Dawn rose over Stettin.

CHAPTER TWO: ERICH

1.

In October 1903, the members of the Jewish community of Stettin were invited to a lecture in the large auditorium in the bourse building. The curious topic was "Zionism and its opposers." Hundreds came, filling the hall to the point of bursting. Even the aisles were packed, crammed with crowding men. Moritz Freyer was invited by the community leaders and at first wasn't sure he would attend, but they insisted, claiming that his presence would bestow an air of respectability. His two sons, Erich and Kurt, wished to go as well, and though the usher standing in the entrance initially said there was no admittance of lads under 20, someone soon whispered in his ear that they were Herr Doctor Moritz Freyer's boys, and they were hastily snuck in and stood wedged against the back wall.

Erich knew many of the people in the audience and waved at them. Among them was also Louis Rosenthal, a community clerk who used to frequent their father's clinic, often unwell despite his young age.

Once everyone had filed in and the doors of the auditorium were shut, the community treasurer walked up to the podium to present the esteemed Herr Doctor Alfred Kalle, member of the Zionist executive committee, and Herr Heinrich Loewe who is also an active member of the Zionist organization in Berlin.

Dr. Kalle spoke mildly, constantly checking the audience for its reaction.

"The Jew," began Kalle, "is a slave of the world. While he might feel as if he is free, as if he is close to his god and to his ancient culture, he is in fact relentlessly oppressed." Apparently feeling the audience was displeased with this bleak picture, Kalle raised his voice slightly. "We are the constant object of animosity and superstition. We are forbidden from running for public office, and we are the first to be blamed and cast aside in the face of hardship." Kurt listened, his face as silent and intent as it most often was, when Kalle added, "We are a people without a homeland. As long as we have no homeland, we will never be free."

At this some heated cries rose from the audience, which so far had managed to maintain its composure, "It's dangerous!"

"It's dangerous! Such talk!"

Kalle said, "You are German patriots. I, too, am a German patriot." The crowd fell silent, hesitant. "And this is precisely why I call for a Jewish homeland. Those among you who feel free in their country, let them live out their lives in peace, but let them also know that in times of suffering the door is opened before them, to a place wherein Jews are free, unconditionally free, in the land of Zion!"

Now Herr Loewe rose to speak, and in a soft voice said, "A week ago I traveled to visit the Chişinău Jewish community in Ukraine. I saw women whose husbands were slain by pogromers as they watched. I saw men who watched Cossacks rape the women they love and slit their throats. I walked to the cemetery with these poor souls and I wept with them! I swore that so long as I draw breath, I will work so that there is a place in the world in which Jewish men and women will no longer be helpless in the face of a cruel militant state. That is the heart and soul of the Zionismus. Chișinău is not the end, there will be other Chișinăus, many others all over Europe."

Loewe's words received a mixed response, both nods of agreement and angry shouting, "Enough of your fearmongering!"

"You fashion politics from blood!"

"Indeed, where does all that donation money you collect end up!"

"Funding Doctor Herzl's excursions abroad! Indulging, staying at hotels!"

"Why, it is downright corruption!"

Several men were already pushing through the crowd to perhaps attempt and remove Kalle and Loewe from the stage, while others yelled still, "This is no way to behave!"

"Let Doctor Vogelstein speak!"

Across the commotion Kurt could just make his father Moritz stand up from his front-row seat. Immediately silencing the growls that rose from the audience, calls for order, appeasement. Moritz raised his hand, saying, "Brothers, friends, what will these esteemed gentlemen think of the Stettin community?"

At this the audience settled down entirely. Marching along the wall on his way to the podium came the rabbi of the Stettin Jewish community, Heiman Vogelstein, an elderly man with a shock of white hair and a brimmed hat. The crowd fell silent. Kurt felt a slight nausea he could not explain.

"We cannot put our heads in the sand," began Rabbi Vogelstein, whose habit of accompanying the prayers with organ music and a mixed Jewish-Christian choir was a topic of much discussion around the family dinner table. "The Jew is now at a point at which his very existence is at issue. We must find a solution, and these dear men, pure of heart, do bring us one – from their innocent hearts, a solution. But it is a false solution, unrealistic. There is nothing for the Jew in Zion. Zion is a starry-eyed dream, a passing fancy. We are Europeans. We are the very heart of Europe. We brought with us to Europe the brilliance of our proud spirits, of science, of the eternal Torah, of Talmudic debate, and –first and foremost – the glory of God. Without us Europe would be the domain of barbarians."

Kurt listened intently, his large glasses glittering in the lights of the crowded auditorium. Erich stood by him, his mouth agape, standing on his toes, straining to see.

"The barbarian fears the Jew," continued Rabbi Vogelstein, "and therefore he strikes our brother, but we shall reach out our hand to him in peace, for the Jew and the Christian are brothers. We shall come to his homes, to his churches, and say, our religion is one religion: Judeo-Christianity. Our motherland is one motherland: Germany. Our world is one world: Europe!"

Heiman Vogelstein looked at Kalle and Loewe. For a moment his gaze seemed compassionate, but his voice was loud, and his pose reminiscent of a choir conductor raising his arms toward the crescendo.

"You Zionists have abandoned religion," he said passionately, "deserted God, divorced both the spirit and the flesh of Judaism, and you have no right to come and preach in its name, and deliver us to a desolate land, where we will become nomads and assimilate with the ignorant Muslim."

The audience erupted into applause, and Vogelstein raised a silencing hand. "We are the chosen people," he stated. "We were not chosen to live small lives in a forsaken land, to found soulless mechanisms of state, to work the barren soil in illiterate villages as the Zionists would have it. We were meant to spread the word of God, for it was we who formulated God, and without us Germany would be a land of idols and demons."

Kalle and Loewe stared at Vogelstein, visibly distraught by the spell he had cast over the crowd. "Germany vomits you from its belly," Loewe seethed, "no one desires your Jewish gospel."

And Vogelstein replied, "The loyalty of the Jew is twofold, both to the motherland in which he lives, and to God, until the coming of the messiah who will bring a world without nations and nationalities. Today, in this great German motherland, we must embrace the hearts of our Christian brothers and render it prepared, work the common God together, and loyally serve the Kaiser."

Many among the audience raised their hands in the air, stirred. Vogelstein burst into song and the crowd joined him.

Kurt could hear the clear, dulcet voice of Louis Rosenthal, who occasionally filled in for the community hazzan, resonating through the hall, "Who is this King of glory, the Lord of hosts, He is the King of glory, Who is the prince of God, Messiah son of David is the prince of God?"

The singing grew louder and now everyone sang together: "Who is the lord of the kingdom, our king and master, Wilhelm the second, he is the master of the kingdom, who is the queen, Kaiserin Auguste Viktoria, noble wife, Amen and Amen and Amen Selah."

The song of worship ended. Shouts of approval rose from the audience, cheers. Kalle and Loewe looked at each other and began moving slowly toward the exit, the audience parting to accommodate their departure. They boarded the carriage that had been waiting and swiftly disappeared. Kurt examined the enthusiasm of the crowd and suddenly, for the first time, noticed Erich, who was deathly pale, and now his head rolled back, and he fell from his chair with a loud crash. He was instantly surrounded. Moritz rushed over to his son and examined him, asking that someone run to the apothecary and fetch smelling salts and moist towels, until eventually Erich recovered, and he opened his eyes.

2.

Erich lay in bed under Theresa's constant watch. Moritz ascertained that he suffered from a psychophysical seizure caused by stress, or perhaps some hidden illness previously unknown in the Freyer family, which had always prided itself on the good health and long lifespans.

Erich remained bedridden for about a week, speaking little and doing less, until one day he rose from his bed and walked outside, Theresa protesting in his wake. Kurt rushed to catch up with him, hurrying through the darkening streets of Stettin, among the linden trees, the plazas and gates. The crooked houses gave Stettin a sense of incompleteness, a city whose beauty must be proven, and in it was a bit of Berlin and a bit of Paris and a bit of Hamburg, but rather than being the sum of these it was their subtraction. Erich reached Kurt and took his hand, and they both turned around and started marching briskly backward – a habit they had recently developed, becoming the source of much entertainment during dinner conversations across Stettin.

"Well," said Kurt, "what now, Erich?"

"Wonderful things are about to take place," Erich stated. "Wonderful things."

"But how do you feel now, you were so ill," wondered Kurt.

"I'm going to do something," said Erich. "Are you coming, or do you intend to make another one of your magnificent speeches?"

Kurt wondered as to the nature of said something, but replied, "I'll come with you. You can trust your brother, you cruel bastard," and they both laughed.

"Right now, we are headed for Herman Jakob's house, and from there you can see for yourself," said Erich.

They climbed the stairs of a house on Turnerstraße and knocked on the door. Herman Jakob received them with graceful hospitality, as they were the sons of Moritz Freyer, more than worthy of tea and cookies. Herman, a short, dispassionate man, was the representative of the Herzl Society in Stettin, and one of the very few believers in the ideas of the Zionismus. He still bore the scars of Kalle and Loewe's shameful escape from the lecture hall in the bourse building, after which the number of Zionists in town diminished even further, and they would assemble only covertly. "Now, what can I do for you fine young men?"

Kurt shrugged, and Erich mustered up the courage to say, "Quite simply, Herr Jakob, I believe it is time to establish a Herzl Youth group in Stettin."

Herman sputtered and coughed, nearly dropping his teacup. "Why this, this is truly… Well," he stuttered, "what in fact, what exactly are we talking about here?"

Erich seemed slightly thwarted by Herman's reaction, but passionately added, "We see things as they are, just like Herr Herzl. The Jews are asleep, it is time to rouse them, and the youth have the power to do so. We have not been spoiled yet, Herr Jakob, we have made no comfortable life to cling to, but wish only to look to the future, to new ideals." He spoke passionately, his face flushed – Kurt, who was looking at him with amazement, once again feared for his health.

Herman was listening carefully now, and eventually turned to Kurt and asked, "And you, Kurt, what do you say?"

"Erich is right," said Kurt. "It is time. Something must be done."

"And what does your father say to all of this?" asked Herman, and they both fell into an awkward silence. He contemplated for a while, then said, "We have a club on Pestalozzistraße that no one is using, you can have it for a trial period."

Erich and Kurt were overjoyed when they left Herman's. They sat in a café and invited their good friend Albert Baer, and the brothers Fritz and Franz Michal, and Willy Greiffenhagen, whom all the Stettin girls were deeply enamored with, and Karl Barić, who had a knack for the written word, and Fräulein Alma Cohen, who Erich and Kurt secretly desired, and after several drinks abandoned the respectful Freyer courtesy in favor of singing her praise.

The Herzl Youth Club was opened with a small beer party. Discussions and lectures took place. The walls were covered with Zionist slogans, newspaper clippings, the landscapes of Palestine, and a huge print of the heavily bearded Theodor Herzl. The second room housed a dusty pommel horse and an exercise ladder, and Erich looked high and low for a sports instructor to train the feeble Jewish boys. Following an exhaustive search, he discovered that he cannot fill the position with a Jewish athlete as there were none in existence, and so he hired one Carl Schmidt to run the Herzl Sports Club, a strapping fellow, suitably blond and blue-eyed. Kurt and Erich dejectedly watched as, after training, Alma took his muscular arm and together they vanished into the streets of Stettin.

Erich was ecstatic, spending hours upon hours in the club engaged in grueling training. He would usually come in last in the short dashes they ran in the alley by the club under the bewildered gazes of passersby, and when they improvised a long jump pit he discovered that his legs will not carry him past a meter and a half. Franz and Willy were both superior to him in these matters, while in the lecture evenings Karl and Kurt competed for the title of most brilliant speaker.

Ten-year-old Käthe, whose wit and cleverness were praised by all, preferred the company of her older brothers to that of children her own age. She often came to the club, listened to the lectures and the lively debates, and howled in laughter at Erich's desperate attempts at the high jump and the long jump. When it seemed appropriate, she would stand in the middle of the room and recite German poetry from memory, and one time even an excerpt from The Basel Program.

"The Jewish people," Käthe spoke the words as if narrating a mesmerizing tale by the Brothers Grimm or from Greek mythology, "the Jewish people deserve a home, a home where they can be free, masters of their actions and rulers of their fate. We, the delegates of the First Zionist Congress held here is Basel, have assembled here to declare the aim of our struggle: establishing for the Jewish people a homeland in Zion."

The others raised their hands in feigned excitement, and Albert clapped, calling, "Bravo, Käthe, bravo, and would you look at that, not a single word out of place!"

Kurt inspired the others to clarify once and for all the question of Zionism. Books traded hands, and they all read Herzl's *Der Judenstaat* and discussed at great length whether a Jewish heritage should be established in the new state there should be no affinity to any religion, and what will become of non-Jewish residents of such a country. Once, Kurt brought a book by Zionist Moshe Hess, who asserted that in the Jewish state there must be social justice. A heated argument ensued.

Karl claimed, "Hess was mixing meat and dairy, apples and oranges."

Alma piped up and said, "Enough, you're giving me a headache, let's go to Kuhberg's for a drink." They went out to the street and walked a stretch in the torrential November rain before climbing down into their favorite wine cellar, deep below ground.

At the wine house, a noisy, raucous party was occupying the long wooden benches. One among them raised his head and loudly said, "Look, the snouts are popping up." Erich looked toward the voice and was horrified to see Reinhold, Fräulein Sarnow's brother, who now held a job at the insurance company. From the darkness of Erich's memory, a bleeding wound tore open, one which had been forcefully closed since childhood, of Reinhold squealing at him, rat-like, "Itzik Jew, Itzik Jew!" And Fräulein Sarnow shrieking back at him, "Do you want to get me fired, Reinhold, is that what you want?" And his reply, "You work for Jews, that's what you do, filthy yids order you around." Erich backed away, pale.

Willy moved toward Reinhold and said, "And what about your snout, I assume its hiding somewhere behind those spots." Reinhold stood up, followed by two of his companions, broader of shoulder and more muscular than him. Karl got up to leave and grabbed Willy's arm, pulling hard, but Willy hissed, "Yes, that's exactly what they want, and you can go, as far as I'm concerned."

Kurt said, "Willy, we will not beat them in this."

Fritz and Franz also edged forward, and Reinhold pushed

lightly against Willy's chest and said, "A fist to that beak will greatly improve its appearance, I guarantee it."

Willy looked him in the eye and punched him in the face. Reinhold reeled back and his two friends lunged at Willy. Fritz and Franz piled on top of them and the room was filled with the racket of chairs splintering and beer mugs shattering.

The owner bustled toward them, yelling, "All of you, all of you will answer to the police unless you stop this instant and get out!"

Erich was braced against the wall of the wine house, shaking, unable to look away from the fight.

Then Kurt spoke, his voice louder than usual, "That's enough! Willy, we're leaving now, or I'm never speaking to you again." Willy stood up and dusted off his clothes, then followed Kurt outside to the curb. After them, battered and beat, came Fritz, whose nose was bleeding, and Franz, panting and sweating. Erich, Alma and Karl came out last, followed by the vulgar laughter of Reinhart and his group, calling after them, "Run away, scared little yids, scurry away."

The rain stopped. Erich, Kurt and their friends sat by one of the fountains at Parade Square and washed their faces as best they could.

"I would've thrashed them," grumbled Willy. "They weren't that big."

"This war cannot be won like that," insisted Kurt.

"It can't be won at all," said Karl.

"It can be," said Kurt, agitated, "but if you start acting like a bandit you eventually become one."

"This is the real world, Kurt," Karl said. "Dream your dreams if you like."

Kurt was silent for a moment, then declared, "It is not a dream.

Good can prevail."

"What sort of Christian nonsense is that?" Karl bristled.

Kurt looked at him and said, "You claim it is a religious notion, but just the opposite is true. I am searching for the connection between good and reason, that is where the key to the truth lies, and I will find it, and when I do all will become clear, all will become simple. It is my destiny, Karl."

Karl watched him curiously and shrugged. Reinhold's group climbed out of the cellar and was fast approaching, cheering drunkenly. "Here comes your truth," Karl uttered, flatly, "and I'll have no part of it." They got up and walked away.

3.

It was late when Erich and Kurt got home. Moritz and Theresa were sitting in the drawing room, each reading a book. Their faces were grave. When Erich and Kurt came in, they both put down their books and glared at the boys who were standing there, ashamed.

"What was that today?" asked Moritz, "What were you thinking?"

Erich flushed red and ventured, "But what do you want? What do you want, Father, that we disappear completely, that we do not talk, do not think, do nothing?"

"Do anything that comes to your mind," said Moritz, "but down here, underneath our feet, something has caught fire, something dangerous."

"Something is already burning," Erich retorted. "And certainly we want to be a part of it!"

Theresa said, "It is never that simple, children."

Kurt muttered impatiently, "Children, children – I'm nearly twenty years old."

"A week ago, they took in Martha's boy, from across the street, for interrogation," added Theresa. "They said he was a member of some anarchist group, and he has yet to return. Martha hasn't slept since. I visit her every day to calm her down. Your father is just worried about you."

Kurt steadied his gaze on her and said, "Father isn't worried about us. He is worried about himself; he fears they'll kick him out of his idiotic Order of Nobility, that they'll start treating him like they treat every other Jew around here; he fears for his income and his status."

Moritz reddened and his mustache quivered. Erich stared at Kurt, stunned. "How dare you, Kurt," said Theresa, "how dare you say such things. Everything you have, you have thanks to your father. You are the reason he works so hard, you children."

"Money," replied Kurt, "money, money, I cannot take it anymore." He went to his room, lay sprawled on his bed and stared at the ceiling.

A while later, Moritz appeared at the door. Kurt raised his head and saw a short, paunchy man, his beard and mustache meticulously groomed. For a moment the man seemed stripped bare of his titles and dignity, and Kurt couldn't help but feel a tinge of compassion. He shook his head, saying, "Mutti was right, I should not have said those things."

Moritz replied, "You owe us nothing, you are a free man."

"I owe you a great deal," said Kurt. "But you must answer me this question that will not give me rest, this question that I pose to myself again and again though is it addressed at you."

"Ask it," urged Moritz, "now is the time."

And Kurt obliged. "What do you really think of everything that is happening, Father, what is your truth? I know what Grandfather's truth was, I don't agree with it, but I know it. I know exactly who Grandfather was, but I have no idea who you are."

Moritz did not reply, and Kurt suddenly found him so old, so very tired. Moritz sat down on the bed, lost in thought, and eventually, slowly, spoke. "Grandfather had one faith, Kurt, huge and whole," said Moritz. "I have many faiths, smaller ones, which I don't constantly reflect upon. Maybe that isn't as impressive. Maybe it is more muddled, but our world is also quite unclear and unfathomable."

Kurt shifted uncomfortably and muttered, "No, you are wrong. One must choose."

Moritz sighed. "You are a bright and precious boy, Kurt, but very young. You must know this one thing. I never harmed anyone, and I never acquired anything through deception, and that is a great deal, Kurt."

Kurt replied, "Not enough, it is not enough, the world is foul, and you guard yourself from it instead of changing it."

"...Kurt, my dear boy," said Moritz after a brief silence, "perhaps you find my world confusing, but you must see that it is not such a horrible world, that there are worlds much worse than mine, and one might even say that we have found the secret to living well, and that's not at all bad. I ask only one thing, that you go out and learn, learn as much as possible, read philosophy, become a scholar whose opinion matters, not because he has a knack for putting pretty phrases together, but because he stands on solid ground. When you have learned, I will respect any truth you see fit and perhaps even come to be taught by you and grow wiser, to become your student."

Moritz stood up and Kurt felt an overwhelming love for him. he embraced his father, a hug between men, though gentle and somewhat hesitant, and Moritz said, "Next year you will go to study art at the University of Munich. That is what you've always wanted, is it not?"

"That would be wonderful," Kurt whispered, "wonderful, Father." He then lay on his bed, excited and confused and eventually plummeted into a troubled sleep. He did not see Erich sneak quietly into the room and stare at him for a long while, his face illuminated only by the dim light shining in from the hallway. Kurt woke suddenly, with a start. Through the beam of light Erich's face seemed dead. Kurt sat up quickly and slurred, "What is it, Erich, what're you doing here?"

"I'm so sorry, I didn't mean to wake you," Erich mumbled and turned to leave.

Kurt said, "You came to tell me something, what was it?"

Erich's eyes were wet. "Father spoke to me. I'm going to apprentice at a store." Kurt stared at him and said nothing. "Whenever I visit Herr Rodrich's homeware shop," Erich went on, "I look at that man and his assistants behind the counter, with their toothbrush mustaches and their ridiculous suits and I think, these are the living dead."

"You don't have to do as Father says. Tell him this plan is unacceptable," Kurt stated.

Erich looked at him through extinguished, pleading eyes. "I was sitting in my room, wondering," he said, "what does one live for, what is one's mission in life, and then I thought, Kurt will have the answer, Kurt knows everything."

Kurt laughed. He stood up, walked over to Erich and folded him in a tight embrace, feeling his brother's small, shivering body diminish in his arms. He walked Erich to his room and laid a moist towel on his forehead.

Erich lay on his bed until morning, his eyes open, wide and vacant.

4.

On October 13, 1906, a lively group assembled at Kuhberg's wine cellar to bid a cheerful farewell to Kurt, who was bound for Munich where he was to study art. The fragrances of autumn swirled in the evening air, the streets of Stettin were full of people, and even the lights in the wine cellar twinkled like stars.

"Damn it, Kurt," Albert was saying, "now you'll come back from Munich an art professor and we'll never have any idea what you're saying."

Kurt said nothing but cleared his throat with something akin to a chuckle. Alma, who had recently broken up from the sports trainer Karl Schmidt, caressed him to the point of blushing embarrassment and crooned, "Ach, Kurt, always so serious, you and that beard will be the talk of all those buxom Munich girls, you'll never want to come back."

"I see you've finally found your Don Juan," Fritz piped up, by now rather inebriated. "At last he can explain the historical nuances of the Impressionismus to some Bavarian ditz while she contemplates all form and manner of sausage."

"Oh, get off your high horse," protested Franz, who was in the habit of automatically contradicting his brother. "As if Socrates and Hegel wander the streets of Stettin, imparting wisdom on passersby."

"Whose horse is that, again?" Fritz retorted. "There are idiots in Germany and there are geniuses, and if you seek them out, you'll even find some Jews whose idiocy knows no bounds."

"While this is true," Franz persisted, "the Bavarians are a special breed. It is known that at the very moment of birth, their chubby little fists open to receive the handle of their first beer mug."

"As if we, the Stettin Jews, are any less ridiculous," proclaimed Albert, "going out to the pub to drink a quarter of beer and lose their faculties entirely."

"Starting a sports club and barely managing to lift their arm and leg," followed Willy, who was actually a decent athlete.

"Indeed," laughed Alma, "discussing Natasha and Pierre till they're blue in the face but clueless when confronted with a kiss."

"Really, Alma," Karl scolded her, "before the Jew can even consider kissing, he must exhaustively contemplate all historical aspects and significance of said kiss!"

"This is exactly the argument proposed by Dr. Freud," Erich contributed. "That when we kiss a girl we are thinking of our mothers." This triggered a bout of laughter that rang throughout the wine cellar.

"If you asked Schopenhauer," said Kurt, "he would tell you that a kiss is a weapon, wielded by women to enslave men."

"Ach, Schopenhauer," Albert scowled, "always with his doom and gloom. Whoever reads his books would do well to remove themselves, screaming, from this mortal coil."

"Exactly," Franz agreed. "No Schopenhauer as a rule. And

those who read too much Freud will find come nighttime that they had forgotten everything they knew about lovemaking."

"Yes," said Fritz, "and then he'll go running off to Freud himself – this is how the fellow makes a living!"

"Those Bavarians will find kindred spirits in you lot," Kurt said, reproachful. "What point is there to life without knowledge, without thought? Munich has some of the greatest artistic minds in the world, and I intend to learn everything I can from them. Thus, I will be happy; and I will find love, as well, a great love."

Alma hummed with patronizing affection and stroked his beard again.

"You need to gain some experience first with a number of nice, charitable girls," Fritz laughed, "before you run off to find the love of your life. Here, look to Erich for example – always rifling through those notebooks of his, so he can grow to become a thriving retailer with a hunched back and bulging pockets."

"I will do no such thing," Erich protested. "The very notion is ludicrous. "

"What will you do, then?" inquired Karl. "What do you want to be, Erich? When you grow up?"

"I'll found an association," said Erich. "An association for good people. It will welcome Jews and Christians, men and women, retailers and scientists, anyone who seeks to better humanity."

"Pfft," sputtered Karl, "Listen to this twaddle. Good people. It will be the world's smallest association."

"Certainly the poorest," added Franz. "You can't pay the grocer with kindness."

"Ach, honestly," Alma objected, "Erich proposes such a lovely idea and you all charge at him like a pack of wild lawyers. I want to hear more, Erich dear, and I'd also like to officially sign up and join your association right this moment."

"With respect," Karl intoned, "while I am no lawyer, I have no intention of signing up to anything without hearing some details."

"By all means," replied Erich, his face lighting up suddenly. "This association shall have no institutions, no obligations, and no one will have to prove anything to the powers that be, only to themselves and to their friends."

"That isn't enough," said Karl. "There must be some grand common goal, a central idea."

"Why, Karl," Erich asked, fervently, "why is it not enough? Surely to be good is a grand enough goal."

"Ach, please," Karl bristled, "because it is meaningless. What does it mean, to be good? Our neighbor, Herr Stock, is an exemplary family man, who has been given a reward for his numerous contributions to the town of Stettin, and just this week I saw him yelling profanities at Dr. Vogelstein and his party as they were walking to the synagogue."

Erich considered this briefly and said, "Well, this association will unite all of mankind. The Lovers of Humanity association. Muslims and Africans will join, too."

"Be careful," laughed Albert, "before you know it, so will the Germans."

"'Humanity' is a big word," said Alma. "I am missing the individual element, flesh and blood. Take my father. He works at the Province Ministry of Economics. All his life he toils for humanity's sake, and he's never given me so much as a kiss on the cheek."

"Well, then, your father is out of the club," Karl announced.

"In that case, count out every single father in Germany," said Willy. "Does anyone here know a father who kisses his children?"

"So far this sounds like a nanny association. An achievement, indeed," droned Albert.

"Then I hereby propose it," proclaimed Erich. "The Association of Good People for Humanity and Love."

"This is extremely problematic," Fritz said, indignantly. "An association of feckless romantics. In thirty years, we'll all meet in a soup kitchen and hug each other in tears and infinite love. I'm out."

"This association cannot happen without you, Fritz," stated Erich. "What do you suggest?"

"I suggest Humanity, Love, and Labor," said Fritz.

"And what of the historical aspect?" asked Kurt. "To be a good person? A worthy cause indeed, but to be truly good is to be contemporary, to make a mark on the world, to refuse to become a slave of destiny and be tossed about by life like a wrecked ship on angry seas."

Erich, beginning to despair, grew silent. But soon a new inspiration filled his eyes and he got up and approached the waiter, who was polishing beer mugs by the counter, and exchanged some guarded whispers with him before scribbling some lines on a small note and returning to the table, a mysterious air about him. After several minutes a slender waitress arrived and set a tray on the wooden table, laden with eight glasses of red wine. Erich raised the one nearest to him, unfolded the note and ceremoniously read its contents aloud.

"I hereby declare, on this day, the establishment of a friendship association, the October Thirteenth Association."

Around the table everyone fell silent. Erich raised his voice and the surrounding tables hushed as well.

"We, who are gathered around this table, pledge to be good

people wherever we shall find ourselves, to think and act in any way that we can for the world, humanity, love and labor, and tell one another of our thoughts and actions regarding these four matters once a year, every year, on the thirteenth of October!"

An awkward silence fell. Erich made to sit back down, and Kurt saw the ominous pallor take hold of him. But Alma stopped him, placing her warm hands on his waist and exclaiming, "Ach, Erich, what a wonderful idea." Fritz and Franz and Karl and Willy immediately followed suit.

Albert applauded and said, "Wonderful, truly wonderful." Even Kurt's customarily stern expression softened into a smile. They all raised their glasses and cheered, and Erich was embarrassed and overjoyed. Alma hugged him.

Karl mumbled, "I mean, October thirteenth, such things."

"I have only one problem that you've failed to account for, Erich," said Willy. "According to this pact, from now on we are all obligated to spend the rest of our lives in Stettin, a reality that is absolutely unacceptable."

They all laughed but realized that Willy had raised a sound point. Albert, suffused in a haze of wine fumes, cried, "Why, then, do we not add Stettin to the pact? Here's to Stettin! To our esteemed mayor Herr Bleicher! To the ships sailing on the Oder River! To the Kuhberg wine cellar!"

Erich raised a silencing hand. "Well, I have a solution. Each year, we will each write a postcard to all the members, from wherever we are at the time, in which we will present our thoughts on the four agreed upon topics."

The idea seemed to go over smoothly, but then Willy suddenly protested, "What sort of association only sends postcards, then? Any association worth its salt must hold regular assemblies."

Murmurs of agreement rose around the table, and Alma said, "We'll meet every five years. Wherever we are, we'll get on a train and come. If it is in Stettin then we'll meet here, at Kuhberg's."

Erich jotted down the new revisions on the little note and once they all signed it, he folded it and nodded to the man by the counter. Another tray of wine was brought to the table at once, and again Erich raised his glass for a toast. This time they all stood and solemnly raised their glasses along with him, and his voice rang loud and clear when he spoke, to them and to the other patrons of the wine cellar, "We, the members of the October Thirteenth Association, make this toast to the world! To humanity! To love! To labor! To good human beings! To October Thirteenth! Hurrah!" and the whole lot of them resounded with joy and laughter when they thundered back, "Three cheers to October Thirteenth! Hurrah! Hurrah! Hurrah!"

CHAPTER THREE: KURT

1.

On September 27 1914, three months after Franz Ferdinand was shot and Europe was thrust into the fires of war, a slender young man of about thirty stood in the lecture hall of The Museum of Folklore Art in the northern town of Flensburg, just south of the Danish border and delivered a lecture. A few dozen of the town's residents sat on the round wooden chairs, listening with a mixture of curiosity and suspicion. The man was the young Doctor Kurt Freyer, who had arrived in town just a month earlier to begin work as assistant to the museum director. Rumor among Flensburg's small culture community had it that the man is a brilliant art scholar, and yet, "quite obviously and inescapably," also a Jew.

The title of the lecture was "What is Heroism?," in itself a matter of some absurdity, as the slight Dr. Freyer looked nothing like a hero at all; several of the town's fishermen could blow him away with a sneeze. The esteemed young man softly cleared his throat and began to speak.

"Over the past few months, various events had befallen us, some awesome, some awful. They came upon us with stunning force, swept us, passionately and expectantly, from one day to the next; the joy of victory, the sorrow of loss..." Kurt paused for a moment and looked at the audience, attempting to gauge some initial reactions, then returned to his papers.

"It is necessary to stop, for a moment, from our routine and consider the deeper meaning of our actions, if indeed we are not content simply swinging thoughtlessly from side to side. We must enforce our actions with inner stability. Self-examination is crucial, doubly so at times like these, if we intend to bear the dignity and the joy of that which lies ahead, both triumph and hardship. If so, we must seek an answer to the question of meaning, what meaning does this war carry, to us, and what is the meaning of such a war in general."

A faint hum was wafting up from the audience, an impatient get-to-the-point-if-you-will sort of buzz, and beside him the museum director, Dr. Sauermann, shifting uncomfortably in his chair. Kurt raised his voice slightly. "Let us imagine," he continued, "that some otherworldly spirit would descend upon our world, a spirit from some pure, sublime place, which knows nothing of earthly actions and wills. It looks upon the warring, looks as crops are destroyed and flourishing cities razed, watches as people who had never met assault their fellow men with weapons. The spirit would tremble with horror; it would think to itself that humanity had forgotten its noble calling, its dignity. It would turn to us and ask us what, exactly, is the meaning of all this. What would we say?"

A man in the audience shouted, "This is heresy! You doubt the righteousness of the war effort!"

Kurt, alarmed, hurriedly said, "To begin with, we would say that we are innocent. That we never wanted this. We wanted to live in peace, and wished the same upon our neighbors, but we were attacked; having been attacked, we were forced to defend ourselves."

"Bravo!" yelled a woman from the front row. "Hear, hear!"

Kurt, seeming somewhat desperate, requested with a clipped gesture that she let him finish the thought. "Of course, the spirit would reply, this explanation is comprehensible, it is necessary to act this way, but it is an earthly compulsion. It cannot be the deeper interpretation of your actions. An earthly-material phenomenon cannot be explained by way of the earthly and the material."

Cries of dissent were rising from the audience now, "What gibberish is this?" "What does any of this have to do with the war?" The museum director stood from his seat and requested that the audience permit Dr. Freyer to continue his lecture, which, he assured them, "will prove both surprising and uplifting."

"We would quickly respond to this spirit," said Kurt, "saying: this is our liberty. We fight not only for external liberty, so that our country is not ruled by outsiders, but even more so, we fight for inner liberty, the freedom to develop, to create our culture, to deliver our destinies to the world. This is also our honor: not only to have the respect of foreign nations but to prove to the world, through our action, our aptitude and value."

The crowd listened quietly, and Kurt spotted among the heads several nods of assent. Emboldened, he continued. "Liberty and honor. These, surely, the spirit would accept. It would acknowledge the two ideals, which stem from its own world, as the foundational ideals of our action. It would say: Woe unto those nations which do not go to war when such things are at stake. Their bad ethics will be a burden upon them, so heavy that fighting and triumphing will soon become impossible to them."

The crowd was now held tightly within the spell of Kurt's words, and it seemed as though it would have settled for them, but Kurt went on, down the path he had charted.

"And still, still it is not enough. The question must be posed: Why must the individual suffer so greatly and inflict such suffering upon others, simply to realize these ideals? What is the point in that every individual, despite the horrors of war, struggles to maintain humanity's purity and sanctify these actions? And the answer to this question would be: The point of this war is heroism."

Three men stood up and applauded enthusiastically. They were met with limp, scattered clapping and sat back down.

"What is heroism?" inquired Kurt. "If someone were to ask us that question a few months ago, I think we would not know the answer. Possibly we would propose the heroes of history; seeking some notion of heroism, we would turn to the past. Then we would know heroism through consequence: a hero is that who performs great deeds, with permanent outcomes. Perhaps we would recall the heroes of *Wilhelm Tell* or *Der Prinz von Homburg*. But even in them we would not find the heroism of reality, but only literary heroism, the rules of which are a great deal simpler. We would find that heroism is inseparably linked with life, with destiny, for the purpose of achieving great feats. We were so engrossed in the everyday, in the paltry human routine, that the ideal of heroism vanished into the past and into literature. Tangible heroism, actual heroism, would seem outstanding; a veritable miracle."

The crowd was captivated. A curly-haired woman in the first row was gazing at Kurt admiringly, and he felt himself becoming slightly taller.

"Now, in an instant, everything is changed!" he cried, riveted. "Day after day we see our heroes, now. Those who head out into action, and those who return, wounded, marked by their heroism. Immediately, we learn: A hero is that who charged courageously forward, who sacrifices his life for the great ideals: liberty, dignity, and homeland. That is the point: To sacrifice life! For too long we fretted over our puny, everyday existence. Asking each other how we will subsist and from what. Now we can once more recognize the fundamental truth, summed up beautifully by Friedrich Schiller: Life is not the noblest possession."

Throats were cleared in agreement throughout the audience, though here and there appeared isles of doubt. Kurt's lecture was now becoming somewhat tiresome, comparing and contrasting the German soldier to the soldiers of the middle ages or the renaissance, when "paid mercenaries wildly charged the enemy, fearing not for their own lives," while the contemporary soldier "follows the example of the submarine captain. He must not only be courageous, decisive, daringly self-sacrificing. He must also perfectly control the complex operation of the machine entrusted to him." Several people, shrugging, stood up to leave. The museum director glared angrily at them, and Kurt hurried to introduce a new idea, one he believed held tremendous significance.

"Viewed from this perspective, can military heroism be considered the only form of heroism? But today we find a new concept of heroism. The first design of this concept is given in Goethe's *Iphigenia*, a work of pure, supreme human dignity. The fact that it is a woman who heralds this new heroism will forever be a source of pride and inspiration for our women, the women of Germany. This is the quiet heroism, which is not tested in battle, is not displayed or advertised, and which wins no praise. It is the heroism of the scholar and the artist, as he toils in a secluded workshop to fulfill his destiny, to bring his work to completion."

The woman in the first row stood up and clapped enthusiastically, calling back past her shoulder, "Listen to him, listen to this man."

Kurt blushed and waited for her to retake her seat. His voice was strong and confident. "We each face the demand to preserve ourselves in this daily struggle, to not be petty, to maintain the purity of our inner being, never to relinquish the sanctity of our souls. We must exhibit this quiet heroism when we bid farewell to our loved ones as they go to war. We must not burden them or harm their faith. And the greatest demand will present itself when reports of casualties begin to arrive. Then we must persevere and remember yet more fiercely the noble ideal these victims had given their lives for. This heroism demands of us repeatedly a fresh willingness for victims, for sacrifice, for acts of comradery. If we each adhere to these ideals, a new, prodigious era will evolve, an era of true greatness: The people are the heroes! We've experienced this once before, a century ago. Today we feel it once more, when the people stand united in service of a single mission. We are not drunk with empty phrases and hatred but imbued through and through with the radiance of the common goal."

Kurt pause briefly, and the audience wondered for a moment whether he was finished, but his voice soon rose again, filling the lecture hall. "If, then, Germany wins its victory and peace," he asked, "and grows and flourishes, will we again become as we once were? Small, mundane, unheroic? Let us hope not. We must maintain the heroism thrust upon us by our current predicament. We must pass it down to our children, so that one day they may say of us: those were the men and women who lived in 1914!"

Kurt finished speaking and the audience applauded and began making its way to the exit. The woman in the first row came up to him and, obviously moved, told him how refreshing she found his lecture, explaining that her husband was serving on the front and she can hardly sleep at night.

His words had encouraged her, she said, and asked whether "Doctor Freyer would be so gracious as to join her for a cup of tea and discuss some questions that had come to her mind during his most delightful address." Kurt blushed and thanked her, laughing a little, his thick spectacles glittering. The museum director also seemed pleased, shaking Kurt's hand vigorously.

In one corner of the room two men tossed him unnerving glances, and as he left the lecture hall he heard them whisper, quite audibly, "There's the tirade of a Jew for you, give them enough words and they'll convince you the earth orbits the moon."

Kurt walked the street winding away from the museum, along the row of poplars, his fingers in his coat pocket twiddling with the written speech he had just given, pondering whether they would agree to print it in the local paper, and perhaps from there the words would fly on to the posh drawing rooms of Berlin, and to the military encampments at the borders, and who knows, perhaps he will be summoned to speak them in the presence of Kaiser Wilhelm, if only the Kaiser could be torn away for just a moment from the business of war.

2.

Word of the Jewish doctor who calls for the German people to sacrifice their lives for honor and homeland was somewhat late in arriving to the enlistment offices of the Kaiser's army, leaving Kurt to peacefully pursue his work at the museum. Every day he would walk from his house on 38 Marienhölzungsweg to the museum, write scientific papers and suggest ideas for exhibits which would demonstrate the recent developments in the world of art, impressionism versus expressionism, but his suggestions were usually rejected by the museum director, who apologetically explained that "Here in Flensburg the people are interested in another kind of art, art appreciated by *hausfraus*, which reminds the people of their town's legacy."

The war had reached other countries, new fronts were opening, and Kurt began to wonder whether Germany had fallen in love with the act of war and forgotten its purpose. Some Flensburg homes received notices from the Ministry of War and Kurt sought for the spark of heroism in the eyes of mothers and fathers who had grown prematurely gray and old as he watched. Anna was busy raising their one-year-old daughter, Charlotte-Renate whom everyone called Lotte, born in Halle an der Saale, where Kurt had also held the position of assistant director. In Flensburg another member joined their family: Hermina-Frederika, known to everyone as "Minchen."

The Western Front was growing more turbulent by the day, and Germany needed more soldiers. In the winter of 1916, Dr. Kurt Freyer was summoned to the recruitment office, where the Kaiser's clerks were waiting. Walking toward the station Kurt could see the disappointment flash in their eyes as they took in his delicate physique.

One of them whispered to another, "Put this one behind a ma-chine gun and he'll fly hurtling away with the first cartridge fired."

When he provided his surname one of the clerks ask, "*Jude?*" Kurt nodded reluctantly, and the clerk jotted something down in his large block of white paper before consulting briefly with his colleagues and informing Kurt that he would be sent "to the second line of the Western Front," where he would assist the war effort in any way deemed necessary.

It was difficult, from the German military camp on the French border, to observe what was going on there, in the war. Trucks carrying supplies and ammunitions passed through the camp, and occasionally large groups of soldiers stopped there for the night, before heading out to the nearby front. The soldiers con-gregated in large groups, chatting, singing a bit, exchanging pro-fanities and tales of the various women they purportedly encoun-tered in their travels. Kurt would stand out of the way, listening.

One time a somewhat inebriated soldier dragged Kurt into the group, hugged him tightly and introduced himself, "Max Schwer-in, at your service."

"Doctor Kurt Freyer," Kurt politely replied.

Max laughed exuberantly. "So, Doctor, don't you feel like join-ing us, tasting some fresh blood?"

Embarrassed, Kurt squirmed free of his embrace and said, "They made their decision at the recruitment office, and what I feel like makes little difference."

"God is looking out for you, you fool," said Max, "God, not the recruitment office, because he knows you've got some sense in that big Jewish brain, and he needs someone to tell future generations about this damn bloody idiocy." Max took a pencil and a piece of paper from his pocket and jotted down some words. He handed it to Kurt, telling him, "When the war is over, you come to this address. If it's me who opens the door, I'll invite you to a dinner you'll never forget, roast pork and wine galore! And if it isn't, you give this letter to my wife, because I don't trust the military post, and if she cries you give her that old German comfort, and believe me, she is a fine cut indeed."

Battalion after battalion, brigade after brigade passed through the encampment, some of them in trucks with soldiers singing in the back, laughing and swearing at Kurt, who was often posted at the gate. And as the days and weeks elapsed, the convoys started flowing through the camp in the other direction, carrying tired, benumbed soldiers, staggered with the horrors of war. Dusty, mud-stained Ambulances also began arriving at the camp, which now housed a special wing for soldiers who were labeled "Physically unimpaired, but no longer suited to serve on the front lines." Kurt and the young officer Franz Schulendorf were soon appointed to register these soldiers and see to their needs. Franz had gentle, forlorn features. Kurt would sometimes see him gazing at him in a way that, at times, made him briefly suspect Franz's intentions.

For days, Kurt and Franz would talk to the soldiers who found their way to the camp. Of some, those who sat and stared at the night air, Franz would say they left their souls in the trenches. Others would rage and yell and curse their officers and even the Kaiser. Kurt would try to silence them, but Franz told him, "For the angry ones there is hope still."

Kurt quickly grew fond of Franz. Among the returning soldiers was also Max Schwerin, his face frenzied, and spotting Kurt from afar he cried, "Look, it's him, my Jewish doctor! My letter, do you still have it? Or have you already visited my wife for a good bit of German comfort?" Kurt chuckled as he always did, a gentle, comforting sound, and Franz smiled as well.

Max approached Kurt and Kurt smelled his acrid breath, a mouth unwashed for many days. He recoiled, but Max moved closer, his lips nearly touching the smooth skin of Kurt's head.

"You're sitting here at the damn Ritz, Doctor Freyer, and missing out on the most unforgettable sights! Blood! Fresh blood, thousands of Germans and Frenchmen charging at each other with rifles and bayonets drawn and the blood bursts straight from their chests! And after that, glorious sights! Chopped organs like you're at the butcher's back home, what say you? To never see such a thing – you might as well have never been born at all, yes?"

Kurt tried to say something, but Max raised his voice to a shriek, "Would you like to hear more, Jude? Would you? Have you looked into the faces of the dead? Not one, not two, you little book-rat, thousands, thousands of dead faces, oh, the sight of them! Terrified, you would think? Horrorstruck? Hardly! Merely astonished, they are, even smiling, or just looking like bigger fools than they were in life. Go from this place, go into the war, Doctor Freyer, go into the trenches, and if you survive you will emerge from it the wisest man alive!"

Kurt felt slightly nauseated.

Max gripped him and hissed, "You want to know the secret, don't you, how a fellow like me is still alive when his entire brigade is laid in stacks out there in the meadow? It's a simple thing, really..."

Kurt stood up, indignant. He tossed the letter Max had given him and went to his room with a heavy heart. The war seemed to him a tedious, pointless affair. He spent the following days reading some books he managed to hastily shove into his pack during the last, wonderful leave he had taken in Flensburg, following which he had been informed in a letter from Anna that a new baby was about to join Charlotte and Hermina. Apart from Franz, whose company was also becoming less frequent, the soldiers and officers of the camp tended to keep their distance from him. He had already sought audience with the camp adjutant and requested that he consider transferring him "somewhere his unique skillset could provide greater use," though he had no idea which skills those would be, exactly, unless he would be invited to lecture the senior officers at headquarters on the fascinating topic of "shape and color in early renaissance art."

The radio and the newspapers spoke of new peace initiatives and a sharp joy simmered through his body, a joy he had not known since the time he saw the warm and loving Fräulein Anna Heymann standing at the dock of the train station in Munich, where he had gone to school with her brother, Otto, and knew that he had found the love of his life, the mother of his future children, and that his world would forever be whole.

In the evenings, if he had his room to himself or was posted to guard duty, he would read Hegel, whose work he had recently come to know and was very much drawn to. Unlike Schopenhauer, of whom he also read a great deal, but whose bitter contempt of human beings repelled him, Hegel was clear, enticing. His description of the virtues of the spirit, the climb from the gloom of ignorance to victorious reason fascinated Kurt, though when he pondered the course of his own life he found in it no gospel of reason; the evidence supporting Schopenhauer was far more compelling.

In that case, thought Kurt, *I must look at history in its entirety, not merely my own life: to climb the tall hill proposed by Friedrich Hegel and from it to see where Europe is headed, and Germany with it.* In his tight handwriting, he wrote notes upon notes in little black notebooks he carried everywhere and found absolutely no one in the dreary camp smelling of gasoline and burned oil to talk with about these crucial matters.

One night he was at the guard post and Franz Schulendorf, whom he had not seen in many days, approached. He apologized, telling Kurt that he was transferred to another camp due to military matters, but has returned and is glad to see him here again.

"What are they saying out there?" asked Kurt. "Any end in sight?"

Franz looked at him and said, "Out there they know nothing. You have the answer, Kurt, you tell me."

"Nothing good will come of this war," Kurt stated. "Certainly not for Germany."

"You are a wise man, Kurt," Franz replied. "You see beyond things. Tell me, what do you think caused this war, where does such an idiotic matter suddenly come from, to suck the wealth and lifeblood of Europe?"

"Well, it is a war between nations," Kurt said, sensing a sour odor rising from the words, "a territorial war. Germany was forced to defend itself, but things spiraled out of control."

"Nothing spiraled out of control, Kurt," Franz quietly replied. "This isn't about nations. Kaisers, generals, they are all pawns." Kurt listened attentively. Franz glanced into the distance and then hissed, urgently, "I'm speaking with you because you are an intellectual, but you must tell no one of this conversation, not ever."

Kurt said, "What is this, what are you thinking?"

"Who controls the world, Kurt?" Franz' voice was deep, warm, as if whispering in a lover's ear, "Think, think! Who benefits from the war machine? Who sits in large offices, in big cities, sits and accumulates more marks and dollars every day? War is good business, Kurt, but for whom? For the Capital! they set the war machine in motion, they are funding it, and they will not let it end, unless we stop them."

Kurt looked at him apprehensively. "And how would you stop them, Franz," he asked, "when that would certainly mean another war?"

"Indeed, it would, Kurt. Indeed, another war. The final war," said Franz, and his pale face glowed and his eyes burned. "The war on Capital, the war that will change everything. Great things are happening regarding this matter, Kurt, immeasurable things!"

Kurt looked at Franz, whose excitement made him smile. Franz grabbed Kurt's large head on both sides, pushing the frame onto the flesh of his temples, placed a long kiss on his lips, and disappeared.

3.

The war spread across many fronts, but the soldier Kurt Freyer was transferred somewhere his intellectual prowess would be of more use. He was posted to the German military's coding school, in the heart of Berlin, where he taught both green and veteran soldiers the secrets of Morse code. He spent his free time wandering in the many bookstores of Berlin, and began nurturing a small library in the teacher's barracks at the coding school which housed his Marx and Engels writings, and prime among them *The Capital, The Communist Manifesto*, and Lenin's *What Is to Be Done?* The Russian revolution of November 7, 1917 had captured his imagination, and he tracked it by every means available to him.

In the evenings he read, sprinkling the pages with penciled notes in his tiny handwriting. He even had in his possession, making sure to keep them well hidden, propaganda booklets and agendas of the Spartacus League, headed by Rosa Luxemburg and Karl Liebknecht. He hungrily devoured Marx, though his books teemed with complex, at times unclear ideas, while Kurt himself was exceedingly fond of clarity: his own work on folk art, which had made a lasting impression on the academic art history community, was described as "crystal clear." In the margins of the crowded pages of *The Capital* he often wrote, "clarification needed," or "this can certainly be rephrased as to be better comprehended by readers."

In the mornings Kurt spent his time teaching Morse code. The pupils would learn the signs using the heavy black coding device that stood on the table, and he would write them on the blackboard as well. The classroom now accommodated young soldiers, recruited when the fronts had already begun closing one after the other, and they listened to Kurt's explanations about the principles of coding with extreme attentiveness, as if it were a matter of supreme scientific importance. The school was part of a large military complex, usually surrounded by squads of training soldiers, with officers constantly coming and going.

On one November morning, shortly after the war ended, a soldier barged into Kurt's classroom and enthusiastically cried,

"Doctor Freyer, you must finish your lesson, quickly, right now!" Kurt went to the window and then ran out to the main quad. His pupils, exhilarated by their unexpected freedom, flowed out in his wake.

Out in the quad, something unbelievable was taking place. A long line stood, made of straight-faced officers in formation, some of their heads bowed, others raised proudly forward. Soldiers unknown to Kurt, who had perhaps come from another camp, were walking among them, ripping off their ranks. Several officers from the base were brought in to one of the halls in the barracks, and the soldiers eagerly raided the offices, pulling documents from cabinets. Rankless soldiers were everywhere. Proclamation leaflets, like black crumbs, fluttered and scattered all over the base. The new soldiers went room by room, person by person, shoving the black pages into the hands of Kurt's pupils, red-bound booklets of "The Red Flag" which Kurt used to buy from the newspaper stands next to the base.

The soldiers occupied the classrooms, exchanging orders and reports, nervously listening to the radios they carried. Kurt observed this, moved, ecstatic. He attempted some questions, some kind words, but they looked at him suspiciously and one of them kept saying, "Revoluzion, revoluzion."

The surrounding streets were filling with rhythmic shouting. Leaving the base, Kurt stumbled into a broad march, men and women carrying placards down Ku'Damm, headed by a petite, familiar woman whose presence set his soul alight. He marched with them. Someone shoved a wooden sign into his hand reading "Long Live Lenin." Other rallies flowed into theirs from the adjacent streets, like brooks joining a wide river, unthinkingly, unpredictably, and Kurt felt uncomfortable at first in his uniform, fearing he would be branded a double-agent, but the people around him seemed overjoyed at his presence.

Come evening he languidly returned to the camp, but entrance was no longer permitted. He wandered around Berlin, the streets covered with paper, wooden signs, military vehicles and police. His legs took him to the home of his sister Käthe and her husband Albert, his childhood friend. They offered him hot tea and a warm dinner and sat well into the small hours of the night discussing whether the red revolution would indeed surge from faraway Russia straight into the streets of Berlin.

The base soon returned to the control of the military, though the signaling lessons were not renewed. The protests in the streets died away, as well. 1919 came into the world hopeful, freshly cleaned of war. Kurt was asked to return his uniform and happily complied. In the Flensburg train station Anna stood waiting for him, smiling her loving smile. Before her stood, like the tubes of a pan-flute, Lotte, six years old and looking somber and pensive in her round glasses; Minchen, sweet and talkative; and two-year-old Susi, of whom Anna wrote to him "has twice as much mischief in her than the other two combined." In their home on Marienhölzungsweg, Kurt took off his uniform, never to wear it again.

The next morning, Kurt went down to the town's museum as a matter of course. Flensburg was a town well-suited for a stroll. It has none of the wide, interminable buildings prevalent in Berlin or Hamburg. A kind, country wind blew through it, hailing from across the border, from the Danes, and the market as well felt like a playground. Along the shoreline walked the same families Kurt already knew, the same but for being three years older. Flensburg seemed to hardly have noticed the war, and for a moment Kurt felt that he had perhaps found a true home to end his wanderings from town to town, from museum to museum.

Dr. Sauermann greeted him at the museum gate with the same restrained amiability he had always treated him with. He congratulated him for his part in the war effort "which, outcome of the war aside, is crucial, as one must contribute to the homeland and not merely receive from it." He invited Kurt to his office, where they enjoyed a hot cup of tea prepared by the museum secretary, who also greeted him warmly.

"And how have things been here, in the museum, these past few years?"

"Nothing out of the ordinary, as strange as it might seem," said Dr. Sauermann. "In fact, our collection has grown by several new pieces of ancient furniture. If you like, I can show them to you when we've finished here."

Kurt sat silently for a brief, awkward moment, and finally dared say, "Well, as far as I'm concerned, I'm prepared to come back to work tomorrow morning."

Dr. Sauermann shifted uncomfortably in his chair. Kurt had the feeling that something untoward was about to transpire. He shot an anxious glance at the tall window of old his office overlooking the garden, which he had occupied for two years and still bore on its door the sign reading "Dr. K. Freyer, Assistant Director." The room seemed unoccupied, and for a moment he was relieved. Dr. Sauermann straightened and said, "Herr Freyer, I'm afraid we can no longer afford an assistant director."

"Impossible," stated Kurt, "and what will become of the duties I performed here."

"Regarding those duties," Dr. Sauermann drily replied, "we have found temporary solutions during the years of your unfortunate absence. However, though it pains me dearly, I now no longer have the means to employ you."

Kurt stood up and made to leave. The old museum director stood as well and approached him, suddenly gentler, sorrowful, and softly said, "Dr. Freyer, in about a year I will retire from this position, and it is my opinion that you are the most suitable man to inherit the director's seat. But this decision, as you well know, is not mine to make."

Kurt replied, "I thank you for that, from the bottom of my heart," and he stumbled unsteadily out to the garden. He walked up the boulevard, toward his house. In the foyer there was a large parcel which had arrived from Berlin, filled with books he had purchased with his dwindling funds.

Kurt stood on his balcony and looked out at the street. Occasionally someone would walk by, a hoary old man, a woman tugging on a dog's leash. Flensburg seemed foreign, now, another town where he had lodged for a year or two, never putting down roots. Just as Hagen had been, where he had also been assistant museum director while he completed his doctoral thesis on "Gothic-Style City Gates of Northern Germany," and as Halle had been, where he had spent another year as assistant director of the museum, and Berlin, where he taught Morse code to soldiers, and even Darkehmen, where he was born, and since then had visited it perhaps once or twice. His thoughts altogether skipped Stettin, the town of his childhood and youth.

His three young girls were already fast asleep. He lay in bed and gazed at length at the high ceiling, and the shifting shadows of wind-blown trees moving upon it.

"What do you say, Anna, what will we do now," he wondered.

"Well, what of it, Kurt," said Anna, "This is how Jews always live, wandering from town to town, following their work."

"It is unbearable," said Kurt, and plummeted into a troubled sleep. The following morning he got up and wrote a letter to the Flensburg city council, nominating himself for the position of museum director: "Upon the retirement of the previous director, my dear teacher and mentor, Dr. Sauermann, at the end of this year, and with his warm recommendation as he will gladly confirm, following my accomplishments as assistant museum director from 1914 until my recruitment to the army in 1916." He went straight to the town hall and delivered his letter to the secretary of the Department for Cultural Affairs.

Having accomplished this, Kurt went to the café near the town hall. Rosa Luxemburg and Karl Liebknecht glared at him from the front page of the Flensburg daily paper, followed by a detailed account of their arrest, and "the immediate termination of the immoral rebellion which seeks to undermine the very foundations of the German Republic." It further said that "Herr Liebknecht and Frau Luxemburg were shot and killed by Berlin police forces following their attempted escape from arrest."

Kurt Freyer, who was not a bitter man by nature, and had always believed a great hope shone at the end of all things, fell into despair. The waiter at the café asked if he would like something else, perhaps one of their delectable sandwiches, but the image of Rosa Luxemburg, who he had seen marching in Berlin only months ago, clung to his thoughts. Her eyes peering from the paper seemed to contain a stark condemnation, of whom he did not know, perhaps of him, of Kurt Freyer, who still has not divined his purpose in the world, who still seeks a key to the truth, though here was that very key, handed to him again and again and again.

In the summer of 1919, he received a letter from the Flensburg City Department for Cultural Affairs regretfully informing him that he had been found unsuitable to the position of museum manager, and wishing him much luck in finding a position appropriate for a man of his many talents. Later that week, Anna and Kurt Freyer packed their belongings and their three daughters and left for Berlin, which all roads lead to.

4.

In Berlin, the family of Kurt Freyer lived in a modest flat on Keithstraße, not far from the large Gedächtniskirche on Auguste-Viktoria-Platz, which Kurt loved to observe, studying its structure and the complex reliefs of its spires. They received some help from Otto Heymann, Anna's brother, who was by now manager of a large bank, and inwardly Kurt chuckled that until capitalism is defeated, having a rich family member was perhaps not so bad. Käthe and her husband Albert Baer, who made a fine living from his work as an insurance lawyer, lived in a large house on Albrecht-Achilles-Straße along with their son, two-year-old Gabriel, a clever and astute child, and their newborn, Rachel. The Baer home served as a favorite stomping ground for Germany's Zionist community, as well as important guests from Palestine.

Once, when Kurt was over for dinner, a woman arrived at the house, in a loose, flowing dress and a wide-brimmed hat.

Albert proudly introduced her, "Here, Kurt, is a very important woman from Palestine, where she started a commune where people live according to the very principles you believe in."

The woman stood up, bowed deeply, and said, "Miriam Baratz. And you are?" She later told him in great detail of Degania, the magical commune on the banks of the Kinneret, where people hand over their salaries to the communal treasury.

Kurt listened, fascinated, and after some time ventured, "Still, this can only work in a rural setting. How will you stop capitalism from taking over the new, urban society that will emerge in Palestine?"

"One must redeem oneself before redeeming the world," Miriam said, and her reply invoked many thoughts in him.

He had hardly seen Erich since he joined the army, but now they met often. When the war ended, Erich was attempting to choose between two women he had been dating. Kurt, having found the love of his life quickly and easily, had no advice to offer regarding such matters. He listened patiently to Erich's romantic misadventures and was amused to note to himself that his brother, who started the Herzl Youth Club, seemed entirely unperturbed by the attempt to choose between two distinctly non-Jewish women.

Erich eventually chose Hilde. She was half-French, which he adored, for Erich had always been a Francophile and spoke French fluently. The couple purchased Hoffman Publishing on Blumenstraße 22 and lived in the flat on the second floor of the building. Their daughter, Yvonne, was born there. The three siblings and their families would go out on weekends to the surrounding woods or a nearby lakeside, celebrate birthdays together, or gather at the Baer house for the Passover meal. The children's favorite was the yearly visit to Stettin, to see Aunt Trude and Uncle Martin, who often served the parents as the butt of a joke. Anna, finally liberated from the Nordic tedium of

Flensburg, was finally happy, and the younger generation seemed to conveniently arrange itself into a sort of geometric series: Lotte and Minchen and Susi, Gabriel and Rachel, and Yvonne. Year after year they lived side by side, growing like weeds, and each of them, at the age of seven, heard the Tale of the Egg Miracle, which had now been passing in the Freyer family for more than seven decades.

Berlin was their home. Glamorous, sophisticated Berlin, the heart of Germany. Berlin of the broad streets, the ancient city gates, the theaters and museums, Berlin of the plazas, Berlin which is a world in itself one can travel through, which is endless and wants for nothing, needing nothing but itself, and perhaps a decent river. The bookstores on Ku'Damm beckoned Kurt and Erich, who read the same books and discussed them heatedly, walking down the city's streets and occasionally stopping to argue at a nearby bench. They had nothing close to the wealth and comfort they had back in Stettin, but Kurt thought, *here, something of the richness of that life, of those days, has returned to us. We are together. Germany no longer repels us so. We have survived the war.*

During the day, Kurt worked at the Hebräer Company book publishers, who bought and sold Jewish literature. In the evenings, he would retire to the small room that had become his study in the little apartment, reading and taking notes. The mark, of which the Freyers hardly had an abundance of in the first place, turned to dust. Erich and Hilde barely managed to keep Hoffman Publishing open, printing new and old books. Kurt, who had become quite fed up with his work at the Hebräer Company, where narrow-minded booksellers customarily barked orders at him, as if he had never left the military, managed to purchase a small shop on Prager Square and began selling and buying antique books. He called his store "Utopia."

Kurt Freyer's Utopia soon gained a small following. Book collectors would come visit, sit and browse his latest findings, sell him a priceless Heine manuscript or an exceptionally rare first edition of *Die Leiden des jungen Werthers*. Socialist literature passed through his store from France to Germany and back. Once a true gem came into his possession – a first edition of *The Poverty of Philosophy*. On the first page shone the signature of Karl Marx himself. Word of the unique piece spread like wildfire among the collectors of Berlin, and one day a pale, bespectacled man appeared at the bookstore, looked around cautiously and, seeing they were alone, asked about the book. Kurt amiably inquired where he had traveled from, and the man replied, "Comrade Mendel, at your service, administrator of the Marxist Library of Moscow." Thrilled, Kurt had hoped to discuss with him the young revolution, barely five years old, but comrade Mendel pleaded, "The book, if you will, please, for I am very much in a hurry, very, very much in a hurry." He handed Kurt the high asking price with no attempt at negotiation, wrapped the book carefully, and disappeared.

On October 13, 1926, the members of the October 13 Association convened in the Kempinski wine cellar in Berlin, which, despite having very little in common with the Kuhberg wine cellar in Stettin, was nonetheless bustling with young people and lively with laughter and chatter. Nearly everyone was there. Karl Barić, whose essays had already gained some traction in certain circles and received mixed responses. Fritz and Franz Michal, who together had started a successful herring and preserved meats business, came accompanied by two cheerful young women.

Alma came as well, by herself, and seeming like life has not been kind to her, though the remnants of her beauty were still visible.

Albert and Käthe came as well, and the gang received them with applause and catcalls, "Well, you dirty old cradle-robber, you hunted her down after all."

Käthe teased, "I was the one who hunted him down, you morons."

Kurt and Anna came as well, and Anna proudly told everyone that Lottchen is old enough to babysit her sisters. Erich, the association's founder, came with Hilde, who was somewhat somber but spoke wisely and to the point. Willy Greiffenhagen's seat remained empty. Willy, the heartthrob of Stettin's adolescent girls, had died in the trench war, charging bare-chested at the enemy.

They sat at the wine cellar for a long while, but it wasn't until they were about to go that Carl said, "I don't intend to move an inch before Kurt answers me one question. Succinctly, if you will." They all looked at him curiously, and a mischievous smile glinted in Kurt's eyes.

"After the brawl at Kuhberg's," Carl went on, "Kurt and I sat by the fountain and he declared that he will not rest until he finds the key to the truth. It's been more than twenty years, Kurt, and it's high time you shared your findings."

Everyone dutifully looked at Kurt, who seemed focused and exultant. "You don't want an entire lecture now, in this racket," he said.

Alma, laughing, replied, "If you can't tell us your truth in a couple of sentences, it's hardly worth much."

Kurt took a deep breath and said, "Anna's brother is a bank manager. While I obviously know truly little of banks, I do know this: To open a safe, at least two different keys are required. One is not enough."

"This is getting complicated already," muttered Franz.

Franz's wife chided him, "Let's listen. We might leave richer than we came."

"The first key was given to me by Friedrich Hegel," said Kurt, and Franz's wife looked at him with wide, startled eyes. "I came to him after nationalism failed me, as did the wind of war which swept me away like it did everyone else, as did Zionism which attempts to tear the Jewish people away from their history. Hegel gave me a fresh perspective with his views on the rise of reason over time. He taught me that the spirit of the world contains within it the common foundation of all humans, and though he does not reject nationalism, he explains why it is not everything."

Kurt fell silent for a moment. The others looked at him, awaiting the rest.

"But it was not enough," Kurt spoke again, as if reading from a lecture he had written in his small study. "I owe the next piece to a mysterious man I met during the war. He opened the door to socialism and Marxism for me. I believe reason exists down here, in human society, in economics, not only in the heavens or the minds of people. The other key is therefore in the writings of Karl Marx."

"But Marx is a communist," Franz's wife blurted out, and Franz hushed her immediately. Some of the patrons occupying the surrounding seats seemed to sense that something important was taking place among the opinionated party and hurried to crowd around them.

"Kurt will never change," said Käthe. "Everything is so organized with him; he cannot accept the chaos inherent to our world."

Kurt's face darkened. He shifted uncomfortably in his seat and said, "The last year has been difficult for me. The world was not kind to me, and the reason of Hegel and Marx seemed a cold, faraway matter. I thought to myself, if life is foul, what good is the truth. If the truth distances us from ourselves and holds no comfort in this life, how can I receive it, and how can I pass it on. And then a third key came to me."

Alma stared solemnly at Kurt.

Albert said, "You have spun us a tale worthy of Scheherazade, but we have no intentions to wait until tomorrow. The third key now, if you will – and off to the bank."

Käthe elbowed him reproachfully.

"All will be revealed now, Albert, and I thank you, all of you, because it was not until now that I can finally see things with a clarity I have been seeking for years. The third key, my dears, was given to me by Baruch Spinoza. When I had just opened Utopia, I purchased a small collection of this wonderful philosopher's work, which the Jews have foolishly ostracized and boycotted. I read and read, enchanted. Step by step he unraveled the great questions of being and with an ingenious flick of his mind reconnected them. Even God, who I have always found to be a preposterous creature, a tyrannical king conceived by human weakness, was construed by Spinoza in a way I could find palatable. When I reached chapter four, Ethics, in which Spinoza tackled the questions of humanity, everything fell into place. The reason heralded by Hegel was no longer a matter to be settled by history but something given to each and every man and woman; and the spirit, which in Hegel's possession became a sort of mysterious specter, with Spinoza came back to dwell in the living human heart, corporeal and feeling. Suddenly, I was there, too. Logic and emotion, body and soul, history and the individual fused together. Thus, I found a balm for my life's hardships, and a guide to follow onward."

Scattered applause rose from the surrounding tables, and Karl said, "The trouble is that to achieve these keys you must spend your whole life studying."

Kurt retorted, "It's not that complicated, this cannot be the exclusive domain of scholars."

"You are a precious man, Kurt," said Alma, "But you live in worlds the rest of us cannot touch. Anna, I envy you."

They went out into the evening chill and said goodbye. Erich suddenly pulled Kurt into his arms, embracing him tightly, muttering, "Kurt, Kurt, my dear Kurt." Hilde took Erich's arm, embarrassed, and dragged him along, and together they walked up the street and away.

5.

The final days of the Weimar Republic found the Freyers content, if not wealthy. Hilde and Erich ran Hoffman Publishing, which specialized in socialist and humanist literature. Käthe and Albert ran a thriving household in the heart of Berlin, and their eldest son Gabriel was expected by all to achieve great things. They would still visit Trude and Martin in Stettin quite often, mostly on summer holidays. In 1929 they came together to mourn the death of their mother, Theresa.

Kurt had been laboring over a short book on his Spinoza, and eventually sent it to a small publishing house, where they were deeply impressed by the sharp, clear style and the spirit of "hope and faith" interlined between its pages. The book found its way to the shelves of university libraries in Berlin. Fifty years later it could still be found in the library of the young Tel Aviv University. Utopia on Prager Square closed, and its business was transferred to the family's apartment on EislebenerStraße. In the evenings, after Kurt counted the pittance he had made in another day of antique book dealing, he would make notes, as German scholars do, on pieces of paper, small and large, that he attached to the margins of books. A large collection had been slowly growing in one of the closets, of art paintings, mostly reproductions, each meticulously numbered and accompanied by many comments.

On March 30, 1933, a few weeks after Hitler became Kanzler of Germany, Hilde wished to ask Kurt about a manuscript sent to their publishing house by a young art scholar regarding the political influence evident in the work of several painters, a topic Kurt was often occupied with. They met that evening by the Tiergarten gate, and from there went to the Gedächtniskirche, walked for a while along Ku'Damm looking at display windows, and ended up in a small café. Hilde ordered tea with milk, and Kurt indulged in coffee with whipped cream. When the waiter brought them their beverages, along with some chocolate cookies, Kurt sighed, "Just like the good old days."

Hilde replied, "Yes, just like the good old days."

"How is Erich?" Kurt inquired. "I haven't seen him in several weeks now."

"To be honest, he could be better," said Hilde. Kurt looked at her worriedly and she added, "He scares me. Something in the way he walks, in his choice of words, and he's been making mistakes with the business, forgetting sums."

"The situation is getting at him, he's always been like this," Kurt soothed her.

Hilde said, "Yes, the situation, it's the situation, and maybe not just the situation."

"What is it, Hilde, what is going on?" asked Kurt.

Hilde replied, "Not now, Kurt, it isn't a good time."

He said, "It's never a good time," and they fell silent for a while.

When Hilde got up to leave, a drumbeat sounded in the distance, growing steadily closer and louder. Kurt raised his head toward the sound and Hilde looked sharply at the corner of the street and gasped. Coming from the west, spanning the entire Ku'Damm in breadth, slithered a brown-colored dragon of men. They marched in rows, men who seemed to all have the same face, the same hair, and the repetitive chant growled from within the dragon as if following a hidden metronome, *Sieg Heil, Sieg Heil.* When they came closer to the café Kurt saw to his horror that the first few rows were carrying white placards with stylized black letters reading "*Juden raus*," and again the metronome beat, Sieg, Hail, Sieg, Hail. Kurt froze and Hilde placed a steady hand on his shoulder. When the procession marched past them, the footfalls echoed in Kurt's ears, and for a moment he was petrified with terror and apprehension. When they disappeared up Budapest Allee, he downed the remainder of his coffee and looked at Hilde for a long while.

"These marches," she said, "it's the same every day now, unbearable. Don't you think, Kurt?"

"The marches are just a façade," said Kurt.

"What are you saying, Kurt," asked Hilde, "what do you mean?"

Kurt stared into her eyes until she looked away. "We need to leave, Hilde. All of us. Immediately."

"Have you spoken of this to Anna?" Hilde wondered.

Kurt said, "We spoke a bit, we weren't sure, but now it is clear to me, crystal clear, Hilde, we must leave, within the week we must get out, sell everything as long as we still own something, and go."

"And where would you go, Kurt," Hilde asked, "you can't be thinking of Palestine?"

"Amsterdam now," Kurt said, decisive, "Amsterdam now."

Hilde sat down silently, and Kurt said, "You know you must come with us." She was fidgeting with the handle of her teacup and squirming in her chair.

"But this is impossible, Kurt," she said, "impossible, and I ask that you do not mention this to Erich, things are hard enough for him as it is."

"We will go to Amsterdam," Kurt stated, "and you will as well, Hilde, there is no other choice."

She twiddled her thumbs nervously and spoke quietly, as she could feel the eyes of the other café patrons pushing like knives into her back. "You will not take us out of here, Kurt, do not even think of it."

Kurt said, "You will come to this by yourself, one day you will understand."

"This had nothing to do with me," said Hilde, "nothing at all. I despise the Nazis, but those bastards will not make us leave, that is a victory I will never give them."

Kurt's wise eyes settled on hers, and she thought she saw in them a glimmer of amusement, and she said, "You, everything is always so clear to you, isn't it, have you no doubts, never any doubts?"

Kurt said, "Doubts are for the ignorant, Hilde."

"Ach, rubbish!" cried Hilde. "All this truth of yours, the rise of reason, Kurt, it is absolute nonsense. You just saw your reason marching up the street, and if Hegel were alive, he would be marching right at the head of that column and throwing Spinoza into a windowless cell!"

"Reason has enemies," said Kurt.

"Ach, please," Hilde seethed. "Nothing but an invention, a massive lie, and you and Erich, the two of you are just like Don Quixote and Sancho Panza. Look around, look at your life, you could have been a brilliant professor, a museum administrator, and what are you, a penniless book merchant, this is what you've come to, wandering from town to town, Amsterdam now, and you know it's just a stop on the way to the desert of Palestine. What will you do there with all that wisdom? Who will even know what you are talking about?"

Kurt said, "You're upset, Hilde. Talk to Erich about this."

But Hilde was resolute, declaring, "I am not going anywhere, Kurt. Not me, or Yvonne. I will not uproot my life because of some marches and some rules that will be overturned tomorrow."

Kurt was silent, and Hilde added, with a sudden tenderness, "Erich will stay here. I will keep him safe, this will pass, this surge will pass, I'm sure it will."

They walked toward Zoo Station, where the tram stops on its way east to Alexanderplatz. They said goodbye at the entrance to the station. As Kurt was turning to leave, Hilde grabbed him by the shoulder and said, "Now it's time that I ask you the question I've been wondering about for years." Kurt laughed his warm laugh, humming amiably as he always did, and she asked, "How do you take it? Everything is collapsing, crumbling around you and you stand there grinning amid the ruins. What is your secret, Kurt?"

Kurt looked at her uncomfortably and his face darkened. "To ask such a question, Hilde," he muttered. "What sort of a question is this."

"Don't say you haven't thought of it," she pressed, "you with all your reason."

"Not like this," Kurt whispered, "not like this."

"Yes, well," Hilde mocked, "without a quote from Spinoza you cannot even look into yourself."

"That is not fair," Kurt protested.

"Were you never angry?" Hilde asked. "Never wanted to stand up and scream? They destroyed your dreams, they stole your life, and now those brown barbarians are chasing you away."

"And what good will come of screaming, Hilde?" he said. "What good?"

"It isn't about screaming," said Hilde, "it is about the pain, Kurt, the pain."

"I am a man of faith, Hilde," Kurt slowly intoned, as if something had been revealed that had nested for years, a trapped bird in the dark slopes of his consciousness, and now emerged simple and whole into the world, "nothing can change that."

"Faith is quite the luxury to have in this mad existence," said Hilde. "Who can afford all this faith?"

"Quite the opposite," Kurt insisted, his face brightening. "It is just when we are circling the mouth of the abyss that we need faith most of all. Without it there is no hope, Hilde, and then the barbarians will truly have won."

"Well, then," Hilde said, bewildered, "another speech. And I have to run home now and make dinner for Yvonne."

Kurt was appeased, now, and his voice was warm and low when he said, "Look after Erich, Hilde. Whatever happens, keep him safe."

Hilde stared at Kurt. Her face grew determined, hard and expressionless, and she disappeared into the train station.

CHAPTER FOUR: HILDE

1.

On May 10, 1933, Erich Freyer got off the tram at Frankfurter Allee in Berlin, a broad boulevard leading from Alexanderplatz to the eastern suburbs. It was around 4 p.m. and a cool spring wind caressed him. Erich crossed the street and started down Schillingstraße, on the path leading to his house. He was a short man who had gone prematurely bald. His face customarily arranged itself into a bewildered smile. At thirty, he looked older than his age, and now, at forty-seven, his hands were prone to tremble. A round-faced woman walked opposite him, carrying two baskets. He nodded toward her and said, "Good day, Frau Rauch." She glanced at him suspiciously and hurried on past him. Erich smiled and nodded again.

On the corner of Schillingstraße and Blumenstraße, four young hooligans ran, shrieking fearfully, as two men in brown chased them, one potbellied and the other small-sized and elderly, waving a baton. Erich turned to Blumenstraße, where he saw a small wall of backs as people crowded in a circle around something he could not see. Erich walked faster, a deep frown casting wrinkles all the way up to his considerably receding hairline. He tried to peek over the wall's heads and shoulders, and they looked at him silently and moved aside, making way. Erich passed between them and stood in front of number 22.

Tall, arched, somber windows adorned the building's façade. In one of them stood the neighbor, Herr Brower, watching the spectacle. The curtains of their own apartment window were drawn wide open, and Erich momentarily feared that Hilde would catch a cold, but then saw that she was standing in front of the building, at the entrance to Hoffman Publishing. She was speaking, businesslike, with a portly man in a brown uniform. His shirt was well-ironed, and his trousers neatly tucked into his boots. A small group of similarly dressed men stood around him, surrounding Hilde. Erich's foot collided with something, and he tripped and fell into a large, soft pile. Hilde ran toward him and held him. He looked at her and moisture came to his soft eyes. She helped him to his feet, and they walked to the side of the pile he had not yet looked at.

"The books, Erich. The books," said Hilde.

"I was at the bank," Erich muttered, "I only went to the bank."

"I know, Erich, you went to the bank. Come, drink some water. Would you like me to make you a cup of coffee?"

Erich did not reply. He looked at the pile and his eyes dried. The entire width of the pavement was strewn with books. Open, torn, tattered, books fresh from the printers, journals written in his handwriting, a thick Russian-German dictionary and history books with frayed edges, thrown on top of each other, the fallen leaves of the chestnut already beginning to cover them. Hilde looked at him and he raised his gaze to meet hers. Her eyes were harder than he had ever seen them, and she immediately looked away.

Erich and Hilde walked into the small office of their publishing house. The table's glass top was shattered, and several books were still scattered at the feet of the empty bookshelves. Erich sat on a chair and placed his small, slightly trembling hands on the desk. Hilde rifled through the closets, some of which still contained file folders, an album full of newspaper clippings, un-filed letters. Out the window they could still see the stout man delivering some final orders and turning to leave along with his small group of men. Only two young men remained, one in a brown uniform and another who sauntered around him, wild and cheerful, remained by the pile of books and drove away the quickly diminishing crowd. Hilde stood up and started dusting the remaining books. She then tipped her head, indicating an empty shelf, and pointed upward, and Erich said, "Well done, very well done, ach, Hilde, very good," and fell silent again. The veins of his scalp were pulsing blue, threatening to burst. Hilde started talking, slowly, quietly, and Erich could hear that old tune in her voice, the tune of clanging metal, which always made him excruciatingly furious.

"I heard them," she said, "saw them from the window. At least thirty of them, you know how they are, like you said, Erich, or-ganized barbarism. They took the books, threw them out, came and went, and you'll ask if I did anything, Erich, well what could I do, what would you do, I ask you, what would you do, Erich, you know they cannot be stopped."

Erich said nothing. He ran his fingernail along the line of cracked glass, as if he wished to shatter it again. "And you, you aren't even listening," Hilde cried, "You never do, you never listen."

Erich said brokenly, "Of course I listen, Hilde, of course I am listening."

She shot him a sharp look and came to sit down opposite him. "I went down to meet them," Hilde spoke quietly now, as if the storm had passed. "I went down, and I asked, 'what are you doing, what the hell do you think you are doing?' So, one of them, he was their commander, he didn't say anything, he just handed me this paper, this document." She retrieved a folded piece of paper from her coat pocket and opened it and placed it on the table, and Erich glanced at it, read the edges of the sentences, the white-hot words, and felt that the page was on fire, burning with a great flame. He rose from the chair, walked several steps and stumbled. Hilde held him and muttered, "Not now, Erich, be strong, not now."

He raised empty eyes at her. "I'm going to Paris," he said.

Hilde grabbed her head in her hands and stared at him.

"Paris," she said, "and what will you do, then, in Paris? Who is waiting for you in Paris? You learned some words in French and now you think Paris is waiting for Erich Freyer."

Erich looked at her with the wise gaze she used to love so much. "I am going to Paris, Hilde. Tonight." He pulled some pale paper bills from his wallet, placed them in her hand and left the publishing house without so much as a glance to the second-story window of his apartment. The two men standing guard around the pile of books that were slowly, almost surreptitiously, fading in the cold light of the spring sun, looked at him, and one of them followed him a way. Erich hastened his steps, once more heading for Frankfurter Avenue, and hurried to the bus station leading to the Anhalter Bahnhof. The streets were full of men in brown, flowing now like a thick and frothing muddy river, out of the small streets and into the main roads, massing in squares, getting on and off buses. Little trucks laden with books moved honking through the broad streets. In Alexanderplatz men in brown uniforms were gleefully waving books around. Laughing, they threw one at Erich, who sat in the bus with his nose pressed against the window.

The bus rattled along the Unter den Linden. The brown men were walking through the streets, singing, converging to a single destination which Erich could not yet pinpoint. The bus stopped at the station near the Opernplatz, and Erich looked on the broad plaza, delimited by massive buildings, gates and spires, and saw as the muddy river surged into it. Several trucks stood in the center of the plaza and large boxes of books were being diligently unloaded from them and thrown onto the white tiles. In the distance he could barely make out distant silhouettes running out of the Humboldt University gates, all carrying books. Erich's lip trembled.

The bus continued on its route. The passengers, solemn men in brimmed hats coming back from the office, women carrying small purses, laughing, jaunty adolescents, got on and off. The events outside were squeezed into the air of the bus and referred to by no one.

Erich got off the bus into the exit hall of the railway station. A human swarm flowed around him. He hesitantly walked to the counter, nearly turning away at the last moment, but reached for his wallet and asked the ticket clerk for a one-way ticket to Paris, on the night train, and the clerk stressed several times that the train would be leaving at precisely eight o'clock. Erich looked at the large clock at the center of the station and the blood thrummed viciously in his temples. He then sat down at the large café and an elderly waitress served him a roast goose sandwich with pickles and a cup of coffee overflowing with whipped cream. The announcer declared the trains leaving for Vienna, Frankfurt, and Munich. The voice sounded distant, dull.

The clock read seven-thirty. Erich got up and slowly walked toward the platform, where he saw Hilde, holding an overstuffed brown suitcase.

"You should not have carried that all the way here," he said.

"You silly man," said Hilde, "you thought I'd let you leave for Paris like this, with nothing but the clothes on your back?"

"I'll write you," he said.

"They took the books," Hilde said. "A truck came and took them. A good thing. I didn't want Yvonne to see that."

"I'll write you," Erich repeated. "We'll have a good life."

Hilde didn't reply. She touched him lightly and he seemed as though he intended to kiss her. She withdrew from him, turned around and slowly descended the large station staircase until she disappeared. Erich boarded the train and sat in an available seat. He looked out the window. His hands shook.

2.

Outside, a deep darkness had fallen. The lights of small hamlets occasionally shone in the distance. Few passengers boarded at the stops. At one of them, a noisy group of men in brown shirts entered Erich's car, singing a drunken tune at the top of their lungs. Some of them eyeballed him suspiciously, sniggering and whispering. One of them, red-faced, approached Erich, rubbing his nose and swaying toward him like a dancer.

He dozed in the dim lights of the car. When he woke the car was empty, the train was rattling among grassy meadows and French villages, and a pale dawn was rising. Behind him he heard two young women chatting in French. Erich loved the French language and took great pride in being the only Freyer who spoke it. He held the German language in much lower regard. "We speak in drums and trumpets, and the French in pianos and flutes," he once told Kurt as they sat for coffee and whipped cream at Ku'Damm.

Kurt laughed, saying, "Yes, that's what they have, light, fluffy words. The German touches the deep foundations of humanity and history. That is why we have such a hard time with words: we cast them from iron."

"Ach, nonsense," protested Erich, looking genuinely offended. "When it comes to language, we Germans simply have no appreciation for aesthetics."

Kurt produces his customary low chuckle, half laughter and half hum, and they left Ku'Damm and headed toward Albrecht-Achilles-Straße for evening tea at Käthe's house, hoping that her husband Albert will settle the argument. Albert listened solemnly, pondered the matter briefly and decided on the invention of a new, impossible language, which no one can speak, but will "finally make it so that Europeans can understand one another."

"Oh? And which language might that be?" Erich scoffed.

Albert pursed his lips, looked at them both, winked at Käthe who was standing, amused, by the kitchen, and said, "Well, I am referring to Hebrew, of course!"

Erich was dozing again. His sleep was unsettled by dreams, fire and the screams of people burning, and he awoke when the voice of the announcer declared that they had arrived in Paris. For a moment he wanted to stay on the train now returning to Berlin, to stay there, sleeping, as it ran back and forth between the cities, but the conductor insisted that he vacate. He took the brown suit-case and got off the train and his tired legs carried him toward the exit. For a long while he simply wandered the streets of Paris. Eventually he sat, breathless, on a bench overlooking the Seine, and unfolded a tattered postcard he retrieved from his pocket.

A rosy-cheeked guard sat at the gate of *Les Debats* newspaper. Erich asked in unmistakably school-learned French that he point him to the office of Karl Barić. The guard looked at him suspi-ciously, mumbled something into a large telephone receiver and told Erich to sit. A bespectacled man, slightly taller than Erich, came down the stairs. They stood looking at each other, Karl with bafflement, and Erich with shame, his eyes glistening. Karl stepped forward and embraced him tightly, and Erich waved a trembling hand still clutching the postcard.

"October Thirteenth," Erich said, "you've not forgotten."

"I have not forgotten," whispered Karl.

"You left right after the meeting at Kempinski's, you bastard," Erich said, "before it all started, and to Paris of all places, and now look at you, a famous journalist."

"For seven years I got your postcards," said Karl, "and Fritz's, too, and Alma and Albert. How are Kurt and Anna?"

"They're in Amsterdam with the girls," Erich replied.

"Amsterdam," said Karl.

They both fell silent for a while. Karl shook his head, saying, "Let's get something to drink, Erich. You must be tired."

And Erich said, "Yes, I am, very tired." They left the newspaper and went to a nearby café.

"Well, how have you been," asked Karl, "difficult times?"

Erich said, "Yes, indeed," and again they fell silent. Eventually Erich raised his eyes to meet Karl's.

Karl asked, "What is it, Erich? Has something happened?"

Erich replied brokenly, "They closed the publishing house. They closed Hoffman."

"Oh," sighed Karl, "you, as well."

"They threw the books out, Karl," Erich continued, "Hilde said a truck came and took them, that it was a good thing that Yvonne didn't see it."

"They burned your books, Erich," Karl said. "They burned them tonight, at Opernplatz."

Erich paled. His face twisted, some foam dribbled from his mouth as he mumbled, "Such a thing, what can you say about such things." He reached a trembling, begging hand to Karl Barić. "Perhaps they didn't burn it all." he whispered. "They can't have found all the books, they don't have enough people to burn all the books."

"They will write new books," said Karl, "and those that haven't burned will disappear. No one will read them. No one will sell them at bookstores. Goebbels spoke there, at the plaza. 'We will clean Germany from filth,' he said, and they stood and tossed books into the fire. All night they stood and fed books into the fire, and dancing, and singing. Our reporter in Berlin told me he had never seen such a sight, never in his life."

Karl placed his hand on Erich's shaking, bony arm. Erich raised his eyes and there was innocence in them. Karl had always wondered about Erich's innocent eyes, were they a mirror, was Erich of all people meant to keep the flame of innocence, or perhaps they reflected his childlike terror. Perhaps those innocent eyes were nothing but a warning of the fall to come, of the desperate foam that would come to his lips, but right now Erich was lucid, determined. "I want to open a publishing house, Karl, here in

Paris," he said. "Hilde and I will publish French translations of German books, an Internazional of new European poetry, study books for the Socialismus. You need it here, too, Karl. France is confused, I read the papers, I know, Europe is losing its way. I'll bring Hilde and Yvonne. We will have a life here, a good life."

Karl had gone silent, and after a while said, "Come, Erich, we'll find a place for you to put your suitcase. You need sleep. How much money do you have?"

"I've brought two-thousand francs," Erich said, and Karl nodded. "That will last you a bit. Maybe in the meanwhile you'll find a job."

Erich looked at him and Karl nodded again, his face growing very grim.

"I can write anything," Erich said, "news articles, columns."

Karl said nothing. He hastily signaled a taxi. They took it together to Porte de Clichy and stopped by the Hotel D'oreale, which looked more than anything like a dilapidated apartment building. Karl booked a room, paid for the first week and bid Erich farewell.

That evening Erich and Karl met for dinner at a small restaurant near the Seine. Erich had cleaned up and was fresh and hopeful. He looked at the river, at the small lights glistening upon the water and the small boats sailing in it. An accordion player approached them and played a tune Erich did not recognize. Karl leaned back in his seat and said, "Erich, I may have work for you."

Touched by this, Erich gushed, "How generous, how terribly generous of you," but he fell silent upon seeing the darkness in Karl's eyes.

"I have a friend in a pharmaceutical company," Karl said. "They have an opening for a translator. They want to sell medicine in

Germany, you would be perfect for them, Erich. With that head of yours, you could help them. It's paying work, you could afford rent…" He placed a small piece of paper in the palm of Erich's hand. Erich stood up, mortified, bid him a rushed goodbye and went down to the metro tunnels. In his small hotel room, he sat on the unkempt sofa and a brief, harsh sob tore from his chest. He then fell asleep and remained that way for a morning and an evening and a morning.

On the third day Erich went outside. For a long time, he traveled around the suburbs of Paris. The people walking the streets seemed like strangers again, and their language foreign once more. At the L'hygiene pharmaceuticals factory in the Parisian industrial quarter, the work manager sat him in front of a little table with a stack of pages filled with compressed French and a stack of medical books and dictionaries. The personnel manager promised him a weekly wage of two-hundred and fifty francs "as these are difficult times, and a raise will certainly be possible a year from now."

Every day, Erich made coffee, cooked a soft-boiled egg on a kerosene stove that a previous tenant had left in the room, and then took two metro trains to work. At lunch hour he went to a small workers' restaurant and ate bacon and fried potatoes. In the evening he went back to the hotel, where he would write long letters to Hilde and his little Yvonne, whose appearance he could barely recall, and his beloved brother Kurt in Amsterdam, and his sister Trude in Stettin, and Albert and Käthe, who had immigrated to Palestine with their children. On Sundays Erich wandered the streets of Paris, looking at the people walking past him along the Seine, and sat for long hours at the Tuileries Gardens. Once or twice he saved up enough francs to go to a theater show at the Comédie Française, and then took the deserted metro back to the hotel.

People speaking German would pass him sometimes in the dark halls of the D'oreale. A small German-speaking family lived in one of the rooms with a round-faced boy. Erich invited him to his room one time, but the boy ran off without so much as a thank-you.

Erich occasionally met with Karl, whose own hardships were becoming more prevalent all the time. In one of their meetings Erich mustered up the courage to ask, "Perhaps now, Karl, perhaps now," but Karl was silent, and Erich shook his head. "I understand," he said resignedly, "You do not want me in your paper. I will not become your yoke, Karl. I will not burden you."

"It isn't that at all," said Karl, "not at all. Every week more Jews come from Germany to Paris. They go from paper to paper, knocking on every door, publishing houses, law firms, accountants, architects, they are pouring in, journalists, university professors, engineers. No one wants German Jews here. At the paper they tell me, you are an albatross, Barić, every *juif* in Germany is coming in your wake. They think that if *Les Debats* is funded by Rothschild then *Les Debats* will be a Jewish paper. That's what they say to me, Erich."

"And you," Erich blurted, suddenly furious, "you already belong, six years and already you belong, it is a matter of time, Karl, only time, I need time. Hilde will come, she is half-French, you remember, she will feel at home, where else could she feel at home? And Yvonne will receive proper schooling. Ever since Hitler, we can no longer put her in those awful schools."

"Paris is a hard city," said Karl. "You mustn't think it is easy for me here. The ground is shaking. The air is becoming poisonous."

Erich said goodbye and decided that he would not meet him again.

Summer came. In the evenings Erich would cut out rent ads from the paper and write hopeful letters to Hilde, and for Yvonne he would attach little rhymes he wrote her, like he used to recite for her in Berlin every night before she fell asleep. He once wrote to her:

A bird once sat to rest a bit,
up on the tallest tree it knew.
'Hello,' it said, 'my name is tit,'
'Mine's Tour Eiffel, how do you do.'

He would read them aloud to himself several times before sealing the letter.

The head of the L'hygiene sales department had told Erich that the company was pleased with his work, and as promised they would discuss his salary come winter. He made some casual friends who like him lived in small hotel apartments in Porte de Clichy and made their living in various odd jobs.

One day they found Erich in his office, white-eyed and agape on the floor of his office. He was taken to the hospital, where he lay in his room and wordlessly stared at the ceiling. Karl sat at his bedside for a long time and eventually said, "You must go from here, Erich. Leave this place."

Erich shook his head.

"I spoke to everyone," said Karl. "Kurt arranged an apartment for you in Amsterdam, not far from his own." Erich raised a questioning gaze at him, and Karl said, "They'll be there. Hilde and Yvonne will be waiting for you in Amsterdam, everything will be fine, Erich, life will be good."

A week later Karl and Erich stood together in the train station. Autumn was fast approaching, and Karl said, "October Thirteenth, Erich, don't forget!"

For the first time in many months the innocent, touching smile returned gently to Erich's pale face, and his lips trembled. "October Thirteenth, Karl," he whispered, "October Thirteenth."

3.

Erich slowly came off the train, brown suitcase in his hand. Yvonne ran to him and hugged him; laughing, she said, "Papi, I thought you were lost."

Erich stroked her hair, saying, "Ach, don't be silly, my little golden girl."

She said, "They talk so funny here in Amsterdam," and started babbling in mock Dutch.

Erich said reprovingly, "Yvonne, you must learn this language so you can go to school."

"I don't want to go to school," Yvonne giggled, "I want to be a florist!"

Her father smiled broadly and recited a short poem he wrote her when she was eight, and she joined him:

Flowers, Herr, flowers, Frau -
come and get your flowers now!
Daisy, lily, and carnations –
lovely blooms for all occasions.

They both laughed. Yvonne dragged him to the end of the platform where Kurt and Hilde were standing, looking at them, Kurt's face radiant and wise, Hilde's quiet and solemn.

Yvonne stopped laughing. Erich approached Hilde. She stared at him for a stretch long enough to unnerve him and then hugged him, saying, "It is good to see you, Erich."

Kurt placed his hand on Erich's slumped shoulder, smiled, and laughed his characteristic low hum of a laugh. "There, now, Erich," he said, "finally back with us, we're all together again."

They drove to a small apartment in Amsterdam's southern quarter. They were joined by Kurt's wife, Anna, and later by Minchen and Susi. Erich noted, "You have grown so much, young women already."

Minchen said, "There is no time to be children in this world." Hilde served coffee and butter cookies.

Erich looked out the window. The one-story houses along the street had tiled roofs. Grassy pastures stretched behind the row of houses, dotted by grazing cows. Past the meadow he could see the street where Kurt, Anna and the girls lived. Suddenly Erich remembered to ask, "And how is Lotte, where is she?"

Anna said, "She's in Berlin, in Beit Hehalutz. We worry for her."

"Ach, nonsense," said Hilde, "No need to worry about Lotte, she always knows what to do."

At night Hilde held Erich and he felt his life force returning, flowing into him and out of him, felt the loneliness of Paris crumbling away. Berlin and Paris seemed to him now like a dense, dark metropolitan, seeped in smoke and the stench of beer and poison fumes. In that moment he belonged, with every fiber of his being, to this place in the outskirts of Amsterdam, which had no name and shone with unblemished magnificence. He was intoxicated by the mingling smells of grass and cow dung and cooked sausage from the nearby houses.

Erich woke at 5 a.m. The perfumed air slammed into his nostrils. He left the house and wandered around the neighborhood. He nodded at the milkman, who squinted at him suspiciously. The paper delivery boy, a young man with pockmarks on his face, passed by on his bicycle and whistled at him. A thickset man with a red face walked his dog.

When he returned, Yvonne and Hilde were still asleep. Erich sat down writing short lines on graph paper:

Where have all the good days gone,
into the dark lands they did roam;
but alas, this made them sad,
so back they all came running home.

He reread the lines to himself and smiled before placing it softly by Yvonne's bed. He went and settled into the sofa, picked up the book which lay in front of it and sat there for a while, reading.

Kurt was now a partner in a used and antique bookstore in Amsterdam. Every day he took the tram into the city, and Erich would go with him and help in the store. At lunch they sat in a café near the large canal and sipped sweet Dutch coffee. Come evening the family gathered for dinner.

Minchen and Susi took little Yvonne fully under their wing. Minchen, an 18-year-old who knew everything there possibly was to know, used to read to her from history and poetry books she would bring from the store, so that Yvonne wouldn't fall behind on her schoolwork. Yvonne, fascinated, hung on her every word.

After dinner the grown-ups would retire to chat in the living room, with Minchen occasionally joining them and making remarks, as Yvonne and Susi went out into the cold autumn air and played hopscotch under the streetlamp.

One day Lotte arrived from Berlin and the excitement was great. Lotte, Kurt and Anna's eldest, was preparing to travel to Palestine, along with her friends, and live in a kibbutz. Yvonne asked Erich where Palestine was. Erich jotted down some calculations on a piece of paper and then said, "If we leave right now on foot, and walk east at an angle, and make no stops save for eight hours of sleep and for an afternoon nap, in three months' time we will have arrived at Palestine."

"And we wouldn't even have to swim?" asked Yvonne, astonished.

"We would need to take a boat to cross the Dardanelles," he informed her, and she bubbled with laughter. Erich wrote her a quick poem:

Who and what are Dardanelles?
If you know please come and tell –
Watch your step or you can bet
that your trousers will get wet!

Erich flourished in Amsterdam. He was smiling again, and even gaining weight. Hilde found some work sewing and embroidering, even making enough guilders to cover the rent, and barely enough to live from. Occasionally she went to the center of Amsterdam, to browse the display windows, leaf through books in stores, try to sell some of her embroidery, and return with a small gift for Yvonne and Susi. In the afternoon she would write long letters to her mother in Glauchau and her friends in Berlin. At nights she retired early to their room and Erich, who would come in later following lengthy and exhaustive conversations with Kurt, would find her lying in bed, snoring lightly, her face pursed, her body wrapped in a long, heavy nightgown. For a while he would lie beside her, staring at the floral ceiling, and eventually he would walk to the small living room and sink into the sofa, contemplative, and fall asleep until first light.

Erich and Hilde used to listen to the radio together, but nearly every show was in Dutch, which Erich deeply loathed. When they turned the large knobs, the German language came on the air and they sidled near the radio to hear better. Erich would sigh and say, "More propaganda. Goebbels, it's all Goebbels." One time, a shrill cry pierced the radio, shrieking words and broken sentences, so jarring that Yvonne, who had been rolling around on the carpet in the next room, came running into the living room, alarmed. Erich reached for the radio, saying, "Him, him I cannot listen to."

"I want to hear," said Hilde.

He fumed, "What is there to hear, we are done with him."

She said, "I don't know. He is there now, but it cannot take that long, how long can it take, Erich?"

Erich was silent a moment and Hilde raised her eyes to look at him, her face once again grave. "I don't know," he said quietly. "No one can know these things; Germany has gone mad."

Hilde paled. She got up, went to the radio, turned it off and said, "But what will we do, Erich, what will we do?"

"What will we do?" Erich's eyes were lowered. "Now we wait, Hilde. Wait and see."

"We can't wait forever, Erich," she whispered. "We can't."

"We will go back to Germany," Erich stated. "When it's over, we'll go back."

"You can't go back now," she said, "you know you can't go back."

Erich had gone completely white now, only the veins in his head pulsing blue. Impotent rage gripped him, and he screamed, not hearing his own screaming voice, "Jew, Jew, Jude, Jude, say it, say the word, now you are ashamed to say it, Hilde."

"I am not ashamed," Hilde replied. "You are the one who is ashamed."

"I am as much a Jew as you are a Christian," Erich said, no longer yelling. "How many times have we discussed this. We are both free human beings, we have no church, we have discussed this, Hilde."

Then Hilde was shouting, uncharacteristically, "Ach, nonsense, utter nonsense, you know it is. Lies. You lie to yourself. To yourself. You're not a Jew? Look at you. Look where you've ended up. Look where you must go to, into the desert, that is where you must go now."

Erich's entire body was shaking. Hilde stood up and left the house, returning later to find him sitting silently, staring at the ceiling. She hugged him and said, "I am sorry, Erich, I am sorry, everything is so hard, I simply don't know what to do."

Erich said nothing. In the morning Hilde found him slumped in the same chair, unresponsive. She tried to talk to him, then ran over to Kurt and Anna's, terrified. "Come, Erich, come lie in bed, we'll bring you some tea and biscuits." Kurt and Anna tried as well, but Erich did not reply, and looked as if he did not recognize any of the people in the room. Yvonne, frightened and sad, they took to Kurt and Anna's home, where Minchen looked after her.

Kurt telephoned the local sanitarium. A doctor and two

orderlies came and took Erich to their car. Kurt went along with them, his hands ceaselessly caressing his brother's. Hilde stood at the door to the house, looking at the car as it drove away, her face hard and bright, like copper.

4.

Kurt visited the sanitarium every day. He would talk to the doctors and even managed to speak with Erich a bit, who by now had begun sipping the soup served by the muscular Dutch nurses whom he would scrutinize as they made his bed or took his temperature. One of the doctors kept asking him inane questions in German. Erich had asked him repeatedly to leave him alone.

One day the doctor came and said, "Herr Erich Freyer, certainly today you intend to be cooperative." Erich shook his head and the doctor asked, "How did you arrive in Holland, sir?"

Erich said, "You know, Germany, everyone is mad there."

The doctor shook his head now, saying, "No politics today." Erich fell silent and thought, *this doctor is an idiot, everything is politics, he has not learned yet that all life is politics, he will, they all will,* but he said nothing, simply smiled and experienced the elation of this thin anger he felt for the doctor, *thinking, oh, this idiot, oh, what an idiot he is,* until the doctor eventually asked what Herr Freyer was smiling about.

The nurses then gave him some sedatives, which came upon him like pleasant restraints. He slept like he had not slept since May 10, when they had closed Hoffman Publishing and burned his books in the plaza. A sleep he never had in the dilapidated hotel D'oreal in Porte de Clichy. A pure sleep. When he woke from it a deep depression settled over him. He rose from his bed to walk the halls of the hospital and entered the doctor's room.

The doctor stood up to greet him and said, "Come now, Herr Freyer, this is hardly beneficial."

"I am cured, Herr doctor," said Erich. "I must go back. We have problems to solve. Decisions to make. Me and my wife Hilde and my daughter Yvonne have crucial decisions to make, which you, Herr doctor are ill equipped to assist with."

"We will simply take some tests, Herr Freyer," persisted the doctor, whose patience was clearly tapering in the face of this small, strange immigrant with the inexplicable illness. "In several days. You have undergone an extreme psychophysical crisis; you might not even be able to stand by yourself."

"Today, today," said Erich, and left.

Kurt's face was grim as he came into the sanitarium reception hall, but Erich was already dressed, smiling, and prepared for the future. They returned to Amsterdam together. When Erich came into the living room in his and Hilde's small apartment, the blood was pounding in his temples. He wandered restlessly about the rooms and returned determined to the living room, where Kurt sat contemplating.

"Where is Hilde?" asked Erich, and then added, "She must have gone to Amsterdam today."

Kurt did not respond.

"I should have told her that I was coming," Erich grumbled. "We have much to discuss."

Kurt tried to interject but Erich went on, "She took Yvonne into town with her, but I'll write her a poem, I'll write a poem, see, 'A little girl went to the city–'" He collapsed onto the couch.

Kurt went into the kitchen and poured him a glass of water.

On the table lay several unopened letters. One was from Karl Barić, who wrote Erich to tell him how fortunate is was that he had left Paris in time, as the situation there has grown so dire that even the pharmaceutical companies were firing immigrants. Another letter had arrived that morning from Hilde's mother, in Glauchau. And there was another one, a closed envelope marked only with the words "For Erich."

Erich slashed it open with a copper-coated letter opener. His eyes misted over slightly when he recognized Hilde's sharp, clear script, the letters larger than usual. He raised it closer for a better look, but his hands shook, and he placed it back down. Kurt gave him the glass of water and he sipped from it slowly. The few letters in Hilde's handwriting seemed to flare like small fires into the air of the room. He gave the paper to Kurt. Kurt eyes swiftly scanned it and he placed his hand on Erich's trembling shoulder.

"You read it, Kurt, I cannot see very well," Erich said. Kurt looked at him with his wise gaze, and Erich could feel himself shrinking.

"It does not matter exactly what it says," Kurt said.

"It matters," said Erich, "it matters."

"What matters is that you rest now," Kurt replied.

Erich raised his voice slightly, "You always know best, but now, read."

Kurt shrugged and sighed. "There is nothing for us together," he read, his voice measured. "You go to your Palestine. We are returning to Germany."

"That is all?" asked Erich.

"That is all," nodded Kurt. "And a signature. Hilde and Yvonne."

Erich was silent. He seemed to absorb every word into some

dark space amid the shadows of his consciousness. He took the note and read it again.

"Hilde and Yvonne," said Erich. "Imagine that."

"They came to say goodbye," Kurt said. "Two days ago. I asked Hilde to wait for you. To speak with you."

"She did not want to wait," said Erich.

"She did not want to wait, Erich," Kurt echoed. "This is Hilde, you know Hilde."

"You are right," said Erich. "This is Hilde."

The sharp afternoon light glimmered behind the locked shutters. Erich looked at the window and then sank into deep contemplation and seemed to have fallen asleep. Kurt covered him with a thin blanket and sat on the sofa, studying him. Erich awoke with a start and Kurt saw that his eyes were moist, and his lips trembled.

"And Yvonne," Erich spoke the name hoarsely, almost breathlessly, "Yvonne, what did she say?"

"She was very sad, Erich, I think she was extremely sad," said Kurt. "She was quiet. But I could see how deeply sad she was."

"Did she cry?" Erich wondered.

"Yvonne did not cry," Kurt said. "Freyers do not cry."

And Erich said, "There, finally something worth saying. Freyers don't cry."

Minchen entered the room, her face grimmer than ever. She kissed Erich's cheek, took the note and read it, then hugged him and said, "Uncle Erich, you are still our Uncle Erich, we will never leave you." Anna and Susi also came into the house now to embrace Erich and kiss him on his bare, damp forehead.

After that Erich fell into a deep slumber. He slept for two days and two nights. The empty room crushed his eyelids. His heart was empty, and his mind was empty. The memory of Germany was erased from his mind in those days of sleep, and with it, Hilde and Yvonne were carried away on the wind, and Hoffman Publishing was taken as well. The suburb on the outskirts of Amsterdam became a nameless place, neither destination nor origin.

On the third day, Kurt came to him, spoke to him and held his hand. Erich got up, washed his face, drank sweet coffee. They walked out to the street and strolled together, hand in hand.

"What would Father say of all this," Erich wondered, suddenly.

Kurt abruptly stopped walking. Without warning he burst into laughter, uncharacteristically long, half rolling hum, half unending expectoration. "Honestly, Erich, finally a question worth asking, a truly outstanding question, what would Father say of all this."

CHAPTER FIVE: YVONNE

1.

Yvonne stood in the center of the small church on Bismarck Allee in the heart of Glauchau in Saxony, where she lived with her mother since they'd left Amsterdam in the summer of 1935. She was fifteen now and had grown fond of small, rural Glauchau, girdled by hills and forests, though her dreams at night were still Berlin dreams, taking place in the halls and the rooms of the house on 22 Blumenstraße.

Hilde sat in the first row of the hardwood pews, looking at Yvonne intently, and Grandmother Charlotta sat next to her. Several old ladies from the neighborhood sat in the back rows, as well as a balding man who sat there carefully studying Yvonne and taking notes in a small notebook. The minister facing Yvonne was reading a prayer, and after that he dipped his pale, meticulously clean hands in the silver baptismal font adorned with angelic reliefs, and splashed water on her face, on her shirt, on her hair, saying, 'I now baptize you in the name of the Father, the Son, and the Holy Spirit.' Yvonne peeked back and grinned at her mother and Hilde signaled her to turn back around and she did, and her eyes filled with importance as she looked at the priest. The priest spoke another prayer and the three women left the church, followed by the disapproving gazes of the old ladies still sitting in the back row.

Yvonne said, "That really was quite short,"

Hilde said, "I told you, it's nothing." They walked through the streets of Glauchau, Hilde expressionless, Charlotte with a heavy step, Yvonne skipping lightly on the cobblestones. They sat to celebrate the occasion at a café, and Hilde ordered them coffee with whipped cream.

"Yes, that was nice and proper, certainly proper," said Charlotta.

"That was adequate," said Hilde, "certainly adequate."

Yvonne looked at them, clearly amused, then haphazardly crossed herself and said, "That priest was certainly a huge windbag."

Hilde hushed her angrily, scolding, "That is enough, you ungrateful girl."

Yvonne and Hilde lived in a small, two-bedroom apartment in the eastern suburbs of Glauchau. At night Hilde pulled a small bed out from under her own, in which Yvonne snuggled up and slept. During the day Yvonne went to school and Hilde sat in the niche in the living room in which she had put her sewing machine and worked on an ever-growing list of orders, as she became known around town as a swift and precise seamstress. Yvonne hated school. She sat in the very back of the class and the teacher hardly ever addressed her. She was forbidden from participating in the morning roll call or going on field trips, "Due to special instructions from the Federal Ministry of Education." Sometimes Hilde and Yvonne spent the afternoon strolling around town or at the market plaza or visiting Grandmother Charlotta. They traveled to Leipzig twice a year to visit the city museum. In summer they would go visit the Czech border to trek through special spots in the forest or sit by the river.

Come evening, the streets of Glauchau, illuminated by the

murky light of gas lamps, would grow empty. Few cars traveled the rutted roads, and the cafés in the center of town closed early. Every evening small squads of men in brown shirts marched through the streets, hailing from the local Sturmabteilung branch, and Yvonne ran to the street to stare at them fervently as they passed. She then mostly read books, which were already starting to pile on the apartments few shelves, and the local paper, *Glauchau-Zwickau*, which brought detailed news from the region and the entire country, imposing ceremonial photographs of the party members or visits from important political and military leaders. She spent no time with her fellow classmates, who were members of the *Hitlerjugend*.

Yvonne would write a letter nearly every day. She wrote to her Aunt Trude and received warm, sympathetic responses. Trude invited her to visit them in Stettin, as they used to each summer, and Yvonne craved their magical strolls in the Buchenwald, which the forests of Berlin and Saxony combined could never rival. She missed wandering around the town square and even recalled her curious peeks into Marin's piano sanctuary. After every letter from Trude she asked her mother, "Maybe we can go to Stettin after all, Trude would be so happy." Hilde would say, "Not this year, it is impossible."

She also wrote her father, Erich, who was still living in Amsterdam. She would ask how he was, if he had recovered from his illness, and he replied with long, longing letters, telling her about his life, always promising that soon they would meet again, and added some lines for Hilde, which she read quickly before placing the letters in a box for safekeeping. He stopped writing Hilde directly after a brief exchange between them, on official notary paper, in which the matter of their divorce was settled unceremoniously, with no meeting required.

One day, the mailman brought her a thick envelope covered in strange English postage stamps and seals, and Hilde said, "This is from Palestine, Yvonne, your father is in Palestine now." Yvonne, now a quickly growing sixteen-year-old, examined the letter from all angles and sniffed it, and Hilde sighed, "Honestly, what is it that you think you are doing?"

"I wonder what Palestine smells like," Yvonne said.

Hilde scoffed, "Ach, nonsense, such nonsense."

When Yvonne eventually read the letter, she found it slightly vague, even confused. She read every word in her father's shaky, unadorned handwriting, her father who she had not seen in six years and whose round face and green eyes were already escaping her memory. She instantly sat down to write her reply, asking that he write to her about Palestine, what kind of place it is, and whether he works at the orange orchard, and if so, how do Palestinian oranges taste? She remembered the oranges from heated discussions on the subject at Käthe and Albert's apartment in Berlin. She then took a tattered photograph from her school cabinet and examined it intently. Hilde and Erich standing on a lakeshore, Hilde's head facing upward, her hair short and pulled back, wearing a black, sleeveless bathing suit and sandals, smiling uncharacteristically, a smile both questioning and accepting. Erich is slightly hunched over her, his right hand holding her left, which she is holding tight against her body, wearing a black bathing suit that covers him from his shoulders nearly to his knees, barefooted, his cheeks flushed and his bald spot gleaming, and he is looking up to the same mysterious spot as Hilde, and he is smiling broadly, a smile more proud than happy. On the margin of the photograph Erich's rushed handwriting read: "Here we are on vacation in Wannsee, Sep 12th,1926. Wonderful sunny day. Yvonne loves to come here and play in the sand."

One day Yvonne came home from school and immediately started rummaging through the cabinets until she eventually found a long rolled up sheet of paper. She started excitedly plotting lines and squares on it, and when Hilde emerged, somewhat groggy, from the bedroom, told her, "Help me, I'm missing a lot of names."

"What do you need all this for?" asked Hilde.

"I'm so busy right now," and Yvonne said, "I need it for school. I forgot the names of Father's grandparents."

"Later, later," said Hilde, "I'm busy right now," and she went back to the sewing machine to complete the dresses and shirts she was repairing.

When the two of them sat for dinner in the small kitchen, biting into sausages and fried potatoes, Hilde quietly said, "You cannot fill out all the squares in the drawing, Yvonne. I hope you understand that."

Yvonne went out to the living room and placed the large drawing, meticulously sketched and colored and replete with small drawings of people, on the table. Hilde stood beside her and placed a hand on her shoulder, and Yvonne said, "But I cannot just erase Father like that, and what sort of family tree is this, with no father?"

"These are bad times," said Hilde.

"You always say that," Yvonne grumbled, "But you erased him, too, just like everyone else."

"Not everything is so easy to explain," Hilde whispered. "It wasn't like that."

Yvonne repeated, "You erased him, he was sick, and you didn't want to take care of him, and what if he had died in that hospital in Amsterdam?"

Hilde sat down, her arms crossed, and said nothing. Yvonne coaxed her, "I'm not angry, Mutti, but please tell me, explain to me what happened."

Hilde said, "There was no future for us, your father could not return to Germany."

"We could have gone with him to Palestine," Yvonne persisted, "I wouldn't have minded, at least to see how it is there."

Hilde's reply was terse, slightly impatient, "I had nothing to do there, what could I have done there, Yvonne, you tell me."

Almost unnoticed, Yvonne took the photograph from her schoolwork cabinet, and Hilde, shocked to see it after it had disappeared years before, when they returned to Glauchau by a two-day train ride. She asked, "Where did you find that?"

Yvonne said, "Perhaps you would like to erase this as well?"

Hilde suddenly snapped, "Now you've gone too far."

Yvonne said, "I'm sorry, Mutti, I just want to understand," and Hilde burst into tears. Yvonne was dumbfounded. She had never seen Hilde cry in front of her, had barely even seen her eyes moisten, not even then, in the train station in Amsterdam, when they stood on the platform and waited for the train to take them back to the homeland, two women with brown suitcases.

Now Hilde was suddenly wracked with short, smothered sobs, and just as abruptly, she stopped them, and stated, "It is over, Yvonne, what your father and I had is over."

Yvonne said, "I don't understand."

Hilde said, "I cannot explain it."

They fell silent again, for a while. Eventually Yvonne said, "But you loved each other when I was born."

Hilde looked at her with eyes wide and astounded and said, "I don't know, we were not young when we met, we wanted to marry and have children, perhaps two, we wanted to do things, do something to make a better Germany, but love, I don't know, Yvonne, love is a matter of luck. Perhaps you will have more luck with love, and then you can come and teach me how it feels."

Yvonne got up and paced back and forth through the small apartment, and then snatched the large family drawing she had labored on all day from the table, crumpled it into a ball, compressed it and tossed it into the little trash bin in the kitchen.

2.

On November 9, 1938, Herr Franz Gommel, a corpulent man with a paintbrush mustache, owner of the office supply store Gommel and Gommel Ltd., left his store on Sachsenstraße in Glauchau early in the afternoon. Before the horrified gaze of Fräulein Yvonne Freyer, who assisted him with some cleaning and organizing and worked the register and even assisted shoppers when needed, he marched to the nearby pharmacy, owned by chemist Moritz Schneider, and with a large club that was tossed in a corner of his store shattered the pharmacy's glass display window to countless tiny shards.

Moritz came out of the pharmacy, shaking violently. Dozens of people gathered around, eager adolescents, police officers, neighbors. Yvonne rushed out of the store and heard Herr Schneider asking, his voice shrill with terror, evoking laughter among the crowd, "Why would Herr Gommel do such a thing?"

Gommel was shrieking, "Filthy Jew, I owe you no explanation!" He slammed his club into Schneider's forehead.

Gommel marched into the pharmacy and smashed the shelves with his club. Bottles of medicine shattered and spilled onto the floor, raising a sharp stench. Groups of young men and boys, and some distraught women as well, followed Gommel into the pharmacy, tore out the counter and started pulling out drawers from cabinets. The floor of the small shop was becoming obscured by multi-colored pills and tablets, shattered bottles, torn documents. The light bulbs were also shattered one by one, and finally they left, skipping over the destroyed ruins of the pharmacy. One by one they tripped over the prone, shivering body of Moritz Schneider. Rivulets of blood flowed from his forehead and nose. No one approached him. The city folk stood silently around him and listened as death rattles gurgled out of him. A woman came running to him, sobbing quietly, dipped her hands in the blood from his face and said, Moritz, Moritz, looked around and brokenly whispered, *hilfe, hilfe* – help, help. The spectators went on their way. The eager adolescents ran to another store down the street, broke in, and dragged out the owner who was paralyzed with fear. Herr Gommel returned to his store, put back the club and stood calmly behind his counter, until he saw Yvonne staring at him with blind, uncomprehending eyes, and said, "Now make yourself scarce."

Several days later Yvonne took the train to Berlin, carrying a brown suitcase with a few books and clothes and stationery paper and envelopes and some toiletries and of course her baptism certificate. Hilde waved her goodbye from the platform. The train parked briefly at a station at Leipzig, and when Yvonne arrived at the Anhalter Bahnhof in Berlin which she had not seen in five whole years, then a golden-braided girl and now a seventeen-year-old young woman with her fate in her hands, her heart expanded in her chest and a joyful cry nearly escaped her.

Yvonne left the train station and began making her way toward the house of her childhood friend, Friedl Jacobus. The streets were filled with police officers and everywhere groups congregated of agitated, furious people. The walls all along Yvonne's path were covered in writing, black and red, Jews out, Death to all Jews, and swastikas large and small. Broken glass and Hobjects still piled high on the cobblestones, and here and there she saw large, blackening bloodstains. The joyful cry caught in her throat, and when she arrived on weak knees to the house.

Friedl unlocked the seven bolts fastening the door and hugged her. He said, "Yvonne, Yvonne, I never stopped thinking of you." For hours they sat and told each other the stories of their childhood and did not hear the noises from outside for the rest of that night.

Yvonne found a job in the outskirts of Berlin, and there met the war, in the Luckenwalde Luftwaffe base, a large, busy place, in which the air constantly smelled of fuel and grease, but the echoes of gunfire and the thunder and crack of exploding munition shells was nearly absent. Nor were the people running around the camp particularly eager or particularly desperate, as was common during wartime. The enemy was far, the war a collection of rumors. The radio broadcasters spoke of the military's progress and success on all fronts.

Yvonne was surrounded by spirited men and by women who worked beside her from morning till evening, typing and office managing and manufacturing and packaging. She wrote brief, rare letters to her mother in Glauchau, and received from her concerned letters which had been opened and read on their way to her. She had kept the last letter she received from Palestine, before the war had started, though it was written in trembling handwriting and so vague she could hardly learn anything from it. And still, her father wrote her, the day of our reunion draws near, he is certain of this, though he cannot for obvious reasons provide an exact date.

She nearly never left the camp. In the evenings she would collapse, exhausted, on her bed in the women's dormitory. On the weekends, if there were no special duties or emergencies, she would go sit near the dining room where a group of people from the camp would often get together and chat. Occasionally a resourceful officer would bring a small treasure of chocolate covered walnuts or liquor, which Yvonne was not particularly fond of. She was an amiable young woman, prone to laugh, and sharp in conversation, and when the men casually touched her shoulders and cheeks and thighs she did not protest, but after a while she would grow distant and head back to her room.

One weekend she headed out to Berlin along with the engineers Max and Berthold and a couple of her friends. Max would often come and go from the office she worked at, and he had brought his friend Berthold, a tall man of around forty, whose hair was already streaked with gray. He had warm eyes and listened intently when Yvonne spoke. The broad city streets were empty. On the roads moved mostly military convoys laden with soldiers and gear. The planes departing Luckenwalde noisily passed overhead. Many of the stores were closed, the windows clouded over with dust.

As they drove through East Berlin, Yvonne suddenly asked the driver to pull over. She ran to one of the houses, dashed up the stairs and pounded excitedly on the door that carried no name.

A dour, thickset woman opened the door and demanded, "What is it, what do you want."

Yvonne said, "I'm looking for my friend, Friedl Jacobus, she lived here with her parents, Martin and Nelly Jacobus."

"There is no Friedl here," said the woman.

Yvonne implored her, "She used to live here, perhaps you know where they went."

The woman said, "I must ask that you leave immediately," and closed the door and bolted it.

Yvonne came back down, stunned. Berthold leapt from the car and rushed over to her, asking, "What happened, Yvonne?"

She said, "They're not here, they went away, where did they go?"

"They were Jews."

Yvonne did not reply. Berthold hugged her shoulders and led her back to the car and sat beside her. She broke into bitter tears, unending, the violent sobs of a woman who, like her mother, had never learned to cry.

Berthold said, "You must cry now, finish your tears, do not come to camp like this." She looked at him and he nodded his head ponderously, and his lips curved into a kind smile, bright and compassionate. The passage of forty years had ringed his face, and his hands were large and warm, and his thighs were hard, a man's thighs. Their fingers slowly met in the darkness of the car and she caressed his hands, which were becoming warmer, and he said, "Yvonne, are you crying still?"

She said, "No, enough crying, that's quite enough, Yvonne," and they both laughed.

By evening they arrived back at the camp. Berthold ran off

to work and Yvonne went to bed and, for the first time in her adolescence, was happy.

3.

Her days in the camp were short now, and the nights long and joyful. Yvonne's body had blossomed and unfolded, and every morning the pleasures of the previous night would coil through her in warm waves. When darkness covered the camp, she would sneak into Berthold's room, and leave it at dawn, for a final nap in her own bed before heading to work. Berthold loved her languidly, attentively, and taught her what he knew of lovemaking. She called him Bertie. "Bertie my big man, *mein großer mann*." He would laugh and say, "And you are my tiny woman, my *Pünktchen*."

There was a photograph of a woman on the dresser in his room, dark-haired, laughing. He nearly never spoke of her and Yvonne decided not to ask. One night she told him of her father, Erich, whom she had not seen in nearly a decade, and his face darkened briefly. That was the last time Erich Freyer was mentioned in the small room, smelling of washed skin and the delicate fragrance of perfume that Yvonne had managed to find in one of her trips into town.

The war, which thus far had been a noisy rumor, took place in distant lands, among people Yvonne never knew, nor would she ever know, columns of names and numbers she encountered during the day in the typists' office at the camp, in the Luftwaffe operational orders, and in information on new planes commissioned and other planes that had been lost and never came back, and with them the men dispatched from the camp to the various fronts, all over Europe.

One evening she told Berthold, "I don't think the war will last much longer."

"What makes you think that?" asked Berthold.

"It must lead to either victory or doom," said Yvonne, "don't you think?"

Berthold laughed, saying, "What will we do with that victory? Will every German be given a little chunk of the world to rule over? And what of us, which chunk will we take?"

"I shall be the queen of Palestine," Yvonne blurted out, and instantly regretted it.

Berthold made a face and said, "And what about some Norwegian fjords? Have you ever been to Norway, *Pünktchen*?"

She said, "The winter is too cold, and the sun hardly ever shines."

"Palestine is too hot," Berthold chuckled.

She laughed and said, "Look at us, fighting already, can you imagine when the war is over?" Berthold fell silent and she said, "You must think about it."

He sat up on the bed and suddenly looked old and sad to her. She wrapped her arms around him, and he said, "You should go now, *Pünktchen*, I'm tired today, I'm so tired." Yvonne got up, dressed quickly and walked out into the cold air of the camp.

Over the next days she did not see Berthold at all. He had signed up for night shifts in the armory and maintenance duty. After that she returned to him, and they spent their nights peacefully, in a lovers' routine, and one time she threw up in the office and went to the camp physician. He took many tests and when she returned to him several days later he closed the door, looked at her severely and asked if she'd recently had sex with a man, and she sat on the Spartan chair and murmured, "But we were careful, we were so careful."

"There are options," said the doctor. "As you surely know, though, you are at the end of your fourth month, so the window of opportunity is nearly closed." Yvonne raised pleading eyes at him and he shrugged and said, "No one will force you into this course of action, but as you know, times are hard, and what future does a child have, born in a military camp in the middle of a war." With some concern he added, "You must know who the father is."

Berthold was crouching under the wing of a cargo plane in the large repair hangar. She waved at him and he approached her, growing stern, and somewhat indignant, as he had told her not to come there. She looked at him and placed his hand on her belly and he said immediately, "How wonderful, this is absolutely wonderful, Yvonne, my Yvonne," and kissed her cautiously.

That night they lay side by side on the bed. He placed his hand on her belly and kissed it softly, warm, delicate kisses. Yvonne was confused and happy, her apprehensions piercing into her like knives. Come morning she snuck to her room and slept for a day and a night and another day.

Terrible rumors had been arriving from the war, tearing through the false veil of radio propaganda, through the encouraging speeches and orders of the hour sent to the soldiers on the front and at the camps. Hilde wrote Yvonne of a family she knew from Glauchau whose four sons were lost in the multiplying fronts, and of the mailmen walking through the streets carrying envelopes from the Ministry of War, knocking on doors. *Each day, weeping and anguished cries sounded from one of the houses,* Hilde wrote, and anxiously wondered about Yvonne's wellbeing and did she need anything during these difficult days.

Berthold was warmer than ever, but restless. He once told her that the engineering department in the maintenance hangars is growing smaller with more and more engineers being sent to the fronts, and she tightened her hand around his. She could feel her womb grow, as her child turned in the waters of life, and at times longed to bear a son who would bring redemption to the world, and then thought to herself that males have no future in this world, and anyway if the war continues the average lifespan for men will no longer exceed twenty-five, and women will rule the world.

One night, Yvonne said, "We haven't decided on a name."

Berthold said, "We don't even know if it's a boy or girl."

"No, Berthold," Yvonne said, "a surname. You know it is your decision."

Berthold did not answer. The next night he was busy with another shift, and Yvonne saw him in the morning from afar, heading toward his room. All three nights that followed, he was deeply immersed in his work and she dared not disturb him, and instead counted the days until the weekend.

On the fourth night Yvonne was plagued by nightmares and yelled in her sleep. When she woke, she saw by her bedside a white vase which had not been there previously, and in it the wildflowers that grew on the outskirts of the camp, and beside it a folded sheet of white paper. She eagerly opened it. Nine words were written there, nine words that flew screaming from the page like black ravens: *My love, I've been sent to Bulgaria, take care,* and at the end his curling signature, a pseudo-gothic *B*.

Yvonne sat on her bed; her clear eyes raised to the ceiling. The beat of a baby's heart resonated from her belly.

4.

The German war faded into the depths of humiliation and loss, wallowed in some final hopeless battles, and died with millions of German soldiers who rotted in POW camps, with their eyes lowered and their beards grown wild. They thrashed, terrified, from the propaganda broadcasts, which had become wild and alarming. The cities of Germany were demolished, one after the other. Stettin, whose remaining Jewish population was sent to the concentration camps, was eroded by dozens of aerial bombardments that laid its streets to waste and tore gaping holes in the ancient buildings. Leipzig, where Martina had been born in the summer of 1943, was showered in fire and brimstone. Dresden was obliterated by thousands of tons of black bombs.

Yvonne worked at the fur factory and lived with other young women who had been separated from their families in the bare-walled, moldy barracks of a military base in Leipzig. Martina lived in a Leipzig orphanage, and Hilde visited her often there, becoming something of a second mother to her. The American army entered Saxony, and the streets filled with pamphlets declaring that Nazi laws were void. The Glauchau community leaders called to its few surviving Jews to return and receive work and housing. Yvonne and little Martina returned to the gray city, now glinting with new life. The memory of Berthold, declared MIA by the authorities, began to fade. She did not have a photograph of him, and the nine-word note was lost. Berthold's name did not cross Yvonne's lips again.

Martina's first years in Glauchau were also spent in an orphanage, along with other German children whose fathers died in the war and mothers did not have time to look after them during those difficult times. Young people took to the streets, started clubs and movements and sang songs that had been forbidden during the dozen years of darkness. Yvonne made a living from various odd jobs and made her way to the Anti-Fascist Committee, which had drawn many young people and founded branches across Saxony. The committee attracted mostly ex-members of the resistance, transformed into heroes by the war, some Jews who had survived hell, and bored men and women. There were also some sycophants who had found a way to slither into the new government, and ex-members of the *Hitlerjugend*, among them several of Yvonne's old classmates who used to stand and scream with adoration for Hitler during the school roll calls while she stood off in some corner, ashamed.

Hilde was about sixty years old now, and her mind was as sharp as it ever was. Her life revolved around little Martina, whom she visited every day at the Glauchau orphanage. Yvonne left the house early in the morning and returned at night, exhilarated. One night, Hilde was still up reading a book when she returned, and she told her excitedly, "Ach, Mutti, you should have been there."

Hilde put down her book, took off her glasses, and looked at Yvonne silently for a long moment before saying, "Just be careful, Yvonne, be careful."

"Careful of what?" Yvonne wondered.

Hilde said, "Someone is pulling these strings, someone is using you."

"But it is strictly a non-partisan committee, that is the whole point," said Yvonne.

"The politicians, Yvonne, they will ruin everything," Hilde

insisted. "Erich and I were just like you, once, we thought that educating the people on equality and humanism will make them better, but our politicians made sinister deals and fought idiotic wars, and now look, look at the calamity they have brought upon us."

Yvonne listen and noted, "Strange, how strange that since the war you hadn't mentioned Father even once, until now."

Hilde said, "I think of him sometimes."

Yvonne said, "I'll write him a letter, I'll write one today, now that writing to Palestine is legal." She immediately sat down and wrote a long letter in which she told him excitedly about the Anti-Fascist Committee and asked if there is a branch in Palestine as well. She wrote him about his granddaughter Martina, born to a father who died in the war, and already talking and skipping about. She asked him if perhaps he knew what became of Trude and Martin.

In April of 1946 a letter from Palestine arrived at Yvonne's house in Glauchau. Unlike the letters predating the war, which had been dim and confused, this one was long and written in lofty, flowery German, colorful storytelling German, ornamented with verbose descriptions of the scent of oranges in the magical Magdiel, a Moshav in the heart of Palestine, where he currently dwelled, and he asked for more details, if she could, about his granddaughter Martina, and whether she is talking already, and is her Freyer heritage clearly evident. The letter was ten pages long and Yvonne read it hungrily, Erich's image slowly reappearing in her mind's eye. He wrote to her of Trude and Martin, whose fate was made known to him through the testimony of the few surviving Stettin Jews. Martin died of his illness at the hospital in Głusk two months after they had left Stettin in a cargo train headed for Lublin, as ordered by the authorities, and that it was obvious he had been "Truly fortunate to die in his bed."

Of Trude, wrote Erich, he knew only that she could not sit by his side as he died but was flung around along with the other Jews from town to town, to Lublin and to Bychaŭ and to Bełżec. She might have died on the journey, as it was a hard one, and might have even taken her own life, though he did not think so. "It is more likely," he said, "that she lived a hellish life in Bełżec along with other Jews, from Stettin and elsewhere, and sent to the camps in October. We know what occurred in Bełżec because of the testimony of Doctor Mussbach, a Stettin physician who managed to hide and survive. He spoke in great detail of the morning of October 28, 1942 in which the SS broke into the Jewish housing in Bełżec. Everywhere were sounds of gunfire and desperate shouting. The poor people were shoved about like animals. Families were torn apart. Anyone still able to work was sent to the concentration camps. Children and old women were sent to the gas camps. The doctor said: 'When we came out of hiding the atrocity was revealed to us in all its horror. There were bodies everywhere, they were piled in the cemeteries, mountains of corpses, with these hands I pulled a living, breathing baby from under the dead. They lay in their beds in the hospitals, shot in the head, all of them.'"

Yvonne's hands began shaking as she read. She gave it to Hilde, who read it carefully, her face sealed, and when she finished, she said only "Dogs, vicious dogs," and another bitter line was etched into her face.

"But how can this all be," Yvonne spoke eventually, "how, without us knowing anything?"

"We didn't want to know," said Hilde.

"For five years I was part of the war machine," Yvonne said, "while Trude suffered such pain…"

"You could have been there, too," said Hilde, "another victim. You could have been there, Yvonne, with Trude and with Friedl. Do not forget that your life was given to you by sheer circumstance."

"I've not forgotten," said Yvonne, "and this committee, this is my path, Mutti."

"Nothing good comes of people congregating in groups," Hilde said, her face tight, "that is where war is created."

"How do you intend to better the world, then," asked Yvonne, "by yourself?"

"Always look into your own heart," said Hilde. "Good exists only within the individual human soul."

Yvonne wondered, "And when you look into your own heart, Mother, what do you see?"

Hilde shook her head slightly, silently, and said, "There is a dark stain there, but I am a good person, you know that, Yvonne."

They sat silently awhile, and suddenly Yvonne said, "Write Erich, Mutti, write him back, he is waiting for a reply."

"I will, Yvonne," Hilde said, placating, "I'll write him before the week is over."

Yvonne got up and deposited Erich's letter in a small wooden box, closed it, and placed a light kiss on the flower reliefs carved into the lid.

5.

So few men arrived at the meetings of the Anti-Fascist Committee that sometimes Yvonne felt she had simply come for the chitchat. Oftentimes she thought to herself that she belonged to a lost generation, in which all men had disappeared into the war and the women were doomed to loveless lives, unless some new law was passed that permits more than two people to marry, and that would be most unthinkable in Germany, whose legislators had never been accused of possessing overactive imaginations.

One time, a passionate new member arrived at the meeting, a man, and was instantly and unsurprisingly swarmed by the women. Yvonne inched toward the center of the crowd and peeked in as the aforementioned man made a rousing speech glorifying the working class and the Soviet alliance, for apparently "it was only thanks to their courage and the spirit of their wonderful army that Hitler and his collaborators were defeated." He raised his arm, exhibiting a bluish tattoo of a serial number. "Four years I sat in the *ka tzet*! I was beaten! starved! Do you know what it was that kept me alive? Faith, the faith that evil will be vanquished and that beyond that door awaits a brilliant new world!"

To the sound of cheering women, the young man grabbed his guitar and started to play, and they joined him as he sang. He bowed when he finished, and the women applauded enthusiastically. Yvonne backed away, somewhat daunted by the man delivering speeches and singing like a performer on the plaza. She was surprised when he approached her and earnestly reached out for a handshake, saying, "Lothar Kilmer, at your service. But call me Kolya!"

"How nice to meet you," she said. "My name is Yvonne."

"Come with me," Kolya said commandingly, "Coffee's on me!"

They sat at one of the new cafés which had recently opened on Glauchau's main road and she said, "Why did you ask me, though, when there were so many lovely women there?"

He stated, "There is wisdom in your eyes. I like those eyes of yours." She became self-conscience and he confessed, "And anyway, I did not even tell the truth back there. Well, not all of it, that is." Yvonne tensed, and he added, "I had faith, yes, but luck as well, and in this life you need luck, plenty of it. Meet me tomorrow at five? If you do, I shall tell you a little story about not-so-little luck."

She laughed and accepted, "Tomorrow at five, then."

Kolya remained in her thoughts all that night. He appeared in her dreams and she tossed and turned in her sleep. The following day she practically ran to the café, straight from work. Kolya was there already, humming a jaunty Russian tune and puffing on a cigarette. Yvonne sat down and he said, "I managed to escape because the Gestapo captured me as a political prisoner. If the bastards would've taken me as a Jew…" he made a sharp gesture with his hand across his throat.

Yvonne said, "Then you are Jewish?"

"Half Jewish," he nodded, "Protestant mother, Jewish father, though he never believed in God, not for a single day of his life!"

Yvonne wanted to say something, but he seemed more ardent than ever. "We are building a new world now, a world in which it will not matter who is a Jew and who is a German, who prays to Christ and who fasts on Yom Kippur! Who is rich and who poor! Do you understand, Yvonne? I see in your eyes that you do, that it is as clear to you as the midday sun!"

"As if the whole world will become one family," Yvonne said, then quickly amended, embarrassed, "Ach, such nonsense, how can the world become a family?"

But Kolya said, "No, you are right, so right, and so it shall be. The world will be one huge family, the family of all humans, and you, Yvonne, you will go from town to town heralding the new world, the family of humanity! How wonderful!"

Kolya seemed on the verge of delivering another speech, but Yvonne suddenly said, "My father is also Jewish, and he is in Palestine right now."

Kolya stood up, threw his arms out to the side and said, "Yvonne, this is impossible, we are obviously soul mates, only death shall us part."

Yvonne laughed, "Don't you think you are rushing things a bit, Kolya."

He frowned and said, "Tomorrow, here, meet me here, at five."

The next day at five, Kolya was sitting at the café waiting for her, as if he hadn't moved since the day before. When Yvonne approached the table he leapt up, pulled out the chair for her and sat back down opposite her. This time he told her about the anti-fascist underground, of which he had been a member for as long as he can remember, in a special cell headed by a woman named Anya. He spoke of Anya with an air of sacred devotion, mentioning that "she could have been a mother to us all, in age as well." She commanded the cell with wisdom and determination, though they were nearly captured several times, and then came that day, that bitter, cursed day. He paused for breath and said, "And that, Fräulein Freyer, we shall further discuss tomorrow at five." And he was off.

The following day Kolya was waiting as usual at the café. This time he told her how his group was captured one night by the Gestapo, who followed information provided by "A rat which had penetrated our cell" and whom he, Kolya, had always suspected. "But there was no getting rid of him." He told her of the torture he endured, and the interrogation rooms in which he revealed nothing, "Though they had trained us that it was better sometimes to say something, so they don't kill us," and of his good friend Max, who was hanged in the camp as he watched. He would tell her "tomorrow, same time." And so they met, day after day.

Once Yvonne told him, "Kolya, you talk and talk and never listen."

He said, "Ach, Fräulein, how utterly insufferable I've been! Please, you speak now, and I'll be as silent as a mouse!"

Over the next few days Yvonne told him of her life in Berlin and Amsterdam and Luckenwalde but did not mention Berthold. She spoke of her daughter Martina, whom she hardly gets to see, because she is growing up at the orphanage, and of her mother Hilde, who believes that all the world's woes come from people assembling together and forgetting that virtue lies within one's own soul.

"Well, with all due respect to your mother," said Kolya. "This is nonsense."

"You will need to elaborate," said Yvonne, "because I do not know what to tell her."

"Alone we are small, petty things," Kolya proclaimed, as if lecturing. "One is important only to oneself. Only together does the good in us emerge, don't you agree?"

"I do agree, Kolya," she nodded, "but only when we are together can the evil emerge, as well."

"Precisely," said Kolya. "And therefore we must choose between good and evil, and there is only one choice, the Big One, the choice our generation has been entrusted with is that between ultimate good and ultimate evil!"

"I think that is probably what Mother hates, how 'ultimate' everything has become."

"Hilde is a bitter woman," determined Kolya, "from a lost generation. But we are not lost, we are building a new world, a new world, good, and the name of this good is Communism, and we have already vanquished evil, fascism, but there is so much more work to be done, by all of us, this is our destiny, a glorious fate, Yvonne, one which has brought you and I together to complete this great work!"

Yvonne looked at him, moved, captivated, and Kolya leaned toward her and took her hands tightly in his. His inquisitive face, scoured by suffering, softened. He took her to a small apartment and kissed her entire body. The bitter wells washed away into sweetness and her body longed for him. Afterwards he lay on his back and was uncharacteristically silent.

She said, "You are suddenly so quiet, Kolya."

He sat up suddenly and said, "I must go now, but meet me tomorrow at five because I have something important to say to you, please make sure to shut the door behind you."

Yvonne lay there for a long time after he left, silent and knowing. The gates of heaven opened before her and Kolya's words and the heat of his body reverberated in her head all that night. The next day she hurried to the café. He sat there waiting for her, like he did every day, and he had placed a small glass on the table with three roses in it, and Yvonne thought, what now, what will I do now, and her cheeks were flushed and her heart pounded.

"You know of course that I love you deeply," said Kolya.

She said, "I know."

He said, "I know who you are, Yvonne, I see into your heart."

She said, "Perhaps we should take it slowly, Kolya, one step at a time."

He said, "I will think of you always."

Suddenly she was distraught and she said, "What do you mean, Kolya, what does that even mean?"

Kolya looked at her. He was no longer jaunty, and the mask was gone, leaving his face somber and his gaze penetrating as he said, "Tomorrow I am getting married."

Yvonne looked at him blindly and thought to herself that obviously she had been wrong about him all along, and perhaps he had simply been driven mad in the horrors of the concentration camp, and she wanted nothing more than to get up and leave.

"You must be thinking," said Kolya, "this madman, to come and bore into my soul like this and then run off and marry another?"

"That is precisely what you are doing," breathed Yvonne.

He said, "It is Anya, of which I've already told you so much, and I am marrying her tomorrow, and I will always think of you."

Yvonne was silent and Kolya said, "You must wonder, what is so special about her, this Anya who is old enough to be my mother, that this man who claims to be madly in love with me would marry her? Why would he do such a thing?"

She did not answer and he continued, "In that matter I can say only that I gave my word, and I, Kolya, am a man of my word, and now, love of my life, I must go, do not cry, there is no reason to cry, you are happy! I see this in you clearly. You are a happy person, a wise person, and no harm will come to you!"

He went away. Yvonne followed him with her eyes, and then left as well and walked slowly up Glauchau's main avenue. People passed her, old people who lost children to the war, newly born children, young people who have found and regained the world they had lost, beaten and battered but still whole. She walked toward the orphanage, hugged little Martina whom she had not seen in two weeks, and went back out into the street.

6.

The Russians came to Germany, and the Anti-Fascist Committee scattered to the wind. Yvonne reported to one of the party headquarters which were popping up in every town, where the newly appointed clerks took an immediate liking to her. Comrade Amy Kohn appointed her editor of the women's section in the Saxony daily newspaper, which was published in Dresden, and so she moved there with Martina and Hilde. Yvonne gained a reputation as a flexible, responsive editor who nonetheless was diligent and loyal to the party line. She was only 28 when they made her editor of the Zwickau daily newspaper, and so she moved there, a city as gray and silent as the other southern cities that lacked the everlasting renown of Weimar and the urbane glamor of Leipzig and Dresden. After that she traveled to Suhl, where she was editor of another daily paper for five years. She spent most of her days at the paper, with the editorial staff, or at gatherings and meetings, mingling with the party members.

The Anti-Fascist Committee was cutting a wide path right down the middle of the new world, across the centers of Saxony cities, through the plazas and assemblies, festooned with monuments of Lenin and Stalin, as well as Walter Ulbricht, the wise and solemn leader whom Yvonne had come to know, and who had become fond of her. On the horizon she could just imagine the rounded spires of the Kremlin in the Red Square, the center of the new world, which had everything: it had a language, it had a god, it had holy scriptures and epic heroes, and it had bitter enemies out there, across the wall, where the devouring demon of capitalism ran rampant.

In the backyards of this wide path, ugly housing cooperatives grew. The streets and sidewalks grew crooked, the stores shelves were stacked with bland, disorganized groceries, and a desolate gloom fell over the cities come evening. The citizens of the German Democratic Republic had brought Ulbricht's vision to fruition, founding small families which lived in tiny government housing apartments, a man and a woman and a child and a dog and, if they were well-off, a little car in faded pink or blue. In the mornings, the citizens would flow out to the factories and depots and schools. The republic's young people congregated in the universities or were ejected straight from military service to the repair shops and warehouses. On the weekends the forests and lakes of Saxony filled with vacationers. On the new holidays of May 1 and November 7, rallies and military demonstrations were held. Hundreds of thousands of people in simple holiday garb came pouring from the housing cooperatives, from the villages and towns, and among them intermixed thousands of undercover police, uniformed police and party operatives. Life was not joyful, but it was not miserable. The desolation brought no pain, and the fear was not so much an adversity as it was the new law of this new game. After those horrible years, the days of bombings and hunger and letters of death, life here was comfortable, despite its inherent despair.

The builders of the new world now helped themselves to abundant handfuls of its fruit. These people were determined, self-involved, and armed with a powerful self-inspection mechanism in which even the smallest step out of line invoked destructive punishment with certain, invariable results. Among their ranks, former underground members and new ideologists mingled with bureaucrats from the old regime who had passed, furtively and unscathed, to serve the new regime, even providing it with several divisions which require an established legacy of evil to function. There were more than a few Jews, as well, who struggled to hide their Jew-ness in a world that supposedly had no race or religion or nationality, and yet their Jewish heritage smelled of distant danger, suspicious glances both real and imagined. And many women inhabited this new world, as an entire generation of men had been erased from the face of the earth. Women who had lived without love and made their homes and families in the new world, with the Party.

This was Yvonne's world. And though she knew no love, and her body had accepted the fact that it would know only the touch of her own hands as she showered, or in the small hours of night when no one saw or heard, her world was Hwhole. The suffocation she felt that day, when Kolya left, had been replaced over the years with a ripened calm, a certainty, a serene knowledge of what is right. Recalling his parting words to her she would think, *Kolya was right, I am wise and happy, and no harm will come to me.*

Kolya had become a sought-after journalist and political commentator, whose views on the state of the world and the fight against imperialism filled the pages of the Party periodical. Yvonne saw him often, and when they passed each other on the street he would salute her brightly and his eyes shone when he said, "Always a pleasure, Fräulein Freyer." His wife, Anya, was rarely spotted in public. In March 1953, Yvonne poured out into Suhl's broad Stalin Allee along with a huge human mass heading for the funeral parade marking the death of The Sun of Nations, who had passed away in Moscow, when Kolya suddenly appeared at her side. They marched together and he said, "Some people do not die, Yvonne." A shiver went through her because, since his marriage to Anya, who was growing old at his side in one of the party housing projects in Dresden, he had only ever addressed her with that other appellation, so saturated by self-loathing and hope, "Fräulein Freyer."

Hilde never came out for the holidays and the rallies, withdrawing more and more into the privacy of her home. The revolution found no hold in her heart. Nearing seventy now, the sum of her life had been a gaping, bleeding wound, cut open that day when they burned the books from the publishing house she had bought with her hard-earned savings on Blumenstraße in Berlin, and in that wound the love of her life still dwelled. She and Yvonne received many letters from Palestine, which had by now become the State of Israel, from their cousins Lotte and Minchen and Susi and Rachel, and from Aunt Käthe in Kiryat Bialik, and Erich, who resided now in a German retirement home in Ramat Gan, also wrote them in great volume, and they replied. When the little state was officially recognized and immediately became a target for all red nations, Yvonne was conflicted, but still wrote to her astounded cousins, presenting her doctrine on western imperialism, of which Israel had now become a tool, and even those letters eventually grew few and far between.

On November 19, 1956, several days after the failure of the

combined British, French and Israeli efforts in the Egyptian Sinai desert, Yvonne received a letter from Israel.

My Beloved Yvonne,

Silence has returned to this country, and we have just celebrated our Rubi's 11th birthday. Things are returning to normal. There are slight restrictions on life and freedom of movement which cannot be helped, but other than that I am perfectly settled. About a month ago we even celebrated the fiftieth anniversary for the October 13th Association, though, apart from Albert and Käthe nearly no one came. Please tell Meme, she will be very pleased to know.

Does Meme remember Professor Walter Friedlander? Could Meme perhaps send me all the addresses for the people who were involved in Hoffman Publishing? This is very important to me, for the matter of reparations.

Regarding this matter, the reparations, I intend to visit Berlin quite soon. Of course I would very much love to meet with you and Meme, and meet your little girl, and stay a while. You are the first to know of my plans to visit. The next time I am in Kiryat Bialik I shall inform Käthe and Albert and the others. I did not want to say anything before I had resolved the details. What do the two of you think?

My best to Meme and Martina,
Erich

Yvonne read the letter late in the evening. Hilde, who had been reading in her room, came out to sit with her. Yvonne said, "Well, he wants to come to Berlin, to see us."

Hilde said, "What are you going to do?"

"He calls you 'Meme,'" said Yvonne.

Hilde raised her voice, again asking, "Yvonne, what are you going to do?"

Yvonne replied, "And you? What do you want, what do you think?"

Hilde said, "I don't know, I am tired, Yvonne."

Yvonne placed a kiss on Martina's forehead, now fast approaching puberty, her face happy and content even in sleep. Then Yvonne lay in bed for a while and tried to draw portraits of Erich that would differ from the one photograph of him she still had. Then her dreams were troubled: Erich came to the door, but his mouth was foaming, and his face was white, and orderlies in white coats surrounded him. She woke up, awash in a warm current of memories, and Erich's beautiful eyes looked upon her as he rhymed, a little poem he had written her: Yvonne, Yvonne, my little one, here's your teddy bear, it isn't going anywhere; and Hilde is standing behind him and he turns around and screams, a hard, shrill cry.

The scream woke Martina; she sat up on her bed, confused. Yvonne got up and set a kettle on the stove, but by the time she had made the tea Martine was asleep again and Yvonne sat alone, silently, in the kitchen. Dawn came and Hilde came out to sit with her. Yvonne took some paper and jotted down some quick words.

"Dearest Father, this all sounds very difficult to arrange, but if you manage to come you are more than welcome to stay here for a few days."

She raised the letter and was about to rip it up, but Hilde took it from her, read it, and said, "Is this what you want?"

Yvonne stood up and said, "I don't know, it is hard."

Hilde told her, "No good can come of this. I don't have to tell you this. You know your new world well. Your Jewish father will come visiting from Palestine and after a week the entire Stasi will live here with us and we will never be rid of it again. And after he is gone what will become of your life? There are many people who want to see you fail."

"I can take it," said Yvonne, "I will not fail. But you, what do you want, Mutti?"

"I don't know," said Hilde. "I am afraid. I thought nothing will ever scare me again, but he does, something about him scares me now."

"He never scared me," said Yvonne, "I always found him exceedingly kind."

"He is a good man," said Hilde, "But a madness lurks in him that I could never explain, a demon that emerges in crucial moments and destroys everything, turns him into an instrument of ruin."

Yvonne frowned and said, "He beat you."

Hilde, horrified, said, "No, never, what are you thinking?"

"I don't understand, Mutti," said Yvonne, "I don't understand what you are saying."

Hilde sat in the corner and dropped her head into her hands and said, "Yvonne, we must be together on this, we must look out for each other."

Yvonne left for work. In the evening she returned, quiet and unclouded. She sat by the table at once and wrote, "Dearest Father, we cannot receive you here. Twenty years cannot simply be erased. Mother has been troubled by difficult memories since you left us, and as for me, I am part of a new world in which you have no place. I ask that you forgo your plan to visit and am certain the matter of reparations can be more easily arranged from Palestine. Yours, Yvonne." She sealed it in an envelope and sent it the next morning.

On February 2, 1957, Hilde received a letter from Israel.

My Dearest Hilde,

It is very quiet in our retirement home, but outside a storm is raging. I too am feeling turbulent and tempestuous from the letter I have just received from Yvonne, based entirely on a flawed understanding of things. But I am not angry with her. What could she possibly know of matters that took place 22 years ago? She is obviously mistaken to think that it was I who left you. Of course, she was only a child then. Furthermore, I do not think she possesses the knowledge and expertise required to advise me regarding my reparations.

It was wrong of me to address my intent to visit Berlin to Yvonne rather than you. I behaved pathetically and failed to stress that it is just as important to me to see you as it is to see Yvonne, and Martina as well.

Disclosed find a copy of a letter you wrote me in 1946. This letter has never left my thoughts, and amid last night's storm, I read it again and thought of us. Now more than ever I know that the love we had can never grow cold, no matter the years. I believe we agree on this.

Love,
Erich

Hilde unfolded the attached paper, saw her handwriting photo-copied on stationery paper, and read it. Her hands shook and her face flushed with blood, and she tore the paper to shreds. The flakes fluttered softly onto the tablecloth. Hilde stood up and yelled into the empty room, beside herself, "Madness, madness, damn it all, damn this demon that haunts me." She paced across the room in a frenzy, and then sat down abruptly and wrote in a frenzy, on an old typewriter, on thin paper.

February 15th, 1957

Dear Erich,

I must once again remind you that we divorced twenty years ago. We lead separate lives. We have nothing in common. Yvonne is no longer a child but a grown woman. She has a family of her own and every reason for concern. Why do you not accept that we are opposed to this visit? It is our right, and perfectly justified.

We would ask that you conclude this ridiculous letter exchange which as you can plainly see leads to nothing good. I wish you well,

Hilde

After that day Yvonne and Hilde never spoke of Erich again, neither fondly nor with scorn, and his picture was never displayed in their home, until Hilde died 18 years later, about 90 years old. Erich also sent them no letters, and they only learned of his death in the summer of 1967. Yvonne placed some roses in a vase near her bed and looked at the face of her mother who had grown very old and weary, and the font of memories welled up for a

RUVIK ROSENTHAL | 163

moment. It is fate, Yvonne, she said to herself, and one does not contend with fate.

7.

Berlin was good to Yvonne. She reached the "age of freedom," at which time sixty-year-old members of the democratic republic were declared senior citizens and released from various restrictions. She was editing 'Für Dich', East Germany's top women's magazine, as well as the illustrious 'Sibylle' fashion magazine, the covers of which featured beautiful models dressed in the finest Paris fashions. She lived in an apartment in a neighborhood that housed high-ranking party officials, journalists, political clerks and economists. Her childhood home on Blumenstraße 22 had been badly damaged during the war, but still stood. The May 1 marches passed in the avenue below her apartment and drained into the nearby Alexanderplatz, above which loomed a huge fresco of workers and fighters raising their fists in victory.

Martina married a young reporter by the name of Norbert, and they raised Robert, their little boy, in a small apartment in an obscure Berlin neighborhood. Kolya moved to Berlin as well and became one of the mainstays of *Neues Deutschland* newspaper. Rumor had it that his wife, Anya, who was entering her ninth decade, was very ill.

The revolution began to drift away from The Cold War, but still held strong, and even though new winds blew through it, they did not blow into Germany. The other side of the wall, built the same year Yvonne moved to Berlin, was a distant place, a place of memory, and to Yvonne an object of contempt, certainly not envy. The land of Israel, where her family lived, also grew distant, and for many years no letters, news or sign of life had come from there.

One Sunday in May of 1981, the love of Yvonne's younger life stood on her doorstep, eyes shining through thick spectacles, and his face alight with the same eager determination, both old and adolescent, which had so enticed her in the distant days of their love. Kolya was holding a sizeable bouquet and asked her permission to come sit in the living room. Yvonne apologized for not writing him after the death of his wife, hurried into the kitchen, found some simple cookies and brewed a large pot of tea, and sat down on the floral sofa.

Kolya instantly stood up and with great pomp, as if facing a huge Alexanderplatz crowd, declared, "Fräulein Freyer, will you marry me."

Yvonne poured the tea into two crystal teacups, served him his cup, sipped from her own, raised her eyes at him and calmly said, "Yes, Comrade Lothar, I will."

From that day they led a love-filled life, of which Yvonne often said, "I never had much luck with men, until Kolya came along." They lived in a second-story apartment on the broad-shouldered Frankfurter Allee, part of which had been renamed after Karl Marx, and the back window of their apartment looked over Blumenstraße, from which the building numbered 22 had long since vanished. They drove Kolya's black Volvo down the wide path of the new world, now grown fat and hard, drove to rallies and conferences, and in the summers vacationed in their dacha on the coast of the Black Sea. They enjoyed the good life but never forgot the doctrine of their youth. This Communism come true was the best of all worlds, Kolya was as certain of this now as he was during his youth, and even if this perfection does not face the ultimate evil of fascism, it still faces the evils of capitalism, albeit evil dressed up as a tantalizing lover, offering wealth and freedom but beyond the mask lies a false creature of chaos and oppression, whose defeat is surely fast approaching.

The age of freedom had been kind to Yvonne, who remained a handsome woman despite the passage of years. One day a visiting acquaintance asked her whether she would be willing to renew the written correspondence with her family in Israel, and with the same unfaltering calm she replied, "Yes, I would be delighted." After a while she began to receive letters from Lotte in Tel Aviv and from Minchen, now Michal, from Kibbutz Kfar Szold. She replied, the bad blood from those letters from the fifties all but dried and forgotten.

In April 1982, I walked out of the metro station on Friedrich-straße, which served as one of the border crossings between the two Berlins. It was my first time in Germany. I came to visit Yvonne, the beloved cousin of my mother, Leah Rosenthal, once Lotte Freyer, and her family. I was momentarily blinded by the bright light of the wide, elegant street. I crossed Unter den Linden and ascended to the third floor of the Sibylle Magazine building.

Yvonne rose to greet me, flushed and delighted. "Why, you look exactly like Kurt." Later we sat down and she laughed again and again, a laughter both joyful and abashed, and said, "Well, there you have it, such a thing, and here you are, Rubi." Again, she was silent and then, laughing again, said, "And what do you have to say of this, Kolya?"

We walked together toward the theaters. The gray, church-like structure of the Bertolt Brecht Theater emerged in front of us. Kolya, who was still at Neues Deutschland, now a specialist on African and Middle Eastern affairs, explained to me that "a crucial struggle is taking place in our region, with the future of the world lying in the balance." For lunch we went to Ganymed, where four waiters in tailcoats served us in the empty, shadowy hall. We dined on turtle soup in tiny cup, various fish, potatoes in gravy and a multitude of confections. Each new dish was carried from the kitchen by a new waiter, who obsessed fussily over every detail.

"Bourgeois customs," I noted, smiling.

Kolya fumed at this. "It is quite silly to call such lovely customs bourgeois."

After lunch, in the house at Frankfurter Allee, we spoke of Erich Honecker, a friend of theirs and general secretary of the republic, and his wife was mentioned fondly as well. Kolya brought out his guitar and played some Russian tunes, some of which I had sung during my time in the youth movement. The city loomed empty through the windows and Kolya admitted that the East Berliners spend their evenings in front of the television, just like their counterparts across the wall.

"Communism has not penetrated the soul yet," said Kolya, "has not yet changed the minor customs created by the capitalist world."

"And you find that important?" I asked.

"I find it unfortunate," he said. "But the crux of the matter, Comrade Ruvik, is that Communism is the finest system construed by humanity."

Yvonne did not join the conversation. She merely looked at me, laughing, moved, "Why, it is Ruvik," she said, again and again. "Here you are."

Martina took me on a tour of Berlin, streets filled with monuments of communist mythology, memorial plaques for Marx and Engels, colossal bank buildings, The Bank of Hungary, The Bank of Bulgaria. In the Berlin Konzerthaus, with its massive ancient chandeliers descending from the ceiling, the walls were covered with images of workers and fighters, their lines crude and their colors without luster, here and there the image of Jesus or Mary could be glimpsed among them, haloed ghosts of a world that was supposed to have been destroyed.

We drove along the Berlin Wall, the mythical dam of war, the Wailing Wall of Europe. Its builders did not gift it with the grandeur and monumentality of the ancient ramparts surrounding the old European cities. It was but a thin wall, wretched and feeble-looking, past which lay four meters of minefield, and another wall after that. Occasionally a guard tower poked out from the dry field of thorns stretched between the eastern and western walls, but rather than fear all I could feel was desolation and despair, like the back yards of this city, its narrow, broken streets, lines upon lines of houses blackened with age.

There, in one of those black houses, Norbert and Martina lived in a small flat. Norbert, cheeks obscured by a full, reddish beard, gifted me a small record by the pop band he had started, songs of the 'Blue Planet', the threatened, precarious Earth. Norbert was wary and a bit sad. The stormy winds from Poland did not make it to this city, the display window of red Germany, and certainly not to the outskirts. "We are an obedient nation," said Norbert.

Come evening, I returned to the world I had left via Friedrichstraße station, and over the next few years my mother, Lotte, and my aunts Susi and Michal went past the wall, and the memory of good Uncle Erich returned to the letters of his daughter Yvonne.

The ice that lay between Yvonne and her family in Palestine had been shattered, but the wall was still up. The fire that swept across the east, from Poland to Hungary and Czechia and the Soviet Union, did not catch in Berlin. Nothing could disrupt the love of Kolya and Yvonne, the children of the revolution, the happy, free citizens of the new world.

8.

November 17, 1989, I was sipping afternoon coffee with one of the managers of Museum Judengasse in Frankfurt. Mere chance had brought me to Germany during those days, when the Berlin Wall fell, the very city I had planned to visit the following day. We were joined by a vibrant, light-haired woman by the name of Ulrike, who had just returned from Berlin. She told us in detail of what she had seen there, and kindly offered me some much-appreciated advice.

When Ulrike was about to leave, she offered me a ride to where I was staying, in one of Frankfurt's northern neighborhoods. As we were standing next to her small car, she stared at me suddenly and said, "I know you." We stopped at her house and she pulled down from a shelf a square, orange book, slightly faded. It was, *Oh Barbara, Quelle Connerie la Guerre*, the book of original and translated poetry written by my brother Gidi, Gideon Rosenthal, before he had fallen in the basalt-rich soil of the Golan Heights during the Yom Kippur War, which I had compiled and printed after his death. In the opening page I had written "To Ulrike, Love, Ruvik."

Why I would have written such an inscription for a woman I hardly knew, Ulrike Kolb, who later became a writer in Germany, and who happened to briefly visit my home at the kibbutz where I lived in the summer of 1980, I could not remember, but in that moment I heard the sound of bells. Along with the collapsing Berlin Wall, the walls of my own war had begun to crumble, perhaps heralding at long last its ending. For a moment it seemed that the book had been waiting for me there, in that Frankfurt apartment, a sign that the bloody march of the century was reaching its conclusion, and the days of eternal peace were nigh.

The next day I arrived at the gates of the reunited Berlin. Following Ulrike's advice, I headed for the gate at the Oberbaum Bridge, where swarms of people were passing along, their faces blank, men and women and some children wrapped in grayish jackets and scarves and baseball caps. The wall had been opened for only a week and already here they came into the gates of the dreary and weary Kreuzberg district, inhabited mainly by Turks. By the gate newspaper and souvenir stands awaited them. Some quick thinker had tacked paper crowns onto the children's baseball caps, bearing the logo of an American burger restaurant.

A long queue had formed by the small booth that had been set up by the gate, where they handed out one hundred marks per person. Train No. 1 stood waiting in the Kreuzberg station. Seemingly endless people were already packed inside and still packing, looking out to the beautified streets, sniffing and breathing the smell of wealth, of which the western television sets had told them so much. In the center of town, where the Ku'Damm meets Kantstraße, the city had erected a small tent. The new guests, slightly ashamed in their humble holiday clothes, again queued into a patient, winding line, and left the tent holding a bowl of pea soup.

The cold, fresh air burst joyfully into my lungs, which had never acclimatized to the heat of the Middle East's eternal summer. My legs carried me along the wall. I walked and walked, feeling the stones, marking them in memory before they turn to dust. The cafés were filled with small families, tired from the walk. "*Guten morgen, wo kommen Sie?*" I addressed one man in broken German, and he looked sharply to his wife and daughter, made some gesture with his head and turned his back to me. At the border crossing on prinzeßstraße the car owners pulled over for inspection, the small cars laden with objects and people. They were approached by a skinny man who handed them the CDU newspaper and excitedly declared, "History is happening before our very eyes, my friends, we are making it right now." They took a newspaper and hurried onward, bewildered, anxious, astonished.

I walked along the winding wall with a light step. Colorful art began to appear on its face, and slogans etched in its stone face, and ladders as well, on which young people were climbing with hammers in their hands. They stubbornly struck the stones, making little holes in the wall. As the wall approached the beating heart of Berlin more and more holes pocked its face, and they grew bigger, into gaps. Here and there appeared windows into the hidden world to the east, a thorny field bordered by towering brown housing projects. Red-faced men marched along the wall with t-shirts reading "Tear down the wall." Young women and pale young men in student jackets stood hunched around the small cross erected in memory of Peter Fechter, who never completed his escape across the wall.

Wooden platforms had been raised near Checkpoint Charlie, and people stood on them to peer into the world beyond. The wall ran on and on with me floating alongside it. The ground was strewn with tattered clothes, copper pots and lamps. Poles and East-Germans exchanged new western soups.

A flood of people gushed into Potsdamer Platz. The wall that had cut through the plaza had been breached. A long queue snaked past iron passages from Leipzigerstraße in the east. More and more people were walking past, driving, riding bicycles. One by one they presented their ID and hurried into the joy of the west to the sound of applause arising from the small crowd that was observing and taking photographs nearby. A smile seemed to envelope the entire plaza. Coming opposite to the new arrivals the very first to cross were already heading back to their eastern homes, laden with packages and bags of potatoes, electrical appliances and household goods.

One brook split from the main flood to march along the wall, beside a grove and an open field, toward the closed Brandenburg Gate, from which Unter den Linden boulevard stretched into the east. A stout, red-faced man was playing the accordion and calling out for the unification of Germany. A group of aging men and women was standing by, dressed in white holiday garments, awaiting the gate's opening with sincere, pious awe. Everywhere freezing men and women were sipping from steaming cups of punch and hot chocolate. Music played, night descended, and a new light glowed on the horizon, but the gate did not fall.

The next day I ventured into the emptied street of the eastern city. The eastern wall, which had stood white and barren since its construction 27 years ago, had been adorned that very morning with its first painting, deer and rabbits fleeing into a thick virgin forest. The Brandenburg Gate was surrounded by soldiers and military convoys. Under the parliament building, between

Karl-Marx-Platz and Alexanderplatz, a small protest was underway. No one was celebrating.

I rang the bell in the front door of the building and Yvonne's voice carried from the second floor, a half-sigh: "Ah, Rubi, well, come, come." Kolya sat in the living room, pensive. The guitar was propped against the wall in the corner. Yvonne brought three cups of tea. We sat in silence.

"Well," said Kolya, "it is what it is, dire indeed."

I glanced at Yvonne. Her face was dour. "Yes, what more can be said," she said, her eyes barely rising to meet mine.

"Mistakes were made, yes, undoubtedly grave mistakes," said Kolya, then stood up with a sudden rage. His hands were shaking and sweating. "Honecker wouldn't listen, wouldn't hear, an infuriating expression of failed leadership, and now it will all be so difficult."

"Yes, Honecker," Yvonne sighed, "what can be said."

Yvonne fussed for a while in the kitchen and served a light dinner to the table. Kolya ate sparingly and without appetite.

"We told him to follow Gorbachev's lead," said Kolya, "but he didn't listen – reforms! That's what it took! Reforms, but in moderation, so as not to throw the baby out with the bathwater."

"And would that have been enough?" I asked, carefully navigating the conversation, searching for a chink of doubt in Kolya's armor.

This seemed to anger him fiercely and he once again rose from the couch and said, "Capitalism does not stand a chance, it is but a matter of time before its inevitable collapse, but it is clear now for all to see that the German Democratic Republic was not blessed with worthy leaders, and they have brought this calamity upon us."

I stood up, deciding to take my leave. A cold November sun greeted me outside the door. Kolya quickly composed himself and saluted me, smiling and saying, "I wish you well, comrade Ruvik."

Yvonne said, "Give Lotte my best, I'll be sure to write her."

A passing taxi took me back to the bedecked streets of Berlin through the open border crossing. Everywhere the sound of the infant revolution sounded, but it was a revolution without eruption, without screaming streets, a revolution born with a smile. Perhaps the shadow of a smile would soon return to the faces of those who loved that old, expired revolution, the devoted Communists, Kolya and Yvonne Kilmer.

CHAPTER SIX: MARTINA

1.

During the 1950s, the May 1 neighborhood in the southern town of Suhl in East Germany was a collection of gray, heavy buildings connected to each other via inner pathways. Mostly weeds grew in the yards that had been haphazardly created between the buildings. An encircling road snaked around the neighborhood like a ring, corralling it into what the people of Suhl, among themselves, had nicknamed "The Red Ghetto." There, crowded and suspicious, lived city hall clerks, journalists, ex-military personnel, local parliament representatives and even a few writers, musicians who played for the local symphony, and some characters whose profession remained unknown and provided fertile ground for rumors. When the residents of The Red Ghetto ran into each other in the paths between the houses they would nod politely and hurry on. In the mornings they would customarily trudge to the parking bays, enter their small, ugly cars that reeked of gasoline, drag a child or two off to school, and scatter to their respective offices and military bases for a workday which usually ended only late in the evening.

Yvonne, Martina's mother, worked at *Thüringen*, at a daily newspaper distributed every morning via heavy trucks all over the province, and Martina would proudly see it peeking from every single mailbox in the May 1 neighborhood. At times she would steal a look at several of the papers to check that every one of them sported the same square outline on the second page with the line, "Editor-in-chief: Yvonne Freyer." Little Martina had thick, blonde braids. Hilde – whom Martina would refer to as "Oma," as children did – would always be unraveling and re-braiding them, telling Martina a fairytale about a girl kidnapped by a witch and only her long braids saved her from a horrible fate.

Hilde didn't live in The Red Ghetto but in a small home on the outskirts of Suhl, next to farmers who had completed their life's labor and merchants who had managed somehow to accumulate some wealth despite the strict laws enforced by the Government of the German Democratic Republic. After school, Martina would head to her grandmother's house for a warm lunch, and they would chat while she did her homework. Then they would take the local bus together to the house in the May 1 neighborhood and wait for Yvonne to return from *Thüringen*.

Martina hated school and the bitter, old men who taught there that seemed to hate it even more than she. She swallowed the math and geometry lessons like bitter pills. During history lessons their teacher, Herr Zelner, would deliver the history of Germany in a steady drone, write dates on the blackboard and explain how the worker class succeeded in vanquishing the wealthy German plutocrats with the help of their working Soviet brothers, while out there, in other places, capitalism rages wild. At times he would give a strange sort of wink and make a strange sort of joke: "Such it is written in your books, and of course, only the truth is put in books."

"Out there," across the wall that Martina never saw but still was ever-present, horrible things took place, mysterious things that nonetheless enchanted her, pulled at her. In the evenings she would study the map of Germany provided in her schoolbook and memorize the names of the cities, the rivers, the provinces Frank-Furt-am-Main, Schles-wig-Hol-stein, Sa-ar-brüc-ken. She planned voyages that burst through the wall, drawn on the map in a bold red line that made it look several miles thick, and on those journeys she meandered on to Stuttgart, north to Köln and Hamburg, and eventually parked in Berlin, the ultimate destination, the place where dreams come true, its heart sliced through by the same red dagger.

Hilde would help Martina with her homework, and particularly loved discussing the thick history books that lacked even a single photograph. The story, depicted in them under the premise of "The Weimar Republic and the rise of National Socialism," she summed up in three words: *Quatsch mit Soße*, "Nonsense in sauce." When they were solving her geography homework, she would tell Martina about France, where she was born, where her mother was from.

"But are you French or German," Martina once asked her.

Hilde said, "If I could be both I would be truly happy, but life took my mother here, to Germany."

"And Opa Erich, what was he?"

Hilde fell silent for a moment and said, "Erich was German."

"Then why did he go to Palestine?" wondered Martina.

Hilde told her, "For that, Martina, you are still a bit young."

Occasionally thick envelopes would arrive at the house, with odd stamps with the face of George V, King of England, marred with numerous stamps.

One time in class, Hildegard, a rough-faced girl who sat two rows before her, told Martina, "You know, my mother reads those letters your mother gets from Palestine."

Martina lunged at her and scuffled with her briefly, crying, "Liar, you're not supposed to read other people's mail, those are letters from Opa," and Hildegard giggled and slinked away to the yard.

For a long time, Martina did not know what Opa Erich even looked like. She envisaged the image of a portly old man with a red beard and a lap ample enough to contain her as well as the two sisters and brother she often dreamed she had. Once, when she returned home from school and no one was home, she snuck into the forbidden domain of her mother's bedroom and rifled through the simple pinewood dresser. An old photograph fell into her hands and a shriek of surprise and disappointment escaped her as she looked at the bald, round-faced, jarringly in-nocent-looking man that she had stumbled upon, with young Oma Hilde holding his hand on the shore of some lake. She im-mediately put it back in the dresser, but occasionally returned to peek at it.

Slowly she had grown to love this man, the new, genuine Opa Erich, who according to her calculations was exactly seventy years old, "And certainly had not grown any new hair," she thought to herself, "so he might look just like he did in that photograph with Oma Hilde." She found Palestine in an old atlas in the school library, and was happy to discover that not only does it have a beach, and perhaps it is in essence a single vast beach one can visit all year long, as she had heard that the sun there is always shining, and apart for a few rainy days a year Palestine is a land of eternal spring. She lay in bed and sailed in her mind to the shore of Palestine on a golden ship. Opa Erich stood waiting for her on the beach, they smile at a tanned Palestinian photographer,

Erich in a long bathing suit holds Martina's hand, like in that photograph where he is holding Oma Hilde's.

Over the summer, Hilde, Yvonne and Martina took Yvonne's Lada, a bit larger than the Trabant cars, that hopped like fleas across the cracked and broken roads of the German Democratic Republic, and went on a trip through the province. Dresden seemed nearly good as new, having been rebuilt at great effort following the war's destruction.

As they passed through one of the streets Yvonne said, "Look, this is where you lived, Martinchen, though I suppose the building was entirely demolished."

Martina looked around and upon seeing a large sycamore fig tree a surge of emotion rose in her, and at once the orphanage appeared before her eyes, dilapidated and broken-windowed. Yvonne had sent her there from the Christian orphanage, seeing as "here at least they don't fill the children's heads with that Jesus nonsense." All she could remember now was Helga, the fat custodian, smacking a spoonful of mashed potatoes onto a plate or plucking lice from children's heads with her fingers.

Later Yvonne stood, a glowing smile on her lips, in front of a house that barely seemed changed by time, saying, "Here, Martina, is where it all started. This was my commune."

From there they continued to Leipzig. Yvonne led their small group, nodding occasionally to important party members who all seemed to know her, saying, "Why, this is absolutely wonderful, just look around, these streets, and the parks, a true paradise."

"Ach, please, Yvonnchen," Hilde groaned, "you must know this is nothing but a façade."

"Again with this, Mutti." Yvonne flared up. "What façade? Façades are what the capitalists have in Ku'Damm, fancy stores only the rich can shop in."

"At least there, the people can imagine they are happy," Hilde said, "they can decide for themselves, and if they want to buy a pretty dress they can go find work instead of the state taking care of everything for them."

Yvonne composed herself and said, "In any case, you shouldn't be saying such things in front of Martina." Martina was examining a large monument of a man with a close-cropped beard and pretending not to hear.

"Who is this?" she asked. "Stalin?"

"That is Walter Ulbricht," said Yvonne. "Do you remember, you met him once, at Easter?"

"He is our Stalin," said Hilde, and coughed out a short, nervous sort of laughter.

"How can you say that?" Yvonne protested. "Ulbricht is a good man, and it seems that Stalin did many things a good Communist must never do."

"Really, Yvonnchen," Hilde asserted, "all your leaders are the same – Ulbricht just happens to wear an excellent mask."

They passed by a small hospital and Yvonne said, "Here, my Martina, this is where you were born, but the place was destroyed and had to be rebuilt."

Martina said, "Did Father live here, too?"

Yvonne was silent for a moment and said, "No, Martina, your father never lived here."

Martina asked, "Where did he live, then?"

Yvonne snapped, "These things aren't important, your father is dead, and he isn't living anywhere, and that is enough of that."

Martina felt clusters of questions bursting from her newly developing chest, and she couldn't help but blurt out, "Just tell me, just once, what his name was, if he even had a name, if he even existed, if you aren't just making him up." Yvonne pursed her lips and looked helplessly at Hilde, who was also growing rigid, and suddenly the two women seemed to Martina like strangers, like two witches from an evil land full of evil secrets, and the only thing saving her from their clutches were the two loose, golden braids bouncing on her back.

When they came home an envelope from Palestine was waiting in the mail, and Yvonne said, "It's for you, Mutti."

Oma Hilde went into the bedroom and Martina heard her cry out, in there by herself, "Madness, madness," followed by the steady ticking of the typewriter. Yvonne sat in front of the restless Martina. Hilde stormed out of the room and handed Yvonne both letters, both incoming and outgoing.

"I want to write a letter to Opa, too," said Martina. "I'll write one right now and you can send it together."

"It won't fit in the envelope," Hilde stated.

Yvonne said, "It is impossible, Martina, to send Opa a letter."

Martina stood up and went out to the yard. She sat quietly on one of the benches put there by the dedicated men and women of city hall, so that the fine people of Suhl might rest from their daily labor. She sat there, silent, and an ancient sadness came bubbling up, filling her veins, her throat, her eternally smiling eyes, now brimming with tears. She wept in silence, then went up to her room with neither a glance at old Oma Hilda nor a word to her mother Yvonne, editor-in-chief of the Party's *Thüringen* paper. She soon plummeted into a dreamless sleep.

2.

Berlin of 1961 took in Yvonne and Martina, embracing them like long lost sons. Martina had recently turned 18, no longer a schoolgirl but still the same lovely, cheerful young woman, though the braids had been replaced by long, flowing hair that fell all the way to her waist. She had a sunny, toothy grin and laughing eyes that narrowed into elongated slits. In front of the mirror she would tell herself that those eastern-looking eyes had traveled to her on the waves of wandering Mongolian tribes through her father, whose name she did not know and whose face she never saw, nor did she own a photograph of him, and who perhaps had given her these eyes that everyone seemed to love so much.

Hilde sold her Suhl home and purchased a small Berlin apartment. And so, they lived as they used to, Yvonne at work from dawn till dusk, this time as editor of the Democratic Republic's women's journal, devoted to matters of household management, cooking, fashion, and even romance, though carefully and educationally. *Für Dich* also touched on the subject of politics, for the Communist woman was not content to simply stay in the kitchen. Little by little, they started printing more complex articles, some of them casting subtle doubts on the great enterprise.

Hilde grew older but maintained her freedom of spirit. Upon arriving to Berlin, she took Martina and Yvonne to 22 Blumenstraße, which she herself had not visited in many years, not knowing whether the building was even still standing. It was, though all the joy had left it. The arched front door was broken, and the windows were open, ushering in the draft, pieces of glass still clinging to many of their frames. The roof was crumbled and seemed as if it could cave in at any moment. In the rooms of the publishing house a rat squealed, perturbed by the unexpected visitors.

Hilde, tearful and confused, pointed at a portion of the floor no longer surrounded by walls and said, "This is where you were born, Yvonnchen, your cradle was right here." After that they went outside and looked at the building for a long while and Hilde said, "We did good things here, fine things, Erich and I." Martina's breath caught in her chest with pain and happiness, for her grandfather's name had not been uttered in the Freyer home for five long years, ever since that evil letter, which Martina was never shown, nor was she permitted to write back.

"You never told me what you did here," she said.

"We printed books," said Hilde. "We wanted people to read, to understand, but those petty politicians spoiled everything. One took away justice, another took democracy, and the third, who wanted only power and power and power, won in the end and destroyed everything. Perhaps you should get back to reading, Martina. Truth is in books. Or maybe you could write, you are a good writer."

"Mutti writes all the time," said Martina, "she's an important journalist."

"Ach, *Quatsch mit Soße*, Martina," Hilde said. "History will erase what people write in your mother's papers, nothing will remain of it."

Yvonne said, "Enough, Oma, for once keep your mouth shut."

"I'm old enough," said Martina, "I can hear, and Oma is right, enough politics, I want to be a teacher."

In the evenings Martina snuck out by herself to the streets

of West Berlin, despite Yvonne strictly forbidding it, "Because it could hurt both of us, to great extent." She wandered streets which were not only as broad as the ones in the heart of East Berlin but also filled with people, smelling of delicate perfumes, roasted sausage and beef from the restaurants, coffee with sweet cream, looking into display windows, enchanted. Her legs carried her to the theater box booths and she panicked suddenly and remembered that she cannot return too late at night to her city, which is the same city but on a different planet, a place where one mustn't wander at night unless one is in uniform. Here people flowed through the streets in eveningwear and the women were so lovely, and the night was open to them. Merchants stood on street corners, clowns from the wandering circus performed for passersby as children tossed them coins, groups of people her age ambled by, singing obscene little songs, slightly inebriated, an unsteady beggar was walking toward her. She grew uneasy and took the U-Bahn back to her home, but again and again was drawn to the forbidden city. And now tractors and construction equipment were flowing from all corners of the city toward the imagined red dagger in her heart, cyclopean cranes were joined by construction workers in white uniforms and soldiers and police officers, and walls were erected, thin stone walls, one on each side, and a fallow field lay between them. Martina's evening excursions ceased and only the longing remained.

Martina went to study at a teaching institute in the north of the city, and in the classes long lines of wooden benches popped up in front of her. The teachers were similar to the ones she had in her school in Suhl, but they were harder, more determined, and all around them scrambled clerks and janitors and students who all looked too old for their age. The curriculum was packed with classes on ideology and mass education, physical education, strategy and the history of war, and "combat and preparation for military service," which was held every day in the school courtyard, where a large training facility was erected, replete with barbed wire fences and climbing walls, and a little shooting range, from which the crack of gunfire was constantly heard.

Martina attended the teaching institute in Berlin for a full week, and when that week was over, she came to the management office and declared that she does not intend to continue her studies. Vice Principal Fräulein Zunz, dressed all in black, now looked at her very much like a spider. She looked at Martina coolly and inquired if comrade Martina Freyer has considered the full consequences of such an extreme course of action.

Martina said, "Certainly, Fräulein Vice Principal." Fräulein Zunz wrote something down in the large notebook on her desk and asked Martina to leave the premises of the institute at once, declaring that "the institute no longer holds any responsibility for her fate," which Martina accepted dutifully and with a sigh of relief.

Yvonne listened to her account, troubled, and said, "But how, Martina, can you do such a thing without consulting me?"

Martina said, "Why would I consult you on something like this."

"Everything is harder now," said Yvonne. "Harder than ever, another war might be coming. They just want our schools to be prepared."

"There won't be war unless your friends upstairs want war," said Martina. "Wars don't just happen for no reason."

"That is not true," insisted Yvonne. "Some things are historical necessities."

"And you're still buying into it." Martina raised her voice, uncharacteristically, "You're still cooperating, still publishing magazines telling German women how important it is that they keep knitting socks to support the war effort."

Yvonne said, "That is what newspapers are supposed to do, explain."

Martina said, "*Quatsch mit Soße.*"

Yvonne snapped, "You've been listening to Oma too much."

Martina faced her, assured and unafraid, and said, "It isn't Oma, it's me, I can think for myself, you see this face I got from you and Father, even if you refuse to hear anything about him, this face is a face that can think for itself. Your papers explain nothing."

"You're hurting me," said Yvonne.

"You know the truth just like I do," said Martina. "Your papers are full of lies, you never say what our cities look like, blackened and poor, because there is no such thing as poverty in our Germany, is there? No poverty but no one has anything, people are miserable, why won't you write about that? Why won't you write that our cars stink of gasoline? Why won't you write about what is really happening in those politics of yours? Why didn't you write even once about how much of a bastard Stalin was, when the whole world already knows! All you write about is the capitalists, how bad they have it. *Quatsch mit Soße! Quatsch mit Soße!* It is better there, far better, I was there, I went there every night until they built that damn wall, and one day I will live there, and you can choke on your new world." Martina was choking down tears but now they burst out of her, and she fell into her mother's embrace, sobbing.

Yvonne hugged her and hummed, "Martinchen, Martinchen, you are all I have, I forgive you, when you are a bit older you will see the bigger picture, you will understand what great things we have accomplished here."

Martina wriggled free and went to her room. She laid out a white sheet of stationery on the table before her and wrote a letter.

April 10th, 1963

Dear Opa Erich,

You might not remember me. I am Martina, my mother is Yvonne, your daughter whom you haven't seen in so long.

I think about you often. Sometimes I dream about you. I have a photograph of you when you were younger and I wonder, do you look the same now? You must have grown older, but I know that you are good and kindhearted. I am living in Berlin now, with Mutti. I saw the house Mutti was born in, where you and Oma had a publishing house, and thought of all the good you did together, something truly important for mankind. As for me, I do not know yet what to do with my life. Everything seems so complicated now.

Oma lives nearby and we visit her often and look after her. I love her so much, and I am always thinking how sad it is that life took you away from each other, because you have so much in common. I know that Mutti and Oma cannot write to you, and that this letter might never arrive, but I don't care. Please write me back to a friend's address I'm attaching below, because Mutti must not know I wrote you.

Yours with much love,
Martina

She dug through the drawer and fished out the address in Israel that she had covertly copied from the last letter from Erich, carefully copied it onto an envelope, and snuck out to the nearest post office. She returned later to find Yvonne sitting alone in the darkness of the empty living room, pensive. Martina walked over to her and kissed her forehead and slept very well that night.

3.

In May of 1963, via friends and confidants from Berlin, Martina received a letter from Israel.

April 24th, 1963

My Beloved Martina,

I am unable to describe the overwhelming joy that engulfed me upon reading your letter. I have heard many good things of you, and lo – a letter in your handwriting, filled with such lovely sentiments.

Your letter reached me just in time for Passover, which we celebrate here at Kibbutz Kfar Szold, in northern Israel, where my brother Kurt lives with a very large family. I immediately read your letter to the entire family, and everyone was delighted to hear it, and would very much like to get to know you. So there, now you have a big new family!

I lead an entirely normal life in a retirement home next to Tel Aviv, in a place called Ramat Gan. There are mostly people here who came to Israel from Germany after

Hitler rose to power, and now they are old people, like me. I am very happy here, and for every celebration I write songs. You can ask your mother Yvonne how good I am at rhyming.

How is Yvonne? I would very much like to meet her, but as you know she cannot write me, and nothing can be done on the matter. I would love it if you could tell her of my letter. And I would also be very happy, and dearly grateful, if you could tell Hilde what I wrote, and that she is in my thoughts.

With much love,
Opa Erich

June 1st, 1963

Dearest Opa,

Thank you for your letter, I was overjoyed to receive it, I had been so worried that something would happen to it along the way, and finally I am calm.

I am sorry, Opa, but I could not send your regards to Yvonne and Oma, and therefore they cannot send any back. I am afraid that Oma would prefer to avoid such excitement in her advanced age, and regarding Yvonne – she must certainly never know of our correspondence, as she is a high-ranking Party member, and they might harm her.

You can send your next letter to the address below in Leipzig, where I am starting photography school next week. I have decided to be the news photographer of a nice little paper called the *Tribune*, and they sent me there. The world of journalism is truly fascinating! Have you ever been to Leipzig? It is a large city with many museums, though I would take Berlin any day of the week.

Love,
Martina

July 20th, 1963

My Beloved Martina,

Each letter from you brings me great happiness, and I hope for many more.

It is summer here, and summers are very hard for people like us, who are used to the cold Berlin air. We lock ourselves in our rooms and do not leave them, since we are lucky to have excellent air-conditioning in all of them.

Two weeks ago, we celebrated a very important birthday, Gidi's Bar Mitzvah, he is the youngest son of Lotte Rosenthal, my brother Kurt's daughter. He is a curly-haired and intelligent boy and interestingly, though he grew up without a father, he is not at all a melancholic boy, and so well-liked by everyone. We all sat down for a good meal together and even Rubi came all the way from the kibbutz, he will be going to the army soon, just a month after finishing his final high-school exams. That is how things are here in Israel and it cannot be helped.

I hoped you told Yvonne and Hilde that I miss them very much, because you did not mention it clearly in your letter.

Much love,
Opa Erich.

January 1st, 1964

Dearest Opa,

I have not written in a while and for that I hope you forgive me. My life is very interesting and in constant flux. I finished my studies in the Leipzig studio and now I am back in Berlin and working as a photographer in the paper. Each morning I go out wherever my editor sends me and photograph what he tells me to. I think I am pretty good.

I am no longer living with my mother; I live with some friends here from the paper in a sort of commune. Mother is working very hard and I hardly ever see her. We had a bit of a falling-out, but now we are good friends again.

Your loving granddaughter,
Martina

April 1st, 1964

My beloved Martina,

Your letter took a long time to reach me, but I read it several times and was happy to hear you have returned to Berlin. I think of Berlin often and wonder if it looks the same as it did 30 years ago. You know, some say that Unter den Linden is the most beautiful boulevard in the whole world! Oma and I walked there together just after we met, and it was so long and lovely that we hardly noticed the passage of time, we talked and talked and made plans, and families with children were walking there as well and suddenly I felt, I want that, I want to walk with a woman who will be mine forever and a carriage with our baby in it. I told Oma, that's it, I have made up my mind, I want to marry you, and Hilde kissed me, one little kiss, but I haven't forgotten it to this day, and she said, Erich, why have you waited for so long? It was love, no question of it.

Please, could you give Oma a kiss for me? It would make me exceedingly happy. Please tell me if you have.

Much love,
Opa

June 5th, 1964

Beloved Opa,

It is odd that you write of love, because I have just found a great love of my own, and I am overjoyed to tell you about it. His name is Norbert, and he is very wise, and he plays guitar and writes songs, and I will tell you two secrets about him. First of all, he is a year younger than me, so I am a bit old for him but still he loves me madly. And second: he is not a member of the Party! He doesn't even care about the party. A lot of young people these days have grown tired from politics and hate the damn wall, but I should not say anymore because they are already giving me some trouble. Could you imagine – I brought along a translator when I came to take photographs in some factory, and when they saw that his ID read "Jewish" they would not let us in! It is a strange sort of country, this Democratic Republic of Germany.

Opa, I know you want to meet Yvonne and Oma, but it is still impossible, under no circumstances can they know of this correspondence, that would be a grave mistake, for all parties involved. I hope you understand.

I love you very much,
Martina

October 3rd, 1964

My Dearest Martina,

I was very glad to hear you have found love. I have a strange belief, and most people must disagree with me on this matter, but I believe that love never dies! Though it might hide, or become ill, I know with utter certainty that the love Oma and I shared is merely dormant, and may awaken still, though so many years have passed.

This which I have written I can also prove. I am attaching a photocopy of a letter Oma wrote me some years ago and I ask that you read it and judge for yourself, Martina, for you are a grown woman now and wise, can love truly end?

Opa

Martina checked the envelope and found a yellowing photocopy of a letter in her grandmother's handwriting.

May 14th, 1946

Dear Erich,

I was happy to read your letter to Yvonne and find that you are living somewhere nice, with orchards, and not in the desert we always imagined when we spoke of Palestine.

We have not met in many years, and a great deal of anger remained between us. Now the war is over, and I wanted you to know that I am no longer angry, and that I sometimes think of you.

We had hard times, but good times as well. It would be a shame if, because of what happened, we would forget the many good things we achieved together. We gave something to humanity, because eventually everything that happens crumbles into the dust of memory, and only books remain. Perhaps if more people would have read our books, Europe and Germany wouldn't suffer such a terrible disaster.

Yvonne is very successful in her work as a reporter, and I am helping her raise little Martina. Erich, you have a clever, adorable granddaughter, with laughing eyes. When she grows up, we will tell you more about her.

Love,
Hilde

Martina buried the letter deep in a chest drawer in her room and attempted writing a response, but could not, and many months passed before she wrote him again.

February 20th, 1965

Dearest Erich,

I must again apologize for not writing you for so long, everything has been happening so quickly, there are so many surprises and joyous occasions! Believe it or not, Norbert and I got married. It was a civil ceremony, because they don't like churches that much here and they closed nearly all of them down. But all our friends were there, and Norbert has a little band that plays songs he writes himself! The boys from the band played in our wedding, and threw red flowers at us, so that no one can say anything. Now we need to find a house, because we have a little money, but the houses in Berlin are so small and ugly, and to get a house in a good area we will need a lot of money, and in a city this size, we will need a car, too.

I was deeply moved by the copy you sent of Hilde's letter. It seems the two of you had something truly special. I met her yesterday and she seemed a bit tired, but I suppose that makes sense when one is nearing eighty and has had such a difficult life. She came to the wedding, of course, and was very happy.

Much love,
Martina

April 3rd, 1965

My Martina,

When I received your letter and read of your wedding to Norbert I danced with joy, and walked around our retirement home in Ramat Gan with a great big smile, eventually the administrator asked if I was perhaps ill, she must have thought that poor Erich Freyer had lost his mind! and I told her, my granddaughter Martina got married, and in her wedding there played a live musical concert. She was very happy as well and sends you her blessing.

I hope Yvonne was at the wedding as well, since you didn't say in your letter, and that she is happy for you. This would be something special for her – she was never married, and that must be difficult. I always thought of Yvonne as the sort of lovely girl everyone would want to be friends with, that the minute she grew up a bit she would be surrounded by men and simply have to choose, you, away with you; you, go to hell; and you – you are the one I want! But fate is sometimes stronger than nature, don't you agree? I have been thinking of Yvonne so much lately, and I do not even have a photograph, only the one she sent me right after the war, and she is such a serious woman today, 45 soon, can you imagine?

I am stopping now because I am tired and my hand shakes a bit, could you write me more?

Send my best to everyone,
Opa

July 23rd, 1965

Dear Opa,

Thank you for your letter. Life is a bit hard now, we are both working long hours and have all but forgotten about the wedding by now.

We found a house in a Berlin neighborhood we didn't really want to live in, the houses here are very dirty and the people are hard, they never say hello, always rushing off to work, but there was no choice. We must work very hard and if we are lucky, we might be able to move from here. There is obviously no talk of a child at the time.

But Opa, still, if you wish to come to Berlin and visit us, it is finally possible. Our apartment is small, but you could stay with us, we would be so happy to see you and we could talk and talk, and you can rest here a bit. Think about it,

Yours,
Martina

January 16ᵗʰ, 1966

Dear Martina,

I was a bit sick and could not write, but I am better now. It is strange, come winter I suddenly feel fine, as if I were back in Europe. And winter here is not so bad. There has not been snow in Tel Aviv for more than 15 years, you would have to go to Jerusalem to see any, and I am too tired for that. But in the winter, nice, hard winds blow through the trees, and it makes a sort of music, and when it rains my heart leaps with excitement like I am a boy running down a boulevard in Stettin, tossing my coat over my head so as not to get wet, my brother Kurt running after me, and after him walks Fräulein Saranow, holding an umbrella. Have I ever told you about Fräulein Saranow? I doubt she is still alive, and if she is, she is probably in an old peoples' home, like me, counting the days.

Sometimes I felt it is already over, Martina, that I am exhausted, being a person is hard work and one never knows when it will end, how much more is written in this mission's orders. And me, I will be eighty next year, and my brother Kurt recently turned eighty, and we celebrated his birthday in Kfar Szold, and Käthe's, who is seventy now. Everyone was there, and I wrote down my life's story, which is also their memories, all of ours. For days and nights, I wrote and wrote, telling everything, even the Tale of the Egg Miracle just as my father Moritz told it to us, 75 years ago exactly! Has your mother told you the story of the Egg Miracle? Because we all swore to pass it down to the next generations.

Every letter from you brings me strength and happiness, please, send my wishes of peace and love to everyone, Erich

March 1966

Dear Opa,

We wish you a happy holiday. We received your lovely letter and will properly reply to it soon. In the meanwhile, spring has come here, but it is still cold as April sometimes tends to be. We want to take a trip to the nearby lake. Norbert wants to fish, and I plan to take my camera and walk around. We look forward to it very much.

Have you celebrated Passover yet, Opa? Do they have Easter bunnies there, too?

Much love from the Berliners, dear Opa,
Martina

4.

On July 5, 1966, an old man, short and shaking slightly, holding a leather bag, knocked on the door of Norbert and Martina Kaiser in one of the southern neighborhoods of East Berlin. Norbert opened the door and was about to tell the man he had come to the wrong house, and perhaps assist him, as he was obviously confused, as the elderly often are. But the man smiled knowingly, a kind, ponderous smile.

"Then you are, Norbert," he said, and his lips trembled, as if he wanted to say more.

"Yes, that's right," said Norbert, puzzled, but his eyes widened as realization slowly dawned.

"I am Opa Erich," said the man, "I am your wife Martina's grandfather, and you, Norbert, you are like my own son, you are my son, Norbert."

Norbert's face glowed, and he said, "Please, Opa, come on in, if only we'd known, we had no idea." He took Erich's arm and walked him slowly to the empty living room. Erich looked around with some disappointment, and Norbert ran off to the kitchen. Erich heard excited whispering, perhaps a hushed shriek of surprise, and then she was standing in the kitchen door, right in front of him, an attractive woman with long, flowing blonde hair, thin lips and a small nose, her eyes squinted by laughter.

Erich stumbled toward her and said, "Yvonne, Yvonne." She embraced him and he muttered, "Oh, Yvonne, so this is what you look like, ach, such a beauty you've become, after all these years."

She gently helped him to the couch and sat in front of him, saying, "Opa Erich, I'm not Yvonne, I'm Martina, your granddaughter. You must be exhausted, let me fix you a cup of tea." She got up and went into the kitchen, flustered and dumbfounded, followed by Norbert. When she reemerged, she was carrying a steaming kettle and some cups and a plate of soft cookies.

Erich was silent, and Martina said, "But Opa Erich, why did you not say anything, I would've picked you up at the border crossing."

Erich said, "It is you, Martina, here, I have the address right here and the driver was very nice and took me all the way here and I paid him four marks."

She said, "When did you arrive in Berlin?"

Erich told her that he arrived the day before and was staying with his friend Karl Barić who used to be a famous reporter and was kind enough to offer his hospitality. Of course, he must return to Berlin before evening, but tomorrow he will come see them again, and surely then he could see Yvonne, who probably lives nearby.

Martina said, "Rest now, Opa, we'll talk about that." His tea had cooled a bit and he sipped. His lips trembled and the veins in his head turned bluer, and for a moment Martina was worried, but he seemed to calm down, and as he sat there looking at Norbert and Martina, a smile came to his lips, a restful smile.

They sat and talked, then, for a long while. Martina told Erich of her childhood in the southern cities and took out a small package of photographs. He eagerly flipped through photos of Yvonne, who had grown into a confident woman, yet did not look as cold and determined as one might expect of such an important person. For a long time, he stared silently at a photo of Hilde, who had grown very old.

Martina said, "Take it, you can take it."

He asked, "And when can I see Yvonne?"

Martina said, "We'll talk about that tomorrow, come, we must get you to the border, it is very late."

The next morning when Erich arrived at Checkpoint Charlie, Martina was already waiting there and hurriedly drove him away from there in the little Trabant she and Norbert shared. They drove along the wall, which left a deep impression on him, and then stood awhile in front of the house on 22 Blumenstraße, which somehow had not yet been demolished, merely crumbled into ruin, tiles missing from its roof, and in the windows hardly a single pane of unbroken glass. Some crows burst screaming from the front door where Hoffman Publishing used to be. Erich's eyes were red and wet, and the veins visible on his small, bare head again turned a deep blue, and his mouth twisted into a pained smile. She took him back to car and hurried home. On the way they passed endless rows of ash-blackened houses, and he looked and looked, seeking his Berlin that he had loved so much, and could not find it.

Back in the house, Erich burned with a fever. Martina placed cool compresses on his forehead, brought him tea and toast with butter. Norbert returned from work and sat with him. Erich dozed and occasionally would weep silently. By the afternoon, though, he had recovered enough to sit up, and say to Norbert and Martina, whose hearts had broken for him already, "Tomorrow is the last day, and perhaps Yvonne will find some time to see me, after all." Martina and Norbert said nothing and drove him back to the border crossing.

On the third day Erich seemed recuperated and high-spirited. The laws of the riven city permitted no more than those three days, and the guards on the eastern side were already becoming more thorough in checking his papers, wondering what could bring a confused elderly man to cross the border, back and forth, several days in a row. Martina was also waiting for his anxiously, uncomfortably, tossing glances around to see if some uninvited individual wasn't following her there to find out what she herself was doing, exactly, day after day by the border crossing. Again they drove through the streets of Berlin which he now knew and no longer relished.

At their house the three of them sat down and Martina said, "Opa Erich, I am overjoyed that you came to visit, but you must know that you cannot see Yvonne."

Erich wiped sweat beading on his forehead and said, "She does not want to see me." He was silent a moment and echoed, "She does not want to see me, I should have thought of that, this I did not think of."

"No," Martina objected, "it isn't like that."

"Why, then?" said Erich. "This is very confusing."

"She does not know you are here," said Martina. "And we cannot tell her. This is what we decided, Norbert and I, and if you'd have said you were coming I would have told you, Opa, Yvonne cannot see you, no one can know that you are here."

"I do not understand this," said Erich, "I do not understand any of this at all."

"They are always watching us," said Martina. "This place, people aren't free here like they are in Palestine."

"But I am her father," Erich whispered. "And I have not seen my child in 30 years, since she was a girl, I am just an old man, of consequence to no one."

Norbert stood up and said, "You are a Jew from Israel, Erich. To them you are dangerous, very much so. And you are a danger

202 | THE LAST VISIT TO BERLIN

to Yvonne as well."

Erich was lucid, now, and hard. "If she were to find that I was here and did not see her," he said brokenly, "what will she think then."

"She won't," said Martina. "I am so sorry, Erich. She can never know."

It was noon and Erich said, "Perhaps I should go now, this is no good, no good at all."

Martina said, "Perhaps it would be better if you hadn't come, how hard this must be."

He was shaking. A thin sob rose from his throat, a wheezing sort of sound, and he said, "I had to come, I could not stay away, and now I will go, but I have one last, small request from you, my dears." Norbert and Martina listened and looked at one another.

They drove along the black streets of Berlin and entered a neighborhood unfamiliar to him. The car slowed and Norbert said, "Here, this is where Oma Hilde lives, in that house over there." Erich squinted, struggling to see. No one was walking in the street, and the windows of the houses remained shut, a bright, cool July sun looking over them.

The car stopped again at Checkpoint Charlie. Erich Freyer stepped out of it and now his eyes were dry and his lips tight and his body tired, worn with grief. He straightened and walked toward the booth, leather bag in hand, step by step, under the painful gaze of Norbert and Martina Kaiser who stood hand in hand, an old man whose days were done, of consequence to no one, and his life's mission, which he did not yet know, and no sign had yet been revealed to him regarding it, ended. He looked back, a final glance, and disappeared.

CHAPTER SEVEN: HANS

1.

The year 1933 stormed into the lives of the German people, relentlessly, but the outskirts of Berlin received a brief respite. The defeated fled and an ominous silence settled onto the streets, disturbed only by the steady, unnerving steps of groups of men in brown as they marched up and down the pavement.

Hans Rosenthal, a tall, handsome man who had just turned 27, spent the ever longer days of March wandering the city, breathless, anxious, scared. His friends had scattered, traveled to the country, vanished entirely, and even their close family refused to say what had befallen them. The front of the party club he would visit each day to argue passionately and read poetry and excerpts from plays he had written about the lives of the workers, was locked, and someone drew some thick stripes and the word "Closed" on the door. The time of the brusque, brutal slogans was past – a single word was enough, now, a stripe of spattered paint, two crossed lines, an exclamation mark, a swastika. Germany had stripped itself of the words that, until the month before, had flowed in abundance from every podium, in the Reichstag, in the papers, in the now purged and empty bookstores.

He was walking down Kantstraße when a loud, chattering group crossed over from Leibnitzstraße, five men, three women. As they grew closer the chatter, it seemed to Hans, transformed into a drunken song. Their faces twisted and the drunken singing became a crude shout. Walking across the street, they had noticed him. A man with a vicious face approached him and came very close, so that their chests were nearly touching. Hans looked away, disgusted.

The man raised his arm into the air, sneering with pride and contempt. "*Heil Hitler.*"

Hans' hand remained in the pocket of the long coat he took when he wandered through the countryside, trying to sell artwork to the villagers in the market days. Deep in the pocket his hand grew hotter and hotter and he said nothing. The rest of the group exchanged glances and simultaneously joined the salute, and speaking as one, taunted, "*Heil Hitler.*" Hans wanted to turn around but the blood flooded his chest, his burning hand, his handsome face, his soft eyes, his aquiline nose, his full lips, and a voice spoke from within him which nothing could stop, "*Heil ihn selber*, hail him yourself."

The vicious one came even closer, his face nearly touching Hans'. "What did you just say, piglet?" he asked, sharply, threateningly. "We could not quite hear you."

Hans stood tall and ashamed. The women took a step back as the five men started laughing and mocking him. Passersby were congregating round them. Hans was paralyzed with fear. Within him, a small child burst into tears.

From the crowd someone yelled, "I know this red scum!" The men were very close now, enough to feel their breath on him. Long fingers were prodding at his shirt and at his neck, tearing away buttons. Fingernails dug into his flesh and the yelling pounded into his brain, red scum, Jewish pig, we'll handle you like we handled your Thälmann. His leg burned as a booted foot kicked him, hard. More and more people were gathering around him. He looked behind him and there, in the crowd, a large gap which would surely be filled any second. Hans leapt desperately for the deliverance of the gap, and a thunder of footfalls came in his wake as he fled. A tram stopped right next to him and he lunged for it. The bloodthirsty mob shrunk away into the distance like a flock of demons.

Lotte let out a small cry when she saw her brother Hans come in. He hushed her. Their mother, Gertrude, came out of the kitchen and looked at him, her face hard, severe. Lotte brought the first aid kit she used in her job as a nurse in the city's sanitarium, cleaned the blood stains from his neck, bandaged his leg and asked, "What happened, Hans?"

"Never mind," said Hans.

"Look after him, Lottchen," said Gertrude and finally addressed him, commanding, "Hans, you will not leave the house."

Gertrude went out. Hans' younger sister came in, glanced at her brother and said, "What have you done now, then?"

Lotte scolded her, "Please, Metta, he is in pain."

Metta said, "At least he's doing something." She laughed, and Hans slammed his door in her face.

Gertrude came back an hour later. Hans was already sprawled in his narrow bed, brooding, his long legs dangling off the edge. She stood in his doorway, Lotte's head peeking out behind her.

"That's it," she declared. "You are out of here." Hans sat up, indignant. "In three days, you are off to Libau."

Lotte's mouth fell open and Hans blurted, "Damn it, Mother, what does Libau have to do with anything."

"I enlisted you in a delegation of Jewish students," said Gertrude, "and until then you are not to leave the house. There is nothing left for you in Berlin."

"I am not a baby," muttered Hans. "What the hell is this?"

She went back to the kitchen and scrubbed the crystal glasses which the smell of the steaming afternoon tea still clung to. Gertrude had sharp features, eyes that were always wide open, and high, round cheekbones. When she stood up straight she was the beautiful and glamorous, like she used to be, the loveliest girl in Neustadt, whom the young student Louis Rosenthal fell desperately in love with, and only through interminable toil and begging managed to eventually charm into marriage.

Hans scrambled up after his mother, saying, "Perhaps we can dedicate more consideration to this matter, make inquiries, I cannot simply—"

Gertrude glared at him, the eagle's glare he knew so well from childhood, the one that always scared him off to shelter, to the unmade bed on the second floor in No. 11 Pestalozzistraße in Stettin, to the gardens above the Oder from which he could observe the boats drifting down the river and imagine himself boarding one and sailing to England, where he would be greeted by not only William Shakespeare but Jonathan Swift and Charles Dickens. But this time Gertrude's eaglelike glare was sharper than ever, mercilessly scouring his face, flitting around the room. The street Hans wanted to escape to was locked behind seven bolts. He retreated, stumbling, back into his room, where he sat, his head between his hands.

Lotte came in and asked how he was. He shook his head and she just sat there silently for a while, as she often did, and then said, "Where is it, exactly, this Libau."

Hans went to one of the drawers and pulled out a folded map with badly tattered edges, pointed at the serpentine coastline and said, "You see, Lottchen, this is Latvia, and Libau is here, on the coast."

Lotte said, "Well, if you go there you could visit Russia, you're always talking about Russia and I always wondered what it is like there, really, the people and the streets, and how they celebrate the holidays."

Hans stood up and started pacing up and down the room, flourishing the little map. His handsome face lit up again and he said, "Why, Lottchen, this is wonderful, just wonderful." Lotte shrugged and left the room.

In Hans' black notebook letters blossomed in his elongated handwriting, like a procession of train cars hurtling onward. He wrote and crossed out and wrote and crossed out, and the room was filled with sunlight.

2.

The large shuttle docked at Libau Harbor. Hans looked at the addresses on the harbor depots and the passenger docks. The dockworkers hollered at one another in a language that sounded foreign, yet familiar – the same language as on signs around the passenger docks, which occasionally received a small addition in German. The clerks in the small immigration office at the harbor entrance addressed the group of merry students flowing out to the dock in sluggish German, grade-school German. Libau is a sunny city, and Hans thought, they take this light for granted here, and he remembered longingly the light saturating Stettin's Parade Square, and the dawn reflected from the shipyard on the

Oder, near where it spilled into the sea, where the ships left on voyages everywhere, and here, to Libau, as well.

A rotund man in a top hat led the group of bundle-carrying students down the streets of Libau. Hans was also carrying a bundle, packed for him by Lotte, and later submitted to meticulous examination by Gertrude. After she left the room, he removed an entire suit from his bundle and instead packed some notebooks and pencils and several books that were already forbidden in Germany. He took the voluminous *And Quiet Flows the Don*, which he had been reading slowly, in small sips, and *The Mother*, which he had read again and again, always returning to the yellowing pages stained with the mess of many lunches.

The rotund man introduced himself as "Mr. Abraham Cohen, clerk of the Libau Jewish community." He spoke German with a Yiddish accent that made him sound pleading, mendicant suppliant, and made Hans slightly nauseated. Mr. Cohen told the new arrivals that he would be delighted to introduce them to the local Jewish community, to hear and be heard, and he is very hopeful that some of them would be willing to tie their own fates to the town of Libau and attend its excellent learning institutions to study important professions and become lawyers, engineers, even rabbis. Hans thought that it had been very long since he was surrounded by so many Jews at a single time, yarmulke-wearing Jews, pale-faced Jews, Jews who rejoice at any mention of Talmudic debate, and now this clerk, this "Abraham Cohen," and his name which seemed to afflict every Jew out of three. This rushed journey to Latvia seemed now to be another one of the punishments his mother insisted on penalizing him with for failing to learn the laws of life.

In the evening the group congregated for an event attended

by the community leaders, who nearly fell over one another as they strained to man the podium for a sliver of a speech. Then they took to the streets of Libau, and Hans meticulously examined the storefronts and the façades of the houses, struggling to find the trace of the Russian soul which had supposedly reigned here for so long. Betwixt the thunder of German drums and the raging storm that was Russia, little Libau seemed like some sort of mistake, and the Libau Jews an ineffable blip of existence. He returned to the inn and scribbled in his notebook until darkness came to its rooms.

The next day, the students had a tour in the community synagogue and several other institutions and schools across town, and ate their fill of murky noodle soup, potato porridge and a slice of veal, the community women terrifying in their determination to cater to their every need, growing more dogged as evening approached. The men in his group, most of whom were younger than Hans and seemed to him gullible and lost, flowed into the great Libau banquet hall, which the community had some rented for the night with its meager funds. The band started playing dance music and in burst with a cheer every Jewish girl in Libau, wearing white blouses and blue skirts, and everyone was swept into the dance circle, large groups and couples. The hall fell into a warm, decadent chaos. He saw pale, slender girls that danced coyly and shot anxious, expectant glances at their partners, and buxom, rosy-cheeked girls who reminded him of the Russian peasants he had seen in pictures from the revolution's books, that danced vigorously, lewdly. He stood, smiling, near the wall, and hardly even noticed the short, sweaty, enthusiastic girl that pulled him from the wall and swung him into the circle of dancers, and he obliged despite his innate clumsiness. But she danced wildly, like a storm, her fiery eyes lancing into him, eyes the likes of which he had never seen. He could not look away from her, the sounds of revelry around them grew distant, only the music remained, and her footfalls. Then she pulled him away to a corner of the banquet hall and they looked at each other.

"You seem to have swallowed your tongue, big man," the girl said, laughing wildly.

"And what would you have me say?" asked Hans.

"First," she elected, "the name. Hans, Max, Franz, one of those names that play like machine guns."

"Right on the mark," he said, "it's Hans! Hans Rosenthal!"

"I am Nechama," she said, "An annoying mouthful of a name, but well-intentioned." Hans looked at her curiously and she said, "What do you know, a Jew who doesn't know Hebrew. Nechama is a very good thing that comes upon you in your time of despair, just when you need it most. What do you say to that?"

"Nechama," said Hans, "right on the mark, again."

"I know," she said, "I always am. What great despair has brought you here, Hans Rosenthal?"

He said, "It's a long story, Nechama, and it is very loud in here."

She pulled him out to the windswept and salt-smelling streets of Libau. He told her about his life as a merchant in the countryside, about the Communist Party whose clubs have been closed and about Germany which had become a poisoned, leprous place, dangerous to people like him. He spoke of his mother, Gertrude, describing her as "A real piece of work, a Woman of Valor, God help us." He told her of his sisters, his sister Lotte who was soon to be an old maid but still would not leave the house, and his little sister Metta, who God had blessed with a high, pointed nose.

Nechama laughed and occasionally elbowed him lightly. They

sat down on a small rock and looked out to the pier. Hans said, "And you, Nechama, you've told me nothing about yourself."

She said, "The story is sad, and I am happy, that is Nechama, and that is enough talk." She stood up so that she was slightly taller than him and brought her full, soft breasts to his mouth and he drank them in deeply, an avalanche of fear and fury falling out of his chest and tumbling onto the sand. She ducked slightly and kissed him, no woman had ever kissed him like that before, and the longer the kiss grew the tighter their lips clung together and their breathing grew heavy and Hans was swaying, like a drunkard, and their hands and their thighs joined into the joy of the kiss, as well. The horrors of Berlin faded; an old world died.

They spent the next few days never leaving each other's side. The love story between the "old student" from Berlin and Nechama, the orphan who lost her father in the Great War and her mother when she was but a baby, the orphan girl who had spread her wings, the songbird of the German Gymnasium, became the talk of the community. Their wedding, which took place but a few weeks later, was officiated by the Chief Rabbi of Libau, and attended by everyone.

The day after the wedding they took the shuttle to Rostock. Gertrude and Lotte were waiting for them at the Stettin train station in Berlin. Nechama ran over to Gertrude and hugged her, saying in perfect German, "Ach, you really are something, Hans told me so much about you." Lotte stood awkwardly as Nechama kissed her as well, then went back and pulled Hans along with her like a girl pulling a boy.

Gertrude took Hans by the hand and whispered sharply in his ear, "I hope you know what you are doing, Hanschen, marrying this little girl."

He said, "Enough of this talk, Mother."

She added, "At least it isn't some red *shiksa*."

The tram rattled through the streets and as they went deeper into the city, a cold terror gripped Hans. Everywhere were locked gates, black swastikas painted on the walls, anti-Semitic bulletins in huge capital letters. The streets were filled with men in uniforms, and Hans saw Nechama flinch. That night, as they were squeezed together in his bed in the small apartment on Goethestraße, she whispered, "We are leaving here. I cannot stay, this place scares me."

"Where would we go?" asked Hans. "Back to Libau?"

Nechama said, "Palestine."

Hans leapt out of bed. "Palestine, never, what are you thinking?"

Nechama said, "Palestine is a land for Jews, and it has sunshine and oranges and villages where people live in communes, and little cities of its own. And certainly no swastikas everywhere."

"Ach, really, Nechama, to take all the Jews and squeeze them into one place, that is an utterly terrible idea," Hans said, reproving. "Jews are citizens of the world – they should be leading the *Internazional*."

"I don't understand any of that, Hans," fumed Nechama, "but people should live where they are wanted."

"Everything is happening here, in Europe," Hans insisted. "Here, this is where the war is being fought, the war on the character of the world, while over in Palestine the Jews are building themselves a golden ghetto with British rifles pointed to their heads."

"Fine," said Nechama. "Then it's your turn, my wise old man, where would you like to live, because I most certainly will not be staying here in Germany."

Hans stroked her cheek and embraced her young body which

yielded to him again and again. He looked up at the ceiling and said, "Russia. The Union of Soviet Socialist Republics."

Nechama let out a sort of horrified shriek and he said, "We will live in Russia, Nechama, learn Russian."

Nechama burst into laughter and said, "*Cherez moy trup.*"

Hans frowned. "Over my dead body," Nechama translated.

He laughed as well, this time, and said, "There, you speak Russian already, teach me!"

Nechama said, "You will never learn Russian, they'll eat you for breakfast, they are a nation of peasants, and their red tsar, the one with the massive mustache, is a peasant tyrant. I know them, Latvia was never able to get free of them."

Hans went out to the street. The house fronts were closing in, falling over him, the whole world became a huge ghetto, a ghetto of ghettos, Germany became a ghetto whose few exits were rapidly closing, and Palestine a sunny ghetto, laden with Jews. Even the small apartment he shared with his mother and sisters and fiery little wife, of whom he knows nothing, also became a ghetto, a prison with embellished walls. His stories and poems will never be published here, and the collection of short stories he got published by Albert Breuer Publishing through the skin of his teeth, *A Man Wants Out*, had also disappeared from the shelves. *Hans Rosenthal*, he said to himself, *there is no place for you in this world*. Suddenly a smile came to his lips and he patted his trousers and happily skipped back to Nechama, who was lying in bed with her eyes wide open, and held her close and said, "It will be fine, everything will be just fine, I have an idea."

The next day Nechama and Hans Rosenthal, a tall, handsome man and a bright-eyed, petite young woman, went to the British consul in Berlin. They meticulously filled out a request for an immigration license to Palestine. They then went to the Embassy of The Union of Soviet Socialist Republics and carefully filled out a great deal of forms, including another request for an immigration license. After they left the embassy they sat in a small restaurant and ordered a large sausage for each of them, with a generous helping of sauerkraut. For dessert they had apple wine, clinked their glasses, and went out to the street, locked in an embrace.

3.

In May of 1936, Hans and Nechama had a daughter, and named her Yaffa. It was their first spring in Palestine, in the small agricultural colony Rehovot, where they shared a small studio apartment. Every morning Hans went out to the employment office and was sent to perform various jobs in the orchards, among the orange and lemon and grapefruit trees. Gertrude found a nice house near the Tel Aviv beach, and hung little notes in German around the neighboring streets: "Seamstress and Repairs, Gertrude Rosenthal."

Lotte found work as a nurse and lived with her mother, and Metta wandered around Tel Aviv for several weeks, took the bus out to the small towns in the periphery to observe the character of the Zionist endeavor, and informed her speechless family that she is returning to Germany, as she has no intention of living out her life "among Asiats."

During the evenings, Hans attended the meetings of the Communist Party of Palestine, which mostly took place in Tel Aviv, and often spent the night there. Nechama was drawn to the town life of little Rehovot, where many were captivated by her fiery eyes and sharp tongue. Yaffa would accompany her in her carriage or placed in the care of neighbors. Nechama despised Hans' "Little Party with a big mouth," and would hear nothing of it. When Hans could not make it to the meetings in Tel Aviv, or when no work could be found for him, especially in winter, he wrote poetry in black notebooks, in his dense handwriting. Poems about the crisp, green-leafed orange, about the wildflowers in which the orange pickers find no value for "not a single vitamin is contained within them," and about the sirocco breathing its hot breath, blinding the eyes, burdening the soul, sowing melancholy.

"And why do you wail so / Thus spake the sirocco / never changing, by any name / I shall always be the same / from the sorrow in your heart / through your own will, you must part."

When Hans was engrossed in his notebooks Nechama would often peak over his shoulder. One time she snuck up on him and abruptly said into his ear, "Say, which are your favorite, oranges or lemons?" and burst into her unrestrained laughter.

Hans blushed, opened his notebook and recited with perfect diction: "Knowest thou the land where lemons blossom?"

She laughed some more and said, "The land of Rehovot, of course."

He flipped through his notebook and read more.

"A wilderness in the blistering sun / under the branches of the lemon / We work, our hoes strike ground—"

"How," Nechama interjected, "how can you write poems about hoes? The man who invented hoes should be found and unceremoniously executed, and you write poems for this instrument of torture."

"And what would you prefer I write about, Nechama?" asked Hans. "Indeed, what?"

"About me!" Nechama announced. "Have you even written a poem about me? Poets write about the people they love, not about hoes!"

Hans said, "All right, and say I do write a love poem to Nechama Rosenthal. Thousands have written this poem before me, but no one has ever written about hoes!"

"If you cannot write a poem about Nechama Rosenthal that no one will write in your place," declared Nechama, "it is better that you do not write poems at all."

In the Party meetings, Hans sought a remnant of the old storm, the beating heart of the red party he had felt in Berlin, but in Palestine there were other people, mostly foreigners, troubled with other things. Some were "Eastern Jews" who came from the towns of Poland and the Ukraine and soiled the profound discussion on the questions of the Internazional with expressions in the Yiddish he so loathed. Others were Arab leaders whose language he did not speak.

Heated arguments would erupt, during those long meetings, about the violent clashes that erupted in Palestine before the Second World War broke out. Some claimed it was "a struggle against the enslavement of Zionism to found a revolutionary government of Jewish and Arab workers," and others argued that it was "a struggle against British imperialism," a claim which Hans found somewhat befuddling. Occasionally, one of the branch leaders gave a speech about the latest developments in the Soviet Union and bring the most recent, wholly impressive data about the success of the Soviet economy even in the most distant regions. Many of the discussions involved matters regarding the

Hebrew worker and regarding this a great deal of scorn was directed at the *Histadrut* labor federation, that "claims to represent the workers but in reality enslaves them to the needs of the nation and chauvinistic ideology." Zionism was mentioned only cynically, contemptuously, referred to as a "colonizing movement" or "a creation of bourgeois nationalism."

Hans' reputation as a poet had also reached the Party, and as in everything led to debate. In one of their evening meetings he suggested to read a new poem titled "The Pioneer Begins to Think." His use of the word "pioneer" already incited some disapproving glances, but Hans read, elated:

Beating down, the sun stares / At our strength and blood it tears / Born to suffer, our aching backs are never done / our hands ache and bleed and the day is just begun // Striking rock with hoe and pickaxe/ An unyielding earth resists their impacts / But hard and painful, submits as well / stone by stone the strikes compel / Another plot of land, we have conquered thee / but of this suffering we shall never be free // It is all for nothing, our lost sweat, our pain / we toil for nothing, we suffer in vain / all the fruit of our labor is rotten / Into crude, grabbing hands it has fallen / and with it into the fine sand fell / The dreams of our youth, lost as well.

A small riot followed.

"Ach, such sentimentality," cried out one comrade.

Another added, "If I did not know you, I could have thought this the work of some Zionist poet."

"I am a *proletar*," Hans protested emotionally, "I exemplify Communism with this very body, and you, when was the last time you labored for anything? Need I remind you that in essence Communism is about the workers, their suffering, their blood and sweat!"

"The essence of communism is fighting the Zionist oppressor!" cried another comrade.

"The essence of communism is the *Internazional*," said a bespectacled man, "and its embodiment is the *Komintern*, and you, all you care about is your dreams, and what of the praxis?"

"But this is nonsense," Hans said, growing desperate, "what does the essence of Communism have to do with this; it is only a poem, and here, I have written another one, titled "A Jewish Worker in Palestine."

Another hail of disdain rained down – "There, there you have it, the Jewish worker, and what of the Arab worker? Enough, no more poems."

Hans, agitated, said, "There are Arab workers at my orchard and Shkolnik, the citrus grower, bleeds them dry, and I talk to them, we eat pita and olives together."

"Write about them, then! About them!" said one of the Arab members.

"I will write about whom I wish to write," Hans seethed, "Even if you would not hear it. Next to the Arabs work Yemenites. They are a slight, lean people, each strong like five workhorses, they work ever so quietly, but let me tell you, they go to synagogue every morning, and the synagogue is on my street. I see them walking on Saturday with their Siddur and they invite me to their weddings, and I will write poems about these Yemenites if I like, though they have never so much as heard about our *Internazional*!"

An awkward silence settled over the room. An elderly man, still bearing a thick Russian accent, took it upon himself to break it, saying, "Comrades, Hans is a poet, and the revolution needs poets. Our friends in the Soviet Union understood this, and therefore allowed poets to write even when they did not necessarily write what was expected of them." Addressing Hans, he added, "All the comrades wish to know is whether your poems, especially those describing the toiling in the fields and the citrus, do not perhaps contain a modicum of, shall we say, romanticism, and I daresay even bourgeois romanticism. The orange is after all nothing but a chemical creation, completely material, merchandise that allows the perpetuation of capitalist enslavement. Why, poems such as these could have been written by someone who has nothing to do with the revolution."

Hans was silent for a moment, then said, "This entire dispute is futile and impossible. I came to this country begrudgingly, and if there is a point to my life here it is to fight against all that is evil, and if I have observed such evil I will write about it, even if it cannot be found in the official Party line."

"And yet, the comrades wonder," said the old man, "whether perchance you have developed doubts regarding the revolution during your labor in the orchard, doubts which possibly might undermine the struggle which is so important to you, as it is to all of us."

Hans stood up, emotional, and said, "I have no doubts. But it is difficult. It is difficult here for me, comrades, and you, you are not helping, not at all."

It was still early in the evening and Hans decided to return to Rehovot, though he had planned to spend the night at a friend's house in Tel Aviv. He took the last bus, which clattered along between the sandy hillocks, stopping at the central bus stations of Rishon LeZion and Ness Ziona. It was night when he at last climbed the steps to his small house. He opened the door and heard choked panting and a familiar muttering voice. The light went on in the bedroom and a man bolted out of it, dressed in obvious hurry and holding his shoes in his hand. Nechama was lying in bed, her face flushed, her eyes burning brighter than ever, beautiful, pleading. Hans stood for a while in the doorway, looking at her, at the old student's little orphan who had grown into a woman he no longer knew, then closed the bedroom door and plopped his head down on a pillow by little Yaffa's bed, where she slept soundly. He fell into a troubled sleep. Come morning he left for work, and all that day struck furiously with the hoe, his enemy and beloved.

4.

In 1940, Hans and Nechama left Rehovot and moved to Arnon Street in northern Tel Aviv but saw progressively less of each other.

During the days they placed Yaffa at a daycare center owned by Herman Boneh, a red-faced, businesslike man who took in orphans, foundlings, homeless children. The odd jobs grew scarce, but the words flowed easily from Hans' pen, and he completed a satirical novel inspired by the great Jonathan Swift, about Gulliver's journey to the land of Palina, where he attempts to negotiate peace between the "Palinians" and the "Alinians."

One day, early in the morning, two British sergeants appeared at their door and asked that Hans, who was still bleary-eyed with sleep, to accompany them to the police station, where an officer informed him that he was flagged as "an activist in an illegal political organization," and therefore will be brought to the detainment camp in Mizra and held in administrative detention "until the matter can be settled in court."

For two years Hans remained in the Mizra detainment camp near Akko with his comrades from the Palestinian Communist Party. He made some other friends from the Hagana and the Hebrew resistance. After the grueling work in the orchards, his time in imprisonment was almost pleasant. Occasionally Nechama sent him short letters, accompanied by drawings from little Yaffa. His black notebooks filled with poems, which he would often read to his friends.

When he was released, he returned to the house on Arnon Street. It was noon, and the air was heavy with the heat of August. The rooms were empty, the bed unmade, some coffee mugs sat in the sink. He went to Herman Boneh's daycare center and waded among the children until he spotted Yaffa. She stared at him, astounded, and he approached her and said, "Yaffa, my girl," and she shied away at first from the tall man whose face had become a distant silhouette in her memory. Herman said, "It's Hans, Yaffa'leh, it's your father," and she hugged him, still somewhat suspicious, but his eyes were kind to her.

He chatted with Herman a bit, Yaffa on his lap, and then returned home. Nechama was back from work. He tried to take her in his arms, but she submitted to the hug only briefly, and then sat down and stared at him as she would at a stranger.

"It's over, Hans," she said. "I must ask that you leave now."

He shifted his weight uncomfortably and said, "You know I have no place to go."

"You can sleep in Yaffa's room until you find one," said Nechama.

He did not reply, but looked at her, bewildered and lost like a child. She said, "It was a game, Hans, it was all a game."

"That is not true," Hans objected. "How can you say that?"

She said, "We both wanted to escape, but all we did is build another prison."

Now Hans smiled his warm smile and said, "There, prison – now that is a perfect metaphor, impeccably timed." The eternal flame glinted in Nechama's eyes and she laughed wildly, the laughter he loved so much, sweet and unrestrained. He kissed her as a father might kiss his daughter and left.

He wandered the streets for a while, awash in memories. Images of his journey with Nechama to the land of Palina, the little competition they had, in which the British empire defeated the Russian Revolution in the certificate race, and that day he uncharacteristically lashed out at the Soviet Embassy, asking if the revolution does not want *proletars* from every nation joining it, and the clerks looked at him diligently and wrote something in a black book that appeared from thin air. His body was hungry and empty. He was wearing the same coat he left the camp with that morning and felt like a character from one of those red flyers he would hang as a teenager in the streets of Berlin under the cover of darkness, a child of the revolution, without a home, without a past, his entire existence a nameless future, laden with plump, low-hanging secrets. He sat at a café in Dizengoff Street and scribbled down a poem that had been bumping around in his head his entire time in the camp, shoved it into his coat and went down to the Party branch.

Emil was sitting there by himself, sipping cup after cup of Turkish coffee. He stood up and hugged Hans tightly.

"They let me out today," said Hans.

"I know, they let a few comrades out. And how do you feel?" Emil asked. "Free as a bird?"

Hans said, "I wrote a new poem."

Emil said, "Read it to me now, the comrades will be here soon and none of them are in the mood for poetry."

"It's a poem about Zionism," said Hans, and Emil grew very solemn.

"That's a bad name," he said. "Read quickly."

And Hans read.

A bed of flowers on moist earth / and the air is suffused with toxic fumes/ their colors luminesce, their beauty utter mirth / for as long as the death vapor plumes // thus Zionism grows, under threat, from the obscene / war and pogrom are its fertile ground / they are the core of its existence, its routine / a sick world keeps it healthy and sound // will we allow the poisoned earth / for the lovely flowers that from it sprout? / No, no! We must drain the poison out! // And in its place, in an earth clean of poison / All the nations of the world can grow under the sun / in all shapes and colors they shall bloom as one.

Emil, whose German was excellent, applauded and said, "Beautiful poem, hide it, hide it deep in your coat."

"I don't understand," said Hans, "what is this..."

Emil's face was dour. "Everything's changed while you were away," he said. "The Jews in the Party have lost their minds. There have been rumors about Jews being killed in Europe and they forgot everything, forgot about what caused that war back there, forgot that it was imperialism that started it all. I talk to them and suddenly they are no longer my brothers, suddenly everyone is just looking after their own family in Europe, what has happened to them, like petty bourgeoisie in your little towns. I did not join the Party for this. And this poem of yours, they will not listen, because the poison you write of has seeped into their souls as well."

"And you, what do you think?" asked Hans. "Will you listen?"

"I listen and think to myself," said Emil, "What lovely flower are you talking about, Hans Rosenthal? Zionism is a lovely flower? Zionism is a monster. I listen to your poem and think, Hans Rosenthal is like all the other Jews. In the moment of truth, he will not be at my side, he will be with his people, in the moment of truth we will come apart, and that moment has come now, and you must decide what side you are on! This poem will not save you, Hans."

People were coming into the room, now, whom Hans recognized, but seemed grim and abject after the two years he had spent apart from them. They greeted him, sat in two separate groups and hardly spoke at all among themselves until the clarification ceremony began, smelling of ancient courthouses. One after the other they spoke, hard words, little gravel-stones. Hans got up and left with no intention of returning.

That entire week, Hans Rosenthal sought out a room to stay in and work to subsist on, and the memory of the detainment camp faded and dimmed. He wandered the small towns, read little ads pinned to the fronts of houses and found a nice room for rent in the agricultural colony of Kfar Saba, surrounded by orchards, in the home of a childless couple. He used to sit at the café by the orchards, and the poems wrote themselves. Once, early in the evening, after he had been wandering the orchards for a while, he sat down and wrote a poem that astounded and amazed him, and then he read it again and again, and laughed a bit, unnerved, and buried it deep in the drawer by his bed.

5.

Europe was plunged into blood and fire, but in Palestine the opposing factions continued warring among themselves, each struggling in their own way against the British rule. The Palestinian Communist Party split into a Jewish party and an Arab party. Hans no longer felt the absence of the nightly discussions at the Party branch. From his seat in Kfar Saba those matters seemed like empty words, insubstantial, spoken by fruitless idlers.

On the days when he could find no work in the orchards, he would go to an obscure library where he had found a cache of German books. There he would avidly, fervently read anthologies of the converted Jew Heinrich Heine, *Ethics* and other writings by the outcast Jew Baruch Spinoza, and the holy books, the dim memories of which had only recently returned to him. Along with them, after many years of oblivion, the image of his father returned to him, Louis Rosenthal, who died in the prime of his life from diabetes, standing in the synagogue wrapped in a great white tallit, singing hazzanic verses. He read again in the Communist Manifesto, which he knew almost by heart and loved every line and every letter in it. He joyfully discovered the book 'What Is to Be Done?' by comrade Vladimir Ilyich Lenin, in which the instigator of the revolution elaborated on the various strategies by which Communism shall emerge victorious in Europe and all over the world.

During the long winter days, when the workers were sent home, Hans sat with the landlady, a restless and attractive woman, drinking tea and talking on hard fabric couches that inched closer and closer to one another until their legs were touching, and more than touching. After several weeks of this they found themselves entwined in the couple's queen-sized bed. She was a soft, hungry woman and Hans a warm and love-starved man. Sometimes at night she would sneak into his bed, and when he marveled at her audacity she said, "Don't worry, he knows that if I am happy, he is happy as well." The rumor of the house in which such wanton activity was underway quickly spread around little rural Kfar Saba.

Every few weeks Hans would visit his daughter Yaffa in Herman Boneh's daycare, and then visit his mother Gertrude on Yehoash Street, two houses away from the daycare center. Gertrude would spear Hans with her eagle eyes and sigh, and he would say, "I have a good life, Mother."

Lotte Freyer, whose official Israeli name was Leah, though none of her friends ever used it, had recently left Kibbutz Givat HaShlosha and was working as a nanny at Herman Boneh's day-care center. After Hans would spend some time playing with little Yaffa, he would stay and talk with Lotte, who was already looking forward to his visits. They would talk at length, on and on until Herman would roar at her, "Lottchen, work now, flirt later," and Hans would head back to Kfar Saba, where the landlords were expecting him for dinner and nighttime promiscuity.

The font of Hans' poetry seemed as though it would never run dry, and the days he spent reading in the German library bore poems that no longer spoke of hoes and lemons, nor of poisoned flowers, but led a lengthy, passionate and astonishing conversation with those other Jews, Heine and Spinoza, which grew evermore distant from the hated, miserly Jew, bound in stale tradition. These poems remained unseen and unheard and they formed into tall stacks in his drawer, pages upon pages of galloping lines in sharp, eloquent script, a hidden treasure perhaps never to be unearthed.

On one of his visits to Tel Aviv, as he was chatting as usual with Lotte Freyer at the daycare center, he noticed a man standing in the gate, about sixty, listless, looking at the children with befuddled eyes. Lotte approached him and affectionately greeted him, "Ach, Uncle Erich, it is good to see you, perhaps you'd like something to eat, Hans, let me introduce you, this is my uncle, Erich Freyer."

Erich huffed and said, "Well, I took three buses."

"How are Käthe and Albert?" asked Lotte.

"They are well," Erich said, his voice low, "but Käthe says I should leave there, what do you think of that, Lottchen?"

"Perhaps you really should find something nearby," said Lotte. "It might be good for you."

Erich sat down, weary. Hans asked him where he was from and Erich said, "Kiryat Bialik, I am staying there with my sister."

Hans said, "No, from where did you come to Palestine."

Erich's lip trembled and his eyes grew moist. Hans immediately regretted bothering this man he did not know, for whom the burden of life was clearly so great.

"Well," said Erich, "I have a small family in Glauchau. Do you know where Glauchau is?"

Hans said, "Certainly, I used to go there often for work, I sold paintings there."

Erich said, "That is good, well and good, because I know

nothing of Glauchau, and have never been there."

Hans asked, "Then, where did you come from?"

"I come from Stettin, on the Oder," Erich said emotionally, his eyes sparkling. "It is where I spent my childhood. And you, young man, have you ever been to Stettin?"

Glowing, Hans held the old man's trembling hand and said, "What do you mean, have I been there? I was born in Stettin, just like you, born on Turnerstraße, and then we moved to Pestalozz-istraße, and perhaps you knew my father, Louis Rosenthal, the community clerk?"

Erich shook his head skeptically, but the spark glinting in his eye ignited. Lotte, who had gone to calm a wailing child, returned to them, and Hans told her, "Lotte, he is from Stettin, what do you say to that?"

"Of course," Lotte laughed. "Was there ever a doubt in your mind?"

They dined on mashed potatoes laden with fried onion and some overcooked chicken breasts. Hans stood up to leave and said, "So, are you looking for a place around here?"

"My sister says that would be best for everyone," said Erich. "I've been staying with them for six years now, ever since I came to Palestine. A man my age, you know, it is very hard to start over."

"I know," said Hans, "it is hard when you are younger, as well."

"It is indescribably hard," said Erich. "And Käthe, my sister, it is hard with her, as well."

Erich was very pale, now. He began to cry nervously, some-what childishly, saying, "There is nothing left, nothing left for me, and I have a child, Hans, a daughter named Yvonne, and I haven't seen my wife, Hilde, her name is Hilde Freyer, I haven't seen her in eight years, and I do not know that I ever will."

Awkwardly, Hans said, "We all have our troubles, I also have a daughter and I only see her once every couple of weeks, and my wife lives just around the corner here, but she is no longer with me."

Erich calmed a bit and said, "But you are a young man with your whole future ahead of you, and Käthe, my sister, she says that I must leave, and I think to myself, she is absolutely right, Erich Freyer has become a millstone around her neck, but where can he go, an old man like me whose life has ended long ago."

Hans composed himself now, and said, "I'll look after you. There is a place in Kfar Saba for people like you." Erich mumbled something in gratitude, bid farewell to Hans and Lotte who were looking at him worriedly, and left, vanishing around the corner.

6.

One night, in May of 1944, Lotte Freyer sat among friends from the Jewish faction of the Communist Party in a small apartment in Tel Aviv. They discussed matters of great importance, but unlike the dreary, somber discussions on the Palestinian Communist Party, the dialogue here was lively and open. They spoke of the future of the Hebrew settlement in light of the notion of the Jewish state which had been growing more popular, a matter which concerned the group, but in which certain advantages could also be found, as long as the new state be founded on principles of justice and equality.

Hans Rosenthal, who had begun to long for the art of his youth and once more sought a place where his poems would be heard, found people after his own heart here. Kfar Saba seemed provincial and faraway, now, and his quaint love triangle had lost its charm. He worked in various odd jobs in the British military and occasionally came to the Party meetings, where he slowly grew to love the people there, who in turn grew to love him. And on that particular night he had come as well, but this time went straight to Lotte Freyer and said, "I am looking for you." Her face shone brightly, and they remained there for a while, listening, and then he offered to escort her to her small room on HaYarkon Street. The sea wind blew through them and they made love as if they were born entwined, and they knew that their love is right and whole and will never be extinguished.

Later Hans raised warm, pleading eyes at Lotte and said, "Lotte, my love, let us return to Germany together."

Lotte laughed and said, "What are you thinking." A shadow passed over her eyes, and perhaps a stab of longing, and they did not speak of it again.

Hans and Lotte were married on an afternoon, in tandem with Eli and Rega, a couple of friends from the Party gang, in a brief ceremony that Lotte attended already very much pregnant, passing the single ring between the two couples. They found, with great difficulty, a room for rent in an apartment owned by a converted Arab, at the very edge of HaTikva neighborhood in South Tel Aviv. The Great War had ended. The scattered Jews of Palestine began to seek out their lost kin, and there was not a household that did not suffer many deaths. No news had come of the fates of Martin and Trude Hendelson, but Freyers are not in the habit of false hope. Metta, Hans' sister, who escaped the extermination camps by the skin of her teeth after her pride had flung her back into Germany during the reign of terror, arrived by circuitous means to Shanghai, where she married a seafaring Jewish waiter by the name of Herbert. Along with their son, Ronny, she eventually returned to the land of the Asiats.

On November 7, 1945, about six months after the great war had ended, on the 28th anniversary of the Communist Revolution, I came into the world and was named Reuven, a name I did not like, and everyone around me managed to bypass through various nicknames. Following the German pronunciation, I was nicknamed Rubi, with a B, and if it weren't for pure chance it would have been my name to this day. Along with my parents, Hans and Lotte, the Party's favorite new lovebirds, I moved to a small shack on Pinsker Street, surrounded by a fallow field, other shacks and mounds of rubble, in which people lived and children grew. The members of the Tel Aviv branch of the "Hebrew Communists" would often congregate in this shack, an offshoot of the Party led by Eliezer Preminger, nicknamed "Yossi" after his name back in the days of the Communist underground, who later became a member of the Israeli Knesset. I was a yellow-haired baby, and to this day the shards of memory still glint in my mind, of cheerful voices, a commotion of people surrounding the crib in which I stood and listened to animated discussions about the future of the revolution and the state of the Hebrew worker.

Father found a job in a small power plant and the font of his poems dried out, perhaps for a while, perhaps indefinitely. He would read his previous poems to the gang, nearly all of whom spoke German. His poems were dearly loved, and compiled into a small German book titled *Pardess* the Hebrew word for "orchard," which had seeped into the German poems along with her sisters, such as *"pardessan,"* "citrus grower." Father never wrote in

Hebrew, and I never heard him speak it. All around me were German-speakers, and that language, musical, decisive, trickled into my child's thoughts and resides there to this day, awoken with surprising vigor whenever I am back among German-speakers.

I loved Father with every fiber of my being, a love of immeasurable magnitude. When I was three years old, I saw him walking up to me from afar. I ran down the path of broken tiles leading from the shack to the street corner, and in one hand he held that which I wanted more than anything, a red tricycle, and with the other hand he hugged me tightly, and I hugged him back, and did not leave the seat of my tricycle for many days.

My Aunt Lotte lived across the street, this time separately from Grandma Gertrude, whom we would visit occasionally in her house on Yehoash Street, surrounded by fruit trees. When we heard the thunder or bombs or war sirens, Mother would pick me up and take me to Aunt Lotte's shelter, where we sat crowded with other men and women and children I did not know, and when the noise had passed we returned to our shack.

The Freyers were scattered all over Palestine. Michal and Susi, Kurt's daughters, started a kibbutz in the Hula Valley named Kfar Szold, after the Israeli leader of the Zionist Youth Aliyah. Kurt and Anna tried to make an independent living in the town of Gedera, but financial difficulties eventually led them to join their daughters on the kibbutz. Käthe Baer found it hard to endure life with her brother Erich, who grew more despondent and introverted every day. He would sit in the house for hours, staring at nothing, or aimlessly wandered the paths of Kiryat Bialik, or drifted among family members in the north and south, a cloak of misery shadowing every aspect of his gait, his deeply lined face, the imploring pain in his eyes.

One spring day in 1945, Käthe finally acted and drove up to the settlements of the Sharon, where she knew several German Jews who had set up farms there. She told two friends from Magdiel the tale of her brother and her predicament and they agreed to provide him with a room and food in exchange for help on the farm.

It was evening by the time she returned to Kiryat Bialik. Albert and Erich were drinking coffee with milk in the little orchard behind the house. Erich was unusually spirited – giddy, even.

"Well," said Albert, "Erich received a letter from Glauchau, and guess who sent it?"

"Ach, Albert, you and your nonsense," chided Käthe.

"The young lady who sent it," said Albert, "is none other than Yvonne Freyer, and she tells that he has a lovely little granddaughter, already walking and talking!"

Erich blushed and sipped his coffee, and Käthe said, "Why, Erich, that is wonderful, what is her name?"

"Martina," said Erich, "Martina Freyer, what do you say to that, Käthe?"

"Well, then, Erich, I suppose you would welcome yet some more news," said Käthe. Erich looked at her anxiously, and she told him about the new life waiting for him in Magdiel. He began pacing excitedly up and down the small apartment, and then disappeared off to a long stroll, returning long after the sun had set. The next day he got up and packed his suitcase and left for the bus station.

Erich had some lovely days in Magdiel. In the mornings he would work vigorously around the farm as if he were a young man, and in the evenings he sat with his new family and told them stories about his life in Germany, his motherland and theirs.

At once, with Promethean resolve, he had cast off the cloak of misery. A year later he rented a room in the nearby town of Ramatayim, and every morning at six he set out on foot on the path leading to the settlement, his pack full of morning newspapers that he distributed among the houses. With a mixture of satisfaction and astonishment, the Freyers told one another that Erich had been reborn.

7.

No rest came for the Hebrew Communists. The new state was established and the hated Ben-Gurion, who many years before had actively sought to remove the Palestinian Communist Party from the *Histadrut*, was now prime minister. On November 7, the group convened in Hans and Lotte's shack to mark the revolution's 32nd anniversary as well as little Rubi's fourth birthday. Samuel Ettinger was there, who later became a prominent history professor, and Haim Gissis, who was a wise scholar, and Asia and Dutzi Zur who were very close to Lotte and Hans, and Eli and Rega Levi, and Walter Grab, who sold purses in a small shop on Allenby Street and knew entire history books by heart, and, after he was accidentally discovered by Professor Zvi Yavetz, became a world renowned scholar in German history.

People came to the shack by foot, from the streets of Tel Aviv which were no longer so small, but mostly empty of vehicle traffic and draped in silence. In the wee hours of night, the rustling water of the Zina Dizengoff fountain, the heart of the city, could be heard from the shack, and the wind blew in from Mahlul

neighborhood and the Muslim cemetery. The house was routine-
ly filled with the sounds of speech and chatter and I, no longer
a golden-haired infant but a dark-haired, skinny boy, fell sound
asleep during my own birthday party, an infant's sleep.

Hans summoned the attention of the guests. His only book of
poetry had been published five years before. After that he dab-
bled in journalism, occasionally writing for some little-known
Austrian paper, and published stories about the life of the unem-
ployed in the Hebrew Communist paper. This time, said Hans,
he wishes to read a few poems that he had written back in 1943
and shown to no one, apart from one poem he read to Emil from
the Palestinian Communist Party, but that was around the time
of the great divide and he felt the time was not right.

Hans opened a chest drawer in the corner of the shack and
took out a stack of pages which had already begun to crumble
and read slowly, line after line, the entire collection of poems,
Hans Rosenthal's Jewish sonnets.

I am a Jew, and a Jew was my father / But I never took
interest in any of that stuff / The Bible and God's voice I've
neglected to honor / Germany had given me more than
enough / and along came Hitler, and my world fell to destruction / To be a Jew became my fate, and with that fate I
struggled / From my people's fruit a kernel of truth I rustled
/ I threw away the shell which had no function // I saw then
how the wicked, prideful tongue / of nationalists and swin-
dlers and priests / has into hate and viciousness the name
of Judaism flung // And today I say I am a Jew and feel no
shame / My Judaism is no fate, and in its name / I declare
war on all forces of darkness and their claim.

Silence fell. Mother was stunned. Hans looked at their guests, abashed, feeling that perhaps, once again, the time is not yet right, that perhaps he had been misunderstood. But he read more, on and on he read and the astonishment surrounding him grew thicker. He wrote of Heinrich Heine who, like Hans, was a Jew who left the shell but returned to the kernel, and of Baruch Spinoza, who refused to leave spirit and truth in the hands of the priests and holy books. He read a poem about the binding of Isaac, whose ultimate victims were Hagar and Ishmael, and another about the Maccabees, and the heroism of Betar, and of Vilna and Warsaw, from which news about the horrors of the Holocaust had already begun to trickle in during the poems' writing, and finally a poem about the ghetto walls.

"This one is a bit long," he said. "I hope you don't find it tedious," but around him he saw inquisitive, expectant faces.

The Ghetto walls were erected around us as borders / they separate us from the rest of the world / Guards are watching us, posted at all corners / lest we try to escape, we are always observed // Behind the walls we were born, and within them found glory / We did not despair, though leave we could not / and the walls that were built from the rock of the quarry / were transformed into walls of thought.

"You wrote this six years ago, Hans," said Haim after Hans was finished reading. "And do you stand behind what you wrote, today?"

"Why would I not?" asked Hans.

"These poems are fairly nationalist," said Eli, "perhaps even religious – I always though you could not be further away from that. You more than all of us."

Hans blushed and retreated into himself. Walter said, "This is not a criticism, Hans, poetry takes us to all sorts of places."

But Hans shook his head and said, "No, no, it isn't like that, it is something else entirely. I abhorred Judaism, I abhorred everything about it, but when the Party dissolved I realized that I had taken the easy way out, that I had not grasped this abhorrence and am therefore stuck with it, neither swallowing not vomiting."

The group fell silent and so did Hans, and the conversation seemed to have run its course, but then, Mother's eyes widening in bewilderment, he said, "My father was a petty clerk in the Stettin community offices, I do not even know what it was he did there, exactly, one of Rabbi Heiman Vogelstein's many sycophants, a hazzan with the voice of an angel who was allowed to rise to the podium and sing only when the chief hazzan was kind enough to fall ill, and he guzzled down these crumbs, and he was grateful. At home he sat and watched like a pining boy as Mother prepared that fatty, kosher food I could not stand, and every time I brought a book home that was not a holy book he would make a face. We had nothing in common. His world was seeped in the heat and sweat of the synagogue at prayer time, in the conspiracies the community wallowed in. I hated being at home, I hated being outside. I hated my childhood. And I never knew why."

Some members of the group nodded. Perhaps the story was not unlike their own memories of home. Mother looked at him and her eyes were longing and wise.

"When I met my Communist comrades in Berlin," Hans said, "it was a moment of elation, of pure joy, of redemption at long last. The walls crumbled, no more nations, no more my-god-versus-your-god, no more rich families everyone grovels before, begging for charity, falling over themselves to sit as close to them as possible in the synagogue. You know, I wanted to live in Soviet Russia, to be a part of the revolution, of a world without walls, without an upper class and a lower class, but they did not want me. Imagine that."

Preminger looked at Hans, smiling astutely, and asked, "Indeed, and yet, what happened when the party dissolved, Hans? What happened then?"

"I am not sure how to phrase this, exactly," said Hans. The group observed him, inquisitive. He began talking, slow, measured sentences. Mother looked at him and her face had never been more radiant.

"For the first time," Hans intoned, "for the first time I went into my hatred rather than running from it. I wanted to fathom it, to study it. It was hard. So hard. For me, to write in a poem 'I am a Jew' rather than 'I am a human being' or 'I am an orchard worker' was like drilling a tunnel through a mountain. My hand shook. Twenty times I started writing, then erased it and started over."

Now Hans grew confident and his words filled the shack and washed over the small crowd. "When I finished writing the sonnets, I was so happy. Everything became clear. One cannot run from oneself. A Jew cannot run from his Judaism because it will follow him anywhere, just as a German cannot run from his German-ness, for he is suffused in it, his skin and his flesh."

Walter looked at Hans, smiled slightly and said, "Now, it isn't that simple, Hans, of course it is never that simple." Hans looked at him curiously and Walter added, "The problem, Hans, is that one cannot separate the Jew from the German, that is the whole problem, that they are inseparable."

"You've just said something truly amazing, Walter," said Hans, "and so I'd like to share something with you that I have ever told anyone, from my days in Kfar Saba, when I wrote the sonnets. I used to go out for a stroll in the evenings, then, after sunset, through the orchards. On one of those days, perhaps it was the chill that reminded me of the cool Berlin air in the end of summer, perhaps the orchard seemed to me like one of the forests that surrounded Stettin, where I would escape as a boy, but I was suddenly gripped by such longing. I went to a café in Kfar Saba and wrote a poem that I have never read to this day, not to anyone, because I was ashamed. I have it here. I will read it now, and please, do not be angry."

The group looked at Hans curiously and affectionately. He fished a folded sheet of paper from a closet standing in the yard of the shack. Mother laughed and said, "You managed to keep it from me, too, you sneaky man. What other secrets are you hiding?" Everyone laughed, but Hans looked at them, and his eyes were filled with shame, and they settled down. He then read, in a clear, sharp voice.

Will I ever see Germany / My country, my beloved / I shall sail there rowing dream-oars / a free nation shall greet me to her shores // A red army is beating her now / the day approaches, the goal is nigh / To my country peace will find its way / with it grows the yearning to return to her someday / for only when Germany is free and mended / can my exile in this foreign country truly be ended / and the blood of my brothers, slaughtered on her land / between me and my beloved cannot stand.

Silence filled the shack. Preminger shook his head. "You are lucky," he said, "to have failed to follow your heart not once, but twice, or there would have been nothing left of you."

They all stared at him, perplexed, and brokenly, his voice an odd mixture of confidence and panic, "You know perfectly well what the Germans did to the Jews and to all of humanity, and I know today what the Communists did in the Soviet Union, and you mustn't think the two are so different."

At this several members of the group, Hans among them, looked at Preminger disapprovingly.

"We have been deceived," said Preminger. "Our revolution has been taken over by villains. They killed millions of innocent people, tens of millions. Always, they have been doing this, and now as well. They persecute the Jews, the intellectuals. The KGB controls the Union, and you, Hans, you would not survive a month there."

"What are you talking about?" said Izhak, shaking with fury, "This is propaganda, you've not witnessed any of this with your own eyes."

"I know," said Preminger, "I heard more and more, and would not believe it, but now I know for sure, and the truth shall be known, it cannot be buried, not ever."

Preminger fell silent and none of the others answered his claims, but a tuned ear could hear a thin sigh of relief rising into the air. Great faith could empower the weary, make them lighter, propel them into the heavens, but here, among the Hebrew Communists, faith itself had been growing weary for some time, the patches holding it together were unraveling, and now finally succumbed, its contents spilled out with a resounding silence. A sound rang through the stillness: the crying four-year-old Rubi, the child of the revolution born on its day of celebration, and now wakened by the sudden silence in the room. His crying prompted sudden laughter among the group, a drawn-out, thunderous laughter which spilled out of the small shack on Pinsker Street, up Bograshov Street, over oceans and lakes, and according to rumor echoed all the way past the thick walls of the Kremlin.

The group dispersed, each to their own home, and Lotte said, "Hans, how could you keep these sonnets a secret from me?"

He said, "I was a bit ashamed. What did you think?"

She said, "I don't know, perhaps you've gone too far. But I accept it."

"I wouldn't write something like that today," said Hans, "but back then it sounded truer."

And Lotte said, "You've not written in a while."

Hans gazed at her and held her hand and said, "Poetry comes from a tempest, Lotte, from anxiety, and now that we have each other, and Rubi, and the gang, everything is coming along, perhaps coming along too well, and sometimes I feel that my role here is done, that I have nothing more left to say."

"Your role is only beginning," said Lotte. He looked at her questioningly and she placed his hand on her belly and said, "This summer Rubi will get a brother, or a sister – which do you prefer?"

They squeezed each other's hand like lovesick adolescents. Hans laughed and cried and said, "We have a good life, Lotte, we have such a good life."

8.

In the final days of 1949 Hans went out by the shack to get some air after Saturday's lunch and vomited his meal. When he lay down to rest a bit, his torso was racked by violent, repetitive spasms. The next morning, he could not get up from bed, and blood spotted the little toilet. Mother called one of her party friends and together they rushed Hans to Beilinson Hospital in Petah Tikvah, where he was kept for rest and observation.

The doctors quickly discovered that the patient Hans Rosenthal was suffering from colon cancer and told his wife. After various treatments they decided to perform an operation, as a colonoscopy that had scoured his innards revealed a "concave tumor with a stiff base attached to the dorsal wall of the rectum." Many years later I explored the linguistic environment of the Hebrew word *se'et*, "tumor," and found it in Leviticus: "When a man shall have in the skin of his flesh a rising, a scab, or bright spot." I found it relates to the gerund *laset*, "to bear" or "to carry," from Deuteronomy: "You are too heavy a burden for me to carry alone," and its cousin, *shet*, derives from *Sho'a*, "Holocaust." But for the doctors it was merely a signifier, marking Father as the owner of a malignant growth that must be surgically removed. The operation was performed in two phases. The medical report of "Hans Rosenthal, profession: menial laborer," the first operation was deemed a success, and "recovery proceeded without complications." The second phase was carried out two weeks later, and again a satisfactory recovery was reported, and "the perineal wound healed relatively quickly." And indeed Father came home, and I knew nothing of his pain. Despite his illness the house was not filled with the stench of medication and secretive whispers.

The new baby was growing in my mother's womb, and I knew nothing of its existence either, or perhaps I did not want to know. Life grew and life diminished side by side. The house was in turmoil, but I had no part in it. Nor could I know of the struggle waged over the baby's future existence. Aunt Lotte, apparently serving as Grandma Gertrude's emissary, spoke to Mother and tried to explain to her how hard it would be to raise a baby with no profession and no provider. Father eventually prevailed, saying, whatever happens, keep it.

On June 30, 1950, the second medical report read "P. Hans Rosenthal was brought urgently to the hospital exhibiting paralysis of the lower limbs. Fever was fluctuating over 39°C. His general condition is poor. Treating physicians suspect metastasis in the spinal cord."

After a while, the severity of his condition seemed to relent a bit, and on July 9, in the morning, he was brought back home. We were living in a two-room basement apartment on Israelis Street in Tel Aviv. Father lay in the bed he and Mother shared, his face sallow and a bewildered light not yet extinguished from his eyes. Mother was practical, determined, self-involved. I was at Herman Boneh's daycare, like I always was. Baby Gideon, born five days before, was asleep in his crib, and his birth, like his father's waning life, passed with a thin, gentle silence. A baby like any other baby, he slept, woke up fussing, suckled a bit and fell back asleep.

Mother went to bring some things from Mr. Pupko's grocery store, which smelled of herring and cucumbers, and the counter was dusted with flour powder from the dark bread that the neighborhood women bought in halves, haggling in Yiddish. She returned with half a loaf, a glass bottle full of milk and a pack of margarine. Hans was sprawled in bed, occasionally letting out pained moans, and Mother said, "But you must be a little bit better? Otherwise they wouldn't send you home."

Hans said, "A little bit better."

Mother looked at Gideon and said, "He is a calm baby, like Rubi was."

Gideon woke up screaming in mockery of this premature praise. Mother picked him up and rocked him, stroked his golden head, and brought him over to Hans. Hans smiled, but his face was emaciated and his smile bitter and fragmented.

"Lie down, Hans," she said, "Lie down, now. You'll have plenty of opportunities to hold him."

Hans looked at her and sobbed a bit, a thin, gentle sob, and Mother said, "No, not now, just don't, Hans, please don't."

But he would not stop, and he said, "We had a good life."

Mother placed Gideon back in his crib, went to the kitchen, rummaged through the cupboard and poured some boiling water into a teacup. In the water she placed a perforated spoon-like instrument, shaped like an egg, full of black tea leaves. Her eyes were dry, but for a single moment her body was overtaken by that forsaken, vile sensation that dishevels the blood. A wild fury gripped her, nearly causing her to drop the cup to the black-and-yellow tiles of the kitchen floor, and she screamed in German into the bowels of the sink, "Oh God, oh cursed God," and returned to the bedroom carrying the hot cup of tea. Hans lay there, looking at her helplessly, moaning softly, tears still clinging to his eyes. The crying had faded, risen like vapor into the heavens.

Mother heard the ringing of the ice cart and hurried outside.

A short ice-salesman in long khakis came down after her, carrying a square, dripping block of ice, and placed it in the ice
box that stood in the small foyer. Outside an onerous July heat
stood in the air. The memory of the snow that fell on Tel Aviv in
the winter had long faded, but the dim basement apartment was
slightly cooler than the hot wind of the street.

Gideon was sleeping soundly, but woke when Hans let out a
broken, merciless moan, his entire body convulsing. "*Ich kann
nicht mehr,*" he said, "I can't anymore, Lottchen," and tried to rise
from his bed.

Doctor Siegfried Steckelmacher, the dedicated physician from
Ramot HaShavim, came to see Hans. He spoke to Mother in a
low voice and immediately ran down the street and asked the
pharmacist on the corner to urgently use his phone.

"You need to go back to the hospital," Mother said, "maybe
this was a mistake."

Hans said, "No, I wanted this, truly I did."

After a while a white ambulance arrived at Israelis Street, which
was otherwise empty of vehicles. Two paramedics in white uniforms came out of the ambulance and ran to the basement. One
of them supported Hans from under his upper back and the other
one held his arm. They rose slowly from the basement apartment
and marched down the street as if carrying a man crucified. After
them came Doctor Siegfried Steckelmacher, and Mother. Baby
Gideon was left alone in the basement, still sleeping soundly, his
face illuminated by the dusty beams of light shining in from the
window. The ambulance went on its way, to Father's dwelling
place during those last few months, the Beilinson Hospital in
Petah Tikva.

Mother went back down to the basement and did not look

at the baby. She sat on the sofa where I lay nestled in her arms during the many nights in which Father lay in a cold, hard hospital bed, and yearned for the tears, but they would not come.

In the afternoon I came back from Herman Boneh's daycare. I found Mother troubled, exhausted. She said nothing when I arrived. And I did not know that Father was here today. That Father had come to say goodbye.

CHAPTER EIGHT: GIDI

1.

The basement apartment that Mother, Gidi and I shared was like many other apartments in Tel Aviv, little-big apartments, their tiny space divided by many walls so as to provide rooms aplenty, a little dining room, and the corridor leading to all the rooms, known as a "hall." Our hall was three paces long, but it had room for a humble coat closet, a hat stand, and an antique chest, which back then had been estimated at over a century old, and was passed down from Freyer to Freyer just like the Tale of the Egg Miracle. Thick pink duvets were stored in it during the summer, and it was covered with vases, little figurines and crocheted doilies.

Left of the hall there was a glass door. Behind the door was a room whose door led outside, to the low front yard shared with the rest of the building, to the dumpsters where the residents emptied the day's waste. Hungry cats lurked there for each new delivery, and at night yowled lasciviously. And there was a closet in that room, as well, and two beds.

Right of the hall the door opened into the living room. Above our head, nearly aligned with the ceiling, people would enter and exit the building, at times peeking curiously through the elongated window at their feet. In the center of the hall, in the corner between Mother's bedroom to our room, there was another door, a gateway into the mystery of the basement, which was not ours but merely entrusted to our care. We nearly never opened the door, and when we did there was a brick wall there that you had to squirm around to enter a dark, dusty space, crammed with scraps and debris, broken bits of wood, furniture that had been tossed in there during the apartment's several decades of existence, all covered in a thick layer of dust. Another brick wall was erected under the high, narrow window leading from the basement out to the entrance path, and still a thin beam of sunlight always found its way in, carrying a million specks of glimmering dust in its wake.

At night the living room became Mother's bedroom. There I lay on a small bed in the middle of the room, with no wall to cling to, during the first months after Father's death, after I had been banished from my mother's bed, and in my place, in that tender heart of warmth, lay the little newborn prince that had usurped me. Mother had decreed there was no room in her bed for two of us. At night, a horde of Indians came charging at the door of the apartment. They pounded at the door with the butts of their sharp spears, and I explained to Mother that they are about to break in, and she must immediately hand over the new baby to them, lest we both suffer a gruesome fate. To this day I am haunted by vicious specters whenever I see a baby, howling battle-cries and the clashing of spears, give it away, hurt it, toss it out the window.

Father was gone and no one would speak of him. A terrible secret had settled over the house, who had taken Father away, what were the motives for this heinous crime, and how, in place of the man I loved so much, was there now a chubby new baby, who might be in cahoots with the bandits? There was only one way to solve the riddle, to eradicate the curse and to reclaim my own stolen dignity, and that was to bring a new man to the house. The dream of Father himself returning and making everything right again was too sweet, too painful, forbidden. There was a man who for a time came in the evenings and spent time with us before we went to bed. I had deemed him a worthy candidate, and then he disappeared, too. The house was standing on three feet and threatening to tumble down at any moment, and nobody cared.

We went to visit Grandma Gertrude nearly every week. She was living in Ramat Gan then, with her daughter Lotte, who had grown so old by her side that it was difficult at times to know who of them was mother and who the daughter. Gertrude's reputation preceded her into the green neighborhood between Herzl and Bialik Streets, where people lived beside tree-shadowed foot-paths, and upon her arrival she started a German Scrabble club. We would drink tea in crystal cups and Grandma Gertrude tried in vain to instruct me in the delicate art of shoelace-tying. The portrait of a stern-looking, monocled man hung on the wall, and I decided that he was none other than Grandpa Louis, who I discovered had died of diabetes a few years before the invention of the insulin shot. Sometimes we would visit Nechama, my sister Yaffa's cheerful and affectionate mother. She lived alone in a shack in Nordiya, which seemed to me like a kind of magical gnome village, glittering with tiny lights. She was at our house often, as well.

Mother quickly acquired a new profession: Social worker. Every morning she rushed to drop me off at kindergarten, and little Gidi, who had just started sprouting princely golden curls, at Golda the nanny's place on Ben-Yehuda Street. From there she would run off somewhere, and return in the afternoon, restless and fervent. I went to first grade at Har-Nevo. Mother would go with me on the number 62 Bus, ask the driver to wait a moment at the bus station in front of the school, quickly walk me across the street, and get back on the bus. In school I found a girlfriend, and we would sit and kiss each other during break time as the other children stared at us and laughed. After school I would usually go to her house and come evening I would return to the riddle-house. Mother was already busy making dinner, little Gidi waddled between the rooms. There was no one to talk to, and I did not know how to ask.

Then, along came Uncle Erich.

He was around seventy at the time. He lived in a red house, a sort of windowless tin shack in the heart of Ramatayim, and on Fridays he would come to visit. Gidi and I were shunted to Mother's room, and he got ours. Every Saturday we would visit the zoo: Uncle Erich, pleasant, quiet, determined in his new role; Gidi, the crown prince who had by now begun to gain my disgruntled affection; and me, a skinny boy in shorts pulled up as far as they would go and a plaid shirt. We walked slowly, the rhythm of children and old men, measuring Israelis Street which had all of a dozen houses on each side, cutting through Gordon Street into the murky Reines Street, then walk for a while in the scarce shade of the trees of Kakal Boulevard, past the guard that we had nicknamed "The Fat Zoo Man," who stood there every Saturday, nodding to the visitors as they came and again upon their departure. Mother was waiting for us with lunch, of which the crowning jewel was the Hollandaise sauce served on a pile of rice and a white chicken leg. Hazzanic verses would play from the radio from the second-story window above our porch, letting us know it is two o'clock.

Uncle Erich was the perfect solution to the riddle. He could be loved like a father without him even having tried to become one, without Father's ghost suddenly popping up to protest. He spoke only German, and there was something feminine about the way he walked. He would talk to Mother eagerly, at length, but I was swiftly losing my German, and so he hardly ever spoke with me, opting instead for a shy, eternal smile. He often imparted lessons, with manners being a favorite subject of his. The most important of these was The Pencil Lesson. A pencil in German is, exhaustingly, *ein bleistift* – a "lead pin." In order to ask for a pencil, according to Uncle Erich, one must recite a long, courtesy-laced petition, which was forever imprinted on my mind, and Gidi's, and any child in the family who ever had the fortune of asking him for something: *"Bitte, lieber Onkel Erich, sei so gut und gib mir einen bleistift."* Please, beloved Uncle Erich, be so good as to give me a pencil. If I had known, at the time, to fathom the inner workings of a grown-up's soul, I would have noticed the glint in Erich's eyes as he listened to the weekly recitation of The Pencil Litany; a fleeting, invaluably precious glint of happiness.

2.

Every year in the beginning of spring the three of us, Mother, Gidi and I, went to visit Kibbutz Kfar Szold, in the Galilee. It was a five-hour drive, with the bus stopping briefly at Hadera, Afula and Tiberias, from which the bus wove up along the meandering road rising from the Sea of Galilee. After that we would take another bus at the Kiryat Shmona station, which carried us among small villages. At the very end of the road, between eucalyptus trees and huge white wildflowers, at the foot of the Bashan Range, the bus panted and weaved its way into Kibbutz Kfar Szold, which dipped in the misty heat of the Hula Valley and smelled precisely like spring.

In Kfar Szold our distant little cluster from the Tel Aviv fringe reunited with the larger family. My mother's sister was there, Minchen, who in Israel was called Michal, and her husband Shim'on Stern, who was a tall, posh man, a renowned educator in The United Kibbutz Movement. My Aunt Susi lived there too, the younger Freyer sister, with her husband Moshe Grünfeld, a musician who was a source of great personal pride to me, having composed a song that became famous throughout the Palmach and the youth movements: "Kfar Szold Will Be a Great Kibbutz Tomorrow." A plethora of cousins waited for me there, each of them like a sibling to me, among them Susi and Moshe's Dina, innocent and beautiful, whom I loved a true love that has not faded to this day.

In the afternoon the three of us went to Grandpa Kurt and Grandma Anna's house. They used to live in a Swedish shed placed on wooden stilts, and only many years later they moved to a small stone house, with a loquat tree growing in the yard, ripening toward our arrival in spring. Kurt would look at me and Gidi through his large glasses, sometimes smiling, sometimes laughing his low, humming chuckle. The walls of Kurt and Anna's little house were laden with books, like the shelved walls of books in the homes of religious scholars, but they weren't Talmud and adjudicators and Maimonides, but Goethe and Schiller and Heine and Thomas Mann, and of course *Das Kapital* and the other works of Marx and Engels and Spinoza and Lenin and Feuerbach and massive art books, books so huge it took two men to lift one, Michelangelo and the Prado Museum book, everything Grandpa Kurt managed to miraculously carry on his travels through Europe and Palestine, where they also moved around a great deal before finally settling in the Galilee kibbutz founded by their daughters.

In Kfar Szold, Kurt sat in the kibbutz library and wrote his books, book after book, a monumental body of work in which he laid out the history of plastic art, which he knew like the back of his hand, through the gospel of Karl Marx, who is commonly thought to have "brought Hegel down to earth," though some claim he had set him upside-down. Now art itself, paragon of beauty and spirit, was being set straight by Doctor Gershom K. Freyer, as he was known in Israel, explaining that every work of art is founded in the material and the economic, and that both creator and audience are people with social consciousness. During this historical examination, he later wrote, "I had employed the doctrine of Stalin in writing the first volume, but not the second."

Anna, who did not find her place in the new Jewish world, lived beside him, patching up the old socks of the kibbutz members. When she would commence in idle talk with her friends, who also arrived too old to Palestine, Kurt would take out his hearing aid and immerse himself in a book, and in this manner he lived out his life, reading and writing.

On Passover Eve we sat around the long Seder table of Kfar Szold, in a brightly lit hall. On the stage a little band played chamber music, all members of this small kibbutz which had undergone a stark divide in the 50s. Every year they would play the gavotte from Johann Sebastian Bach's Orchestral Suite No. 3, a delightful melody that frolicked joyously across the bright and attentive Seder hall like an envoy from another world, from courtrooms of counts and European drawing rooms. The melody osmosed into my blood and still today it continues to erupt from inside of me.

Among the musicians sat Uncle Shim'on who played the cello, and his eldest son Yohanan who had taken up the cello as well. Gabbi, Susi and Moshe's eldest, played the violin, and Moshe himself conducted. Many years later the younger generation of the kibbutz had decided to retire poor Bach from his Passover eminence, and I felt as though the holiday had been desecrated.

When they were done playing, Shim'on came down from the little stage, opened the Kfar Szold Haggadah which had a large cyclamen drawn on the back, and became the Seder officiator. In a clear voice, musically, he ordered, "Wrap the *Maror* in the *Charoset* – and eat." The snap of breaking *matza* crunched around the hall. We read the Haggadah and sang Passover songs sung by generations upon generations of Jews, from "*Ha Lachma Anya*" to "*Dai Dayenu*," and songs brought into the Seder from Europe, just like Bach was, and became imbued in it as naturally as if they had been given handed down along with the Torah on Mount Sinai.

"How lovely art thou, O spring," I sang passionately, year after year, "In the field, in the meadow, the buds blossom! A revelry of life; How lovely art though, and how pleasant, O spring!"

Mother never sang. The music that had been passed down the generations had skipped her, but her face shone brightly, peacefully. Gidi sat beside me, both close and distant, a child I was meant to serve, for he shall inherit the crown. Was he gripped by the same sense of divinity that gripped me when the band played the sacrosanct music of Bach? Did he also ponder the meaning of "Take *kezayit* and eat"? did this large family solve the riddle for him, as well, the ever plaguing Riddle of Three, that had hovered above our small family, above the basement apartment on Israelis Street? And perhaps his riddles were different? Perhaps Erich to him was not a new father but merely a loving uncle, an obvious presence, leaving him to seek a father elsewhere? Perhaps a man born without a father has no need for one? The riddles were legion, and I knew not how to ask them, and by the time I did, I found them strewn all around me, useless, lying in the great, wide river of the forgotten.

3.

On October 30, 1956, Mother sat at the kitchen table and opened the daily paper *Al HaMishmar* printed by the United Workers Party. The headline was plastered across the entire first page in big, square letters: "The IDF has taken up position around Sinai." Mother let out a bitter cry, startling me. Gidi also hurried into the kitchen, his eyes questioning. The memory of that wail remained with me, to rise anew every time a newspaper headline declares a new war. We didn't speak much of war at home, but Mother would often say that "Rubi will probably have to go to the army, but surely by Gidi's time things will be different."

That morning Mother informed us that that day we would be staying home. We attended the workers' children's school on Lassalle Street, along with the sons and daughters of the noble workers of Israel. Gidi was in first grade, and the princely glamor he was born with had not dimmed with time. That afternoon, Tel Aviv was filled with the whine of a siren. At once the basement became the beating heart of life in the building, the curse swiftly lifted from its dark, mysterious depths. The residents of the building walked one at a time into its gloom, which even the murky light bulb could not vanquish. The landlord came, as well, Mr. Shachor, who once grabbed me in the stairwell, pinched my cheek and said, "Do you know your name in Russian? Rosislav!" and a boy came who had been so mean to me that I dared not even poke my nose outside and now was sauntering through our apartment in the custody of his parents, and our basement floor neighbors came, Mr. and Mrs. Spielmann, with their daughter, Zehava, whose entire world fell to pieces when she had finally found a man she wished to marry and he died from a cruel disease promptly after their engagement. Everyone assembled into the basement that was supposed to protect us from the bomb sent by the enemy, whose name I did not even know. Enemies were not discussed in the Rosenthal household.

From that day, the war became a devil that had come to live in our home. Mother's cry had marked the moral border between good and evil. War, any war, is a pure and absolute evil, which delivers only futile misery. War is always senseless. War has masters, and they are the kings of wickedness. The only worthy war is the one on war itself, and even this supposedly just war can never justify bloodshed. "Operation Kadesh," known later as The Sinai Crisis, conceived by the leaders of two declining powers and one baby-nation, a decision for which to this day bizarre excuses are still being made, had become the paragon for the evil of all wars.

The line demarked by Mother's cry echoed in me also when

our counselor in HaShomer HaTzair youth movement told us that our group, which through some odd tradition was called a *gdud* – "battalion" – would be judging comrade Joseph Vissarionovich Stalin, the late leader of the Soviet Union, for crimes he was convicted of just two years before, during Khrushchev's famous speech at the 20th Congress in 1956. The bill of indictment pounded me like a tam-tam: mass murders, show trials, innocents becoming enemies, blood and blood and blood spilled on the altar of great ideas. Indignant and distraught, I joined the prosecution, and my *gdud* embarked on an exhaustive inquiry, which ended in the sort of compromise that seemed apt back then: Stalin was cleared of the charges relating to his blood-soaked revolution, but not of those involving what used to be referred to as "perversions," for which he was accused of dabbling in during his final years.

Evil had been clearly marked, and yet, when the Israel Defense Forces informed me that due to my puny weight and what must therefore be limited physical prowess the military has no need for my service, I asked the doctors at the recruiting center for a "combat" profile. I was eager to join my *gdud*, my battalion, and particularly, I wanted to join the 50th battalion of the 933rd Nahal Brigade. This personal war also ended in compromise, with my profile no longer listed as "limited," but as "poor." And so, in accordance with half my mother's prophecy, I went to the army.

We celebrated Gidi's Bar Mitzvah according to family tradition, this time in a new apartment on the fourth floor of a building on HaBashan Street, in North Tel Aviv. An opulent meal of delicious and very much not kosher food. Grandpa Kurt, who was now seventy-eight and had recently published his book, *An Introduction to Marxist Thought*, which had become a must-read among left-wing circles, made a speech in slow Hebrew, very similar to the one he made on my birthday, at my Bar Mitzvah.

"Gidi, my beloved grandson," said Grandpa Kurt, "you have finally reached the age of passage from childhood to adulthood. To be an adult is to begin to understand the world and begin to understand the meaning of truth and of good, and, primarily, that you have an opportunity to partake in human history, and even to mold it.

"Know this, dearest Gidi, that history is not but a sequence of blind, random events. History progresses, ever forward even at those times we may fear that it is retreating to evil places or taking a circuitous path. History is a war between good and evil, and good will prevail, because good is represented by reason, and reason is the origin of truth. History, dear Gidi, is the story of reason's triumph, and we humans must each choose, whether to support reason in its ascent to ultimate victory, or become bound to evil, dark, ignorant forces. This is the meaning of humanism.

"I look at you, Gidi, and I see the seed of good within you, I see the sense of reason within you and I know that you will choose well. I wish you *Mazal Tov*, truly, good fortune from all of us, and also from Grandma Anna who regretfully could not come with me today to your party."

He pronounced the Hebrew word *"tevuna,"* "reason," doubly stressed and with an extra, celebratory vowel thrown in after the T, and finished with his customary humming smile and throat-clearing. Gidi was clearly moved but did not get up to kiss his grandfather's cheek, as such behavior is frowned upon among the German-Jewish families. I looked at Gidi, who was still a child, but the innocent, somewhat severe reason of Gershom Kurt Freyer, an evolution of Hegel's reason of spirit and Spinoza's reason of mind, was already evident in his quickly maturing features. He looked at Grandpa Kurt, and Grandpa looked at him, and a silent exchange of love and reason passed between them. And for a moment my heart went out to my brother Gidi. Though we were very distant, it would have been fitting that I show him some degree of affection, on this, the eve of his adulthood.

4.

During the summer of '68, Israel was vast, overgrown and overflowing with spurious dreams. The yeshiva boys dreamed that the redemption of the whole land of Israel was at hand, and the scepter of Zionism that had fallen into secular hands will soon be returned to them. HaShomer HaTzair alumni dreamed that the moment of reconciliation had finally arrived, and the conquered land will finally be returned to its Palestinian owners. The Mapainiks, Israel's lords and masters from the Workers Party of the Land of Israel, hated dreams, and appointed as their ruler the high priestess of dream-hating, Golda Meir. Playwright Hanoch Levin placed her in the bathtub, but she sat in her kitchen instead, cooking thick broths of hatred and hubris.

Gidi was by then a tall lad, light-haired, opinionated, pensive, still glistening with his princely anointment. The army received him happily, as he was neither "limited" nor "poor" but entirely combat-ready, and served in the Nahal along with his friends from the youth group, who were intended for Beit Kama, a kibbutz in the north of the Negev region. He developed a reputation as a soldier who is all thumbs, blundering, always awkwardly adjusting the multitude of bags and kits instruments that the military loaded on him, and he had even scribbled a kind of rough poem about himself, a "*tokmak*," a sad fool whom the army "closes in on like an octopus / run left, squad commander / run right, sergeant / run back, platoon commander / run forward, weapon jam / and he would really like just to dig a hole and fall down it / and shove his head in it / and leave it there 'til further notice."

Toward the end of his service, the military decided that Corporal Gidi Rosenthal will be stationed along with a large group of other Nahalists in the Armored Corps, and he was transferred to the Armored Corps school in Julis, in the south. Gidi wrote no poems and scribbled no scribbles of the armored monstrosities, but he made some friends down there, Bnei Akiva alums who enjoyed debating the assertive, zealously secular Nahalist after training hours, during the long, dull weekends on the base.

The art of war didn't seem that hard, anymore. The watershed of Mother's cry, cutting through all future wars, was briefly forgotten. The Six-Day War was the last war, and in it a dream was born. After that there were no more big wars whose births and deaths were declared, but everyday wars, in which people died every day, one by one, unseen. Then Gadi Sharoni, who Gidi knew from Beit Kama, died along with nineteen other soldiers in the Battle of Karameh.

At the funeral, Gidi walked tall and heavy along with the other members of the kibbutz, Gadi's family, and the soldiers who survived the battle. Gadi's mother walked there and made no anguished wail. Gidi saw the gaping hole dug in the ground and heard the dull cracks of the shots from the firing squad. The body of Gadi Sharoni cried out from the closed coffin, cries that only Gidi could hear, silent cries of pain, and he imagined himself lying there, wanting out, with no one to protect him from the clumps of dirt being flung at his body. There was no anger in him, only horror.

For a long time, he stood beside Gadi's mother, hearing her sobs rolling around inside of her. Death, which had been a companion to me since Father disappeared, had for a long time skipped Gidi's world, but now that they had been acquainted, Gidi knew that Death had been a constant presence in his life, and that War and Death are treacherous companions, one seducing him with power-drunk iron behemoths, the other lurking in dug holes. He did not have the years I had to learn to survive the presence of Death. Death entered his life at once, and at once Gidi became a poet.

Death lurks at the edge of my mind, far within / a pair of bright eyes perk up like an ear / from my supposedly serene soul, to examine / if the hour for my final tally is here // Like a lion prowling the forest's dense gloom/ it is vicious and gruesome, but ever unseen / it watches my steps from my birth to my tomb / a patron both loyal and obscene.

In the north and south soldiers were dying every day, two a day, three a day, and Gidi would know them through their names in the papers, try to decipher their features in the grainy photographs, and Death was no longer in the edge of his mind, but everywhere. He would look at people in the street and try to figure out if they had lost a son, if the bereaved can be somehow detected.

On Saturdays Gidi would visit Mother in Tel Aviv. They would eat together and talk for a bit. Gidi told her of the dead he knew and Mother would look at him desperately and say, "This must be stopped, how can this be stopped," and after he left she would think to herself, *I will not be able to bear it, not this, I could live with what happened to Hans but not this, this will be too much.*

At Beit Kama Gidi worked at the cowshed and in the fields. His long legs, ungainly at war, were ill-wrought for farm work, as well. Every few evenings he returned to Tel Aviv and to the protests, translating songs by Bob Dylan and Bertolt Brecht, songs about other wars, against the masters of war and the horrors of war, songs about war's victory over love. And most of all, he loved Jacques Prévert.

> Oh Barbara, such a shitty mess is war / and what became of you now / under this iron rain / of blood, and steel, and fire / and he who embraced you / Lovingly / is he dead and gone, or living still.

Of himself he wrote, "I want to live," writing of a boy with bright eyes and light hair holding a dove, but she will not return to him, "naturally reluctant to soil / her wings, white as driven snow / in his bloodstained grasp."

Gidi spoke at length now with Death, who was harvesting eagerly in the fields of war, and Death gave him no signs. Angry and horrified he wrote in his notebook, in bold, round script, a desperate statement of defense, which might protect him from the obscene patron shadowing him.

A man am I
Not a shard of this huge world
Stumbling blindly

Groping
Among crises of nature and madness
My love
The very heavens
She will embrace to her bosom
My laughter
Will explode like fireworks
Of all the sky's stars
And in my sorrow
Bedims the face of the moon
That spreads its light.
I do not seek protection
From the horror of nature, the cryptic
For it is to me
For it is in me
For it is I.
A man am I.

5.

The War of Attrition was over, and its dead forgotten. Life in the kibbutz returned to its usual rhythms. The eldest members of the kibbutz were still at their prime, and the younger people came to visit for a day, for a few hours, taste the racket of the dining room and the torturously early wake-up for the grove and chicken coop work, the evenings spent talking on the grass, the weekly movie on a 16mm projector shining on a white sheet in front of a crowd of couples and groups, and the racket of chatter and coffee cups rising from the portico when the reels were being changed.

Love came and went in the kibbutz like the flowers of spring and autumn, catching Gidi in its wake. Occasionally he went to visit Mother, who was happier and livelier than ever. In the mornings she drove to Ramat Gan for work, were she was known as both vital and proficient among the veteran social workers, and during the evenings she would meet with her many friends from her Hebrew Communists days, known as "the exes." She would be sixty soon and at times she thought to herself, *I have gone through so much, but I have a good life, I am happy, even.* When Gidi appeared she greeted him with a smile, a meal, some conversation, and he told her little and went on to his business with the Peace Movement, which had changed names but not members, returning for the night, and she looked at him and her heart sang for him. Gidi had girlfriends, and he had even written some love poems, as well as translating into Hebrew some written by his favorite songwriters, songs the Beatles wrote about Eleanor Rigby and the Lonely Hearts, and the girl who leaves home, and Desmond and Molly who love each other and the beautiful life. They came and went, none leaving a mark. Mother would not ask about Gidi's loves, as if they had wordlessly agreed that the matter would be best left undiscussed. She thought to herself, he is the smartest and most handsome man in the world, and has so much to offer to any woman who'd be lucky enough to have him, but she did not despair, thinking, when love comes along, we'll know – Rubi found his Tami when he was seventeen and she was a fourteen-year-old girl, and they've been like two little lovebirds ever since. She loved her grandson Hanan, named after Hans, with a kind of madness, but never with hugs and kisses, as such behavior is considered distasteful among the German Jews.

Late in the summer of 1972, Gidi sat to eat lunch at the kibbutz dining hall. A girl with cherry eyes stood at the door, and the eyes looked at him, and past him. The cherry-eyed girl then sat at a table, lost, curious, and looked at him again, this time for a while. Gidi finished his lunch, hurried outside and ran to the cowshed.

Come evening, he looked for her, but she was already engaged in rapt conversation with some men who were eyeing her eyes and white flesh, and then vanished. He asked around about her, cautiously, so as not to be counted in among those men seeking easy prey, and learned that her name is Meira, and that she had come to find out if she could come to the kibbutz after her basic training, for unpaid military service. Then she disappeared for several days, and he had nearly started to forget her eyes, which sought something he could not fathom. When she returned, he awkwardly introduced himself, floundering so horribly that she nearly burst out laughing, and then they found a spot on one of the omnipresent lawns and sat there.

"You don't even know me," said Meira.

"I want to know you," said Gidi. "Help me know you."

"You really shouldn't," she said, "I complicate everything."

And he said, "I like complicated things, I'm a bona fide riddle solver."

Meira laughed, and suddenly kissed him with a fierceness entirely new to him, hungry, feral, and took him by the hand, and they ran to his room and made love like he never knew was possible. Meira said, "You're a snake, you're a good monster, you're a pink dragon."

His face darkened and he said, "What, Meira, what are you saying?"

She said, "Don't ask me, never ask me." She got up and dressed quickly and left the room.

Over the next days and weeks, they never left each other's side. She clung to him, desperate, laughing. At times she would disappear off to some inexplicable place when they were together and he would say to her, "Meira, are you with me?"

She would say, "I am in another place, in another state."

When they made love, he would again ask her, "Are you with me, Meira?"

She would say, "I am floating in another space, another time,"

And he said, "Come back to me, come out of it."

And she would ask, "Why, why come out? I am here, where I am supposed to be." Sometimes she would spiral into a deep sadness, and for an hour or two say nothing. He would leave the room and go sit on the lawn across from it and brood, and then she would be there, standing over him, smiling, hugging.

Then Meira went off to basic training. She wrote him letters that entangled him and confused him and scared him with the love they invoked in him. With each letter he felt that he is closer to rupture with yearning for her. She wrote, "for long moments I think of you and sense you, and then I feel like an aquarium, sealed, and everything outside unreachable," and he was afraid, and wrote her a letter filled with love and longing and many questions, because the thought had suddenly gripped him that she would attempt to take her own life and he would not be there.

"Your letter was like a balm for my soul," she wrote back. "We will be very together, very soon." Gidi practically skipped out of his room, overjoyed.

When she returned to him he loved her during the nights, and during the days he would grapple with the riddle of her, looking for hints in her parents, who raised her like a black diamond that mustn't be touched, and whom she ran from and never wanted him to meet, either. He heard of the religious school she was raised at like a black sheep until she eventually threw God away, and he tried to fathom her mysterious code. At times she would disappear for a few days and then come back, lying in her bed, staring, and he sat beside her, trying to tell her things to which she did not reply. Once, in a forgotten bag, he found some poems she'd written in dense, urgent script:

> Lost in fattened paths woven among sculpted clouds and air offending the dimness of my eyes / my soul is pierced with thousands of piercers cheap ones not at all sharp / I haven't the strength anymore to bear ways / I haven't the strength to bear / I haven't things or skies or dirt / I haven't. / the smoked folds of my brain crawl toward my wrinkled heart

and later she wrote:

> Stirring a cauldron of horrors / and green and yellow chameleons / with tongues or without. / a worm crawled in the desert / of Daniel's journey / with a seashell even / and whispering they chopped off my ankles.

He read and became terrified. Meira came into the room and he sat and looked at her and stroked her. She wanted to cry in his lap but couldn't and said, "Maybe we should break up, I can't stand this love."

"Maybe we should try elsewhere," Gidi said, "somewhere people won't look at us so much."

"Maybe," said Meira. "I don't know, you should never have met me."

And he said, "You are the most important thing that ever happened to me."

And she said, "You are good, you're a good person, and I'm not, I'm a crooked person, everything you see is the skin of evil."

Gidi's wise eyes met hers. "Nonsense, Meira, you are a good person, you're just scared about something, we can solve it."

"Once you solve my riddle you'll go," said Meira and laughed, a hard laugh. "What could possibly be interesting in a solved Meira about whom you know everything. And if you don't solve my riddle, you can't stay."

Gidi said, "Let's try. For me."

And she nodded, weary.

It was summer. Gidi and Meira took one of the kibbutz cars to Tel Aviv along with two suitcases. They huffed their way up to the fourth floor of the building on HaBashan Street, which despite being the tallest building around, its insides were hotter and stuffier that the basement apartment on Israelis. It had a yard and a porch and a little shrub which at the time seemed to me like a mighty tree, which Gidi and I used to climb during the good days we shared and had both forgotten.

Now Gidi and Meira were staying in the room Gidi grew up in, and Mother lived in her own room, which was a living room and a drawing room by day and a bedroom by night. A wall formed between Mother and Meira and grew steadily taller, and Mother thought, he is the smartest and most handsome man in the world, he deserves a great love, when it comes along, I'll know. In the mornings Meira stalked past her, unkempt, confused, on her way to the little bathroom where she would leave clumps of hair and scattered toiletries, and their room was always cluttered with jumbled piles of clothes. When Mother wanted to take something from the closet, she warily picked her way among the trinkets and books and clothing items and thought, when will this end, but said nothing.

Gidi enrolled at the Theater Department at Tel Aviv University and delved into the introduction to drama and the plays, discussing them at length. At night Mother would hear them talking, long, choked conversations, and think to herself, perhaps she will go, and he will live here by himself, that would be nice, to see him each morning, going off to university, until he finds love. When he finds his great love, I'll know.

Gidi started school and Meira would sleep in. Mother found her sometimes when she came back from work, staring, dejected, but they never spoke, and one day Meira got up and left. Gidi retreated into himself and wrote in his notebook.

Love has many faces / but she has lowered her face / and her words are like a stone upon my heart / she does not love me / does not love / and then / she turned her back / love has many faces.

I will see her again, Gidi said to himself. *I must see her again.*

6.

His theater studies provided Gidi with somewhat of a reprieve from the agony of love. He found friends there after his own heart, and a teacher after his own heart: Nola Chilton, who came into his life with the full weight of pain and anger and swept him away to her theater. The first papers he wrote were praised as exemplars of analysis and grasp before he even finished his first year. He continued to translate poetry into Hebrew. From Bertolt Brecht's anthology, a favorite of his, Gidi translated a series of death-poems he could not explicate and could not understand why of the plethora of poems available to him they had caught his attention. The poem about the child Jakob Apfelböck who murdered his mother and father and remained to sit in the house with them, and now the milk-maid wonders, "Whether Jakob Apfelböck will visit / his poor parents' grave once more." He also translated "The Song of the Fort Donald Railroad Gang," running from the storm that threatens to drown them, groping their way "blind as moles in that dark Ohio ground" until the storm finds them and drowns them. Distraught, he translated the poem of the man from Mississippi who lay dying at the foot of a tree in the Hathoury Woods, left by his so-called friends to die alone.

Grandma Anna passed away. Her second life, the thirty-five years she lived out in Palestine, was not a joyful life. Her brother Otto, who was an extremely successful banker in prewar Germany, but by 1939, the noose was tightening around his neck as well, and he packed his considerable funds and businesses and left Germany. He invested his money in Australia and New-Zealand, founding the Heymann Bank Ltd. His children scattered everywhere.

The eleven children of Rabbi Simon Freyer and his wife Zerlina scattered, as well. Rosa Hohenstein remained in Stettin like her niece Trude, and was killed by the Nazis along with her son, who was also named Kurt. Esther Lindner emigrated to the States back in 1865, and her great-granddaughter Linda Eastman married the great Paul McCartney. Apart from Moritz Freyer's three offspring, Moritz' sister Ida Rehfeld also came to Israel along with her son Bruno, the doctor, who became a kibbutz pioneer.

In the spring of 1973, Yonatan, Rachel and Aharon's son, went to settle at a new kibbutz, Gilgal, in the sweltering Jordan Valley. Rachel, Käthe's youngest daughter, had founded kibbutz Beit HaArava along with some friends, including her high school sweetheart Aharon, on the northern coast of the Dead Sea. The young State of Israel later gave the whole region to the Jordanian King, and so they left, broken-hearted, and founded kibbutz Kabri in the green Galilee. Now that the region was returned to the Israelis, Yonatan followed his parents broken dreams and returned to the valley.

In his congratulations on the beginning of Gidi's studies, Kurt, who was no longer in good health and prone to despondent musings over the death of his wife, Anna, and over his life's work that was now truly drawing toward its conclusion, sent him an envelope with two-hundred Israeli pounds in two banknotes. He added a note reading, "To Gidi my beloved grandson, this sum is to buy books that are important for your studies, and as you promised, do tell me as soon as possible which books you have bought and what you are learning from them. With love, your grandfather, Kurt."

Before he started university, Gidi paid a visit to Kfar Szold, where he and Kurt had a lively conversation during which Gidi spoke in a lucid, sure voice. Kurt broke out the Hebrew he saved for special occasions, the languid Hebrew of his grandchildren's Bar Mitzvahs speeches and of lectures on art and society. They spoke about art and Gidi said he wants to study theater.

"The art of theater is a social art of supreme importance," said Kurt, "it has always expressed the deepest wishes of the people."

"It also served to tell the people things they might not want to hear," said Gidi.

Kurt cleared his throat and laughed his laughter and said, "You must also try and understand during your studies whether theater is a bourgeois art. Does it herald the rise of reason, or simply reflect reality as it is."

"That will be very interesting," said Gidi, after some consideration, "but sometimes art must also reflect the absurdity of reality, such as in Ionesco and Beckett's theater." He said some other things about recent developments in theater, with which Kurt was unfamiliar, but Kurt soon grew tired and asked that they conclude the visit. Remembering the topic of their conversation, Kurt noted to himself that he has a grandson that deals in matters of true importance, and Gidi promised that the next time he is in Kfar Szold, most likely when is well into his studies, he will come and tell Kurt what he has been studying and whether he has found an answer to his questions. Kurt never forgot about that promise, and occasionally would ask if Gidi has perhaps mentioned an intended visit to Kfar Szold, as the two of them had important matters to discuss.

Meira wrote Gidi a short letter, and they even spoke on the phone. Gidi's heart still clung to her. One time she called him, terrified and melancholy, and he said, "Meira, Meira, what is it?"

"I'm alone in this house, I'm afraid."

And he said, "Come, come to me now."

And she said, "I want us to go away, away from this city," and asked that he wait for her at the central bus station on Friday morning.

He arrived at the station and saw her there. This time she was happy and fervent, and she ran to him and kissed him wetly, desperately, not wanting to separate, as if she hadn't exited his life indefinitely only three months ago. They took a bus to the Galilee. They spoke for long hours, between Hadera and Afula, and between Afula and Tiberias, filling the blank spaces of the past few months. From Kiryat Shmona Gidi phoned his Aunt Michal and she said, "Of course, please, you're more than welcome, we'll find a room for you."

In Kfar Szold they walked along the periphery of the kibbutz, and at night they remembered how to make love. Come morning Meira got up and left the room, walked into the fields and the rows of eucalyptuses creaking in the autumn wind. The fishponds were like little, square lakes. She walked alone and he came out and ran after her, but she slipped away, and he said, "We had it so good together."

"It wasn't good, Gidi," Meira said. "It wasn't good, it was all a mistake."

"Then why did you want to come with me," he asked, "why did you come back?"

"I wanted to check something," she said. "Don't be mad, I wanted to check where our souls went, our bodies drifted apart but I wanted to check where the souls went."

And Gidi said, "Meira, what are you talking about?"

And she said, "I knew you wouldn't understand."

And he said, "It's up to us, it is entirely in our hands, if we talk, if we love, our souls will also be close, you speak of the soul as if it were some kind of demon."

Meira sat on the edge of the fishpond. A cold wind blew through the eucalyptuses surrounding the pools. "Not everything is up to us, Gidi," she said. "Our souls are not our own, there are forces controlling us."

"Those forces are just people, like us," said Gidi. "The demons are an invention, something we conjured up to escape ourselves."

"The world is full of demons," said Meira, "they are everywhere, leave me now, Gidi, take me away, there is too much beauty here, take me back to our ugly city and never see me again."

Gidi was sullen and desperate. They sat for a while longer by the pond. No one went by, no one saw them there, sitting side by side and not touching each other, and he thought to himself, *where am I going, where am I going with all this, I am twenty-two and have not known great love yet, and the love I have known is pulling me into the abyss.* He stood up, determined, and said, "Come on, let's head back," and they walked side by side. He placed a hand on her shoulder, though it was not a lover's hand, but a doctor's, a concerned father's. She did not ask him to remove it, and he raised his eyes to meet hers and what he saw frightened him. She no longer looked at him but toward some distant place, and there was a hard pain in her eyes. They got their backpacks and hitchhiked back to Tel Aviv, where they parted ways.

That night, in the little apartment on HaBashan Street, Mother saw Gidi hunched over his desk, writing in his round, somewhat childish handwriting, and knew that it was not schoolwork. Her heart went out to him.

When she was ten, she was told about the great lakes. The house was cold, and the lakes were also cold. From the eyes of her mother that told her the story the lakes sparkled, and they were oh so cold. But there was a house on the lakeshore, and the house had a straw roof, and you can sink in straw, and in the winter there is snow, and blankets of snow on the roof, and under blankets of snow you can snuggle up and sleep for ever and ever. And in the window of the house bloom flowers, brown and orange and yellow like the earth, and the earth is floral as well. Even when she did not dream of the lakes they were always gone when she woke. And she was twenty and drank the lakes from bottles, and into the wet cup she would ash her cigarette, throwing dust in the lakes' eye.

Today she is twenty-three and she tries to burn the snow with cigarettes. She sits in the snow and smokes and smokes. She carries her loneliness like a charm in her pack of cigarettes. The tears flow out and she puts out the cigarette, and she lights another. She wanted to sit there like a holy guru and sink into the unattainable serenity, but she just sits there cross-legged and her thought skitters about, nothing like a guru's. Only the hands reach out in unclear, steady directions. To the matchbox. To the bottle of whiskey. She seeks the lakes in the whiskey, but why do you need the bottle, girl, when the lakes are here, just out the door. Just open the door and look into their eyes, and you will see the house with its straw and its blankets of ice. But she knows that if she looks, she will only see herself. And she does not want to see herself.

She looks forward and says, 'Let's go!' and her friend sitting beside her says, 'Let's go.' She is a good friend and has also come seeking lakes. She is also an employee of Lake Seekers Ltd.

And they go. But with them goes another lonely man, hugging himself with the arms of society. Soon more lonely people will come, from all over the city, the world. They will walk in a silent parade to the cold lake. They will look at their reflection and surround the water in a soundless, steady march. They will sing of the reflecting light and the moonlit waters. They will sing of the whisper of reeds and the groves in the distance. And they will not sing of the house with the straw, but they will think of it all the time, all the time. Because a straw house is a matter for children's songs, not grown-ups' songs.

Soon they will come. And meanwhile she goes and hugs herself with the arm of no one. And in her eyes lakes and her eyes are lakes and if only if only she could sit like that in the snow, sit in the snow like a holy guru and marry a god who sits in a straw house and he is oh so hot and the straw burns and burns and is never consumed.

I solved the riddle of Meira, Gidi suddenly thought to himself. *I will not see her again.*

7.

A week after his visit to Kfar Szold Gidi received an envelope at his house on HaBashan Street with his address in the familiar handwriting from the dedication of his book, and in it a brief letter.

> To My Grandson Gidi,
>
> I was deeply sorry to hear that you were in Kfar Szold and did not come to visit me as you promised. I wanted very much to hear about your university studies, and to continue discussing the vital questions that were raised in our conversation of six months ago, before you started your studies. I also wanted to know whether you received the gift I sent you and if you enjoyed it."
>
> Love, your grandfather,
>
> Kurt

Gidi sighed and told his mother about the letter and she said, "You really should write him, his health is not what it was and you are very important to him, he thinks you are the grandson that will carry on his legacy, so he's been saying."

Gidi said, "I didn't mean to hurt him."

Mother said, "I know, Gidi, it happens."

He sat down at his desk and wrote a letter for Grandpa Kurt.

5.11.72

Dear Grandfather,

I just received your letter, and you have no idea how sorry I am for what happened. The truth is that I wanted very much to come see you, and intended to do so on Saturday morning, but it did not work out because I left the kibbutz early in the morning and only came back around noon, and I didn't want to disturb you. The time simply wasn't right. But that does not change the fact that I didn't visit, and I intend to come to Kfar Szold again, soon.

It is also true I forgot to thank you for the gift, and that was wrong of me. But I thank you now, and I thanked you in my heart every time I bought a new book, even if I didn't write a letter. I used it to buy a lot of books on and of Greek tragedies. The complete writings of Euripides, Aristophanes and Aeschylus, and I've started reading them. I have somewhat neglected philosophy and Marxism in favor of theater, but I found plenty of room for philosophy there, as well. I am also taking a class on architecture and art styles as a part of theater studies.

Dear Grandfather, I hope to come visit soon, probably in about a month, and tell you everything in detail. I truly wanted to come, and I am sorry it worked out this way.

Your truly loving grandson,
Gidi

P.S. – since it will take some time to tell you about everything I am studying, I will write you several letters regarding this once I have more time, because right now I am in a hurry.

And indeed, two weeks later, Gidi sent another letter.

19.11.72

Dear Grandfather,

I promised to write you a detailed letter about my university studies, and here it is. I am studying theater, and only theater. Some of my classes are practical, which I am sure holds little interest for you, but I am studying acting according to the Stanislavski method. In the theoretical classes, however, I am learning very interesting things. We reach an understanding of drama via an approach not dissimilar to Marxism's superstructure. The first few lessons involved the theory of myth, though there was no mention of the Marxist approach. Instead we discussed the theories of Miller and Schelling, Lévi-Strauss and Freud. But in the following lessons we touched on the approach explaining the emergence of tragedy, and the changes in forms of drama as a result of social change. I would be very interested to know if, at least regarding the literature itself, the Marxists have something to say about these matters, and what your attitude is regarding the truly great writers and poets – Sophocles, Aeschylus, Shakespeare, Goethe, who were in a sense extremely conservative and religious. Shakespeare even goes as far as exhibiting nationalism in some of his plays. Does that diminish their value? Did they not understand the world as much? Though these men were often devoted to the monarchy, functioning mainly in the confines of the royal court, and still they understood many things that even Brecht and Shaw and Ibsen did not. Or I could be wrong. What do you think?

Looking forward to your reply.

Your loving grandson,
Gidi

P.S.

The great tragedians claim that humans are powerless. That they can never shape their destiny as they choose. That they cannot withstand the evil that descends upon them. Surely you claim differently. What caused them to think this, and what brought about the huge fame that they have accrued, more so than any other artist throughout the generations?

Kurt received both letters and immediately forgave his grandson and sat down to write back, laboring over his reply for a long time.

15.12.72

Dear Gidi,

I was very pleased to receive your responses and shall attempt to comply with your fascinating requests. Regarding Marxist literature on theater, I am attaching to this letter a list of books and papers which should prove very helpful.

In every generation there were artists, and they might be writers, painters or playwrights, who saw the world through black-tinted glass and did not believe it capable of change. To them, what they saw with their eyes, the darkness, the injustice, human suffering, was the world's final and ultimate form. They were blind to the development curve, to the fact that history is changing, that those things that seem evil today can become good, if only humans would act to influence history, rather than remain its victims.

Even those playwrights we discussed, such as Ionescu, who is at least somewhat amusing, and Beckett, which I do not at all understand, what is he trying to say, these playwrights describe what is, describe an image that has no sense or order, and that is why theatergoers have become so enamored with them. This audience watches the play and says, indeed, this is what the world is like, a world of suffering, a nonsensical world. But this is art which can only be appropriate for a time, because the world never stagnates, but is ever-changing, and humans are ever-changing. A war rages between reason and evil and chaos, and in this war each of us, even the playwright, must take a stand, and if they do not take a stand, then they have unwittingly aligned themselves with the forces of darkness, and relinquished their understanding of history.

I know that things seem dark today, and we know things about the revolution that we did not know in the past. Sometimes the best ideas are too big for the people who try to realize them. Sometimes people make history, but do not understand it. But the power of reason is greater than any other force in existence, and human society, along with its artists and playwrights and scholars, will steer it in the right direction.

I hope I have answered all your questions satisfactorily and I await your next letter.

Your loving grandfather,
Kurt

5.1.73

Beloved Grandfather,

I received your letter, and I thank you sincerely for all the material you sent, which I have not yet finished going through. I will not discuss here the problems of Marxism and theater, and in general I have been very busy with the practical challenges of acting and am finding it difficult to read. Our theoretical studies have also shifted from tragedy to comedy, following a keen and interesting summary of the issues of tragedy.

Instead I would like return to a subject we discussed once, and I recently recalled: modern playwriting. Regarding the matters of humanity, destiny, and of greatness or its lack in any given playwright, it seems that the truly tragic elements exist in fact in the post-Brecht plays – Ionescu, Beckett and their successors. This begs the question, should those playwrights who wrote about the actual end of the world and the death of all values be considered merely appropriate for a certain period of time, or something more? Sometimes I feel, in this reality of mine, with all of the education I received, that the only way to love is to escape this vicious cycle of nations and wars altogether, and live someplace quiet, because the entire social-political framework has a kind of tragic destiny that it cannot escape, and will always lead to destruction.

And unexpectedly it is now that we have reached a certain apex in our development that things are so much worse than they were a century or two ago, and the world strives ever closer to its own death. You will disagree, I am sure, but it is very hard to think differently these days.

By the way, I have heard an interesting theatrical analysis of the Israeli-Arab conflict as a tragic conflict according to classical examination. Meaning, the tragic flaw of the nation that followed its hubris, the founding of the State of Israel, was in the fact that it never deliberated nor even considered the Arab problem. This according to the claim that a tragic flaw is not a flaw in character, but in knowledge. I sometimes wonder if the Israeli-Arab conflict could ever come to a solution. I hope so, but I am far from certain.

See you in the next letter, and maybe in February,
Gidi

Kurt received the letter and read it in his sickbed and could not answer it. They had placed his latest book, that had just been published, at his bedside: *Marxist Humanism*. He leafed through it, sent it off to his family and friends with his signature, and, in March of 1973, closed his eyes. He was eighty-eight.

We walked, generations of Freyers, on the path leading to the cemetery, up the hill, on the way to the reservoir where I splashed and wallowed during the distant visits of my childhood. When the rest of us turned and headed back Gidi remained by the grave for a long time, catching up only much later. I returned to my kibbutz, Nahshon, in the Judean lowlands, and Gidi returned to his studies, and we hardly spoke. The evil secret that stood between us since he came into the world had not dissolved, but I could see in his seasoned eyes, in his wise face, that the day of a solution was at hand, that a wonderful friendship is about to blossom between us, and perhaps even love.

8.

On October 6, 1973, which held both the serenity of the Sabbath and the concealed horror of Yom Kippur, Gidi was called to report at once at the improvised recruitment center in Yad Eliyahu. He wore his reserve duty uniform and the tall paratrooper boots and tossed some underwear and toiletries into the reserve duty rucksack that lay abandoned in the corner.

Mother paced restlessly up and down the small apartment, saying, "What can this be, what is really happening," and she was hard and slightly cross and kept saying, half asking, half begging,

"Must you go, must you really go?"

And he just said, again and again and again, "Of course I do, you know I do."

"But call," said Mother. "If you see a payphone you call me, and write me, the minute you get there send a letter," and she shoved into his rucksack some telephone tokens she had found in some drawer and stationery.

And he said, "I'll call."

They went down to the small street together. Some other men in uniform were emerging from their homes and Mother looked at them helplessly. Gidi joined the walkers, and she watched, her eyes spearing into his back. Gidi turned around, smiled, and disappeared. She ran back up to the fourth floor, wracked with an anxiety that would not be soothed all that day, and that night, and all the days and nights that followed.

Gidi took a bus that collected soldiers from everywhere and took them north. The roads were packed with buses and half-tracks and tank transporters, all flowing into the few narrow roads leading north. The ever-growing convoy was humming with alarming rumors, and the radio which had previously gone silent started playing songs that amused Gidi, reminding him of the traditional sing-alongs they used to have in the school up north, accompanied by Meir Noy's infinite accordion, playing the same songs over and over again. He chatted only briefly with the people around him, for being a Freyer he had neither knack nor experience in small talk, but his spirits were uplifted and eager toward something unknown, something big and hard, an exuberance shared by all soldiers in all wars, a moment before entering the gates of the war proper.

The bus brought Gidi to camp Yiftach at the Golan foothills.

Tank transporters were also congregating in the area. In the camp chaos reigned. Gidi announced his arrival, sat down on a rock and looked at the people scurrying among the buildings, at the QM store where large and small packages of equipment were jumbled messily on top of one another, tank nets and towels and gun oil and canned food. He waited, nearly dozing off, until eventually someone called his name. He was informed that he would be stationed in a tank along with tank commander Micha and his teammates Effi and Avi, who were already standing by the tank and making dry, terse acquaintance. They climbed into the tank. Effi, the driver, started the tank which rattled and hummed and started moving and fell silent and went still. A tow truck was sent to tow it into the large workshop which already had several rebellious tanks parked out front, surrounded by soldiers in coveralls.

Micha demanded they be supplied with another tank and was told that there were no tanks and to wait patiently. They found some available beds in one of the rooms and laid down. Micha ran around the camp, urged the men at the workshop and again requisitioned for a new tank. Gidi read a bit in one of the books he had brought, and then the four of them went to eat dinner and fell into a deep sleep until the following day.

For four days and four nights the soldiers at the workshop toiled to fix their recalcitrant tank. Gidi came to know Avi and Effi, opinionated yeshiva boys like the ones he knew back in Julis, where he debated them at length regarding the relationship between man and his Maker, waging a vigorous counter-attack on their "God of Armies" and Holy Torah. He sent Mother two brief letters and asked someone who was leaving the base to phone her and tell her he was okay.

The air was filled with the thin, onerous smell of war, which despite being neither heard nor seen in the city streets was carried to them on the wings of rumor. Gidi knew with certainty that this was the war he had been waiting for these past three years, ever since Gadi Sharoni died, the war whose meaning he sought, the war he had written about and now is a poem no longer, but it is not reality either. He no longer hated it, and for some reason felt no fear of what loomed ahead, merely curiosity, a desire to see the most horrible of all beasts from up close, to peek into its maw, to stroke its flesh-rending talons, to feel its breath and its tensed muscles, and then leave, leave forever, or return to it once again to vanquish it.

On Thursday, October 11, 1973, Micha and Avi and Effi and Gidi climbed into the tank and up to the Golan Heights. The roads throughout the hills were abandoned. Nearly no one inhabited this land, and those who did were now fleeing, hiding in the bowels of the earth. The Golan became a realm of smoke and dust, its roads crushed and fissured by tanks and APCs, and riddled by stray tank fire. The path was marked now with smoking metallic carcasses, a severed caterpillar track, a flipped jeep, a torn item of clothing, black, viscous stains that were not gasoline.

There were no explosions yet. All was silent, and Gidi looked at the tank carcasses and felt they had somehow stumbled upon a garden of primordial monsters that had come unearthed. As for the knowledge that these monsters were carrying people only yesterday, that he himself had somehow mounted such a monster and was galloping somewhere on its back, he postponed it, suppressed it. Into the hollows of his body which had fallen stiff and numb over the four days he had spent in waiting, a light anxiousness was pooling, a sort of nausea, and it grew the closer they got to the sounds of explosions, and the basalt earth was all around them now, rows and rows of black rock that have stood there since they burst from one of the mountain's many maws, and now their rest had been disturbed by tanks maneuvering between them.

On the horizon he could see other tanks, and Gidi saw how a red flame licked out from somewhere and the nearby tank becoming a torch. He saw people jumping out, screaming, on fire, rolling on the black stones. A whistle came from above and grew very loud, and a dull, hard crash propagated toward his body, his ears, shaking him in a hard tremor that felt as if it was ripping his skin from his flesh. The tank stood still then, and silence descended.

It was afternoon. Gidi climbed out of the tank, slowly, his long legs bumping into each other, followed by Effi and Avi. Micha remained seated in his chamber, wide-eyed, still. They came around him and tried to speak to him. Effi touched his throat, his wrist, placed his palm on his heart and said, "He's gone."

The three of them sat there, stunned, and for a long while said nothing. Effi's eyes flitted around. Avi muttered a prayer and Gidi withdrew into himself. They eventually pulled Micha's body from the tank, placed him on the ground and erected a little mound of stones around him. They placed his dog tags on his chest and they sat and looked around.

Now other voices could be heard, nervous ones, in a language Gidi new well from the Middle Eastern studies classes he took in high school. Human silhouettes appeared in the twilight.

"Those would be the Syrians," said Effi. "They see us."

"What are we going to do," said Avi, "maybe we should seize the initiative."

"Initiative nothing," Effi ruled, "we wait for the cover of

darkness and shove off to Khan Arnabeh. It's our only chance."

Gidi said nothing. His eyes shifted among the malevolent silhouettes. Rising from somewhere, from some nameless spirit of the skies, came a full moon, smiling white, prepared to fill in for the sun's absence to the best of its ability, tonight of all nights.

The voices around them quieted somewhat. Effi, alarmed and determined, retrieved a small book from his pack and began muttering a prayer. Gidi looked at him and when he was finished he took the little black book, the likes of which he had never before opened in his life, and leafed through the pages, at the miniscule print, just barely legible in the moonlight, and read, "Yea, though I walk through the valley of the shadow of death, I will fear no evil. For thou art with me." And he read, "What man is he that desireth life, and loveth many days, that he may see good? Keep thy tongue from evil, and thy lips from speaking guile. Depart from evil, and do good; Seek peace, and pursue it." He read the words again and for a moment the malevolent voices swarming around him were forgotten.

Effi stood up and they broke into motion, advancing as quickly as they could at a low hunch, nearly a crawl, across the plain of bare basalt field, and found a rock in the field and hid behind it. Gidi heard other sounds and voices around them, unfamiliar, and looked around but saw no one, only Avi and Effi moving among the rocks ahead of him, flitting from cover to cover. Lights twinkled in the distance, but they did not grow closer, as lights at night often seem, faraway as stars until you are right at their doorstep. At each cover, Effi would point at the southern lights and whisper, "That's Khan Arnabeh, we've got this," and clambered forward, and Avi followed, and then Gidi, slipping and stumbling on the basalt rocks, suppressing with every fiber of will the crippling terror that had already seized some of his organs in its paralyzing grasp, but his legs moved still, and his mind was still clear, and a voice echoed again and again in him, the men of Fort Donald, yo-ho, the men of Fort Donald, yo-ho, and he lunged behind a small rock and remained there for an eternity of a moment and to his horror heard a sound, a click of bolts, a quick guttural command, and a hard noise exploded into his ears, tearing through his eardrums, and chains of fire and iron consumed his body, his chest, his long legs, his overflowing head, his wise eyes, his glasses fell to the ground and a bitter scream tore out, with all that was left in his throat he screamed, the rough basalt cutting the still moving, squirming body. For a fraction of a second the knowledge existed in him, but his head was blank with the horror of it, and the scream also was fading.

The moon stalked off to perform many more missions of light, and Effi and Avi were no longer there, either, but had clambered on, resolute, stunned, toward the lights of Khan Arnabeh. Around the body wrapped in its military cerement formed a glow of silence eternal.

CHAPTER NINE: LOTTE

1.

On October 14, 1973, a Sunday, my cousin Yohanan phoned me from Kfar Szold. Back then I was the secretary of my kibbutz, Nahshon, which lies halfway between Jerusalem and Tel Aviv. Bad news came daily. Fallen family members, friends. Rumors abounded of the war that eats thousands like a fiery dragon. The air was pregnant with anticipation for worse news than what had already been received, and indeed it only became more ruinous.

Yohanan hesitated for a moment and said, "I tried to find out what happened to Gidi. I'm very worried."

I did not know what to ask.

"No one is saying anything clear," said Yohanan, "I'm very worried. They can't find him."

I and Tami, who was at the time my wife and in the final trimester of pregnancy, went to Tel Aviv, to the house on HaBashan Street. Mother hadn't heard from Gidi since that Wednesday, when a passerby from camp Yiftach called her and delivered a message that everything is okay, that he had seen him, and a postcard arrived, everything is okay, nothing to worry about, and a sort of letter on a piece of paper with no envelope which had also arrived, everything is okay, everything is okay. When I came to visit her just three days ago, on Thursday, she was standing by the phone saying, "No calls, no calls, the line has to be free." *I just need one minute*, I thought to myself, *what difference could one minute possibly make.*

Now the two of us were climbing up to the fourth floor, without having announced our arrival, because what could I have said to justify this unexpected visit, and the fact that we had both come, in the middle of the day, lit candles of dread in her eyes.

"Yohanan called," I said.

"Yes, Yohanan," said Mother.

"He said he's very worried," I said. "He said no one can find Gidi."

Mother fell to the cold floor, on the orange tiles in Gidi's room, next to his bed. I never saw her lying on the floor like that, writhing, and she said, "But I love him so much."

"Nothing is certain yet."

"But I love him so much."

We settled her down into a couch in her room and I said, "We'll find out, I'll go and find out, you have to wait until I find out."

Mother sat on the couch and did not cry, only muttered to herself in German, "This isn't me, this isn't me."

Then the phone rang and a man I did not know spoke to me, saying, "I'm Avi's father." I did not know who Avi is. "I'm Israel Piekrash, from Hadera," his voice was deep, clear. "Your brother was in the tank with my son."

I said, "And what about him, what about them?"

And he said, "I'll meet you tomorrow at the Netanya central bus station and tell you everything, be there at eight."

We took Mother to the kibbutz. We made a bed for her and she lay down and said, "But you are good, you are good, you are also good." This was beyond my grasp, all of this, since if Gidi is missing there is only a single task that we all must enlist to now and that is to find him, he must be hiding somewhere, no one knows anything about anything in this war. Perhaps he joined some other unit. Perhaps he had fallen captive. That is what Yohanan said, after all, and tomorrow all shall become clear, and this Israel Piekrash knows many things, surely he does.

Mother lay on the bed and a shadow fell across her clear face. Again and again she said, "Gidi was good, and so are you, Rubi, you are also good." Tami sat beside her and talked to her. Four-year-old Hanan came to the house, and Mother looked at him, saying, "This is Hanan, Hanan."

The next morning, I met Danny, my Aunt Michal's son, known as the writer Dan Shavit, with whom I have had many long, straightforward conversations over the years. Together we went to the bus station in Netanya. Two young women came looking for us and said, "Israel won't be coming, he asks that you come to him." I asked what happened and they said, "They found his son," and went away, weeping.

We went to the address they gave us, where family members and friends from Hadera were already gathering. Israel, a robust, sharp-spoken man, said, "Go up to camp Yiftach and ask around, maybe they've found out something about Gidi." And then he spoke clearly, his voice ringing strong, as all around him choked sobs rose and fell, telling how Avi and Effi and Gidi headed out that evening, after their tank was hit and their commander, Micha, was killed, out to Khan Arnabeh, and all they know of Gidi is that he disappeared into the darkness, and Effi and Avi kept advancing toward Khan Arnabeh, where they encountered a group of Syrian soldiers and fought them there. Avi was killed and his body was found in a pile of Syrian corpses who were about to be buried in a mass grave, but the yarmulke visible on his head revealed him to be one of ours.

I asked what happened to Effi and he was silent for a moment, and then said, his lips thin, biting back words of anger and inquiry, "Effi made it to Khan Arnabeh, and gave his account of what happened."

When we got to camp Yiftach, Yohanan was already there, waiting for us. A thin, pale officer was sitting in one of the offices and muttering things we did not understand, looking through lists without raising his eyes at us, and eventually said, "Gideon Rosenthal, he was in Micha Granit's tank."

I went back home to the kibbutz and told Mother, "They don't know yet, no one in the army knows yet," but she did not answer, merely stared. Her eyes were red, but not from crying. I returned her to the apartment on HaBashan Street, where friends had already begun to gather.

One evening I came to the apartment and they told me, "Effi was just here, he left a few minutes ago."

I said, "How can I speak to him, I have to speak to him."

"Yes, he was here," said Mother, "we didn't really talk."

Day after day I sat at Mother's house and on the Sabbath, she came to our home on the kibbutz. The members of the kibbutz saw her and waved hesitantly at her and did not ask, did not know what to ask. She came and sat with us at the dining room, uncharacteristically withdrawn, somber, red-eyed. On Sunday she went back to work. She was about sixty, and every day she went to work, and every evening friends would visit her, her fellow "exes" who had built a new world with her and now came to weep with her. They all were around sixty, but still in their prime. One day Meira came, aghast, her cherry eyes somewhat dimmed, sat with Mother and said, "It was irresponsible to put Gidi in a tank. Who puts someone like Gidi in a tank?"

Some days passed. No one from the military had come to speak with us, nor did we expect them to. The military was a place we no longer wanted anything to do with, a place stinking heavily of tank motor oil and gunpowder and stifling offices. Mother stood out on the porch and looked out to the street. I sat on the couch in the living room, which since that day had become her only bedroom, and at once, with no outside stimulus, with no new information, the knowledge sliced into me like a hot knife, knowledge which left no place for doubt, and I wept long, wracking sobs, wept loudly and unendingly in the small room, in front of Mother, who turned around and looked at me, alarmed, and said, "Enough, Rubi, I can't, no, Rubi, no." I wept his certain death, his eternal suffering, and my love for him that never came to fruition, his wise eyes, our days together on the way to school and to the zoo, and I wept for Mother and she did not know, just said again and again, "Enough, Rubi, don't, no, don't, I can't." I stopped crying at once and did not cry again.

2.

I started going through Gidi's drawers and notebooks. Bits of paper seemed to flutter out of every corner, fragments of poems, a tidy notebook of his favorite songs and poems translated into Hebrew, things I never saw and knew nothing of. I collected them with the intention of compiling them into a book. Mother came to the kibbutz every weekend, and baby Yotam joined the family. It had been a mere two months since the war and we did not want to name him Gideon so as not to burden him undeservedly, and only many days later I opened the Bible to confirm what I knew and refused then to remember, Yotam, the son of Gideon the judge.

The military bothered to call and inform us that Gidi was "missing." They spoke the word with a sort of reverence and looked surprised when we did not yell or make inquiries, for we knew that this information was a lie, that it was for nothing they left us in the murky limbo wherein dwell those ethereal specters of war, The Missing. Gidi will not return. We will not seek his name in the lists of captives. His decomposing body lies somewhere out there, and will be found someday, and perhaps will not, a body with no name. His spirit is gone from us, and his memory and the knowledge of his existence and that which he left behind are here, in this house. Mother knew this and I knew it and we did not share this knowledge aloud. I assembled the world that crumbled out of the scraps of paper and the words of poems, and at night I would think and dream the book, name it, draw its pages, arrange it in different layouts.

Mother would go to work and return in the afternoon to her house on HaBashan Street, where a kindred spirit always waited. Her sister Michal would be waiting for her and her sister Susi would be waiting for her and they would sit and talk and sit and not talk, and her eyes were dry, but when she went into the shower and took off her clothes and stood under the scalding water, she would yell, Gidi, Gidi, and the cry burst through the ceiling and ascended into the heavens like smoke, and it burst through the walls and bounded around the rooms of the house.

Sofi came for her, wise, impassioned. Mother knew Sofi from her youth in Ein Gev, where she came after working with the pioneer's children at Kinneret Courtyard. Many years had passed since, and they had met rarely during that time. Now she came and spoke with her, and they talked and talked. I hadn't heard Mother speak so many words in my entire life as those they spoke then, and Sofi said, I am here, Lotte, I am staying here, and she brought a suitcase with her clothes and various necessities and stayed over, week after week, month after month she was with her, and they spent nearly every night of the week together, and they even went out together, to the cafés and cinemas, for they were young women, only sixty, and far too close for a man like me to ever come between.

A year later Sofi left the house and Mother said, "She saved my life."

Avi's father would phone me occasionally, decisive, "It's Israel," he would say. He saw me as close and aware, a blood brother, and I fled from him, fled from the fellowship of the bereaved that made me a fellow in the act of war, a partner in what I saw as a conspiracy to deem the victims responsible for their own deaths, to ransom their deaths with life. Israel was a bright, firm man. He would hear none of my excuses and instead invited me to join him and "some friends" to see where it happened.

I came to his house in Hadera, and together we went up to the Golan Heights. We drove down roads, on which perforated tanks still stood, their trunks hanging low, and mounds of stones were gathered up by the roads, and black names were written across the mounds. We drove and drove. We passed Quneitra, which had become a ghost town, and came to the large basalt field east of it and stood there.

"It happened somewhere around here," said Israel.

Each of us sat on the black rock he'd chosen for himself, and I

298 | THE LAST VISIT TO BERLIN

thought, Valley of the Shadow of Death, Valley of the Shadow of Death, a place no one should ever kill or be killed for, a place no one would ever live in, and a silent fury gripped me. Israel looked up from his seat on the rock toward the rows of black basalt, lying on black ashes turned dust, looked into the black, empty horizon and said, "I am glad we came here, now I know that my son did not fall for nothing."

We were silent on the way back. A mustachioed man who came with us and apparently had his share of war said, "That wouldn't have happened to us, we wouldn't have come out of the tank like that, during a moonlit night," and I was again gripped by fury. I did not meet Israel for many years after that, though occasionally he would call on Yom Kippur or Remembrance Day to ask how Mother is doing, and I would reply brusquely, through gritted teeth, that Mother is fine, that I'll tell her, but she wanted nothing to do with the fellowship of the bereaved either. Rarely she would deem to say about someone, "This is Judith, her son fell in the War of Attrition," just that, parsimoniously, as if there was no sorrow, no horror.

Gidi's poems were collected and compiled. Some of them were good, a few even truly excellent, and some I found unworthy. It was spring and the family gathered at Mother's house on HaBashan Street, and we said things, and Mother spoke, a bit, as well. "Such great wealth," Mother said, "and a little piece of iron is all it takes to finish it."

My cousin Dina flattened out a folded piece of paper and said, "We found this in a drawer, it's one of Gidi's, we just stumbled upon it." We looked at Dina. "Only Twenty," she read the poem's title. Silence filled the room.

I did not carry my falling friends and did not hear their mothers' cries. I did not see severed limbs nor smell the dead's demise. But I have lived for twenty years underneath these skies. It was good, and I want more. Just to continue to be alive.

I lie in bed dreaming forbidden dreams under the moon, how wonderful. I walk in busy streets on a bright afternoon, how wonderful. I walk in dark streets and hum a merry tune, how wonderful. And I think – I am only twenty, I am only twenty.

If I live to eighty, I have sixty years, by estimation. I can have two dozen great-grandkids and build another nation.

I am in love, but she loves me not, how sad. I am absentminded and confused quite a lot, how sad. But what truly has my stomach in a knot, how sad: I am already twenty, I am already twenty.

But if I live to eighty, I have sixty years, by estimation. I can have two dozen great-grandkids and build another nation.

Some people fall when they are young instead, how silly. And from a bullet rather than in bed, how silly. For parents whose lives will be hell to the end. How silly. Dead already at twenty, already at twenty.

But I did not carry my falling friends, and did not hear their mothers' cries, I did not see severed limbs or smell the dead's demise. But I have lived for twenty years underneath these skies. It was good, and I want more. Just to continue to be alive.

For a long while after Dina finished reading, we sat there, the daughters and grandchildren of Doctor Kurt Freyer, who had died just over a year ago. In the crowded room on HaBashan Street, the empty place where Gidi would have sat gaped open, and we said nothing. Mother was shaken and distraught. No one cried, because Freyers do not cry, and the dead remain stuck in our throats for eternity.

3.

I did not know how Mother dealt with the grief-filled days. She would open windows into her world only rarely, succinctly. On Friday evenings she would sit with us at the kibbutz, then retire to her room. I used to wonder what she would do in there, now that no one is around, is that where she wraps herself in grief? She never cried in public.

I know grief ambushed her at night. When she lay in bed at night, she would see Gidi, lying there beside her, living-dead. One moment would repeat itself relentlessly: Gidi walking down HaBashan Street in the uniform he had only just pulled out of the closet, walking toward Ibn Gvirol Street, turning around, looking at her, smiling, and her climbing back up to the fourth floor, fraught with anxiety.

Ten days prior to this war that undid her, we celebrated Rosh HaShana on the kibbutz, and Mother told me, "I think I can be happy, I have the two of you, I have a world, I think happiness might be possible," and now this primordial monster descended from the heavens, its wings blocking out the light. She no longer slept at night, but tossed and turned in her bed, pushing away that most vile of images, the moment of his death. "That I cannot see," she told me, "I will not go anywhere near it." I alone was left to relive the moment of his death, over and over and over. I sought out Effi so that he could tell me what happened, exactly, how his death came to him, did he see, why was he left there alone, and I could not find Effi. No one knew where he was.

Again and again Mother would say, "It is a terrible thing that happened to us, but all I can think of is what happened to him, and that cannot be overcome, it is impossible to overcome." And once, in a rare outburst, she said, "And you didn't let me cry, you would not let me cry then, when I knew." I lowered my head and thought, *what was I supposed to do then, what could I have done?*

Two dead men stood between us, but they did not bring us together and did not make us one flesh and did not cast us into the treasure trove of memory to share it. I was a man of words, but they nearly always went to the page. Mother read books and shared her many thoughts with her friends but did not know how to deliver them to me. The two dead men stood between us like a wall, and the evil secret which stood between Gidi and I from infancy stood there, too, a witless yet powerful golem.

We did not ask about Gidi. I got a call once from the military asking whether Gidi had dental records, and if so perhaps there are photographs, and once someone told us he saw Gidi's name at the hastily dug graveyard up north, but he isn't sure it was the same name, because so many had been buried there.

Another month or two passed and they called again from the military to ask that I arrive at the adjutancy base to receive an important notice, as my mother, they said, Mrs. Leah Rosenthal, had requested that I go in her place. I went with my wife Tami to the base and we walked among the offices of adjutants and sergeants until we reached a tired-looking officer. He invited us to sit down, appearing somewhat embarrassed, and once we did, he stood up, clicked his heals, saluted immaculately and sat back down. He said, "The Defense Force regrets to inform you of the death of your loved one, Gideon Rosenthal, may God avenge his blood, who fell in the Golan battles on October Eleventh, 1973." He asked that we sign the notice and looked at us, bewildered.

A year had passed since his death, and the military invited us to the burial of Gideon Rosenthal, may God avenge his blood, in a permanent resting place. We came at noon to the huge military cemetery in Kiryat Sha'ul, which I had never been to. I was blinded by the yellow, arid plain. The long rows of tombstones looked like the rocks of a desert, a place completely inhospitable to human beings.

Across the fence, tall, green trees provided shade for the civilian cemetery, where I walked many years before along with the rest of my HaShomer HaTzair battalion to accompany one of the girls whose father had died. I was about 14, a skinny and despondent boy. We walked down the path, following a gurney that only minutes before, the widow had removed the tallit from, and for a moment I saw the dead man's face, white and stubbly, and then we walked in his procession and my eyes darted left and right, and suddenly fell on one of the graves, and the tombstone read Hans Rosenthal, son of Louis Leib and Gertrude, 1906-1950, and I walked toward the tombstone and stood over it, a skinny, despondent boy, stood there and looked at those letters for the first time, and Leah the counselor saw me standing there and placed a warm hand on my shoulder, and a tear fell from my eye, just one, and I never went back to that grave again.

Now we stood on that barren plain in the military cemetery that someone had dug a hole in, and I had not a single tear to spare. Mother stood in sunglasses and took in the scene, as I did, as if it were not us standing there but characters with no name and no flesh, shadow simulacra. Many people came, people we knew and people we did not, and they all looked at these shadow simulacra that held our image, could not look away from the core of pain that the two of us were. The hazzan sang, and I did not see what they put in there, in the sandy earth of the Kiryat Sha'ul military cemetery. For many years I did not come back to visit the grave, nor did Mother, not on the Memorial Days or any other day.

Day by day the new rules of life were being written, the ones that started the day Gidi had disappeared into the war, and I learned that which had been so obvious, that all my life I fought for my birthright as firstborn, of which I was robbed on that foul night when Father disappeared and the little prince took his place. I learned that I might have given up my birthright then, but now that the heir was dead it was returned to me, and I must accept it, because it is the mission I was always meant for, and a new mission was attached to it now, to live his unlived life. And if being firstborn is a blessing, the burden of the additional life is a curse, nonnegotiable, which cannot be lifted through some heart-to-heart or by practicing apathy. I found that I must beget his unborn children, live in the house he could not live in, though I do not even know where it is. I do not know what sort of wife he would have had. Now she is living with some strange man and does not know how the man destined for her was taken away on a cruel moonlit night. I furiously read the theater reviews in the paper, for his teacher Nola Chilton claimed passionately that he would be the best theater critic in Israel. In each and every moment I was forced to live somehow where he was meant to be and yet somehow, simultaneously, to be where I am, as well, and perhaps that is why I am always in a rush to do more and more, to chop time down into little slices, to grow fruits on every tree, and run from tree to tree to pick them in due time.

In the spring of 1975, the book finally came out, Gidi's and mine, a big square book in an orange cover. *Oh Barbara, What a Shitty Mess Is War*, I titled it. Those were the words Gidi gave to Jacques Prévert line, "*Oh Barbara, quelle connerie la guerre.*" During my work on the book I was horrified to find it all there, in the poems. In one of them Gidi described the blood on the hands of the young boy, in another, the death of the twenty-year-old, and in another the little prince who has gone, never to return. The poems he chose to translate documented his hard conversation with the monster of war that revealed itself to him at the grave of Gadi Sharoni, and he translated from Bertolt Brecht the story of his future death in gruesome detail. The men of Fort Donald running from the flood, and then the man who died in Hathoury Woods, whose friends hurried on, leaving him behind.

> For the woods were loud around him and them / And they saw: him clinging to the tree / And they heard: him screaming at them / They stood there smoking in the Hathoury Woods / And annoyed, watched him go cold / for he was a man, like them.

The tale of his second burial, under a proper tombstone and a dignified, family-attended military ceremony, Gidi told with Brecht's "Legend of the Dead Soldier," of the soldier who is exhumed and redressed in a handsome new uniform so he can be buried properly.

Gidi's friends from the theater department told his story in the student play of their class, which documented him and his friends and me and Meira, who I now saw through other eyes and seemed different to me, closer than she had been.

They talked to Mother, too, Gidi's friends; spoke with her for hours and hours, and she told them things which needed to be said, and still neither of us touched on the core of sorrow. They shaped Mother's words into a monologue of fragments, delivered by an actress who spoke in a thick Jewish-German accent.

"I grew up in a world in which the single most powerful belief was that the individual can do something to make the world a better place," said Mother from the actress's mouth. "The humanist idea that it is not enough that one be a humanist for oneself, but one must also be a humanist for society, that is what Grandfather gave us and the grandchildren, and in that respect Gidi was the grandson."

The actress stressed the "the" in "the grandson" and a shard of indignity passed through me. "The important thing was the faith that human beings are essentially good," the actress continued, "And I think Gidi took that faith with him. I no longer have it. Something broke for me, and I never really believed in anything again. Gidi is a victim, a pure victim to evil, to the evilest sort of politics. This is a mad world. My belief that people can make the world better, that is what broke."

We drove away and I said, perhaps asked, "You really lost faith."

Mother was silent for a while. Then she said, perhaps asked, "And you, Rubi, you still believe."

"I do," I said, "but differently. Faith and doubt always go hand in hand, for me."

"You must have faith," said Mother, "you must do something so that there won't be any more wars, because I can't anymore, I don't know anymore."

I went to bed that night and thought about Mother, and what she had left now, after the two pillars of her universe had collapsed, never to be repaired. Gidi, the source of happiness, was lost. The inherent goodness of humanity, the wellspring of her faith, had run dry. And what was left? Life was left, to be lived, and one does not give up on life, not ever.

4.

Oh Barbara, What a Shitty Mess Is War was a hit. They reprinted and reprinted it. Adolescent girls placed it on their nightstands, soldiers read it during R&R, it passed from hand to hand, perched on library shelves. I personally brought a copy to the library of Tichon Hadash, the high school we both attended, wrote a dedication on the first page and placed it reverentially in the librarian's hands. They read "Only Twenty" on the radio, during Memorial Days and war commemorations. Some of the poems were composed as songs. Once a couple of high school teachers came to the publishing house to ask me about a special price if they bought it in bulk as a gift for their entire class of graduates, and then phoned me, apologizing, "We can't give the students a book with this title."

Mother never stopped working, not for a day. She made new friends playing bridge and started painting in watercolors, delicate and eye-catching. "But it lacks depth," she said. "It has no depth, nothing is deep anymore." Alongside the path of sorrows that her grief had taken her on lurked the green-eyed monster, upon her realization that even after this horrible war so many remained alive, nearly everyone, and Gidi was the only fallen soldier in his class and most likely in his entire year, and she the only bereaved parent among her many friends. Those she knew from his generation returned from the war shell-shocked or wounded, but alive, talking. Her friends and family had several sons named Gidi, and the name Gidi could not be erased from the pool or be sanctified to our Gidi alone.

Soon after the birth of my third child, Noam, the unease of my marriage suddenly boiled over. The evil secrets of my childhood went into the home I had made on the kibbutz, and I knew I must leave it. Mother was uncharacteristically chagrined by this, uneasy, saying, "And what will happen now."

Furious, I retorted, "I have to worry about myself as well, it had to end."

And she said, "I've lost too much, I don't want to lose my family, too." But she kept coming to the kibbutz every Friday, and she thought, at least Rubi is on the kibbutz, with the children, at least there's that, and her anger faded gradually and did not fester.

It was then, when so many secrets had suddenly sprung forth, that I felt I could no longer brush my anger at Mother under the thick carpet of practicality, and it erupted from me like a djinn from a bottle. I asked her why I was not taken to Father's funeral, why I wasn't shown his grave, why no one talked to me.

"I think we told you that he died," Mother said, taken by surprise, "of course we did." And later she said, "We didn't know back then that we needed to take you there, to talk about it, we didn't know the things we know now."

Emboldened, I asked, "And really, why did you never remarry, you had plenty of suitors."

"I didn't have time to think of such things," she said, defensive. "I had to work, I had to raise you, life was so full, and why are you asking this all of a sudden?"

"I always hoped a new father would come," I said, no longer angry, relishing in the small reveal.

She was indeed so surprised and said, "I never thought it was like that, you never said anything."

"There are other things we need to talk about," I said, "I have a lot of anger, I want to talk about it."

And she said, "No, I can't, this I can't."

And I said, "It will do us both good, I want to unearth things, look, we've already started."

And she said, "There are things, Rubi, that cannot be opened, and certainly not now, I need to rest, I cannot follow these things into the depths," and suddenly she was hard and somber and irate. Lotte Rosenthal of the house of Freyer, now over seventy years old, and I, her only living son, were like strangers to each other.

Meira disappeared from our lives and for a while we knew nothing of her whereabouts. Years later we discovered that she looked for Gidi everywhere even before the war was over, volunteering to work at military hospitals in the hopes that by some miracle she would happen upon him, even when we already knew he would not be coming back, even after she came to visit Mother and sat with her and said, "It was irresponsible to put Gidi in a tank."

Gidi's friends from university came to see her, too, and she was hard and furious and said, "There was nothing in the world that could protect him from what happened to him," and she said, "no one loved him enough. His mother did. And maybe me." And then the actress playing her said in her name, "That is the heart of fascism, some people smoke the cigar and pick the fruit, and some people pay the price, huge masses of humans like ants, humans who are the oil in the cogs, and Gidi fell between the cogs, he was the mortar for the wall of victory. No one is allowed to live in a country where Gidi is the mortar in the wall of victory." And Meira also said, "Gidi had such a beautiful, nuanced gamut of expressions, and when I heard that he died, expressions of unspeakable terror came to my mind, and I know that is what his face looked like."

Meira came to see the play at the university, greeted us briefly and vanished. She tried her hand at painting. Her teachers and peers said she was extremely talented, expressive, but she only painted one subject, herself, and always horrified. In the paintings her comely face became twisted, and her cherry eyes became panicked, despicable. Men fell for her and again and again left her. Again and again she cut short her locks of hair that Gidi loved so much. And one day, in the spring of 1989, they found her lifeless body in an apartment in Tel Aviv. She did not leave a note. In her wallet they found a page she had copied from Dante's *Inferno*, and beside her was an open poetry book by the poet Zelda.

He whose heart is / a sweet and aimless flower / blackens / at the unraveling of trust and silence // when the banquet / runneth over / – he will take his own life / with the sick / and with the weary. / Feel thou not disdain for the lost, / made to be an ocean / born to love.

When I received word of her death, I pondered another unsolved riddle which connected those two souls, both close and far apart. Perhaps Gidi was drawn to the chaos Meira brought to his life to test Grandfather Kurt's stubborn Gospel of Reason in the innermost places, and perhaps he attempted to contrast Mother's fierce *élan vital* with Meira's fragile alternative, ever circling the abyss. Could she have returned to him? Had she parted with him? Did she reflect further on the realm of souls she constructed for herself, where Gidi's soul wandered, crying out for her in agony?

Around that time, I was finishing the writing of *The Family of the Beaufort*, a book about six families who lost their sons on the first day of the Lebanon War and became a close-knit group as a result. I took the questions that Mother had answered with clipped sentences, cut short with sorrow's knife, and addressed them to other mothers and fathers, who found value in the fellowship of the bereaved, who drew strength from it, and turned that strength into a fist raised against the masters of war.

I went from family to family. I went to Dita Ben Akiva from Kfar Yehoshua who gave me the merciless truth of a bereaved mother and never let herself forget, not for a single moment, and her husband Yaakov, who slowly retreated into himself as many fathers did. I went to the pure-hearted Yehoshua Zamir, who insisted that he can and will part with his son, Yaron. I came to Raya Harnik, who hounded Menachem Begin every day of his life, and spoke to her Guni through poetry. I visited Mona Sherf at her house in the Jordan Valley, a Job who does not want his cloak, and at the Tavor foothills I met Avraham and Fania Eliel, who spoke of their dead son in simple words laden with imagery, and furious, anguished Yaakov Gutermann. I taught them and was taught by them. In every house I visited they asked me, "And how is Mother, how is Mother coping." The fellowship of the bereaved, which I, too, had tried to escape, embraced Hme now with its hoary wisdom.

The Family of the Beaufort cleared out channels that had long since been closed to me, clogged up. I told Mother of the ongoing conversation Yehoshua Zamir has with his dead son and asked her if she had such conversations as well. She shook her head and adamantly declared, "No, no, I couldn't, that would be wrong." I asked her if she believed in bidding a final farewell, in what the psychologist's term "letting go," and she said, "I don't think such a thing is even possible." We spoke of the anger, because the parents of the Beaufort family were so focused and directional in theirs, and she said, "I was mostly angry at Golda. She did not do enough for peace. She did nothing, nothing. And at Moshe Dayan. For not preparing for war. A terrible anger, sometimes I would feel that Dayan is the devil himself."

And I asked her, "Why did you not do anything with this anger?"

And she said, "It wouldn't have helped, what good would have come of it, and I hadn't the energy for it, no one did."

The Family of the Beaufort became a book. We met at the Eliel's home in Kfar Tavor to celebrate its birth. Mother came with me and they enveloped her, the Lebanon War's freshly bereaved, people who'd lived for seven years in the house of grief, and she, a veteran, from the bereaved of '73, a strong, clearheaded woman. She sat there and listened, and they spoke to her, and of themselves, and she spoke a bit, too.

When we left, she said, "That was good, I'm glad I came," and some luminous bolt went through me and I knew that the anger had ended and become dust. I no longer wanted it. From now on

I am a master of my fate and she of hers. This woman beside me does not crown princes and perhaps never did. All of it was but an error, a false report, a mountain of ashes and dust that I had built with my bare hands and tried again and again to climb, and again and again came the hand to push me back down.

The mountain crumbled. Sitting now beside me in a car sliding down into the Judean lowlands is my mother, Leah Rosenthal, who is seventy-six and very much needs me, and we both share this wound, we both have this common loss, and we both chose life. The evil secret was carried off to where it should have ended up long ago, off to the great river, the river of the forgotten. And even if I do not know how to express love toward her, our lives are interwoven in one another.

Gidi remained our beloved Gidi, the pure victim of evil. The two of us were charged with the weight of his existence. When we go so shall he, and only the books will remain.

5.

I remarried and returned with my wife Edna to my hometown, Tel Aviv. Mother was still working though she was well over eighty by now, taking care of seniors. One day she said, "This is becoming ridiculous, most of the seniors I look after are younger than me." She continued to enjoy watercolors and her bridge group, of which she once told me, "There is a lady in our group, one hundred years old, she is already making mistakes." She went to lectures and once asked for recommendations and went to hear the famous poet Nathan Zach, "Though I do not think I can read his poetry," and sat enthralled through the whole thing.

Zach later told me that he recognized her, "She sat in the front row with a friend, and they listened so attentively that I spoke only to them."

Years later I found the courage to tell her that Meira took her own life. A shadow crossed her face and she said, "Such horrible things, such awful things, it is inexplicable, all of this."

The "exes" grew old. The men perished one after the other and the women remained. Mother had never been sick a day in her life, but her friends occasionally were, and found it more and more difficult to climb the stairs to visit her. We never visited Gidi's grave, nor spoke of it. One day a man came to the house on HaBashan Street. I happened to be there and opened the door. He was about sixty, gray of hair and mustache. He said, "I'm your neighbor in Kiryat Sha'ul, your son is lying beside mine."

Mother peeked across my shoulder and slipped away into her room. The man said, "I wanted to know if you go there, sometimes."

And I said, "No, no, we don't."

And he said, "I understand, but you'd maybe like to know that I've been tending to the grave, I brought a new flowerpot when the old one broke."

Mother paced around her room, troubled, and I said, "We thank you, and we're very sorry, so very much." The man glanced at the woman in the nearby room and left, and even after he left, we did not speak of it.

She only said, "It is meaningless, a grave is meaningless."

In the summer of 1992 Edna and I were looking for a bigger apartment than the one we got when we left the kibbutz. Edna found a tempting little ad in the paper about an apartment on

Ahad Ha'Am Street. On the second floor we found a spacious four-bedroom apartment with built-in closets, balconies and windows galore. A thick layer of dust coated everything; the apartment had been standing empty for nearly a year, and now they were looking to sell. On the floor in one of the rooms bulged a messy little hill of piled books, and on the very top, glowing orange, was *Oh Barbara, What a Shitty Mess Is War*.

I picked up the book and opened it. On the first page was the dedication I had written for our old high school, Tichon Hadash, and inside was the empty library card. Seventeen years before, the teenage boy who had lived in this house checked it out, and it was waiting for me here, in my new home, ever since.

Every year, as Yom Kippur drew near, Mother would say, "On Yom Kippur we'll talk about Gidi," and I never answered. And when Yom Kippur Eve came I would bring her to our house and she would say, "We'll talk about Gidi, we'll talk about Gidi a bit," and the words would dry up in my throat, and she said, "He was good, he was a good man, I think of what he could have been," and again she said, "It is a brutal thing that happened to us, what happened to him is horrifying, inconceivable." Afterward I would drive her home at night. The streets were full of children on bicycles, making the most of the holy day's driving taboo, and the few people walking outside shot hard looks at us as we drove by, at times yelling angrily, and I would return home anxious and bitter.

On the twentieth anniversary of the Yom Kippur War we invited Gidi's friends from the kibbutz and the theater department to our home. We spoke of him and knew that this would be the first gathering and the last, because there is nothing left to remember, because the fountain of memory had run dry, and everything that needed to be said had been. Those were the days of the Oslo Accords and I was eager, optimistic, and I thought, perhaps Mother can find her faith again, and she said, "I want to believe, I want so much to believe."

In the spring of 1993 our Tel-Aviv-born child, Arnon, joined the family. The house was filled with joy. Mother became an eighty-year-old grandmother in a world of fifty-year-old grandmothers, and she showered him with love, but never with hugs and kisses, as such behavior is not the way of German-Jewish families.

On the eve of Yom Kippur 1995, we were sitting together as usual. Suddenly the phone rang, and Mother shuddered because it had been so long since the phone rang on Yom Kippur. It was Rachel Dror on the line, Käthe and Albert Baer's daughter, Mother's cousin from Kabri, and I thought she wanted to say something to Mother, some words of comfort, but she said, "Yonatan was killed," said it clearly, as if it were painless.

Mother looked at me and I saw the dread in her eyes and Rachel said, "He was coming back from Jerusalem last night, they found him this morning on the way from Jerusalem to Gilgal. Is Lotte there, by any chance?"

And I said, "Yes, she's here." Mother spoke to her a bit and came back to the table. We took the road of sorrows back to her house and she did not come visit on Yom Kippur again.

Loose ends were tying off, one by one. Jealousies and animosities faded. Yvonne from Berlin, whose beloved husband Kolya had passed away with the arrival of the 21st century, writes letters to her cousins from Israel and they often speak on the phone. An invitation was sent from the city of Flensburg to the daughters of Dr. Kurt Freyer, previously the assistant director of the local museum, inviting them to come and participate in a tribute event in their father's honor.

Mother and Aunt Michal went to the city perched on the Danish border, where they were honored with warm words and medals of appreciation presented by the city's president Mr. Rautenberg, the museum director Dr. Schulte-Wülwer, and the diligent Bernd Philipsen, a journalist investigating the region's history. During the ceremony they heard how, in 1920, Dr. Kurt Freyer presented his nomination for the position of museum director and was rejected, despite him being, according to the director himself, "the most brilliant and talented scientist to ever operate in this museum." The city's head archivist, Dr. Broder Schwensen, said, "It seems that in 1920, during the extreme nationalist atmosphere of the already troubled border region, there was no place for a free man like Dr. Freyer."

Mother uncharacteristically made a small speech, saying, "My father was not religious, but he had faith. He believed in humanism, in the human ability to make a better life for everyone, a better society. He believed in the triumph of reason."

In the fall of 2001, I went to visit the town of my ancestors, Stettin, which became the Polish city of Szczecin. The Jews were expelled from it before the war, the Germans after the war, other Jews came and suffered and were persecuted and fled, scattering as far away as they could. Regarding this the following rhyme was often quoted among the Freyers, one of Albert Baer's seemingly endless supply of quips: "On the banks of the Oder where once bathed German marauders / Now the Poles come along and spit into the waters."

There, on Głogowska Street, which during the German era was Turnerstraße, I found the house where Father was born, on the first floor, and the house on Bolesława Śmiałego Street where he spent his childhood and adolescence, which then was called Pestalozzistraße. An old couple suspiciously peeked out the window at me. Moritz and Teresa Freyer's estate was in ruins, and where Trude and Martin Hendelson's house stood they had built a new building from the ground up.

Gidi's final moments remained a black box sought by me alone, and the box's owner was Effi Slutski. One day a man called and introduced himself as "the unit's new liaison to the families of the 679 brigade," a number I had managed to forget again and again, but I didn't need it to understand he was talking about Gidi. He said, "I see you never come to the ceremonies."

And I said, "No, we never do, though I appreciate your interest."

And he insisted, "Still, perhaps there is something we can do for you."

And I said, "No, we don't need anything."

Just before I put down the receiver my memory flickered and I hastily added, "Find me Effi Slutski." He was happy to be given a task and called me back several days later to tell me that Effi had been found, and he would be happy to talk to me in any way, but preferably face-to-face. Apparently, Effi had been living for several years in Gush Katif, a settlement bloc in the Gaza Strip that, back then, had not yet been evicted. Disheartened, I decided to postpone the meeting once again to a time when no border will stand between me and the keeper of my black box. After a while I mustered the courage to call, and Effi said, "I'm waiting for you," and he also said, "I'll come visit, I'll call."

Effi came to see me just before Memorial Day, 2001. We sat at a café and he told me of Gidi's final hours, in great detail, and said, "You know I came to your mother's house, during the first week, but you weren't there."

"I know," I said, "she said you didn't really talk."

"We talked," said Effi. "I told your mother that Gidi read from the Siddur before we headed out and she got angry and said, 'That is impossible, that wasn't Gidi.' She didn't want to hear much more after that."

Then he told me how the three of them started moving toward Khan Arnabeh under the light of the full moon, how they crawled from shelter to shelter over the rough bed of basalt, with Syrian soldiers swarming all around them.

"Gidi was last," said Effi, "We waited for him. We heard a scream and he disappeared in the darkness. We didn't see him again."

We were silent for a long time. Effi looked down and said, "I heard two death cries that night, and kept going. That's how it was written, that I should go on, that I should make it."

After Mother lived for a while in a small apartment building near my childhood home in Pinsker Street, she moved to the same Ramat Gan retirement home where her beloved Uncle Erich spent his final years. We took in the antique chest which had passed down the generations. As for the many books in German that had been collected over many years, some of which she had brought from Germany, prose and poetry and art books, we stacked them and packed them in cardboard boxes.

"There is nowhere to put them," said Mother. "No one wants them, even at the Goethe Institute they don't have room for all the *yekke* libraries."

I left the cardboard boxes laden with dusty books next to the dumpsters, which stank of rot and spoiled food. I turned away from them and did not look back.

Mother gave me large stacks of papers and certificates for safe-keeping, notebooks full of notes and stories Father had written, spanning both Germany and Israel. Some of them were printed on a typewriter and carbon-copied to thin, translucent paper that crumbled to my touch. I found many poems there that I did not know, and neither did she, or perhaps she had merely forgotten. When she settled in at the retirement home we sat there and read them together. She explained the meanings of any words I didn't know, and said, "It is beautiful, I never thought it was so beautiful, that it is more than only his thoughts, that as a poem it is beautiful."

For a long time, we sat and read poems by Hans Rosenthal, my father, about whom I knew nothing, who vanished from my life without notice, without warning. When I got up to leave my mother, I kissed her, for the first time in my life.

Made in the USA
Coppell, TX
20 August 2020

33831831R00177